HIGH PLAINS
Tango

HIGH PLAINS

Tango

a novel

ROBERT JAMES WALLER

DOUBLEDAY LARGE PRINT HOME LIBRARY EDITION

Shaye Areheart Books

NEW YORK

This Large Print Book carries the
Seal of Approval of N.A.V.H.

For my mother, Ruthie, who for years has lived in a quiet fog of Alzheimer's disease, but who still smiles in recognition when she sees me and likes it when I hold her hand on winter afternoons.

"In some respects, George Armstrong Custer had a pleasant stroll by the river compared to what Carlisle McMillan went through, and afterward nobody placed any white markers in the thin, red soil of Yerkes County. Never been anything like it, not out here, at least . . . not anywhere else, probably. You name it, we had it: magic, war, Indians . . . so-called witches, for chrissake."

"Mind if I quote you here and there, on the local stuff?" I asked.

"Keep buying the Wild Turkey, quote me all you want. Talk to Carlisle McMillan, too, get it straight from the hombre who went through it all."

—CONVERSATION,
back booth in SLEEPY'S STAGGER INN

———

Hell, we're all just a bunch of dervishes, dancin' around and chantin' till the music ends. But you got to accept the tango runs forever. Susanna Benteen understood that. Not sure if anyone else did. She ain't no witch, like people said. 'Least I don't think so. She dances a sweet little tango, though, I'll say that.

—GABE O'ROURKE,
ACCORDION PLAYER

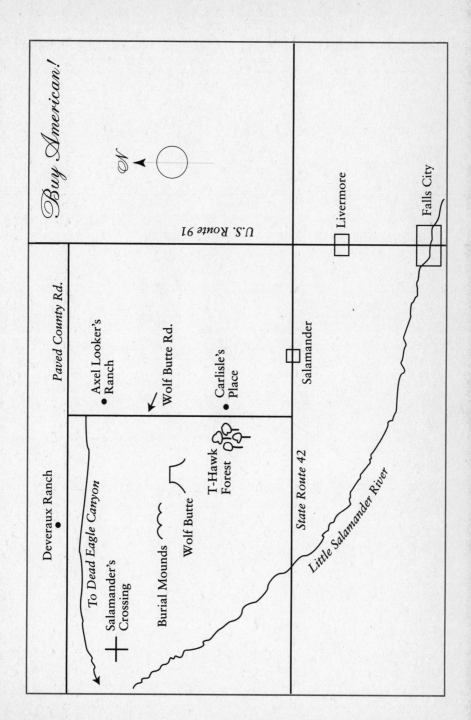

HIGH PLAINS
Tango

CHAPTER ONE

Not exactly a dark and stormy night, but nonetheless: a strange, far place in a strange, far time, distant buttes with low, wet clouds hanging across their rumpled white faces and long, straight highways running somewhere close to forever. In a settled land, the truly wild places are where nobody is looking anymore. This was a wild place.

Enigmatic sign pointing west.

Why did the eagle die? Did anyone remember? Some did, but they weren't talking.

Red dirt road perpendicular to the highway, heading into the short grass and disappearing over a low rise a half mile out.

Other signs, every thirty miles or so, pointing to other roads hinting travel through invisible walls and into other times. If you had a vehicle with enough stamina, maybe turn off on one of them, just for the hell of it. We've all had a fleeting urge to do that.

That's what Carlisle McMillan did. He was in no hurry, a traveler without design, a temporary drifter by his own choice. After turning his tan Chevy pickup off westbound pavement onto what the locals called Wolf Butte Road, he headed south past the Dead Eagle Canyon sign. After a while, he stopped his truck and got out, miles from the nearest little town.

Late August cool. Mist. Carlisle McMillan stood there for a few moments, boots becoming grass wet, sky water on his face and hands.

Easy wind came, went, came again. Silence. Cattails bending, yellow clover riffling as the wind chose. Like a film without a sound track—the silence—only deeper. More like a stone coffin at nightfall when the

mourners have left and dirt has been shov-
eled over you.

The Cheyenne believed this was sacred
ground. Sweet Medicine said it was so. The
hawk sitting thirty fence posts south of
Carlisle McMillan believed it. Anyone who
happened on this place believed it. The
smart money would come with food and
water, perhaps a sleeping bag, in case an
engine failed or a tire relented and the spare
was empty. For nothing out here cared
about you, that much was clear. Nothing
cared whether you lived or died or paid your
bills or danced on warm Pacific beaches
and made love afterward. There was nothing except silence and wind, and they would
be here long after your passing.

The Early Ones were buried here in
mounds, giving the appearance of sea roll to
the prairie. They shuffled across the old land
bridges from Asia when the continents were
connected in the high north. A century ago,
others were buried in this place. Buried
where they fell in the wars of Manifest Destiny, the great westward push. You could still
find metal buttons from cavalry tunics if you
scuffled around in the gravel and looked
close. Other things, too, old knife handles,

human shoulder bones splintered by lance and bullet, pipe stems. If you dug, you would find more, a lot more.

Six inches behind Carlisle McMillan's left rear tire was a tunic button half buried in the mud. The winds of a hundred springs uncovered the button, rain washed it into a creek. The creek carried it onto a sandbar. A bird picked it up and flew toward a nest, dropping it when it turned out to be hard and tasteless. That particular button once fastened the coat of Trooper Jimmy C. Knowles, Seventh Cavalry, who rode behind a man they called Son of the Morning Star. Trooper Knowles thought well of his yellow-haired general and aspired to be a cut-and-paste copy of him. He would have ridden into hell with Son of the Morning Star. And he eventually did.

If you can get past the wind, listen beyond the silence, there are old sounds reverberating here. Distant bugles, squeak of cavalry leather, maybe the low thrum of time itself. And faint images of old riders from a long time ago, mounted on fine Appaloosas, breaking from the shadows of Dead Eagle Canyon, running hard across the roll of green prairie, and turning their ponies for autumn, steam coming from muzzles and mouths.

Sometimes you can even smell things farther out when the wind is just right. That's what they said and still say. You have to lean back and flare your nostrils. Work at it. Then it will come to you. First the ordinary smells of big, open country and after that the faint whiff of old deceptions.

Not far from where Carlisle McMillan stood in light rain and looked out across the rise of nothing, the anthropologist fell to his death from one of the smaller buttes. There had been the sound of rushing air followed by the thump of something high in the middle of his back, causing him to stagger forward from where he was standing and launching him into downward flight. The first eighty feet or so, his fall had a certain purity in its form and velocity, almost graceful. Until he hit an outcropping. After that, it was a Raggedy-Ann tumble for the next six hundred feet. The only sound was his scream, and his only perception was that of the cliff face going by him in a blur of white sandstone. He smashed into rock and gravel at the bottom, neck twisted rearward in such a way that his chin could touch the bottom of his right shoulder blade. None of his colleagues on the plain below had seen it happen or heard his cry.

A pair of dark eyes had seen it, though—the man falling through cool sunlight, the thin and yellow sunlight that sweeps this land in middle spring—but nothing would be said. Nothing, not ever. It was the way of things. That was known long before the horse soldiers rode through here on their way to the Little Big Horn. That was known a long time ago.

Carlisle McMillan leaned on a fence post, looked west, stared at the distance. Great run of empty space, broken only by an occasional butte. The one a half mile to his right, 3,237 feet high, was called Wolf Butte. A woman was dancing there on the crest, but Carlisle couldn't see her.

Bare feet on short grass, she moved. Far off, far down, she could just make out a figure standing beside a pickup truck. Twenty feet behind her, the Indian played a flute, his back resting against the gnarled trunk of a long-dead scrub pine.

A low-slung cloud moved onto the butte, the cold wetness of it touching the graceful arch of the woman's back, touching the curve of her legs. It touched her face and the opal ring on her left middle finger and the silver bracelet around her right wrist, touched the silver falcon hanging from the chain around her neck. The Indian could not see her clearly anymore, only transient sightings through the cloud, a momentary view of leg or breast or the swing of long auburn hair as she turned. But still he played, knowing the cloud would pass, knowing she would come to him.

Far off and far down, Carlisle McMillan shifted his truck into reverse and backed onto the road, grinding into the mud a tunic button that once fastened the blue coat of Trooper Jimmy C. Knowles, Seventh Cavalry. When the cloud drifted away from the butte and the woman again could see what lay on the plain below her, the figure was gone, only the vague image of a pickup truck moving south.

The flute angled down to silence. She raised her arms through the mist to the sky, lowered them, and walked toward the Indian. He was old, but his body was hard like fence wire, and she settled onto him. The wind was light and cool and wet. Close to her, he could smell the sandalwood with which she had bathed that morning. The rain lifted for a moment, and over the Indian's shoulder she watched the hawk flying toward a cliff, the same one from which her father had glimpsed the earth rising toward him.

Chapter Two

Axel Looker wasn't stupid. He just behaved that way. In his bones he knew the scientist fellow was right, even though he didn't like scientist fellows in general. Didn't like them because they clearly were a bunch of radicals feeding at the public trough, funded by Axel Looker's own taxes. Didn't like them because they held you to logic and asked for proof, wouldn't let you get away with the comforting restaurant talk where myths born of self-interest were passed around like ketchup. Passed around and eventually agreed upon with murmurs of assent and nodding of heads, until an enduring fiction was created with which all were comfortable. One departed from this common point of view only at the risk of censure, not to mention expulsion from the back table in Danny's café.

The ecologist had said their days out here were closing down unless they dramatically changed their ways. Told them they were draining the big Ogallala aquifer and overgrazing the grasslands. Said they were letting the soil, which was thin at the outset, blow away in the wind.

They had listened to him, first at a speech he gave in the Livermore gym, where he had nearly been hooted off the stage. Afterward, walking out to their cars, someone said they ought to at least whip up a barrel of hot tar and send his feathered butt back east where he belonged. Things didn't go any better when the ecologist showed up at Clyde Archer Legion Post 227 in Salamander and spoke again. Somehow, though, it was harder to dismiss him when the audience was small and they could see his eyes and he could see theirs. He was thin and earnest, talking quietly. He had charts and numbers, and he had level, steel-hard answers for their questions. It seemed as though he knew their criticisms flowed from the myths they were determined to preserve, and he would have none of it.

They kept looking for gaps in his arguments, but they couldn't find any. That made them dislike him even more.

As with most people, no matter how intelligent, Axel Looker had his own way of putting aside unpleasant evidence that didn't fit with what he wanted to happen. So even though Axel knew the scientist fellow was right, deep down he knew that, he couldn't admit it to anyone, including himself. Over morning coffee at Danny's, the boys tilted back their caps and talked about outside interference in their lives while they absently fingered the crop subsidy checks tucked in their shirt pockets.

On his way home and six miles west of Salamander, Axel turned off Route 42 and headed north along the red dirt road toward the place he and Earlene had farmed and ranched for thirty-four years. The red dirt had turned to a sticky gumbo in late summer rain, and he slowed down, nearly stopping, when he met a tan pickup with California plates.

"Now who the hell is that?" he wondered out loud. Tomorrow he would ask around at Danny's or the grain elevator, see if anybody knew. Looked like an Indian behind the wheel, maybe another one of those agitators forever demanding the land out there be returned to them, filing lawsuits, and claiming it was their land and that it had been stolen from them a hundred and some more years ago. What a pile of cowshit that was. Axel may have disliked scientists, but he absolutely hated Indians, particularly those who argued he was farming stolen land.

When he arrived home, he mentioned to Earlene that it might be time to think about retiring and moving to Florida. He didn't say anything to her about the pickup truck he met on the way back from Salamander. Didn't want to worry her.

Looking back on it, if Carlisle McMillan had known what lay ahead of him, he might not have stopped in Salamander that first night, might have kept right on going through and out the other side of Yerkes County.

"Too damn much grief, as it turned out, for a man doing nothing except trying to find some peace and quiet." That's what he once said.

Easy to understand why he might say

that. His recollections were still clear and hard formed: birds lifting off with a predator's scream and warriors lashed to the trees of April. Boom of shotguns and the hard crack of a long-range rifle. Sirens, men shouting, dust climbing high and fast into morning skies, fires on the crest of Wolf Butte. And the slow, downward slide of anything resembling justice and plain dealing.

Carlisle's jaw tightened when he talked about that part of it. Then he would shift over to a half smile. "But there were compensations. On balance, I'd do it over again."

Of course he would. How many women could you find like Susanna Benteen? Or Gally Deveraux, for that matter. Pretty close to none. Susanna and Gally and what came to be known as the Yerkes County War feathered out the boy. Made him stand upright and lurch forward into manhood. Carlisle admitted it.

He came into Yerkes County from the north late on that August day, stopped and looked at the country around him. The roll of short grass, Wolf Butte to his right. Mist, easy wind, silence. Heading south again on the red dirt road, he hit pavement after a few miles, Route 42. He looked at his map, leaned on the steering wheel and thought about his options. Full dark coming in an hour or so. A little town east about six miles. In the other direction, the next place of any size was Casper, Wyoming, three hundred miles southwest and not much between here and Casper. Turn east.

Fifteen driving minutes later, Carlisle squinted past the slap of his windshield wipers and saw the four cylindrical towers of a grain elevator ahead. Sign on the edge of town: WELCOME TO SALAMANDER, Pop. 942, Elev. 2263.

The sign was battered, needed a new paint job. Three bullet holes were grouped within the O in WELCOME. Problematical greeting.

More signs: church schedules, and the Lions Club met every Tuesday at noon. He moved slowly along the highway doubling as Main Street, the town spreading out a block or two on either side of the commercial district and five blocks beyond it at the ends. Past Duane's Pickup Palace & Lawn Mower Repair, past the Blue Square Drive-In (CLOSED LABOR DAY) and the Jackrabbit Lanes (CLOSED, windows covered with plywood). He shifted down into second with the truck engine whining a little, wipers beginning to drag as the rain let up and late sunlight splayed through the overcast farther west.

Merchants along Main Street were shutting their front doors at the end of the day. The buildings they locked were mostly white frame, some of them well built originally, but in need of scraping and paint now, and part of the roof had collapsed on what used to be the Salamander Hotel. Mixed in with the wooden structures were several fine old brick buildings in late Victorian style, the former home of Melik's Drug as an example. In the spaces between some of the buildings, Carlisle could see houses on side streets and beyond them open country. Not many trees, and small ones at that, water being scant and the soil too thin in most places for deep, heavy roots. Those that had grown to any size had been cut for buildings and firewood years ago.

Carlisle McMillan put his tires against a curb with chunks missing from the concrete, in front of a tavern called Leroy's. Got out, flexed his knees, swung his arms. Long day, thirsty day, 397 miles since dawn. He walked into Leroy's and slid onto the first stool just at sundown, feeling grimy. Leroy was at the other end of the wooden bar, talking to a tall cowboy wearing a Stetson. The cowboy, rakish having been his middle name a long time ago but bilious now more appropriate, smoked a thin cigar and looked as if he were four days past the end of everything. Two men in caps with fertilizer logos on the crowns were bending over the shabbiest excuse for a pool table Carlisle had ever seen. It sloped, it leaned, and the cushions had deep cigarette burns in them.

But it wasn't the worst-looking article in the place. That prize belonged to the old duffer sitting two stools down from Carlisle, left arm crooked on the bar. And lying on the arm was a face with a week of gray stubble. Up came the head, or what passed for one. He stared at Carlisle through crosshatched red eyes. "Who'errr *youvff*?" When Carlisle ignored him, his curiosity escalated, and he shouted the same question, nearly falling off his bar stool in the effort.

Leroy came along behind the bar, cigarette dangling from his mouth, wiping his hands on a dirty white apron wrapped around his waist and hanging two inches below his knees, a rip in the hem causing part of it to hang even a little farther. As he passed the old man, Leroy slapped the bar and said, "Shut up, Frank."

"Fugyouleer-oy." Frank flung the slur in the general direction of Leroy's retreating back before his head smacked onto the bar and he was quiet.

Leroy nodded. Not friendly, not un-friendly, not in the middle or at the extremes. Flat, in the way of no concern for anything or anyone.

"I'll have a Miller's," Carlisle said.

Leroy slid open the metal cooler below the bar, inspected the contents, and twisted his head upward. "Outta Miller's. Got Bud and Grain Belt."

"Bud's okay." Leroy's smelled like every beer joint Carlisle had ever been in, only worse. Sour, acrid, a quintessential place where men came to die, a burial ground for all the old, besotted elephants of Salaman-der.

Leroy opened the bottle and set it on the bar along with a little beer glass, narrow at the bottom and curving vaselike to a wider opening at the top. "That'll be seventy-five."

Carlisle laid out a dollar. Leroy rang the

cash register, slid a quarter along the bar toward him, and walked back to his conversation with the cowboy. "Seen the witch lately?" he asked the cowboy.

"Screw the witch."

Leroy laughed. "Well, lot of us would like to give it a shot sometime."

"Yeah, fat chance," he said, looking down at his whiskey and water, stirring it with his right index finger, high-heeled boot on the bar rail.

"Ever notice that Injun she hangs around with?"

"No . . . what Injun?" He raised his eyes without moving his head, staring at Leroy.

"Old Injun. Lives somewhere out in the buttes."

The cowboy coughed hard and shoved his glass toward Leroy. "Screw old Injuns, too. And speaking of gettin' old and gettin' screwed, put a little more ol' Jim Beam in this."

Leroy laughed again and reached for the bottle. "Jack, I could put nothing but two hundred proof in your glass and you'd still think I watered it down."

The cowboy tilted his head toward Carlisle and mumbled something only half under his breath about "hair longer'n a woman's," not caring whether Carlisle heard him or not. Leroy glanced down the bar while the cowboy shook his head and stirred his drink. Carlisle drank his Bud, wondering just where in the big peculiar he had landed. Silence and wind, witches and old Injuns.

The beer was cold and tasted good in spite of the dismal ambience, even though Bud ranked about sixty-fourth in his beer hierarchy, with Grain Belt further down than last. Six feet away, Frank snored or choked; Carlisle couldn't make out which, decided on both. One of the pool players screamed, "You lucky bastard!" while the other crowed, "Rack 'em up, Arlo." Outside, someone revved up a car engine, the rolling boom from a hole in the muffler ricocheting off buildings along Main Street.

"How's Gally doing, Jack?" Leroy asked. "I haven't seen her for a while except to catch sight of her going through town in the Bronco."

"She's okay. You know women, always goddamn complaining about this or that, never happy with the way things are. Thinks we ought to sell the place and try something else. Christ, by the time we'd pay off the first and second mortgages, there'd be nothin' left."

Leroy had heard it all before. He lined up empty glasses on a towel behind the bar, wishing his lower back pain would go away. Poured himself a shot of bar whiskey to ease the pain, which worked for a while but seemed only to make it worse later on.

Carlisle thought about a second beer, but the company didn't warrant it, and he didn't feel like troubling Leroy again. Leroy stood with one foot on a keg, laughing with the cowboy, not bothering to turn when Carlisle finished his beer and walked out. As he closed the door behind him, pool balls cracked into one another while old Frank snored and choked his way toward oblivion.

"Now just what did we have sitting down there?" Jack Deveraux asked, canting his head and looking toward the door where Carlisle had exited.

"No idea." Leroy turned to wash more glasses. "Some longhair from somewhere. They come in once in a while. No problem, 'long as they keep quiet and keep moving."

As he put his Red Wing lace-ups on the sidewalk outside Leroy's, Carlisle's first observation was that an elderly man was watching him from a second-floor window across the street, above what used to be Lester's TV & Appliance. His second was that Salamander and the sun pretty much closed up shop at the same time.

In the past few months, Carlisle had seen hundreds of small towns, and Salamander was not unique. Other places, lots of them, looked the same with their empty storefronts, boarded-up schools, few young people on the streets. A general sense of malaise, of lifelessness, of things gone wrong.

It was a pretty sunset, though, his first evening in Salamander. The kind you get out in the big spaces, with the western sky turning pink magenta laid up against a dome of azure to the north.

Hungry now, choices limited. Leroy's had advertised Tombstone pizza, which, looking around the main street of Salamander, Carlisle decided was prophetic. Leroy's other specials were beef jerky in a glass jar and packages of beer nuts, all of it amounting to a shade less than the five basic food groups.

Twilight came with a descending chill typical of late summer nights in those parts. Carlisle pulled his old leather jacket from the truck, slipped into it, and walked along Main Street. In the window of E. M. Holley's furniture store–cum–undertaker's parlor was an overstuffed love seat upholstered in blood-red flowers against a white background. He guessed by the looks of things in Salamander that the second half of Holley's empire was outrunning the first.

The windows of Charlene's Variety were plastered with GOING OUT OF BUSINESS signs stating that thread and notions and gifts could be had at rock-bottom prices. Two of the three gas stations were gone, weeds growing where pumps had been. The remaining one was trying to peddle unleaded at three cents a gallon higher than Harv's Get & Go convenience store. Swale's Ranch Supply looked as though it might sell a little wire or maybe some feed now and then, but not much else. There were no fresh tire tracks in the mud by Swale's loading dock. Orly's Meats and Locker Service was hanging in there, Webster's Jack & Jill grocery was doing the same.

On the door of what used to be Schold's Badlands Lounge was a sign reading, "I have moved to Livermore." Just below that sign was another, one that had been fastened there a long time, the bottom corners of it curling back. Carlisle squatted down to read it.

SMALL TOWNS
Crime is scarcely heard of, breaches of order rare, and our societies, if not refined, are rational, moral, and affectionate at least.

— THOMAS JEFFERSON

Salamander's commercial district was two blocks long. In the middle of the second block, across from where Carlisle walked, was a small and faltering neon sign, yellow with black lettering, signaling "DAN Y's." As he crossed the street, Carlisle could see the burned-out N, which cleared up the dominant question in his life at that particular moment.

The door to Danny's was flaking white

wood on the bottom half with a frame of glass at the top. A faded Kools cigarette advertisement was pasted to the glass just below a Pepsi sticker. Above those was a sign advising that, indeed, Danny's was open and would be until eight o'clock.

Seven chromed metal stools with red seat coverings fronted the counter. Three Formica-topped tables ran down the middle, and six scarred booths wobbled along the side of the room next to the sidewalk. In one of the booths, four teenagers were reeling through that horrendous period of life when it seems death will never come and zits will never leave.

Buddy Reems, Carlisle's former partner in Reems & McMillan Construction, had come up with lots of good ideas. One of his best was that all teenagers should be sent to some desolate place, maybe North Dakota. Buddy had it figured out: Pave the entire state and stock it with nothing but fast-food restaurants and skateboard parks and drive-in movies.

Buddy would then sit at a small table on the state line, and those interned would have to pass an adult certification interview with him before leaving. Some, many, most, would never make it. Those who did would have an "A" for "Adult" branded into the flesh of their foreheads so the world could identify and treat them as rational people. All Buddy asked in return for the brilliance of his idea and his work at the interview table was the Clearasil concession for the entire state, into perpetuity, and the right to operate a trashy amusement park he'd call Buddyland.

Listening to Buddy talk about it, Carlisle had thought the proposal contained a lot of merit once you got by its front-end weirdness. Automobile insurance rates would dive, and so would crime rates. Bad music, gone. There were more benefits. Buddy had a long list he'd worked out, but just now Carlisle couldn't remember all of them. Dammit, sometimes he missed Buddy Reems, missed his company and his good ideas. In addition to being a decent carpenter and drinking companion, he was a first-chop social theorist—well, maybe a cut or two below that—and operated pretty much as Carlisle's opposite, saying and doing certain things Carlisle wouldn't.

Waylon and Willie were roaring out of the café's jukebox, bragging about honky-

tonkin' men and the good-hearted, maso-
chistic women loving them in spite of their
errant ways. The plastic, two-foot-high tubu-
lar pie case on the counter had room for ten
slices. Six were gone. Apple and some sort
of cream wonders were left, kind of mournful
looking at the end of the day, their morning
zip just a memory and replaced by an early
evening sag. Carlisle decided the pies were
not a bad metaphor for himself, or for the
woman who came out of the kitchen and
saw him sitting at the counter, oscillating
slowly on a stool.

"Oh, hi. Didn't know anyone was out
here. Can I help you with something?"

Gally Deveraux was tired, felt that way,
looked it. Nice midrange voice. A little wind-
burned in the face, a little sad in the face. A
little thin in the body, maybe, or maybe not.
Long black hair with a few silver strands and
rubber-banded into a ponytail. Eyes kind of
a haunting color, gray or close to it. She
might have been pretty a long time ago, but
now she had the same spare, run-down
look as the country around them.

"Well, I'm trying to locate some dinner,
and this seems to be the last hope in Salamander."

Gally Deveraux smiled, good smile, genuine smile. "We eat *dinner* around noon out here. Suppertime comes about six in the evening, breakfast twelve hours after that. So you're kind of in a cranny, your last hope fading with every clock tick. Here, take a look at the menu and maybe we can work something out."

The menu was handwritten and shoved into a cracked plastic sleeve. The same list Carlisle had found in small-town cafés everywhere in that sector of America: hamburger, cheeseburger, vegetable burger, hamburger steak, pork tenderloin, grilled cheese sandwich, tuna salad sandwich, egg salad sandwich, French fries . . . The fish sandwich had been priced at $2.45 (with fries) but was crossed out now.

Carlisle closed the menu and gave her an easy grin. "What does the chef suggest? The free-range almond chicken with an infusion of rosemary, accompanied by an unassuming white wine, or the veal in cream sauce?"

She smiled again. "If it were me, I'd go for the hot turkey sandwich and a tossed salad on the side, 'specially since I just cleaned the grill and I'm not anxious to mess it up again. That's easy for me to fix and won't jump up and bite you too bad later on. I'm mostly concerned about the former."

"Okay, that's it." Carlisle grinned back. "Black coffee and a glass of water will take care of the liquids. Leave off the house dressing on the salad and bring me a wedge of lemon to squeeze on it."

She poured him a cup of coffee, good coffee, and went into the kitchen. He could hear her opening and closing a refrigerator door, while he tapped one foot to the juke-box and tried to ignore the greasy-haired boy thumping the pinball machine with the palms of his hands. The other teenagers, overcoming their miasma of self-absorption for a moment, were looking at him and giggling nervously. If Buddy had been there, he might have mooned them; he had done that one time in Fresno.

He heard the microwave humming, and the woman had the sandwich ready in a few minutes. Two mounds of mashed potatoes, chunks of turkey suffocating between slices of white bread, and a Thanksgiving kind of gravy ladled over the whole business.

The salad was iceberg lettuce with

grated carrots sprinkled on top. And there was his lemon, looking at him coyly as if to say "You could've had Thousand Island, yet you chose me."

The salad dish was one of those plastic jobs designed to resemble a wooden bowl. Carlisle had seen them before and guessed that somewhere around 1955, a smooth talker had drifted along the Middle Border with a truckload of those beauties and sold them, thousands of them, to all the little cafés in all the little towns. "They never crack or stain, and they look just like those nice wooden ones. You'll be real happy with them, I guarantee it." And so they sailed on, the little bowls, with their cargoes of iceberg lettuce, confident of their ability to outlast everything but an exploding sun.

Carlisle buckled down and got serious about eating. The woman poured herself a cup of coffee, leaned against the soft-drink cooler. "You're not from around here, are you."

Mouth full of mashed potatoes and gravy, he shook his head. After he got the food down, he replied, "No, I'm not. How'd you guess?"

"Well, first of all, you talk in complete

sentences and use silverware. That tipped me off right away."

Good line. She was quick and smart. And he laughed, while probing the gravy's surface. "I used to be from California. Now I'm from my pickup truck."

Bite of turkey, wash of coffee to put it down. For no reason he could remember later on, he asked her if a man wanted to buy a little place around here, who would be the person to see.

"Cecil Macklin has an office in his home, just back of the café and across the alley. There's a Better Homes and Gardens real estate outfit in Livermore. That's about ten miles southeast of here, and they cover Salamander. Cecil works for them."

"Well, I'd just as soon not do the Realtor bit. Any other way of scouting around?"

She gave him a quizzical look. "Everybody else's leaving or trying to, and you're thinking about moving here?"

"Just thinking about it. Trying to fight off the encroachment of what passes for civilization, as long as possible. Salamander seems about as good a place as any to throw up the barricades."

"You've got that right. Just go out in the

street and wave a sign that says 'Lookin' for a Place.' You'll be trampled by people shoving deeds at you."

She refilled his coffee and leaned against the cooler, watching the man while he ate. A different sort all right, in his leather jacket, old jeans, and denim shirt. Brown shoulder-length hair, almost as long as hers, tied back with a yellow bandanna around his head. Dark eyes and slim body with good shoulders. Proper manners. Apparently civilized. Mid-thirties, maybe a little older, olive skin with the first creases from age and sun around his eyes and mouth, hands that had done a lot of manual labor by the look of them.

For a moment, a flickering one, Gally Deveraux wondered about possibilities, then let it go. She had tried that two years ago with Harv Guthridge, who owned the quarry outside of town. Harv knew how to flatter a woman, and Gally had ended up in his bed over in Livermore one night after closing up Danny's. That happened twice more. It wasn't much in the way of good sex, but her husband, Jack, had stopped paying attention to her a long time back, and at least

Harv kept telling her she was just about the prettiest thing he'd ever seen.

Then Harv had started bragging about his conquest, and Gally didn't need those knowing looks when she dropped plates of meat loaf in front of Danny's regulars, so she'd called it off. If Jack knew about it, he had never said anything, and Harv still came by the house now and then to drink with him. Harv hadn't liked being set aside by a woman, so he grinned at her now the way a trapper grins on his way home with pelts over his shoulder. He'd had her, and he didn't mind telling anyone who cared to listen that she was pretty hot stuff when you got her clothes off and got her cranked up.

Watching Carlisle McMillan, she knew there wasn't much point to thinking about possibilities. Shut up, shut down. Put the food on the counter and feel the slow dissolution of anything connected with being a woman. She was becoming one of the boys. Danny's regulars treated her that way. So did Jack, when he had anything to do with her at all. Recognize deadfall when you see it. Make a slow left turn just this side of oblivion, that's the best you can do for now. Still, she wished she were dressed a little better tonight, maybe in the new shirt and jeans she had bought a couple of weeks ago at Charlene's sale, and wished, too, that she had brushed her hair an hour or so back when she'd thought about it. No particular reason, she just wished she had done those things.

But she was tired, and that was probably why she was having these thoughts. Eight hours earlier, before coming into work, she had watched a lone eagle ride one of the last winds of summer. Standing there in a long field that ran all the way to the beginning of afternoon and watching the eagle, she could hear Jack coughing in the kitchen thirty feet behind her. His cough was worse than yesterday, and yesterday it had been worse than the day before. The cigarettes and Jim Beam had him by the throat, physically, figuratively. He was dying. But then he'd been dying for the last ten years. Gally Deveraux had been dying, too, in her own way and for a long time. Maybe ever since she had married him twenty years ago and had come out to the high plains.

Not much resemblance between the man in her kitchen and the one she had married. Sometimes, when she thought about it, she could still see the early Jack leaning against a fence at the North Star Stampede, a rodeo in Effie, Minnesota, fiddling with a lariat. A hard, thin swashbuckler in his boots and Stetson and western shirt with pearl snaps, starched jeans fastened up by a wide leather belt that had "Devil Jack" stamped on the brass buckle. Back then, Jack Deveraux had been a wild rider of broncs and bulls and young women having the temerity to smile at him. Gally and two of her friends from Bemidji State had smiled at him.

He had smiled back in that slow, roguish way of his. "Evenin', ladies." Good eyes, blue and direct.

When Gally had left for college, her mother recited a litany of bad things young women should avoid in the interest of preserving all the good things young women are supposed to preserve. The list was a long one and included star quarterbacks but inadvertently omitted cowboys. After watching Jack ride the bulls that night in Effie, and after three beers from the cooler in his truck, Gally willingly shucked her jeans and smelled the dust on his skin while she straddled him in his truck cab. Jack pulled out for Bozeman the next morning, and Gally went with him.

"Easy," that's what he called her back then. She hadn't minded because it was a pretty good description of her in those days. Besides, early on in their marriage she liked the way Jack said it, kind of soft and loving, as in "Hey, Easy, wanna go dancin' tonight?" He called her that for years after they were married. He didn't call her that anymore. He didn't say much of anything to her anymore.

The eagle had disappeared somewhere in the north behind a rain cloud. When she couldn't see it anymore, Gally walked across dusty, short grass toward the house. She opened the fridge, stared into it for a moment, then looked at the distant, contemptuous man sitting at the kitchen table, coughing.

"Want me to fix you something to eat, Jack? I could heat up the vegetables and roast left over from Sunday."

He was still thin in the legs and shoulders, but now he carried a potbelly that sagged in concert with his splotched, puffy face. He was drinking whiskey straight from the bottle this morning and tilted back his head, took another shot. He swallowed it and said nothing.

"You really do need something in your stomach. Seems like you never eat anymore."

"If I don't feel like eating, I'm not gonna eat. Stop pushing at me about it, for chrissake."

The table was covered with empty beer bottles and two ashtrays full of cigarette butts. Jack and his cronies had spent another night sitting there bitching about hard times, about what the government and shit-faced environmentalists and bankers and European farm policies were doing to their lives.

"Maybe if you'd clean up the goddamn kitchen table once in a while, I might feel more like eating."

"Clean it up yourself, Jack. You and your buddies made the mess."

The old Jack was pretty much gone, but the temper was still there. He swept a stand of beer bottles to the floor with his forearm and went into the living room. One of the bottles continued to spin on its side for a long time, then clinked against a table leg and stopped.

Arms folded, Gally leaned against the door frame of the house Jack's grandfather built in 1915. The house was peeling white and needed care, but there wasn't any energy for that. Energy for whiskey—the procuring of it, the drinking of it—but not for the house. Or for her. No money, either. She had bought her last new dress two years earlier when they were going out to celebrate Jack's birthday, but he had gotten drunk in midafternoon and passed out. She leaned against the door frame this afternoon and looked down at herself in an old denim shirt, faded jeans, boot heels run over, and felt six times bad and worse than that, feeling a whole lot older than thirty-nine.

She wondered how Jack Jr. was doing. He was nineteen and following the second-tier rodeo circuit, firing off a postcard now and then from Las Cruces, Ardmore, and other places where the bulls had straps pinching their genitals and tried to buck off cowboys who had never really been cowboys, just rodeo riders. Sharon was also gone, to a husband who drove for a truck line out of Casper. At first, she would ride with him when he hauled loads up to Fargo and stay with Gally and Jack for a few days before her husband picked her up on the way back, but not anymore. Two babies of her own kept her tied down in Casper now. Even without the babies she wouldn't have come now, because of Jack's drinking and all.

Around noon, Gally walked across the porch and out to the Ford Bronco, started it, and drove along the lane. Rain took up just as she turned onto Wolf Butte Road. Four hours later, Jack followed her into town and went into Leroy's.

In Danny's, another country tune counterpointed by the pinball machine was expiring on the jukebox: "I'm [*bing!*] short on words, but [*bong!*] long on *[bing!bong! . . . bong!bong!bing!]* love . . ."

Carlisle was thinking a contemporary composer, maybe John Cage, could cut through all of that and do something with it. Or maybe Cage would consider it a masterwork and just leave it alone.

"Do you own this place?" He looked at the woman in faded jeans, denim shirt, and old cowboy boots with the heels run over.

"No, and I'm glad I don't, the way things are going around here. Older woman named Thelma Englestrom owns it, took it over from her husband when he died. She's been in the Falls City hospital for the last couple weeks, so I'm working a little more than usual. Me and Mrs. Macklin, Cecil's wife, are sort of keeping things going till Thelma gets back on her feet. Ordinarily I just work here a few days a week, mostly in the mornings, sometimes afternoons and evenings."

Carlisle stared at the pie case.

"Those fellows look a little tired, don't they," Gally Deveraux observed, following his eyes. "Mrs. Macklin bakes 'em fresh every other day. But the liquid runs into the crust and eventually collapses it, kind of like Salamander."

There was something in what she said that was straight and true. Something. He had thought about it before. "Yeah, it does kind of look like that. But I'll take a shot at the apple."

"Want it straight or with some ice cream?"

"Strap on the vanilla. The end is near anyway, right?"

Big piece of apple pie. Big scoops of ice cream. She rested her stomach against the ice-cream freezer, her jeans pulling up tight over a nice-looking rear, and dug out the good stuff, serving it along with a clean fork. She took his gravy plate into the kitchen, rattling around in there. He missed her company. He was in the middle of Salamander in the middle of America in the middle of the world, someplace in a universe still expanding. It had been good talking with her.

Outside, squeal of tires. The teenagers were leaving.

When he paid his bill, Gally glanced up at him and smiled. "You know, I've been thinking about your question . . . about finding a place. An old fellow named Williston used to live on an acreage about eight miles northwest of here. Pretty bare, but there's a nice grove across the road from it and a little house of some kind. Probably in rough shape by now. In fact, it was in rough shape to start with. I remember, though, someone said a lawyer over in Livermore or Falls City was trying to sell it as part of an estate. I can find out for you, if you're serious."

"I'm halfway serious. I'd appreciate any information you can give me."

She sketched lines on a paper napkin with BUY AMERICAN printed in the upper right corner and handed it to him. "No charge for the map. You'll be able to find it okay. It's off in the direction of Wolf Butte, which has a reputation for being haunted and promoting things that go bumpity in the dark. That legend got some additional help when a college professor fell off a nearby cliff some years back and got himself killed. You don't strike me as someone who's too bothered by that sort of stuff, however."

She grinned and went on. "The house sits a hundred, maybe a hundred fifty yards from the road, and it's got a couple of nice big trees right near it. I think there's a little shed or something off to the side. I pass right by there coming into town, but you know how it goes, see something a million times and you forget what it looks like."

Carlisle looked at the map. "I appreciate it. This all seems a little familiar. I think I may have come into town that way."

Gally Deveraux was turning off the café lights as Carlisle stepped outside. The air had a bite to it, and he flipped up the collar on his jacket. He stood there for a moment. Four cars in addition to his truck were parked on Main Street, all of them resting under the mercury vapor streetlamp in front of Leroy's, like horses angled into a water trough. A tumbleweed blew in from the west on a tentative wind and rolled down the pavement. Carlisle watched it pass Charlene's Variety, then stop in front of Orly's Meats and Locker as the wind died.

An out-of-tune Dodge pickup driven by a man in a cowboy hat moved slowly by in a direction opposite that of the tumbleweed, its lights reflecting in empty storefronts. Face dark and indistinguishable under the hat, the man looked at Carlisle for a moment, then stared straight ahead, holding a cigarette against the steering wheel. A rifle was racked across the window behind him. Custom license plates seemed to be the habit around Yerkes County, and this one read DEVLJK.

The wind came again, and the tumbleweed began to move east, bouncing silently along the street in the dust of this place called Salamander. Laughter reverberated softly from somewhere inside Leroy's. Carlisle heard the laughter and listened to the wind, listened to the crunch of his boots on gritty asphalt as he crossed the street. You could smell winter getting to its feet, and Carlisle was still a long way from anything called home.

He started the engine and turned on the

headlights just as a figure in a long cloak passed in front of his truck. The woman was startled by the sound and the lights, glancing for a moment toward where Carlisle sat in the cab. Auburn hair flowed from beneath her hood, and the face, what he could see of it, was strange, an uncommon kind of beauty that started in a man's eyes, then dropped into his belly. She turned her head again and continued along the street, cloak billowing softly in the wind and dust of a late summer heading quickly into early autumn.

He made a U-turn and drove back down the street. The woman stepped off the curb and waited for him to pass. He looked at her again. A lot of people looked more than once at Susanna Benteen. Some even called her a witch.

CHAPTER THREE

Sleepy's Stagger Inn, Livermore. The old man gripped his right leg with both hands and shifted it into a better position underneath the table, grunting a little from both the effort and some obvious pain.

His face twitched momentarily before he went on with what he'd been saying.

"Never been anything like it, not out here, at least."

He fingered his shot glass, angled it up, and looked straight down into the whiskey, what he called the "amber truth" when he ordered it. He shook his head slowly back and forth. "You name it, we had it: war, magic, Indians . . . so-called witches, for chrissake."

"Mind if I quote you here and there, on the local stuff?" I asked.

"Keep buying the Wild Turkey, quote me all you want. Talk to Carlisle McMillan, too, get it straight from the hombre who went through it all."

The old man liked to talk, so I switched on my tape recorder and let him.

"When Carlisle McMillan first rolled into Salamander that first evening, I somehow knew the level of excitement was going to pick up around here. Somehow I just knew that.

"Now, if you're sixty-four, as I was then, living in two rooms plus bath above what used to be Lester's TV and Appliance, there wasn't much to do. Especially if you couldn't get around too well because of the leg you mangled out at the Guthridge Brothers quarry in '75, when you got caught between the blade of a front-end loader and a chunk of limestone. I'd hobble down to the post office in the morning for the junk mail and keep track of Main Street from the window in my parlor. That was about it.

"Since almost nothing happened down there, your mind kind of rotted from concentrating on piffle running to emptiness. But it was that or television, and the street won hands down.

"Anyway, Carlisle went into Leroy's and came out twenty minutes later. He stood around on the pavement a bit, then took a jacket out of his truck. He walked along, looking into windows, cutting cattywampus across the street in the general direction of Danny's. I lost my angle of view on him when he got to my side of the street, but Danny's was the only thing open, so I guessed he must have gone in there.

"I also took my meals at Danny's. Some of them, anyways. Right after I went by the post office in the morning. That way, I only had to negotiate the stairs to my place once a day, which was plenty with this damn leg. Gally Deveraux, who worked in the café, was real nice and gave me secret discounts on the noon specials. She'd send me home with day-old rolls and those little unused jam cartons left over from breakfast, free of charge. Sometimes she told me to go ahead and take extra packets of sugar or salt or pepper.

"So if I ate a lot at noon, I could get by in the evening on oatmeal and rolls with cheese or a little peanut butter and jam. Well, that and a shot of the Old Charter my daughter always sent me at Christmas from

Orlando. Of course, by late March I'd worked my way through her gift, and December started looking like a long way off.

"But I baby-sat Mert's Texaco when he'd take his wife to the clinic in Livermore, and he'd pick up a fifth of cheap stuff for me at the big Piggly Wiggly store over there. That's how he paid me for sitting on my butt and telling people to pump their own damn gas at a nickel a gallon more than Harv's Get and Go inconvenience store charged. The IRS held I ought to report the whiskey as barter income, but I always said piss on 'em. I wish they'd audited me anyhow, just so I would have had someone halfway intelligent to talk to, even if it was an accountant. You know, if those folks weren't so boring, they'd be interesting.

"So, how'd I know Carlisle was going to notch up the energy level in Salamander? Not sure. Maybe it had to do with the yellow bandanna tied around his head and the long brown hair coming out from underneath it, hanging to just above his shoulders. In the twilight, in his leather jacket, old boots, and faded jeans, he looked like one of the younger bucks from the reservation who was trying to forget Wounded Knee, avoid a beer gut, and rediscover his heritage.

"Something about his walk, too. Kind of easy, kind of sure. A walk like that covered a lot of ground in a day without exerting too much effort. There was something about Carlisle that told me the years were pulling at him pretty hard, but I could still tell he was upper shelf, that he wouldn't bend without some real pushing. 'Course, we don't bend none too easy around here, either.

"For all those reasons, I decided to keep an eye on Carlisle McMillan and see if he hung around. As I said, we'd been pretty hard up for excitement. Before all hell broke loose in the form of the Yerkes County War, there'd been only two things worth noting around here, aside from Salamander needing some kind of municipal CPR. One of 'em didn't involve Carlisle directly. The other one did.

"The first had to do with Susanna Benteen. You had to get your mind kind of calm and straight to understand Susanna. Otherwise you'd take her for something she wasn't, like maybe a relic from the old student uproar days of the sixties. We used to watch it all on TV in the evenings back then, and I kind of miss seeing that now. Of course, the bobos over at Leroy's weren't all that sympathetic toward those students marching around and burning flags. But they *were* more or less fascinated with the 'free love' ideas we heard about, which apparently was a nice part of the marching and burning.

"Once you got by that notion and started looking real close at Susanna, your reaction would depend on whether you were a man or a woman, I suppose. A lot of us still remember the first time we saw her. It's easy to recall 'cause Susanna Benteen came riding in on the last Greyhound ever to stop in Salamander. Had a battered suitcase in one hand, macramé bag over her shoulder. The boys at the back table in Danny's looked up from their cards and out the front window. Somebody said, '*Jesus* Key*rist*! Do you see what's coming off the bus out there?' We all turned as one, like we'd been rehearsing it for a long time.

"And Susanna Benteen came stepping off the bus and onto the sidewalk, light as you please. Wore a dress about the color of ripe wheat with a dark green shawl over it, high black boots, and that long auburn hair of hers done up in a fancy braid. She came into the restaurant and asked for a cup of herbal tea. Spoke real quiet and polite. There wasn't much call for herbal tea in Salamander, and Gally apologized for not having any. That was perfectly all right, the regular stuff would do, we all heard Susanna Benteen say. We all heard it 'cause we were all paying close attention.

"Gally served her a cup of hot water and a Lipton's bag with a spoon, trying not to stare at this creature who had wafted in off the Greyhound. But the boys in the back stared. You bet they did. The older you get, the more bad manners are permitted, if not forgiven. That's one of the few advantages of age and its various declines. I was sitting at the counter a few stools down from Susanna and pretending to read a newspaper, but I was staring, too. At the risk of sounding poetic, which I ain't and never have been, a swallow had landed where only crows had flown.

"After she'd been here a while, quite a few of the folks in Salamander started calling Susanna a witch. Some still do. That's one way of dealing with things you don't understand. Partly it's the look of her. The feeling you might be staring at something you haven't seen before. Something beyond the boundaries of ordinary ways of doing things, and *do we ever* hate anything deviating from the ordinary. She represented something the other side of where most of us cared to go, fearing we might never get back to a place that was familiar. And when it comes to Susanna, I suspect there's some truth in all of that, the idea that you might not get back from wherever she might take you. Carlisle McMillan eventually found that out.

"Even though the locals were suspicious of Susanna from the beginning, a lot of that witch business got its start when Arlo Gregorian's wife, Kathy, got pregnant. The fact that she *was* pregnant would have been enough, simply because babies are a real oddity in a town where the majority of residents are old women living on government transfer payments or sucking up interest from CDs, courtesy of Verle and Floyd and Morris and Harold and all the rest of those buggers who worked their asses off to pay for their land and then died at about the same time they burned the mortgage. After which, of course, the wife sold the property that was too much for her to take care of and moved to town.

"No, what made things real interesting was the way Kathy Gregorian got herself with child, as they say. It had to do with Susanna Benteen. See, Arlo and Kathy had been married for over three years with no sign of babies in their future. They were both healthy young folks and were always hanging on to each other at the Fourth of July picnic and such. One supposes, then, they were getting it on at home regularly, doing their best, but no cigar.

"Not being able to have children is a common heartache and not to be made light of, under any circumstance. But in a town full of men thinking of themselves as real stud horses, which, of course, they weren't—just ask the women—the inability to manufacture offspring was the local equivalent of being a hairless eunuch. So Arlo was taking a real beating over at Leroy's about all this. 'Any little ones in your future, Arlo? Need some help?' That's what they'd holler along the bar at him.

"Kathy dragged Arlo three hundred miles down to the big municipal hospital, a journey he'd just as soon had remained a secret. And it probably would have if he hadn't bumped into Leroy down there, who was getting his checkup so he could get his liver medicine prescription renewed. Leroy, with the keen insight gained from years of following his chosen profession, which was serving drinks to drunks, guessed why Arlo was hanging around the fertility clinic waiting room. Upon his return, he informed all his regular drinkers and pool sharks about the encounter, along with his personal supposition that Arlo had been advised to wear loose undershorts and was being required to whack off into a test tube.

"That just made things worse for Arlo, and he was getting desperate, thinning down from working all day at the Farmers Co-op and dealing with a low sperm count at night, wearing his shortcoming like barnacles. By then, Kathy was leaning toward artificial insemination, but Arlo wouldn't hear of it.

"'Jesus-on-the-dashboard, I've got troubles enough,' Arlo told her. 'You do that and the shitheads'll be asking if the Boar Power truck full of refrigerated hog jism came through or what.'

"Kathy, crying and carrying on and close to falling apart, was leaning on her best friend, Leona Williams, for support. Leona suggested a talk with the new woman named Susanna, who seemed to know about all kinds of things. That seemed pretty radical to Kathy, at first, but women have this useful streak in them of doing what it takes to get things done. A streak, I might add, that is entirely missing from the genes of most men, who get themselves all tied up in pride and posturing courtesy of testosterone and whatever else it is that prevents us from being fully housebroken.

"So Kathy went to visit Susanna. Susanna said the problem might be solvable. Unfortunately, Arlo needed to be involved in the process. That worried Kathy, but not Susanna.

"When Kathy told Arlo about this new strategy involving Susanna, Arlo got in his green GMC pickup with the world's largest engine and drove around town for a half hour, alternately considering divorce and suicide. Then he started thinking about alimony, test tubes, the shitheads, Boar Power, and self-abuse, pretty much in that order. Those prospects kind of opened him up a little to new ideas, and he agreed to at least talk with Susanna.

"Came the following evening, Susanna knocked on the Gregorians' door. Kathy, in high heels and the dress she'd bought the previous year for the Volunteer Firemen's Benefit Dance, escorted her in and got her seated on the brocade sofa, which had been a wedding present from Arlo's folks. Arlo was real nervous, given all the rumors about Susanna. None of the rumors had ever been substantiated, of course, but truth didn't count for squat in Salamander, never had, never would. So Arlo kind of churned around, not knowing what to say or do, and finally offered her a Grain Belt, which she politely refused.

"There were a few minutes of stiff conversation during which Kathy tried to make small talk and Susanna merely sat and smiled pleasantly. Arlo crouched on a footstool by the Magnavox home entertainment center on which he was making lifetime payments and trying all the while not to look too directly at their guest.

"Of course, he'd never spoken a word to Susanna after she'd drifted into Salamander and set up shop in the old Nelson place south of the elevator, right on the edge of town. Up close, however, the witch seemed pretty nice, he decided. Kind of harmless.

"Nonetheless, she made him uneasy. Aside from the mantle of darkness conferred upon her by the citizens of a state that brags about having the fourteenth-highest SAT scores in the U.S., she made him nervous simply because she was easily the best-looking woman in Salamander. In fact, Susanna was and is one of the best-looking women you're likely to find anywhere.

"On that score, the ongoing Salamander beauty contest, a minority of the boys held out for Alma Hickman, who ran a beauty shop called the Swirl'n Curl from the basement of her home. But that was more a matter of patriotism than good judgment, and anybody who'd been around at all, or even looked at magazines other than *Farm Implement Digest,* knew that any comparison between Susanna and Alma Hickman was a crock of you-know-what.

"In addition to the hint of a luxurious body moving around underneath her long, flowing dresses and shawls, a real pretty face, and her auburn hair hanging down in a shining braid, Susanna had something Alma

would never have: class. There wasn't one
of the boys who didn't privately dream about
what it would be like to crawl under the cov-
ers with Ms. Susanna Benteen, while they
rolled their toothpicks from one side of their
mouths to the other and watched her when
she came downtown to pick up her mail. But
she paid no attention to any of them and, in
her own way, made it clear they had a better
chance at the Virgin Mary than her.

"They all agreed it was hard to say just
how old Susanna was. The ordinary cues
about age didn't seem to apply to her.
Somewhere between late twenties and mid-
thirties was about as close as any of them
could come to guessing her age, with the
heavy money resting on the middle of that
range. After she was in Salamander a month
or two, an Oriental fellow stopped by to visit
her. Sort of a gaunt rooster, also of indeter-
minate age. Speculation was they were setting up a narcotics enterprise out here far
from organized law. Bobby Eakins, operating without mercy or evidence, as usual,
called her companion the dope slope, not to
his face, of course. The Oriental stayed a
few weeks, then pulled out.

"Folks claimed Susanna bought most of

her supplies from natural food stores on the West Coast and that UPS was her supply wagon. Her garden took care of the rest. A few of the old people started to visit her for herbal medicines when the clinic couldn't make any headway on their complaints, and some of them swore she helped. Talk was that some of the younger women had also been drifting by her place to discuss things beyond the scope of conversation at Leroy's. Some of 'em brought home other suspicious cargo like incense and jewelry and such. Other than that, she had little to do with the town.

"This matter involving Arlo and Kathy Gregorian would probably still be a secret if Arlo hadn't gotten drunk a few months after Susanna did her thing and told Bobby Eakins about what had transpired. Bobby sucked on a Royal Crown at Mert's one hot Saturday and related his version of the story to several of us, including Orly Hammond hanging around waiting for Mert to get back from Livermore with a part for his Chevy. Bobby swore the facts were just as Arlo had presented them to him while under the influence.

"Arlo later found out that Bobby had

mesmerized us with all the particulars and said he'd burn Bobby's single-wide to the ground if he opened his mouth about it again. So Orly and me and a few others were the only ones knowing the total story back then, at least as much as Bobby knew. The rest of the town just put together its own version, which turned out to be a lot racier than anything approaching the truth."

"Need another Wild Turkey?" I asked the old man.

He waggled his jaw and nodded, big grin on his face. I was starting to feel some affection for the old guy. He seemed to talk straight, adding a little color to his descriptions as he went along. I walked over to the bar, got another shot of the amber truth from Sleepy, and set it in front of the old man. He took a sip, wiped his mouth with a soiled shirt cuff, and looked at me.

"Let's see, where was I? Oh yeah, the Gregorians' living room. When things had settled down a little that night, Susanna talked to Kathy and Arlo. Arlo said she'd talked real quiet, sort of motherly. The first thing she told them was that she wasn't a witch of any sort and did not adhere to any satanic beliefs. In fact, Susanna insisted she avoided all organized religions, including Christianity, the Rosicrucians, and professional football. That latter point about religion made Kathy and Arlo a little unsteady for only the smokiest of reasons, since neither of them had been in any church since their wedding day. Though, as Arlo liked to say, he came from a long line of rebels himself, including his grandmother, who stopped going to Mass when they turned the altar around some years back and started inviting in folksingers to entertain.

"Susanna kind of lost Arlo when she talked about the healing power of nature and the significance of moon phases and a lot of other mumbo-jumbo, as Arlo called it. He tuned in again when she got to diet, telling them they were eating way too much red meat and other animal products. She claimed it was bad karma and that the animals consumed had ways of coming back at you with their own brand of revenge.

"Those of us alert to the details of a complex and shifting universe noted that Susanna always carried woven bags instead of an ordinary leather purse. She had one of these bags with her at the Gregorians' and began taking small packages and bottles full of herbs and spices and oils from it, one at a time, all the while explaining how they should be used. Kathy paid close attention, for which Arlo later was grateful, since the instructions were moving by him pretty fast.

"Then she started talking about women and men, and Arlo could make a little more sense of that. She used a lot of words, such as kindness and understanding, and generally admonished them to work on making their conjugal ventures more warm and intimate. Both Arlo and Kathy got clenched up red in the face when Susanna discussed eroticism, focusing particularly on the needs of women.

"Arlo said he wanted to bolt for the kitchen and drink a quart of Grain Belt or lye water or whatever he could get his hands on, but she just kept staring at him in a firm, even way with her big green eyes. He felt as if he were nailed to his stool near the Magnavox. She stayed for nearly two hours, talking real soft all the time.

"In addition to the herbs and oils and such, she gave them a small book on something called the Tao and a set of dietary instructions written in fancy script. Oh yes, she also provided them with certain dates that seemed most fruitful—that seems to be the right word—in terms of conception. Until the first of those dates, which didn't begin for over two weeks, they were to refrain from any bedroom folderol, absolutely. Some kind of warehousing or whatever on Arlo's part.

"Just as Susanna was standing by the door and ready to leave, she looked at Arlo and said, 'Arlo, I don't mean what I'm about to say to sound harsh or presumptuous or any of that, and it's awfully hard to express it in any kind of subtle way. But the fact is that the culture out here makes it difficult for a man to get in touch with himself, to understand what it means to be a man and not just a large boy. But you can do it if you want to, and, having done it, I think you'll feel better about a lot of things. And, Kathy, you can help him by not complaining about the amount of money he brings home and how he could do better for himself than working at the co-op. Arlo has his own self-worth, and you must do your part in helping him to discover it.'

"After she'd left, Arlo told Kathy that the witch's last comment was entirely uncalled for. He knew who he was, yessir, and who was she to imply that he didn't? Didn't he own a GMC with a serious power plant under the hood? Didn't he work at the co-op? Hadn't he scored the winning touchdown for the Salamander Tigers against the Leadville Miners in the 1974 playoffs?

"At the time, the news seemed all bad to Arlo. Not only was the local football team one and six for the season, not only did Susanna's instructions include both abstinence and absolutely no television for either him or Kathy, but in addition he was now asked to become an herbivore for several weeks.

"'Hell, Bobby,' he'd say, 'I'm not eating, I'm grazing. Here I am working for the co-op, and what am I doing? Supporting the stupid vegetable farmers out in the San Joaquin, that's what. If word ever got around about this fag diet I'm on, I'd not only lose my job, people'd think I was a prevert or something.'

"According to Arlo, Susanna's prescribed diet was stringent: no red meat, no meat of any kind, plenty of vegetables and fruits and rice and whole-grain concoctions. Arlo lusted for his breakfast sausage, which was not part of the scheme, and his supper food sort of lay there and snapped at him. But Kathy kept reminding him of the alternatives and said, besides, she felt better eating this way.

"Arlo did admit that his acid indigestion had disappeared and that he no longer got sleepy in the evenings after supper. Since he was allowed only one beer per day and couldn't eat those little beef jerky sticks, he stopped hanging around Leroy's. He conjured up excuses as to why he missed the Legion's annual fall steak fry and, in general, spent more time with Kathy.

"Based on Susanna's austere instructions, they were barred from watching *Dallas* or anything else, for that matter, and there wasn't anything else to do in the evenings. So they started taking walks together or driving the GMC over to the Little Salamander River to look at the sunsets.

"The lack of boom-boom, which was Bobby Eakins's term when he was telling all this, was the worst part. Arlo wanted his candy now and said he was developing a painful constriction in the groin area. It wasn't easy holding him at bay for nearly three weeks, but Kathy's ace card was always the test tube or the possibility that some other man's genes might flow through their child if it came to artificial insemination. That latter thought was particularly daunting to Arlo. As he said to Bobby, 'Christ-in-a-sidecar, Bobby, we might get an Einstein or an idiot, and I don't know which'd be worse.'

"Kathy posted sayings on the fridge from the Tao book Susanna had given them and discussed the meaning of them with Arlo, just as Susanna had suggested. That was kind of hard for Arlo, since his brain had been rotting away ever since seventh grade when he discovered football, girls, and internal combustion engines, not necessarily in that exact sequence. Over breakfast, instead of catching the hog markets and sports results on the morning news, he was asked to consider little gems such as

> *. . . the True Person*
> *arrives without traveling,*
> *perceives without looking,*
> *and acts without striving.*

"And

> *Blunt the sharpness,*
> *Untie the knot,*

Soften the glare,
Settle with the dust.

"During the day, driving the liquid fertilizer truck along country roads, Arlo found himself wondering what it meant to act without striving. That was a tough one all right, and he couldn't get it out of his mind. Kept turning it over and over. Even asked Bobby Eakins what he thought it meant, which was a mistake, of course.

"Bobby's instant interpretation was, 'Shit, Arlo, that's simple. It means the woman's on top and the man's on the bottom.' After which Bobby laughed and said he'd done just that last Saturday night over in Livermore at the drive-in movie, and if Arlo would start drinking Grain Belt again, all things would become transparent. 'Clear as a foggy glass of Salamander water after it's been run through six goddamn million filters,' were his exact words.

"But it worked. Somehow it worked. Within six months, Kathy was wearing maternity dresses. Word circulated that Susanna visited the Gregorians in October and performed some ritual where they'd all got buck naked and danced around an upside-down cross laid on the rug in front of the Magnavox. The Watkins Products man heard this during his stops in Salamander, spreading the news to Livermore and beyond. Since a number of the boys said they'd plead nolo contendere to a charge of low sperm count or just about anything else if it meant seeing the witch in her altogether, an epidemic of insufficient sperm became a real possibility in Salamander for a while.

"Kathy delivered a fine baby girl right on time. She had been thinking of suggesting to Arlo they name the baby Susanna, but Arlo was replacing shingles on the roof when the idea came to her, so she kept quiet. Eventually, they decided on Myrna, which was Arlo's paternal grandmother's name. The christening at St. Timothy's Catholic Church in Livermore was well attended, and when they got to the part about casting out Beelzebub, quite a few of the faithful looked at each other in knowing ways. Some claimed they saw the priest put an extra dollop of baptism oil on little Myrna's forehead and swore he said some additional words in Latin that they'd never heard before. The outcome of this sequence of events, along with little Myrna, was that

Susanna's place in regional history was chiseled into permanence, even though she could have done nicely without it.

"As for this witch stuff, I always thought that was a little harsh. So, being a latter-day sensitive and understanding male with an elevated consciousness, I preferred 'medicine woman' as a general term of description for her. 'Course, I never believed in any of that witch stuff. Still, I have to admit that after the incident with the Gregorians, I kind of wobbled a bit and admitted to myself that maybe Susanna knew something the rest of us didn't."

The old man paused at this point to speak gently with a gray-haired fellow who stopped by our booth, asking for a sip of the Wild Turkey. Pulling two wrinkled dollar bills from his pocket, the old man hollered at Sleepy to give Frank a couple of draws. Frank mumbled his thanks and staggered over to the bar.

"Frank and I used to work together out at the quarry. He was a good, hard worker in those days. Started the serious boozing about twenty years ago when his daughter married an Iranian from Omaha and his wife took off with a sergeant from down at the air force base. He usually does his drinking over at Leroy's in Salamander."

He frowned momentarily, found his place in the story he'd been telling, and continued. "As you might recall, I started out to talk about the only two pieces of excitement in Salamander over a period of a decade or so, aside from the Yerkes County War, of course. All this previous rambling was somewhat necessary as background for major events that cropped up later on.

"The second thrill occurred about two years after the Gregorians' success at adding to the great human tide devouring this lonely planet. I was looking out my window one night, as usual, preferring that to watching some dude on ABC dance around in the end zone after scoring a touchdown. Up to around nine o'clock, the only thing of interest I'd seen was Carlisle McMillan, who'd been around the area for about seven or eight months at that time, park his truck and go into Leroy's.

"A few minutes later, I saw Huey Sverson's old green Buick screech to a stop right in front of Leroy's. He double-parked it, he did. Out jumps Huey without bothering to close the door, and I saw he was carrying a butcher knife big enough for use at the rendering plant over in Falls City. He walked past Jack Deveraux's truck where Devil Jack, as he liked to be known, was sleeping one off, slammed open the front door of Leroy's, and disappeared inside.

"The rest of what happened I got from Gally and a few other generally reliable sources. Their version was subsequently confirmed by each and every customer stopping at Mert's while I was plunked down there a few days later. It seems that Beanie Wickers, who at one time drove a soybean truck, as you might guess, had been diddling Huey's wife on the side while Huey was off with the National Guard on selected weekends. Huey found out, tossed back three or four shots of Jim Beam, and made a cool and well-considered decision to punch Beanie's ticket.

"Beanie saw Huey coming and had a pretty fair idea of what was going on, since Huey was shouting, 'I'm going to carve your ass into sixteen parts, you wife stealer!' or something to that effect. Beanie ran over the top of the pool table and locked himself in the women's toilet. That resulted in a situation having temporary stability, since none of the boys, least of all Leroy, had any intention of disarming Huey, who was swinging that knife around like John Rambo.

"Huey kept banging on the metal door of the ladies' powder room and shouting—in some detail, according to bystanders—exactly what he was going to do with the butcher knife, focusing especially on certain operations he intended to perform on Beanie's private members. While that was occurring, Leroy summoned our local security force consisting of one Fearless Fred Mumblypeg, which is what the town called Fred Mumford. Fred was sixty-nine, wore a silver badge, and drove around in his Olds seeking out such habitual violators as Ernie 'the Gurney' Penrose, a retarded kid with a habit of peeking in bedroom windows.

"Fred got to Leroy's and told the assembled observers that he might be old, but he wasn't stupid. Moreover, as far as he was concerned, Beanie was about to get everything he deserved. That attitude didn't surprise anyone, since Fred was a lay preacher at the Baptist church.

"Now I'd observed that Carlisle McMillan was kind of a quiet guy who didn't much cotton to violence. Said he'd seen enough of that out in California and in the bars around Fort Bragg, North Carolina, when he'd been in the service. But, as we all found out that night, Carlisle had some barb to him when events called for it.

"He watched the Mexican standoff in progress and overheard Leroy say he was going to call the county sheriff. Along with violence, Carlisle had an acute dislike for formal organizations of any kind, and on top of that, he knew what serious law would mean for Huey. So he asked Leroy to hold off a few minutes. Carlisle walked calmly within talking distance of Huey and started saying things in a real level, quiet way, trying to convince him to put down the knife and go home, mend things with Fran, and forget about assholes like Beanie.

"But Huey, in his heightened state, and suffering besides from the memories of his U.S. Ranger days in Vietnam, which wouldn't let him sleep at night, started calling Carlisle a 'long-haired hippie bastard,' two-thirds of which was true, as we later found out, and turned the knife on him. With Gally screaming at him to be careful, Carlisle retreated, reached behind himself, and grabbed a twenty-weight pool cue someone had left lying on the table after Beanie's sprint across the top of it.

"Huey was so wrought up he didn't notice Carlisle had hold of the cue, and when Huey came within range, Carlisle swung that sonuvabitch in a nice firm arc and clubbed Huey on the outside of the left knee. Hit 'im with the butt end of the cue, real hard.

"Huey went into a stagger, dragging his injured leg like he'd been taught in the Rangers, and kept coming directly at Carlisle, at which point Carlisle did the same thing to Huey's right knee, only harder. Huey kissed the floor of Leroy's at about thirty miles an hour, landing facedown in miscellaneous cigarette butts, one of them still smoking, plus the remains from a spilled pitcher of Grain Belt and a slice of Tombstone pizza featuring extra cheese and pepperoni. Carlisle stepped on Huey's knife hand with one of his work shoes and kicked the knife away with the other. That done, he told Leroy to get Beanie out of the women's can and out of town.

"Well, the evening ended with Carlisle and Huey and Gally all sitting in a booth together, sharing a pitcher, and talking. Gally had a nice, motherly way about her when she felt like it, and she was trying to calm and console Huey, all the while cleaning up his face with a bar rag. After a while, Huey started crying, which was a little embarrassing, but given the circumstances and the fact that he was a veteran, nobody held it against him later on. At closing time, Leroy presented Carlisle with the pool cue he'd used to swat Huey, saying that Carlisle had saved him a lot of trouble with the law.

"The next day, thinking they needed to reinvigorate their marriage, Fran and Huey left on a trip to the Five Flags amusement park, which she'd been trying to get him to do for years. Apparently Beanie stayed out of Huey's marital bed from then on and did his drinking over here at Sleepy's.

"So it all ended pretty well, thanks to Carlisle. And in Huey's eyes, Carlisle McMillan could do no wrong after that, saving him, he figured, from prison and losing Fran and never getting to see Five Flags, where he rode the rolly coaster six times."

CHAPTER FOUR

By the scores we keep, what has come to be known as the Yerkes County War was a small war. Small and primitive. You probably saw a brief mention of it somewhere in your newspaper or maybe in a film clip on the evening news, then dismissed it as one of those nasty little quarrels in some distant place having no relevance to your life. Just why the nastiness occurred is complex. A lot of tangled reasons, some of them reaching back a century or more. Would it have taken place if Carlisle McMillan had never come to Yerkes County? Hard to say. The fact is he did come.

On his first night in Salamander, Carlisle McMillan stopped at the convenience store on the edge of town, still thinking about the woman who had moved through his headlights, then waited for him to pass after he made a U-turn and headed east down the main street of Salamander. He carried words in his head, words that came and came again, something about flowers and wind and bittersweet recollections. He couldn't get it straight: Did the words come from his mind or the truck radio, or was the woman whispering them as he drove by? Damn, he thought, this country is playing with my head.

He gassed the truck and went inside. A six-pack of Old Style plus the gas came to $17.87. The store was empty except for a frowsy woman in her late forties behind the cash register and a suit talking on the pay phone near the door. The man was business wrinkled after a long day and sagged against the wall while he talked. Right foot crossed over his left at the ankles, brown tassel loafers, expensive ones, dulled by the day's rain. He sagged a little more when he got an answering machine on the other end and talked back to it.

Hi, Cal. This is Bill Flanigan from the High Plains Development Corporation. I checked in with my office, and my secretary said I should call you as soon as possible. Sorry we keep missing each other. It's [looks at his watch] . . . nine-fifteen at night, Tuesday the twenty-seventh. I'm in Salamander, about ten miles north-east of Livermore. Been up here with Ray Dargen looking over the layout we talked about. I'll be in my office first thing in the morning. Give me a call. I'm anxious to hear about how things are progressing on your end, and we're real excited out here about what the senator's got in mind.

Back in the truck, Carlisle moved along Route 42 toward its intersection with U.S. 91, following a car with a state insignia on the side. The car had pulled away from the convenience store just ahead of him, its accelerator pressed by a brown tassel loafer.

Carlisle turned south on 91, guessing there might be a motel in Livermore, the next town over. There was. The Chief Motel, one of those mom-and-pop places where you ring a bell on the desk and a woman in a green cotton dress with orange flowers on it comes through a door serving as the entrance to the family's living quarters. Carlisle had noticed that at about 80 percent of these stayovers, you could look past the woman's shoulder as she dug out your key and see some guy in his undershirt and slippers, watching television. The significance of that recurring tableau was unclear to him.

The woman looked up at him. "Number twenty-two. Out the door and left, second from the end."

Carlisle was tired, slumping a little, dark brown eyes catching the woman's for a moment. She lowered hers quickly, then brought them up again, watching his back when he left, the little bell attached to the door jingling as he closed it.

She sighed and returned to her living room, where she flumped into a chair beside the man in undershirt and slippers, unwrapped a Butterfinger, and said, "Did you see that man? Something about him kind of gave me the willies. Kind of half hippie, half Injun, half somethin' else, coyote, maybe. Didn't have an address, but he paid in cash. How can you not have an address these days?"

The undershirt said nothing.

The television said, "We'll be back in a

moment after these messages from your local station."

The Butterfinger stuck to the woman's teeth as she chewed it.

Carlisle tossed his duffel bags on one of two single beds spread with frayed chenille, wilted into a chair covered with black, cracked vinyl, and opened a beer. Trucks were rolling down 91 outside as he reached over his shoulder and flipped off the overhead light. The only light in the room came from the quiver of a dying fluorescent bulb over the bathroom sink. He was somewhere west of the Mississippi and east of the Rockies, north of Nebraska and south of Canada. The picture on the opposite wall was that of an Indian brave in loincloth, bay pony mounted, eyes shielded with his right hand held parallel to his brow. The Indian was looking toward a setting sun, and no buffalo were on the plain below him.

Sliding lower in the chair, Carlisle put his boots on the bed nearest him, the woman of the Salamander street in his thoughts again. The face, the auburn hair, the green eyes watching him pass. A woman like that, in Salamander, Middle of Nowhere? He'd seen her before, or a woman like her, somewhere.

Not in the flesh, exactly, he knew that. Maybe in some old dream he should have written down but didn't. Can of beer between his legs, the woman disappeared from his thoughts as his head lopped slowly onto his shoulder.

Like most people, Carlisle McMillan had been shaped through chance as much as intent, by incident as much as cunning. A decision here, another one there. In retrospect, some of them good, others bad. The outcomes of his choices determined by rational effort mixed with unforeseen events arching in over his shoulder on days when he least expected them. The roll and toss of ordinary existence, in other words. Uncertainty, in another word.

And from the start, Carlisle McMillan had lived with more uncertainty than most. A little short of forty years back, he had been born the misbegotten son of a woman named Wynn McMillan and a man whose last name she either never knew or could not remember. From what little his mother told him, he had no more than a vague and

shifting image of the man who was his father.

So in his boyhood wonderings, and even
the same in his later years, he saw the man
only as a dark silhouette on a road bike, one
of the big ones designed for long hauls. The
man rode the coastal highway south of
Carmel, backlighted by a falling sun, crossing a high bridge where the Pacific gouged
deep into the cliffs. And the woman behind
the rider? Her arms around his waist, her
hair riffling back in the wind? That would
have been the mother of Carlisle McMillan, a
long time ago.

She and the man were together only two
days, but two days were enough. Enough to
have created a boy-child named Carlisle.

She remembers the sand was warm
against her back where she lay with him.
She's never forgotten that, how warm the
sand was in late September. And she remembers his strange, quiet ways, some of
the same characteristics she later recognized in her son. She sensed he knew secret
things and heard faint music from a distant
past that was his alone. Yet his last name
escaped her. She thinks he told her once,
but they were sitting by an evening fire, high

on the rim of their lives, drinking homemade beer. And she doesn't remember it.

As she once said, "Somehow names seemed unimportant in those days. I know it must be hard for you to understand, Carlisle, but that's how we felt. I suffer that now, the loss of his name, more for you than for me."

So ran the edge of the tale. She had told him everything when he was twelve. They were sitting on the front steps of their rented house in Mendocino. She put her arms around the thin, quiet boy and leaned her head against his while she talked, her freshly washed hair conspicuous in her blend of mother scents. He listened and loved her for the unrelenting honesty with which she spoke, for the happiness she found in having brought him to be, even for the tingling overtones of mystical, sexual abandon she conveyed in talking about the man. Though at Carlisle's age it was hard for him to imagine anything of that sort, especially involving his mother.

All of this was good, her honesty and her caring, but it was not enough. In his secret places, Carlisle McMillan wished for a father who could give him the reassurance that all the random and powerful feelings thrashing around inside him could eventually be synthesized into a coherent and useful manhood.

And for a long time he was angry. Angry about the ambiguity, about Wynn McMillan mating casually with a stranger who had then ridden north through the coloring trees of a long-since autumn and simply disappeared. It took some living, some thinking, but he finally made a slender peace with it all. Well, most of it.

Still, there was the ambiguity, the sense of being incomplete, and the curiosity about the particular ripple in the gene pool from which he had come. There were those who said he looked part Indian, the cheekbones and the prominent nose, and the long brown hair he sometimes tied with a red bandanna, Apache style. He kind of liked that idea, even though he had no way of knowing whether or not it was true. When people asked, "Do you have Indian blood?" he was silent, shrugging his shoulders, letting them draw their own conclusions.

And there was the tapping. That's what he called it. It had started when he was a child and had stayed with him over the years. Something way back and far down, source unknown. Signals, faint and distant, maybe from the spirals of his DNA, coming when he was quiet inside, sensing them more than hearing them. As if a feral cat were playing with a dusty telegraph key in a ghost-town railway station: tap . . . pause . . . tap . . . pause . . . tap, tap . . . re-peat sequence. That was one pattern, there were others.

It seemed implausible to him at first, chimerical, perhaps, but he imagined his fa-ther was sending some kind of message down the bloodlines to him. He thought of it this way: My father as a person does not consciously know I exist, but his genetic codes know, for they are part of me. The codes know I exist, the species knows I ex-ist. I am of his species and carry his genetic blueprints. Therefore, in a way, he knows. The logic was fuzzy, but it made some kind of sense if he didn't pursue it too far.

So Carlisle came to believe his father was connected to those signals, that he was back there someplace. He listened hard and talked back to them. "Who are you, man? Dammit, crank up the volume, stay on the air. Tell me something about you so I can know more about me. What is it I know that I don't know I know?" But the signals were tenuous, fading almost as soon as they started, and he always felt slightly abandoned and a little sorry for himself after that.

He noticed the signals mostly when he was at ease with himself. A year ago, maybe two, the signals had stopped. Carlisle McMillan had come to a place where he had no quiet moments and was no longer at ease. He was losing himself.

When he was a boy in Mendocino, an old master carpenter named Cody Marx had taught him to swing a hammer and saw a board better than almost anyone. Two decades later, he knew he was violating the old man's trust and it was eating holes in his heart. He constantly thought how far he had drifted from what Cody Marx had tried to make of him. How far? A long way. A long way from the builder of things beautiful and lasting he had started out to become.

Looking back, he wasn't clear on how it had happened. Along the turns of his life, small choices had mounted into large consequences. Focusing on the immediate had led him astray into a corrupt and unpleasant future, one in which he had never intended to live. Somewhere in all of that, the dream of living as a craftsman was lost, Cody's way discarded.

Bills came due. What the hell, take a garbage job just for the money. More bills, another piece of quick work, mediocre work. Get it done, get paid, get out, get on to the next job to pay the next bill. The way of things.

Call it the hard press of reality, Carlisle thought, call it getting by in an uncharitable world, call it anything you want. That didn't pretty it up, the nibbling away at the dreams, the silent, creeping, almost unconscious surrender to the forces of banality. Hardly noticing, concentrating on survival, he spiraled down through the levels of pride and caring, until he finally leveled off at a place he never expected to be.

He came to see himself as just another carnival pony plodding along in a great, trashy parade of things ephemeral, things of no value beyond what someone was willing to pay for them. The market took the measure of things, and Carlisle understood that the markets of that hard, unsmiling time seldom valued quality of the kind produced by Cody Marx. Carlisle's language, his outlook, his posture, all reflected acquiescence to a system Cody Marx had quietly railed against.

Even the occasional woman in Carlisle's life had come to be handled in the same way: nothing permanent, permanence didn't matter. Another woman, an evanescent night or week, and move on, keep up with the parade.

He had fought back the guilt, suppressing the low and persistent mumble of protest within, telling himself and others that times had changed, that the leisurely, self-indulgent world of Cody Marx no longer existed. That worked for a while, and the rationalizations deadened him, like the too much beer he drank in the evenings, like the weekends that were lost in bar talk and bitching.

His partner, Buddy Reems, once said, "Carlisle, it's become a race between people with your outlook and the developers, and you've got concrete in your boots. You're suffering a major friction between practice and instinct, covering up the gap between this bullshit work we do and who you really are. You're trimming your life, Carlisle. Just like we slap molding over the place where two boards meet so you can't see the crack."

Carlisle remembered Buddy's words clearly, and he knew Buddy was right, though a part of him wanted to deny it. He was benefiting from what civic boosters called development, all the builders were.

Buddy's observation occurred while the two of them were sitting on top of a house they were putting up in Oakland. They had just finished nailing roof sheathing to the rafters and were taking a break before hauling up the shingles and laying them down. All around Carlisle and Buddy, new houses were under construction. From the rooftop they could see downtown San Francisco across the bay, where cranes were working thirty stories in the air, looking like big fishing rods in the summer heat waves, spooling concrete and metal up to the guys balanced on high steel. Everywhere, the grading and pouring and hammering were going on.

He and Buddy were on a runaway freight train moving too fast for a workable dismount. How the hell could you get off and not stumble? Payments on the truck and tools. Payments to subcontractors. Rent. A few bucks for serious Saturday night drinking. They were doing a wire-walking act on top of the train, working without a net, knowing a client's default on a lumber bill could send them tumbling.

Buddy had swung off the train, though, and joined a commune in New Mexico. He took up with a girl from Taos who had legs longer than last week, so he said. He also said he'd share her with Carlisle in true communal spirit if Carlisle would come on down.

They stayed in touch for a while, but eventually the commune imploded and Carlisle lost track of him. Carlisle kept on building houses he didn't like for people he liked even less. Days going by, years going by, swinging his hammer and counting his pay, enduring the blind sweat of routine work. Making compromises to bring projects in at budget, maximizing cosmetic style at the expense of craftsmanship, benumbed and losing his way. Trying to forget Cody and failing in that effort.

A voice from somewhere kept saying: *You have to turn like a river.*

Carlisle had always been quiet, but it got to the point that he hardly ever spoke, the torment from what he considered his betrayal of Cody Marx, and himself, tearing him apart. Nights, he sat in his little apartment beneath a yellow evening lamp and thought about it. In the apartment below, an elderly woman watched reruns of *The Lawrence Welk Show,* and the too sweet horns and same-sweet voices sent red, red robins and sunnier sides of happy streets up through the carpet while a gay couple across the hall quarreled endlessly.

Above him, late on Saturday nights, he endured the dull thump of a bond trader bouncing on a fashion consultant, the un-imaginative four-four meter of their desire forming a cadence so measured that you could dance to it.

The woman on the futon was given to pleas of "More!" while the man favored "*Yeeesss!* Ohhhh . . . *Yes!*"

Sirens in the distance,
foghorns from the waterfront,
book in his lap,
drink in his hand,
fly on the lampshade,
the Lennon Sisters in waltz time below,
red, red robins,

and a wavering string of MORE-OH-YESes from above.

Carlisle McMillan sat there, remembering what Cody Marx had said about working to close tolerances in all things, numbed by the savage burlesque his life had become.

On a spring morning, he was thinking again about how far he had toppled from where he'd begun, from the day he first strapped on the old tool belt he was wearing now. Thinking that Cody would shake his head in disbelief if he saw the work, saw the compromises, saw the capitulation to everything he had stood against. *Turn like a river . . .*

Carlisle was laying down subflooring in what would eventually be the sunken living room of a fifty-eight-hundred-square-foot number. A big split-level on which he was doing the carpentry work as a subcontractor. The house was for an executive who worried about the color of logos on toothpaste packages and was paid a third of a million bucks every 365 days in monthly installments for his deliberations.

Voices were coming from the vacant lot next door. Carlisle sat back on his haunches and looked out the open window beside him, hammer in his right hand resting on his thigh. Two men and a woman. One of the men, perspiring and cumbrous, was talking. He was either a Realtor or a developer or the manager of a big construction firm; they all kind of ran together after a while. The other man was rounding in the gut and slumped in the shoulders from deskwork and expense account lunches and a lack of exercise.

The woman was one of those California dreams. On the Eighth Day, and rested from His previous labors, God had built a secret plant somewhere down the coast of that western land for the sole purpose of manufacturing women like her. Thirty-five, maybe, and a lovely tight body wrapped in designer jeans tucked into knee-high leather boots and a light pink sweater that showed her fine breasts swinging upward underneath it. Blond hair halfway down her back fastened with a gold clasp.

Carlisle looked at her, then at the sorry suit standing next to her, and figured she arched her back and smacked her belly against some horse from a local exercise salon, early afternoons, probably, in a good motel. He remembered meeting a guy from

Illinois who swore he was heading west to bring back one of these California beauties lashed like a hunter's trophy to the fender of his car. Carlisle could hear the three of them talking, with the developer-Realtor giving a short, verbal tour of things to be.

"Over there is where the golf course and clubhouse will go. Your lot will be on the edge of the fourteenth fairway. Allison, I understand you like to play tennis. There'll be six courts by the clubhouse, just a short distance from the Olympic-size swimming pool. Of course, access to the entire area will be controlled by guards at the gate. And we're bringing in a chef from London, who will make sure the clubhouse dining room serves only the best continental cuisine."

"Hey, Carlisle, how's it going?" The contractor had arrived, making his rounds. "I promised the Muellers you'd have this in shape by the first of July. Gonna make it, I hope. I might have to pull you off this job for a few days to help out the knotheads working for me south of here. They dunno shit from shinola about building houses. Christ, Carlisle, they put the dormers on the wrong side on two units. And we've got sixteen more units just getting started over in Concord. I'd like you to do some framing over there. Just get this flooring down as fast as you can. We'll run the carpet over it and nobody'll know the difference. How the hell come you don't use a nail gun like everyone else, anyway?"

Carlisle, still on his knees, brown hair hanging over his collar, sweat dripping off the end of his nose and through his faded blue workshirt, squeezed the hammer in his hand and turned his dark eyes up at the contractor. A sparrow had flown in and landed on a two-by-six lying a few feet from him, tail flicking, leaving a small gratuity on the board.

The salesman next door was rambling on.

So was the contractor.

So was Allison Whoever.

So was the sorry suit.

So was everybody in the entire world, it seemed to Carlisle, and as far as he could tell, they were all talking about the same thing: crap. That's what they were talking about: crap, sparrow crap.

"Dancing at the clubhouse on Saturdays, Allison . . ."

"Carlisle, the units over in Concord are el cheapos, so don't worry about . . ."

"Bill, though we can't say it openly, minorities won't be a problem . . ."

"Allison, you'll just love . . ."

"Carlisle, I want you to . . ."

"We'll need room for three cars . . ."

"Get this place buttoned up, Carlisle. We need you in Concord."

Carlisle turned his head and stared at the floor. *Turn like a river . . .*

He stood up slowly, unfastening his tool belt, and jammed the hammer into it as he walked toward his truck. The young man hired by the contractor to be Carlisle's helper had been lugging in a crated stained-glass window, a mass-produced design Carlisle had already installed in two other houses this year.

Walking and speaking quietly, he looked at the contractor and flipped his head toward the young man. "Let him finish it. After that he can do the framing over at Concord and move right on from there with his nail gun, all the way down the coast to Tijuana, make a big circle, and hit Bakersfield on his way back up to Vancouver."

The young man carrying the window

looked at Carlisle, then at the contractor, his face a mixture of anxiety and confusion, waiting for directions. This was a guy who still thought a dovetail joint had something to do with dope and whom Carlisle had to roust from bed three mornings out of six. The contractor was shouting obscenities and telling Carlisle to get back on the job, the young man was holding the window, the people in the vacant lot next door were staring. Carlisle McMillan climbed into his truck and started the engine.

He went back to his furnished apartment, packed his clothes and radio into a couple of duffel bags, and settled up with the building manager. He made the bank just before closing time and withdrew everything he had: $11,212.47. A thousand in cash, three thousand in traveler's checks, two thousand in a check to his mother to help her get by, the rest in a bank draft.

His smaller tools went into the metal box fastened to the bed of the six-year-old Chevy pickup. His books, table saw, and other bulky things were stashed in a you-store-it-you-keep-the-key cubicle, and he pulled out in early evening, with no idea of where he was headed.

He started with the Oakland Bay Bridge, swung north through Sacramento, and eventually picked up a little two-laner across the Sierra Nevada, up into Idaho. Nice country there, but too close to California, too close to the roar of a future he didn't care much about seeing.

The truck seemed to have its own mind at crossroads, so Carlisle had let it go, running east, all the way to the North Carolina coast. At Cedar Island, he took the ferry over to Ocracoke on the Outer Banks and settled down in a B&B to watch the trawlers and catch the wind. But the developers had been there, too, not at Ocracoke, but north and south a little ways, pinching in toward him. He could smell them, feel them. Screwing up Nags Head with their condos and theme restaurants, building on land the sea would never stop trying to reclaim, asking for government help when their houses washed away after they had been advised not to build on the mercurial dunes.

It was worse farther down. On the sea islands, off the mainland from Charleston, the white boys were sweating only lightly in their tan summer suits while slickering everybody, mostly the descendants of ex-slaves who had owned the islands. Carlisle sat on a sea wall next to an old black man and talked with him about it.

The man told him the island people were originally into family and poetry, music and Christian mysticism. Still were to some extent. The world they had fixed up in this sweltry place was one of Brer Rabbit and Brer Gator and fine sea island cotton. Now the white boys, they were into something else altogether. Hard-nosed stuff, that's what they were up to.

"They's ridin' 'round in those little golf carts, just a-figgerin'. All the time they's a-figgerin.'"

The old man wore brown striped pants from a suit that had been new thirty years ago but was now shiny with wear, a blue-striped white shirt with a frayed collar, and a gray fedora. As he talked, he looked out toward the sea islands, his voice taking on a distance that seemed farther away than the islands themselves. Carlisle listened, sometimes looking down at the patterns they both were making in the sand with the toes of their shoes, sometimes looking out to where the old man looked, out to the islands.

What those white boys had done was brilliant, Carlisle admitted that to himself. Ruthless, but brilliant. It worked like this, according to the old man. Offer big money for land, get the avarice sluicing around in the heads of some poor folks, and put an expensive hotel on the site. That jacked up property taxes beyond what the remaining landholders could afford. To pay the taxes, they had to sell the land given to them by General William Tecumseh Sherman after the Civil War. The developers bought the land and put up more hotels and condos and beach clubs. Property taxes rose even more, the cycle continued.

Eventually, an island would reach what the fast guys called "buildout," which meant there wasn't any more room for construction. And the really delicious part? The great-grandson of former slaves, a fellow who used to own a little land on one of the islands, wound up working as a pool boy at the Hilton. He vacuumed the bottom of chlorinated ponds while his mother stared through an iron fence at the graves of her ancestors. She needed a pass from the white folks at the hotel to visit the grave sites. Brilliant—elegant, in fact—you had to allow them that much.

He said good-bye to the old man and drove to what he hoped might be a quiet beach. That didn't work out. The college troops were on spring break, even though most of them, in Carlisle's way of looking at things, hadn't studied hard enough to deserve any break at all, and those studying hard were back at school in the library. He had spent four years at Stanford and knew the real scholars were not on the beaches, even though they were the ones needing a rest, along with construction workers, machinists, and the Mohawks working high steel, none of whom had spring breaks written into their union contracts.

A wet T-shirt contest was in full blossom on a stage near the water, the present contestant being a good-looking girl wearing bikini bottoms and a doused cutoff T-shirt, which had CLOSED MONDAYS printed on the front. In spite of the nonsense, Carlisle couldn't help but admire her breasts. Her nipples were practically tearing apart the thin cotton in an effort to be seen. He supposed swinging your fine tits in front of four hundred howling men did that to some women.

The Sigma Chi and their affiliates were drunk and sunburned and falling back toward the darkness civilization was rumored to have overcome. "Let-us-see-them . . . Let-us-see-them," they chanted with what they took to be clownish understatement, more tongue-in-cheek refined than "Show us your tits!" while a Van Halen tape hammered the afternoon through a sound system designed to communicate with other worlds.

And, eventually, she did let them see. Stripped off her shirt and dignity at the same time, setting free those big, lovely breasts with a suntan line across them, while civilization fell to its knees weeping, along with the Sigma Chi. That done, the crowd started working on her bikini pants, the gentle roar of hundreds of drunks urging her to get rid of those, too. Responding, she moved into a self-conscious bump and grind with strong Protestant overtones, hesitant thrusts of her pelvis—not too much—movements confined by years of parental admonitions concerning moderation in all things.

Somewhere, Carlisle imagined, her parents were sipping cocktails and telling their friends, "Yes, Christina is a sophomore at William and Mary, but she hasn't decided on a major yet. She's mentioned sociology, or maybe art, but we're worried about her lack of direction. And what do you do with a degree in art?" With that body, Carlisle grinned to himself, Christina needn't worry about direction, because a long line of expert advisers would be happy to provide guidance.

He drove south again, walking the beaches where he could get to them via the few public accesses left. Hunkering down for days at a time, reading, thinking, letting his hair grow longer, looking for salvage. In late summer, he caromed off the East Coast and headed inland again. He remembered a place called Chimney Rock wedged in Hickory Nut Gorge, not far from Asheville. He had spent a week there with a woman in . . . he tried to remember . . . long time ago, in autumn. She wanted to take a look at a small piece of land she owned in the southern Blue Ridge. Carlisle had just been discharged from the army and was headed from Fort Bragg to California, so he decided to go with her.

It had been real nice. A fast mountain stream with a pretty lake at the end of it slashed through the village. They rented a chalet with a big stone fireplace and a long front porch. She was a fine woman in her late twenties, a little older than Carlisle. Her husband had left her after finishing medical school, and she was forced to take a job in the maintenance division office at the base. That's where Carlisle had met her.

His carpentry saved him from Vietnam. A colonel took one look at Carlisle's skills and assigned him to the maintenance division. He completed his two years working on the officers' quarters at Fort Bragg, plus a few afternoons now and then at the colonel's home, building a deck out back and a sauna in the basement. Routine hitch, no sweat.

Eleven years later and thinking about the woman, he hit the city limits of Chimney Rock once again. Sunday afternoon, middle part of August. Tourists shambled through stores advertising corncob pipes and "Genuine Cherokee Indian Moccasins" made in Taiwan.

In a motel parking lot, an outfit called the Buccaneers and their assorted mamas were draped over bikes, wearing their boots and leathers, drinking beer, and posturing, working on their nominally lethal appearance and unsettling the Chamber of Commerce sorts peering through window blinds in their real estate offices. Crabby Dick's Oyster Bar was jammed, and fun seekers were writing graffiti on river rocks, telling an indifferent world they had been there, telling it that "Al loves Becky," at least for a little while. Sunday in the Carolinas.

Carlisle figured the visitors would fire up all 37,648 cylinders that had brought them to the mountains for a weekend and would get out before sundown, back to Asheville, back to Charlotte, back to wherever. He was right. By eight o'clock, the main street was dark and almost empty.

He ate ham and biscuits with red-eye gravy at John's pretty fair restaurant and walked along the river afterward, looking up through darkness at the two-thousand-foot cliff giving the town its name. Suddenly he felt lonesome. It was a good place and a good time to be with a woman, but he didn't have one.

He wished Sharon were here on this Sunday night. The images came up in his mind like a quick slide show evolving into a filmstrip. Years before, they had rolled around on a rug in front of the fire. Women always look good in firelight, and Sharon looked even better than that. She wore flannel pajamas and a perfume whose name he couldn't remember, but he could still taste it on her skin.

After her divorce, Sharon had pulled herself together and worked her way through an English degree at Duke, then hired on with a book publisher in New York. He knew all of this because she had always sent him a Christmas card until a few years back.

There was a phone by the park entrance. New York information provided a number, and he dialed it as light rain started coming down. A man answered. Carlisle almost hung up but stayed with it and asked for Sharon.

She picked up, paused after Carlisle gave his name, and said, "Please hold while I take this on another phone."

The flat sound of her voice made it seem as though he had called to order a gallon of paint thinner. He could hear music playing in the background after she laid down the receiver and her voice saying, "Ronnie, sweetheart, please hang up the receiver when you hear me pick up the other one in the bedroom."

She came on again, different this time, bright and warm and glad to hear from him. "Where are you, Carlisle?"

He told her. Told her all the right things and meant them. Told her he was in Chimney Rock in the rain and thinking of her and missing her.

"Oh, Carlisle, right this minute I wish I were there with you. I sold my land out there years ago, but I still love that place. Tell me exactly where you're standing."

He told her.

"I can just picture it. The mountain up behind you. And the river. Hold the phone so I can hear the river going over the rocks."

He did that, looking up at the dark sky.

"Come to New York, Carlisle. I'd love to see you again."

He explained he had reached the point where places containing more than a thousand people and requiring rush-hour traffic reports from Sky Ranger gave him the twitches. She said she understood. They talked a little more and said a warm good-bye.

Afterward, he wished he hadn't called her.

He walked back to his room and read for a little while, then slept. At dawn, he made a thermos of coffee and pulled out, rolling west again in a state of lassitude.

Through Asheville, along the Great Smoky Mountains Expressway, the truck pointed west. Days on the road, one indistinct as the next. Wheels rolling, mind rolling, thinking about Cody Marx.

Out of the southern high country, climbing north into a place of soybeans and hogs and cornfields that stretched beyond sundown. Near a bridge in Ohio, a boy of about eight sat ten feet from the highway, watching the traffic. Two hundred yards back in a field, Carlisle could see farm buildings; probably the boy had come from there. Sixty years ago, a farmer's son would have been watching trains and wondering about the rails and where they went. On that day, wearing a ball cap and old jeans, the boy watched trucks and cars, following the asphalt with his eyes, looking in all directions at once, dreams beginning to form, plans yet to be made.

Farther west he traveled. August hot on most days, unforgiving white sun, hammering sun, lights from ball fields soft focused in

a mix of dust and evening haze, heat light-
ning in the distance. Rain sometimes, windshield wipers scraping the water aside, hiss
of rubber tires on rainy backcountry highways running as flumes through late summer cornfields. Village signs proclaiming
past glories, small victories, old but not forgotten and shown to the world as if that particular kind of history mattered in the future:
1972 STATE 2-A TRACK CHAMPIONS. The sign
was weathered, barely readable.

And the smells, thick and summery: pork
chops on grills, fresh-cut grass in small
towns, greasy steel in the old manufacturing
cities, oily diesel smoke from tractor-trailers,
one with TRUCKIN' FOR JESUS on the rear
doors.

And the sounds. In Bettendorf, Iowa, the
banners screamed BIX LIVES! and old-time
jazz floated out and over the brown Mississippi, over the barge traffic and tugboats:
Shufflin', shufflin', shufflin' down to the land
of dreamy dreams, where she moans the
whole night long and drags me around by
her apron strings just when they're closing
Storyville. In Sioux City, on a Saturday,
cathedral bells of the Angelus rang at sundown while Carlisle pumped his own gas.

Every other county seemed to have a bluegrass music festival under way or on its way. Jim & Jesse and their backup crew headlined a Sunday night concert at a middle-of-somewhere fairgrounds. Hair slicked back and Jesse cross-picking his mandolin over Jim's flattop guitar, fiddle and five-string banjo noodling around behind them. Carlisle stood far back in trees near the concession stands, drinking lemonade, listening.

An overweight man carrying a fiddle case asked him, "You a picker, boy?" Carlisle shook his head, and the man walked away, looking for pickers.

Somewhere west of the Mississippi and east of the Rockies, a little town came up, one of those places with dust in its teeth and a dry rattle in its throat: Salamander.

CHAPTER FIVE

The woman passing through Carlisle McMillan's headlights his first night in Salamander was called Susanna Benteen. As with other men who had stared at Susanna and wondered about the exotic frontiers that might lie beneath her cloak and dress, it was the look of her that first caught Carlisle's attention. On the initial glance, it would have been easy to dismiss her as a relic from the wild Berkeley days. Easy to dismiss her as an older version of those idealistic young people who had fairly crackled with intensity, handing out pamphlets on obscure causes and urging others to sign petitions on behalf of the Secaucus Seven or human rights in countries most people couldn't even locate on a map.

Such an appraisal would have been

wrong. Susanna's mother, a Hungarian national, died when she was four, sending her into the keeping of her father, a scholar whose work in applying Jung's theories of symbolism to the puzzles of ancient cultures took him to wherever humans dig for whatever it was they were before. She had traveled with him, a girlhood of sandals and T-shirts and baggy shorts with elastic waistbands, shuffling off to schools in Cairo or Khartoum, playing with tribal children along dusty excavation trenches near the Nile's second cataract or the great dig at Olduvai. In the heat of aboriginal villages, she sat beside her father while his tape recorder turned, and they listened to tales of dreamtimes past, the swirl of allegory and image rich in her ears. In short, Susanna Benteen was a child of desert nights and desert drums.

When he took a professorship at Yale, she kept his house and cooked his meals, already old in her ways, already a veteran of life on the road. The phone in her New Haven kitchen rang on a bright April morning. The archaeologist in muddy boots and field clothes had spoken to her in level tones, coming down the long lines of Mother Bell from Yerkes County, South Dakota. Her father was dead.

"Fell from a cliff about three hours ago, none of us saw it happen. What can I say. . . . I'm really sorry. He was a good man. We'll take care of things on this end for you."

After stumbling through a boring and incoherent year at Bryn Mawr, she pulled out to discover what was possible and what was not. Communes and compulsions, old cities and third world buses, on her own and moving. Moving.

She lived for a time on the Spanish seacoast, in San Sebastian. The house belonged to a man named Andrew Tanner. She was twenty-three and searching, Tanner was fifty-six, a journalist and magisterial, following his trade to places where men fought one another for reasons not altogether clear. Wherever conflict existed, there went Andrew Tanner with his notebooks, and he went alone.

Susanna remained behind in San Sebastian, waiting for him to return from Entebbe or Beirut or Vientiane. He would sometimes cable her, and she would ride the train to Paris, meeting him there for a day or two while his laundry was done and his ease was taken. She stayed with Tanner nearly three years, growing restless and already thinking of leaving when a cable arrived from Beirut: A mortar round had hit the truck in which he was riding and Tanner was dead. The fathers all seemed to die.

Tanner. She remembers the long talks over wine in the cafés of Paris, over cognac and coffee on the porch of his house in San Sebastian. He was sun-worn and quiet in his ways, living somewhere in another time. Modern warfare, he used to say, was too fast, too machine-driven, lacking what he called the majesty of conflict. He longed for the shouts of centurions, for Napoleon's cavalry moving through early morning snowfall on the plains of Europe, for riders in black robes sweeping down the sands of Arabia.

Tanner had watched Susanna and sensed her restlessness. He had traveled widely and well, and he had seen such women before. The African in the airport at Mombasa, mocha skinned and regal and offering not so much as a look in his direction, the curve of her bare shoulder melding into a slender arm encased in gold bracelets.

Another one, the glint of her crossing from one building to the next in the byzantine paths of a Calcutta market. He remembered the green sari and the long, brown neck and the eyes that came his way for only a moment. One other, perhaps, thirty years back, an Arab carrying a young child and stepping down from a second-class coach in the station at Marrakech. But he had been a boy then and still wondering what it was like to be a man.

"Men will be a problem for you," he had said to her one night. "Finding the right one." Tanner had a cryptic way of speaking, as if he were reading from his notebooks.

"What do you mean?" she asked.

He paused. "There will be few men who will suit you. Most of us remain boys for as long as possible, beating back responsibilities that ought to come with adulthood, substituting whatever specious things we can conjure up as a way of staving off the quite reasonable demands of full-blown women."

In the darkness, the rasp of match against striking pad as he lighted another cigarette. She turned toward him, listening and understanding. He was silhouetted against the dark water of the Mediterranean. Some of the waves glowed with a green phosphorescence as she watched them roll toward her.

Tanner continued. "The reason is simple: Our boyhood pastimes ask considerably less of us than a woman eventually does. The kind of woman you are becoming, or already are, has expectations when she looks at a man. Those expectations go wanting when only a boy looks back."

He hesitated and let his voice circle down until it was scratchy and almost inaudible. "And there is pain and sadness in all of that. The boy feels it, I know that for certain, and I suspect . . . I suspect there is pain and sadness for the woman, too. I think you may find it lonely out there."

Susanna was wearing an off white caftan that lay soft across her body, cognac glass in her lap, rocking slowly in a wicker chair and staring out over Spanish waters. A light wind from the Azores had come up and ruffled the caftan, and she was aware of the soft cotton moving against her skin. Tanner leaned toward her and put his lips on her hair, then went into the house. When she followed an hour later, he was asleep in his leather desk chair, an unfinished manuscript stacked on the typewriter.

The next morning he was gone, leaving a sheet of paper on the pillow beside her. He had written this:

In middle age
I was content,
Striking my bargains
With swift-running light
And telling myself
That I had done
What could be done.
Then, you . . . you again,
After all the years.

I have seen you before
    Out on the deserts,
    Out on the trains,
    Near castle walls
        Where jugglers swallow fire,
And
    Dancing like a fallen nun
    In the streets of Pretoria—
        The arch of your neck,
        The toss of your head,
        A casual show
        Of yellow stocking

When the music turned.
And suddenly . . .
. . . Again
I am fighting
For the hours.
But I can do no more
Than play sweet lamentations
For the death of blue autumns.
That's all I can do now.
And none take notice
Of my winter longing . . .
. . . Or know your secret fancies
Except
The Dancing Master
And
me.

Three weeks later, Tanner was dead. Susanna Benteen pushed on. An Argentine taught her the tango and loved her to insensibility on the candlelit balcony of a Buenos Aires mansion. He had removed her clothing while they danced and continued to dance with her after she was naked while he remained fully dressed in evening clothes, then bent her over the balcony rail, her long hair hanging toward the street below while she screamed into the night with pleasure.

There were many nights like this. He wanted to marry her, offered her money and a position in society, but it wasn't right for her and she knew it and pushed on.

Then came the aging jazz musician in Seattle. She sat in a bar called Shorty's and listened to his tenor saxophone, and she found his blackness against the light peach of her own skin to be part of an intense, quiet eroticism she shared with him. The sound of his saxophone would sometimes reach inside her as if he were there himself.

So her future became the road, and she spent a long time on the road. Her father had taught her about symbols, Andrew Tanner had taught her about the world and its capacity for malice, and an Asian man had given her part of the map for tranquillity. Still, the Indian who came later, after she had moved to Yerkes County, was closer to her in many ways than any other man she had ever known. It was as if the two of them shared a common mind, or nearly so.

All of the men she had cared for, every one of them, shared a common trait: While they did their work, whatever it was at the moment, they were also looking for something else, looking toward some other place.

They were always thinking about that other place, the paste of their relationship with whomever and wherever eventually beginning to crack and release. Each of them was skilled in what he did, yet each of them felt as if he belonged to another time.

And throughout these years, she remained troubled by her father's death, the way it happened, as much as the fact of it. And so the last Greyhound to stop in Salamander brought her down a long, straight highway through April rain and let her off in front of Danny's.

She rented a small house south of the Salamander elevator and began discreet inquiries into the circumstances of her father's death. The coroner's verdict had been quick and sanitizing: The earth gave way where the anthropologist stood; death was accidental.

An editorial in the *High Plains Inquirer* stated her father's death was "an unfortunate casualty in our yearning to better understand ourselves by wresting knowledge from the layers of our past." In a way, that was both a little too quick and a little too tidy, or so it seemed to her; the lid on the incident had been slammed shut. The entire package had been neatly tied, and nothing could be found to indicate anything other than a scholar concentrating on his work rather than where he placed his foot. None of that made sense, for her father was a careful and experienced man who had walked many cliffs in his lifetime.

Beyond all of those circumstances, there was the curious matter of the dig being closed immediately after his death. Funding for the project had appeared certain, then evaporated. The dig at Salamander Crossing was aborted and forgotten in spite of its original promise.

The Crossing was nothing more than a junction thirteen miles northwest of Salamander, near Wolf Butte, where the Chicago & Milwaukee switches sent trains in directions ruled by schedules and cargo. Aerial maps disclosed the presence of several promising moundlike structures, and ground observations indicated vegetation was unusually lush in certain of these areas, a characteristic of subsurface burial plots and middens produced by refuse disposal. Interest in the site was increased by pottery shards found nearby in the cuts made by railroad construction. In addition, several

test pits indicated the possibility of archaeological deposits below.

Her father and others had begun mapping the area in preparation for a full-scale
dig, a research design was prepared, and re-
quests for funding were submitted to federal
agencies. A breathless article in a prominent
natural history magazine stated: "The dig
at Salamander Crossing contains bright
prospects of shedding new light on the cultures of Palaeo-Indian Man and may se-
verely challenge widely accepted theories
concerning overland migrations from Asia
via the Bering Sea land bridges and down
through North America." Academic reputations were at stake, and those enjoying the
perquisites of fame based on a widely accepted hypothesis, which now might be
proven wrong, became uneasy over the
possibilities at Salamander Crossing.

Susanna's father had climbed to the top
of a cliff attempting to get a better view of
the site in preparation for the final mapping
of the area. He knew that spot well, he had
been there before. In fact, one of the photographs accompanying the article showed
him standing on the cliff's edge, the very
spot from which he fell a few weeks later.

The photograph was razor sharp, and clearly the anthropologist had been standing on rock, not dirt.

The rent in Salamander was low, the town was quiet, and the great spaces of the high plains suited her. When her small investigations provided nothing new, she settled in, concentrating on her own existence and treating her father's demise as a mystery yet to be solved. Most of the modest death benefits from his university retirement fund had been spent in her travels. But she made her own clothes, ate simple foods, and started a small mail-order business that sold herbs and unusual jewelry she fashioned from scraps of whatever she could find, shells along the river, stones along the roads.

The result was a subsistence-level income, plus a little more. The locals were troubled, of course, by her ways and by the letters she occasionally wrote to the *Salamander Sentinel* petitioning for the kinder treatment of all things, including humans, animals, and the earth itself. None of this went down well in a place of men who talked cattle prices, who still believed the land was theirs to use as they saw fit and anyone believing otherwise could go screw themselves.

Susanna Benteen's bearing and speech transmitted a sense of herself that was disconcerting to some, to most. Call it equanimity, a quiet self-reliance that enabled her to live evenly and centered in whatever landscape she chose. The range and intensity of her experiences compressed into only thirty-odd years of living had given her the appearance of someone who has been there before. She had come to understand the value of small universes—the limitless worth of well-defined moments, of small tasks with infinite paths to their accomplishment—and cherished them more than larger ones. Those latter characteristics alone were enough to set her off from the people who were beating their way through ordinary lives.

That would be the outside view, and mostly accurate. Yet, as Tanner once said to her, "Some people's lives, most, maybe, are like a flaw on a phonograph record. They never seem to get with anything, repeating as they do the opening measure of a mindless, four-note song. You, Susanna, are different in a way I cannot explain, as if the womb just had been a brief transition from a different world in which you lived a long time before coming to this life. You'll stagger, I think, but eventually you'll get to a special place. The price of that will be aloneness, for people will fear not only you, but the journey it takes to become what you are."

And, as Tanner had predicted, she had come to be by herself in this far place, passing through the long winter nights of high plains America, wanting true friends, wanting the hands of a man upon her, hands moving across her breasts and along her legs, words in her ear, the paradoxical, two-edged feel of complaisance and power that a certain kind of man can stir in a woman.

The Indian was a separate case. Neither man nor boy, but something else. A bird perhaps, maybe a hawk, a shadow figure with whom she could quiet herself temporarily and practice her mystical ways without restraint. Like the others she had truly cared for, he had a sense of impermanence about him, as if he were always looking out beyond wherever he currently stood.

She was thinking of the Seattle jazz musician as she walked along the main street of Salamander on an August night. Heading south toward her house, she prepared to cross the street and waited for a pickup truck with California license plates to pass, the same one that had been parked in front of Leroy's and had startled her when its engine turned over. The window on the driver's side was open, and the driver looked at her when he went by only a few feet away. His face was partially shadowed from the streetlamps, but she could see the fall of long hair tied back with a yellow bandanna. The music from his radio faded as he rolled down the street.

CHAPTER SIX

Carlisle McMillan jerked to hazy wakefulness at four a.m. when a truck backfired on Route 91. He was cold and scratchy and stumbled from the chair in which he'd been sleeping onto the nearest of the twin motel beds, still dressed. After wrapping himself in the spread, he slept again, dreaming restlessly about a rider on an old motorcycle. In the dream, a woman with a yellow feather in her hair reached out for the rider through the wake of his passing.

Three hours later, showered and drinking instant coffee heated by the small electrical coil he carried with him, Carlisle sat at a desk marred by deep cigarette burns along its edges. He wrote to his mother in Mendocino.

Dear Wynn,

I'm still drifting around in a place called America, looking things over. You can reach me, at least for a few weeks, at general delivery, Salamander, South Dakota. I just got in here last night, but this area looks pretty good to me. If things work out, I might be settling down here for a while, get some space between me and the craziness out on the coasts.

Love,
Carlisle

Carlisle pulled back the curtains to check the weather. First light was indecisive, ragged stripes of reds and grays. But sunlight finally powered its way forward, and the sky was clear when he drove away from the motel. Coffee cup squinched between his legs, napkin map beside him on the seat, he headed north along 91 past an old dance pavilion set back from the road and on the edge of a small lake, turned west on 42, and ten minutes later stopped in front of the Salamander Post Office.

He bought stamps, mailed the letter to his mother, and reached for the door. It opened, and the face in front of him was the same face as the night before in his headlights. Her auburn hair was fashioned into a long braid winding around her neck and coming to lie softly on her right breast. Green eyes pointed at him, straight and even.

She said, "Excuse me," smiled pleasantly, and moved by.

Carlisle sat in the truck, waiting for the woman to leave the post office. He wanted to see her again, to look at her in the way one returns to stare at a Matisse print or the way one puts on the Brandenburgs even after a hundred listenings.

Sitting there like a stone. Too obvious, yet not forward enough. Introduce yourself, tell her she is the most incredible woman you have ever seen, ask who she is and where she's going. Hell, say you want her right now, in the truck, in the post office, on the pavement outside, middle of the street. Hard to do, not good at that direct approach. Feeling clumsy and immature around that level of beauty and the sense of a controlled burn seeming to lie beneath it.

He started the truck and moved down Main Street, looking in the rearview mirror. She came out of the post office, her eyes focused on the truck for a moment. The bounce of the truck and sun reflecting in his mirrors made her into a figure dancing through a prairie grass fire. Then she was gone, turning right at the post office corner. He made a promise to do better the next time he saw her, knowing he wouldn't.

Carlisle drove through Salamander and then, six miles west of town, turned north off the secondary highway and onto a dirt road the color of iron oxide. Same road he had traveled yesterday. About two and a half miles farther was a grove on the left. He checked the map again: Turn right at the intersection, go about two miles or a little more, grove on left side of the road, look for old house sitting fifty yards or more up from the road on the right. He found it.

The land had not been farmed or grazed for a while. High weeds everywhere, sunflowers scattered around, cattails bending long and yellow and brown in the ditches. In the grass, meadowlarks carried on, a red-winged blackbird stared at him from a fence wire, and a gopher headed for cover when Carlisle got out of his pickup. He shut the truck door quietly.

A rutted lane of sorts led up to the

house, but he parked just where the lane began and walked along it, feeling like the trespasser he was. He liked the softness of old dirt under his shoes and the August sun on his face, liked the scent of open country in his nose, dense smells from a mixture of heavy dew and sun and wild things growing and a light breeze from the western mountains. High clouds formed random shadows on the ground when they passed before the sun.

As the woman at Danny's had said, the house was in rough shape. But Carlisle was good at seeing what could be. Hammer enough nails, saw enough boards, consider possibilities, and you get to that place where you can see. He walked around the building, looking in through broken windows, banging his hand against the siding, then backed off fifty feet and circled it again. Unlike the big two- or three-story farmhouses built out there to shelter large families, this was a little fellow. About a thousand square feet on the first and only floor, covered by a roof with a forty-five-degree pitch.

A sink with faucets, which meant a well of some kind outside. No toilet, but that didn't surprise him, since he had noticed the privy behind and off to one side of the house when he walked up the lane. That could be remedied. The porch floor was rotten, its roof sagging where supports had fallen away. He stepped inside carefully, watching through shadowy light for holes and snakes that prefer to hang around old places such as this. Some holes, no snakes.

And no basement, which was unusual for this part of the country. Since footings had to be sunk more than forty inches to get under the frost line, the conventional strategy was to just keep going and build a basement. But this structure sat on its footings about two feet above the ground, weeds poking up through cracks in the floor. Nobody had lived there for a long time.

About then he started thinking log cabin and pried back a piece of moldy wallboard to see if chinked logs were underneath. No. Only the normal two-by-four fir studs, but with no insulation in the cavity. Must have been cold in here during the winter and hot in the summer. Whoever put this up had been in a hurry or simply unskilled. Yet the basic structure looked all right, no tilt from a distance. And inside was a huge stone fireplace, a handsome one, with a gunky flue for certain.

After that he examined the two large bur oaks in the yard, one on the south side, the other near the front of the house on the west. Along with their aesthetic value, they'd help keep things cool in the summer. Both trees seemed to be healthy and were inhabited by squirrels that opened up with a broadside of chattering, resenting his intrusion into their lives.

Walking around the property, Carlisle discovered a small creek hidden in high weeds north of the house. Minnows flashed in the deeper pools, and a small turtle dropped off a log when he appeared. Above him, a hawk drifted along on the morning convections, a little hawk of a kind he had never seen before. The raptors had always interested Carlisle, though he didn't know much about them, just liked to watch them ride the shifting air currents. In the high plains, the hawks were only a notch below the top spot in their particular food chain. Their only real worries were the great owls and idiots with shotguns. Or that's what he was naively thinking.

The lane sloped upward from the road at

a pretty fair angle, giving the place good
drainage, and he could see the Little Salamander River southwest of him, flashing
in the sunlight. Wolf Butte was northwest
about three miles, its face white and flat in
morning sun. The grove across the road was
a nice one, covering twenty acres or so,
mostly mature cottonwoods in the low
ground, with oaks and smaller trees of other
varieties where the land sloped upward
again away from the road.

Back to town, back to Danny's. Hungry
again. A dozen cars along Main Street. Salamander trying to do business, trying to hang
on, rooted there in the shadow of unwel-
come changes.

Gally Deveraux was clearing dirty dishes
from the counter while an older woman
worked the booths and tables. He was in
the trough separating coffee and doughnuts
from noon dinner, so Danny's was quiet
except for the four elderly men playing
pinochle at a table in the back and another
old fellow three stools down from him. He
noticed Gally had on new jeans and a
freshly pressed western shirt. Her hair was
hanging straight down this morning, parted
in the middle. She looked better that way.

Her eyes looked better, too, brighter somehow.

"Back for more punishment, huh?"

"Yes. And I've been out to the Williston
place, looking around."

"See anything interesting?"

"Maybe. Did you happen to uncover the
attorney handling the estate?"

"No, but I can do that in less than twenty
seconds right now."

She walked to the other end of the
counter where the old fellow in a gray workshirt and suspenders was reading the café's
communal paper that whistled up from the
state capital every morning. A wooden cane
rested against his leg. Carlisle had seen him
last night. He had been sitting in a window
above Lester's TV & Appliance when
Carlisle came out of Leroy's. Gally bent over
and spoke quietly to the man, for which
Carlisle was thankful. The man looked
toward him through wire-rimmed spec-
tacles, turned to the woman, and said
something.

She walked back to where Carlisle was
sitting. "It's part of an estate, just as I
thought. Heirs to the place are scattered all

over the country. The lawyer's name is Birney. Has an office over in Livermore."

She nodded toward the old man. "He
says there's only two lawyers in Livermore,
so you shouldn't have any trouble finding
him. Now, what can I get you? The special
today is meat loaf, and it's just coming out
of the oven."

When Carlisle paid his bill, Gally gave
him a nice smile and said, "Well, good luck
on your dream house. I hope it works out for
you. This town certainly needs some fresh
blood."

"Thanks. And thanks also for your help.
Not only are you a decent cartographer, but
a helpful broker as well. I'll report back later
on."

She looked puzzled. "What's a cartographer? My ears aren't used to dealing with
more than two syllables at once. I think I
knew that word once, but I can't remember."

"Mapmaker."

"Oh, the napkin. Glad it helped."

"See you later. Thanks again."

Carlisle liked the fact that she asked the
meaning of cartographer. Cody Marx had
taught him that one of the first indicators of
authentic intelligence was not being embar-

rassed by ignorance, as long as there was an attendant desire to learn. Without the second, Cody said, ignorance devolved into stupidity.

He drove over to Livermore and asked a gas station attendant about the attorney's office. "Yep, just down the block on this side of the street. Birney is the lie-yer's name. Getting rich on probating the devil out of all these farm and ranch properties."

Lawyer Birney was in, but busy. If Carlisle wanted to wait, Birney would be free in about twenty minutes. While a secretary clicked her way along the keys of an IBM Selectric, he read a copy of *Agriculture Today*.

Birney, round and prosperous looking. Meaty handshake, examining Carlisle, possible new fodder for the cut and chop of his probate machine in a couple of decades.

Yes, the Williston place was for sale. Thirty acres and the house. Birney was cagey, but he was no California Realtor. "Kinda strange, you know. The Williston place has been sitting there for some time. Now you're the second person asking about it this week. That property'd be worth a hundred and twenty-five thousand over in Falls City."

That was his opening gambit. Clumsy. The Marin County boys would own his butt in twelve minutes, maybe less.

"Let me get this straight," Carlisle said. "I thought the property was northwest of Salamander, not in Falls City. Or are you thinking of moving it?"

Birney turned slightly pink and fiddled with an expensive pen set on the desk in front of him. "Well, no. But I was just trying to say that it's a nice little piece of ground."

"That's all it is. The house is garbage. I took the liberty of walking the property this morning. No bath, no insulation, structurally it's a disaster. More trouble to deal with than the entire acreage is worth, probably. I'll give you six thousand, assuming the title is as clean and tidy as the back of a baby's neck."

"Whoa now, Mr. . . . ah, McMillan, was it?"—Carlisle nodded—"I have a responsibility to my clients."

"Look, Mr. Birney. Let's stop screwing around. Six thousand. A thousand now, the rest in monthly payments over the next three years at six percent simple interest on the balance, no prepayment fee for early retirement of the note. Of course, I'll want to look over the abstract first."

Birney said nothing, studied Carlisle. Then, with well-practiced hesitation, he swiveled slightly in his chair and stared out through translucent orange curtains covering the office window.

Carlisle stood up. "Thanks for your time."

The lawyer sighed and looked at Carlisle. "All right. My clients were hoping for quite a bit more. But it's been sitting around for years, and they want something out of it. I keep trying to explain to them that they could get some cash flow through one government program or another, if they'd enroll it. But they're city folks, and the thought of government paperwork drives 'em crazy, even though it's not all that hard."

Sometimes you luck out. Carlisle hadn't thought about government programs. That was something foreign to him, but he didn't let Birney catch any hint of his ignorance. If Carlisle had known there was income to be generated merely by letting the land sit idle, he might have offered more for it.

Carlisle's old partner, Buddy Reems,

once said, "Carlisle, I've decided to abandon carpentry, get out of this rat race, and go into farming." He was talking serious, looking down at his beer in a San Francisco bar.

As usual, Carlisle bit. "Jeez, Buddy, that takes real money. Land, equipment, seed, all that stuff."

"Nope." Buddy grinned. "Given the largesse of the U.S. taxpayer in funding farm programs, all you need are land and a mailbox."

He laughed, then reached over and slapped Carlisle gently on the face. "Carly, old boy, you're a born straight man. We could put Abbott and Costello to shame." Buddy Reems would've had lawyer Birney for breakfast, after first driving him insane, of course.

Birney the attorney spoke again. "I'll have the papers ready by Wednesday next, if that's all right. Meanwhile you can look over the abstract. I can assure you, however, everything's in order, and the title's clean as . . . as a baby's neck. I'll have to remember that phrase, it's a good one."

"You can have it. I think I stole it from E. B. White."

"Who?"

"A writer."

"Oh."

Carlisle walked down the street toward where his truck was parked, feeling especially tough and smart. Cutting good deals was the modern equivalent of early man going out on a hunt and bringing home the goods. He'd heard that some men actually could get an erection just thinking about making deals, though he guessed they were generally sorry-ass specimens when it came to anything else.

Back to the motel room for a few hours with the abstract. It looked all right. Williston's claim to the land flowed straight down the family tree from his grandfather, who had squatted down there under the 1860 Homestead Act and received clear title. Fifteen years ago, 130 of the original 160 acres had been sold. That sale was clean, as was everything else, and the attached survey seemed dead-on accurate.

He opened the door to Danny's at ten minutes before eight after glancing up to see if the old man was at his post above Lester's. He was, windowed like a Vermeer portrait in a brown and blemished frame.

Carlisle waved to him, startling the old man, but after a moment he waved back, stiff but friendly.

Danny's was empty. Gally was mopping, looking tired.

"Don't panic, I'm not here for anything requiring chefs and waiters in tuxedos," Carlisle announced as he came in.

"I'm not panicked," Gally Deveraux replied. "I have no intention of doing any more cooking today. Wayfarers requesting food, including Mick Jagger and Jimmy Carter if they happen by, are being directed to Leroy's and the pleasures of his menu. If you want coffee, I just unplugged the machine, but it's still hot. You can have a free cup, since it doesn't seem right to charge for something out of a piece of equipment that's been shut down."

"Fair enough."

He sat at the counter while she poured two cups and leaned against the soft-drink cooler as she'd done the previous night. "Well, how'd it go? Are you a future resident and taxpayer of Yerkes County, or is California looking better and better all the time?"

"In answer to your first question, yes, I think so. I'm having the abstract brought up-to-date, and Clarence Darrow over in Livermore will have the papers ready in a couple of days. The answer to your second question is a firm No."

She smiled then, holding out her hand. "In that case, my name is Gally Deveraux."

He took her hand, a worker's hand but a nice hand. "I'm Carlisle McMillan. The reason I'm here is to offer you a beer for your mapmaking and real estate brokering, unless you're tied up or whatever."

As soon as he said it, he was sorry. He hadn't noticed her wedding ring before, wasn't used to looking for wedding rings. Clumsy, putting both her and him in an awkward situation.

He tried to backtrack. "If . . . that's if it's okay. I really didn't think about you being married . . . not that you shouldn't be . . . and just now noticed your ring. I mean . . . I don't mean anything, not trying to start anything . . . Aw, crap."

Gally Deveraux laughed and put her hand over her mouth, trying to conceal her amusement, but she couldn't. She hadn't done that for a long time, laughed out loud.

"Well, that's really decent of you. Drink your coffee while I finish mopping, and we'll brave the wilds of Leroy's in about ten minutes. Be forewarned, though, I'll be on my guard all the way across Main Street."

She laughed again, not at Carlisle, who was obviously squirming inside and entirely uncomfortable, but at the situation. He picked up on that and appreciated it, but he still felt the blood come to his face.

Beating on himself for his clumsiness, Carlisle glanced through remnants of the *High Plains Inquirer* lying on the counter. The logo said it was the newspaper he could count on, so he counted on it. It told him that somebody's hitting streak ended at thirty, that a new movie premiered in London, and that wearing corrective teeth braces had actually become a fad in Richmond, Virginia. With those items in mind, he turned to the Opinion section and looked at the lead editorial.

TIME TO GET GOING

Getting the state moving economically has proven to be a bigger challenge than Governor Jerry Gravatt anticipated. His diagnosis that we have been too dependent on agriculture and its related industries is right on target, but his solutions and those proposed by various business or legislative groups have so far not borne fruit. The chasing of smokestack industries puts us in competition with states that have paid more careful attention over the years to infrastructure requirements for industrial purposes, such as highways. Residents of this state have consistently voted against even slight increases in the state gasoline tax, which would have added greatly to road construction and improvement. And rumors of federal funding for a major new highway through the state have so far proven to be just that, rumors. Moreover, the aging of our population due to the exodus of our young people is steadily eroding the skilled labor force necessary as one component for convincing industry to locate here. Meanwhile, the state's tax base continues to decline as incomes drop and even longtime state industries move elsewhere in search of cheaper labor, better transportation, and relief from the increases in various state taxes being levied to offset the decline in the tax base. It's time for the governor, the legislature, and business groups to stop criticizing one another and start working together. The governor's proposed high-tech corridor from Falls City to the capital is a good beginning. All citizens of the state should get behind this visionary proposal in spite of the high initial costs for the laser and biotechnology centers. It's time to stop complaining, roll up our sleeves, and get going.

While Carlisle read the newspaper, Gally Deveraux mopped the chinked linoleum of a place called Danny's and thought about her life. She had torn her existence down like an old car engine parted out and scattered on a greasy floor. At least once a week she did that, then tried to reassemble it in a way that made more sense. But it always came together in the same sputtering, rackety form: thirty-nine, lonely, running down, no options, a woman steadily becoming invisible to the eyes of men. Even a married woman didn't like being invisible that way, especially to her husband.

She pulled on a denim jacket and began turning out the café lights. "Any time you're ready."

Carlisle held the door for her as she switched off the neon sign on their way out.

"Thanks. I'm used to opening my own doors." She smiled again, and they walked across the street toward Leroy's.

The pool table was dark. So was Leroy's face. Except for old Frank, the town greeter with his head flat on the bar, no one else was in Leroy's tavern at eight-fifteen on a Tuesday night. Sales were not good and getting worse.

Leroy squinted at the longhair that had come in with Jack Deveraux's wife, figuring maybe not say anything to Jack. Jack had a real bad temper, particularly when he'd been drinking, a state in which he existed more or less permanently.

A few months later, when he got to know Carlisle, Leroy would say, "Carlisle, I've developed the typical small-town retailer's mentality, that being 'Please, God, don't do anything bad until I retire, then do whatever You want to the poor bastards who're left.'

God's not listening to me, however, for about a thousand reasons I can think of."

Carlisle ordered two Buds, guessing that Leroy had not yet restocked Miller's. He collected the beers and took them over to where Gally was sitting in a booth, the LEROY'S window sign doodling red marks on her face when it flashed. She sensed that and shifted over in the booth.

He raised his bottle a little. "Here's to squatter's rights, or whatever it's called out here."

She tapped her bottle against his, easy-like. "To squatter's rights, and let's hope they can get to their feet after being in that position for so long." She leaned back in the corner of the booth, tugging on her beer, looking out over the bar.

Leroy fed the jukebox. The first two songs were standard issue—trucks and adultery, eighteen wheels and crawlin' home late at night with lipstick on your collar. The next tune featured some guy with a pretty decent tenor and solid steel guitar work behind him: "Hangin' on the door frame, repeatin' my own name, as if I might forget who I am."

Things picked up a little when the duck-

man came in. Carlisle had no idea who the
duck-man was, but he would see him occasionally in the years ahead and was mildly
fascinated by his behavior. The duck-man
sat at the bar, ordered a beer, and drank it
quietly, keeping to himself. Nothing unusual
there. What was strange was this: Inside the
big overcoat he wore winter and summer
was a live mallard. Every so often he would
peel back his coat lapel and the duck would
stick out its green head. The duck-man
would tip up the bottle, and the duck would
take a hit of Grain Belt, then disappear back
inside the coat.

Carlisle looked at the duck-man, then
over at Gally. She shrugged and grinned,
taking a hit of her own beer.

He wanted to ask her about the woman
with the auburn hair, but he didn't. He'd
learned a long time ago that asking a
woman about another woman, with any hint
of interest attached, not only came off as a
little tacky, but generally elicited bad information.

Instead he said, "Tell me more about the
ghosts out at Wolf Butte."

Gally looked at the ceiling for a moment,
then at Carlisle, noticing how warm his eyes

seemed. A little sad, maybe, but warm and good. Maybe the kind of man who wouldn't see women as trophies.

"Well, I think I mentioned the college professor who fell off a cliff right near there. That was some time ago. There was a lot of hoopla in those days about the Indian mounds out in that direction, and all kinds of scientific types were rolling in and out of Salamander for a few months. Men and women both, all nice folks. Dressed in hard-working clothes, real polite when they came into Danny's to eat. Cleaned their boots on the curb before they came in, which Thelma appreciated, still mentions it occasionally when she's chewing out some cowboy tracking ungodly stuff into the café. Quite a crowd, they were, laughed a lot and seemed to have a good time.

"Rumor had it that the Indians were getting pretty upset about what was happening out there on what they consider sacred land that should be theirs under the old treaties. Wasn't long after that the professor got killed, and the project was abandoned. Nobody seemed to know why.

"A year or two before the professor died, a survey crew was camped at the foot of

Wolf Butte. Four of them all staying in a big tent. In the middle of the night, a chunk of rock peeled off the butte and fell smack right onto their tent. Squashed the lot of them, though one guy lived for about a week before dying. It's a mercy he died, shape he was in. Everybody said they should have known better than to set up camp that close to the rock face. Another crew came in and finished the job, that's what people said. Never heard anything about what they were surveying for."

Carlisle said nothing and waited for her to continue.

"It gets stranger and stranger. Some of the old-timers claim there was a series of such incidents out there when this area was first settled. All sorts of peculiar goings-on back then, according to what I've heard— fires on top of Wolf Butte at night, sound of drums, a huge bird circling the butte, a hairy creature called Big Man stalking around the countryside, all kinds of stuff. Some people say the stories go back much further. The Indians themselves say the stories are ancient. Something about a priestess called Syawla. The old-timers believe there's always some-one or something out there watching for intruders. Legend has it that he is called the Keeper and is the son of Syawla. Keeper of what, I'm not sure. Keeps watch over the sacred ground, I guess. That's about all I know. Kind of gives me the shivers when I drive by that area on my way into town."

Carlisle sat quietly, thinking for a moment. "That is pretty strange. Makes me even more interested in the Williston place. Who owns the land around Wolf Butte?"

"I'm not sure, exactly. Axel Looker's ground is right north of there. On the west side, I think some of it's government land leased to ranchers for grazing, some of it's owned by a corporation, so people say. The company has one of those nondescript names that's hard to remember. Aura Corporation, something like that."

"Aur . . . what? How do you spell it?"

"Like it sounds: A-u-r-a. I have no idea what it stands for. I asked Jack, my husband, once, and he didn't know."

Carlisle fingered his beer bottle, rocking it slowly from side to side. "You can see Wolf Butte rising in the distance from the Williston place. Maybe I'll get some binoculars and see what I can see out there. Want to plunder the moment and have another beer?"

"Sure, let's plunder." Gally smiled, finished her beer, and handed the bottle to Carlisle.

Carlisle slid out of the booth with the empties in his hand. As Leroy dug out two more beers, the duck-man watched Carlisle sideways, tugged his blue stocking cap lower, and pulled his coat lapels together until they overlapped.

When Gally and Carlisle came out of Leroy's, the streets of Salamander were quiet, and Carlisle noted the old man was gone from his window above Lester's. He said good night to Gally and opened the door of his truck while she walked toward her Bronco across the street, humming an old tune, the name of which Carlisle couldn't quite remember. But a few of the words came back to him, something to do with dance pavilions in the rain.

CHAPTER SEVEN

"Need another one?"

"Nope, I'm okay for now." The old man sat with his back against the wall of a Livermore tavern, his better leg stretched out on the seat of a booth, bad leg underneath the table. He grinned and looked at the ceiling, rapping his cane quietly on the edge of the seat.

"When Carlisle McMillan bought the old Williston place northwest of Salamander, the locals thought he was around the bend. After buying it, he embarked on one of the great scrounging expeditions of all time. No place in the county was safe. He rummaged old barns and ransacked the dark corners of the discount lumberyard in Falls City. Axel Looker brought in daily reports on the increasing amount of material Carlisle had lying around, and in three weeks, people were driving by just to see the stuff. Some took along binoculars since the house sat back a bit from the road. The more emboldened of the locals shifted into four-wheel drive, went right up the lane, got out of their vehicles, and asked, 'How's she coming?'

"Carlisle was always polite to the visitors, even though he was frantically trying to get the place closed up tight before winter. Given the late start he'd gotten, that was a real horse race. He'd keep right on working, trying to answer their questions while he sawed and hammered and tongued and grooved and mitered and shingled.

"Talk on the street, over at Danny's, in Leroy's, and down at the elevator was all about Carlisle and his project. It started out pretty uncomplimentary, the talk, that is. 'Not enough acres to graze cattle or grow winter wheat.' Or: 'That house never was nothing more than a glorified line shack and a bad one at that.' Or: 'Seen the little house on the prairie lately? Darn, I hate to stand around witnessing stupidity in motion.'

"After a while, though, the tone kind of altered. Folks had taken Carlisle for some sort of hippie deviant right at first, but those

who'd been out to the Williston place said
he seemed to know what he was doing.
Said he used a Skil circular saw, which in-
volves guiding by hand a blade turning
faster than eight zillion times per quarter
second, better than most people could cut
with a table saw. Said he could drive a roofing nail with two shots of his hammer and
never miss. Said he wore a leather tool belt
that looked like it'd seen considerable wear
before he came to Salamander. Some of the
women said they understood he looked real
good with his shirt off and hair tied back
with a leather shoestring into a ponytail.
That's what Alma Hickman passed on after
talking to her customers at the Swirl'n Curl.

"Some nights he'd drag into town just
before Danny's closed and eat whatever
Gally had available, two or three helpings of
it. Most of the time, however, he camped
out, cooking for himself on a little butane
stove he'd bought at the Falls City Wal-
Mart.

"People also noticed Carlisle's appearance changed some once he got to working
on his house. In spite of it being early autumn when he started, he acquired a real
deep suntan, though his skin was kind of

dark to start with anyway. He also straightened up some, and his jeans seemed to fit
him somewhat looser around the middle.
Even his walk took on a different character,
the way that happens when a man finds
purpose in life and something to live for.
Carlisle apparently was getting himself in
shape, physically and mentally."

As the old man said, when Carlisle McMillan
bought the Williston place northwest of Salamander, the locals thought he was around
the bend. But then they didn't have his outlook on life, which is not surprising, since
even he wasn't quite sure of what his outlook
was at that time. And, more important, they
had never studied under Cody Marx, an
artist of his own kind in a town full of artists
and literati.

In Mendocino, the place of Carlisle's
growing, Wynn McMillan offered cello lessons and worked part-time in an art gallery.
Gradually, their little rented house turned
into Mendocino's version of a salon, a modest copy of the one Gertrude Stein had engi-
neered in Paris thirty years earlier when she
provided a place for Hemingway and Pound

and their cronies to hang out after they finished working for the day. So Carlisle grew
up around people who used big words and
analyzed what they were doing to the point
that what they were doing ceased to exist as
anything intelligible to an ordinary observer.
At least that's how it seemed to him.

He had seen books of Monet's paintings
by the time he was four. The music of
Mozart and Haydn and Schubert was
played by local musicians in the living room
while he lay in bed reading about Tarzan and
following the adventures of Zane Grey's heroes. Schopenhauer, Shaw, and Spengler
were discussed by people leaning against
the refrigerator or banging around the stove
while he fixed peanut-butter sandwiches for
himself on Friday nights.

"Hello, Carlisle. My, you're growing up
fast."

"Hi, Carlisle. How's school going?"

"Carlisle, I'm cooking Thai for this unruly
mob. Where does your mother keep the
turmeric?"

The one great strength of these people,
and Carlisle was always grateful to them for
it, was how they treated the circumstances
of his birth. The fact that he was misbegot-

ten simply made no difference to them. Schopenhauer was important, but the fact that Wynn McMillan had rolled naked upon the sands of a California beach with a man whose last name she could not recall and produced a boy-child afterward was not important in its moral implications.

Cody Marx did not frequent Wynn's salon. If he had been invited, he wouldn't have come. Cody didn't use big words. In fact, he didn't use many words at all. He just happened to be one of the world's great carpenters and let his skills do his talking for him. Even though he was not asked to participate in long evenings of chamber music and literary criticism, he was the first to be summoned when anything to do with building was required. If you couldn't get Cody because he was tied up with other work, you simply waited until he could get to your project. That is, if you were one of those people insisting on perfection.

Cody Marx was far more than just a good technician. He looked at things with an artist's eye and a philosopher's mind, understanding that Zen and precision are not at odds, though Cody likely never had heard of anything called Zen. And his work demon-

strated it. If you showed him a picture of
something—a house, a room, cabinetry—
that someone had already built and said,
"That's what I want," he would politely turn
down the project and amble off. Cody didn't
build copies of other people's work. Cody
built Cody's work, period.

The way you dealt with Cody was to put
up with his pipe smoking, describe in general terms what contribution to your life the
finished product was supposed to make,
and then stand back and leave matters to
his creativity and skill. The other thing you
never, ever, did was to put a deadline on a
project or try to hurry him along in his work.

Word got around about that latter idio-
syncrasy of his after he walked away from a
kitchen job he was doing for a local banker.
The banker's wife complained to Cody in a
rather unsubtle fashion about his slow, methodical ways, saying she couldn't cook or
entertain or anything else with her kitchen
torn up the way it was.

Without looking at her or speaking, he
gathered his tools, left, and refused to finish
the job until the banker agreed to take his
family on an extended trip, a journey that
would not terminate until Cody sent them a

postcard declaring the kitchen was finished. Of course, their new kitchen with its custom cabinets, fancy built-ins, and subdued exactness of fine craftsmanship was admired by everyone. The most lavish praise came from a British department store executive and his wife who visited the banker's home in Mendocino after they had all met on a winter cruise, the one taken while Cody was remodeling the banker's kitchen.

So Carlisle was there on the north coast, mowing lawns and scraping paint from expensive boats owned by summer people, unhappy with odd jobbing. He had never much liked repetition, never liked doing things where he didn't grow in some way while doing them. It had always seemed to him that after living another twenty-four hours, you ought to be a better person than you were when the day began. Like an anchored gull, that's how he felt, flopping around on the surface of things, tugging at his anchor chain, and trying to beat his way upward into full flight.

He heard Cody's name mentioned by his mother and her friends and picked up on the considerable reverence that always surrounded any discussion of Cody's work. His

mother's friends, while able in their own intellectual and artistic trades, did not possess
manual skills of the kind producing immediately practical outcomes. That being so,
they were given to displays of respectful
awe when it came to people such as Cody
who could produce those outcomes. Great
auto mechanics fell into the same category,
though at a somewhat lower level than Cody.

Having technical skills and using them to
make things of utilitarian value, things that
lasted, was an idea that appealed to Carlisle.
The Mendocino houses Cody built in his
younger days were models of good construction, standing strong and quiet through
the years. That's what everybody said.
Everything in plumb, no tilts, no leaks that
were his fault. Banisters that never loosened,
tiles that never worked free, ceiling joists that
hung for decades and never drooped.

The Cody anecdotes were told and told
again in his mother's living room. They were
known as "Cody stories" and "Cody's Way."
One of them in particular impressed Carlisle
and ultimately changed his life. The man
who related it was a local poet, a man who
knew something about things hidden and
meanings submerged and who once re-

marked, "Cody Marx knows where the bones of shoddy work are buried in the walls of Mendocino County." Cody had been building an addition onto the man's house, and the poet had watched him sand pine support studs that would be concealed in the walls. Nobody would ever see them, sanding didn't make them any stronger or cause them to function any better, so the man asked Cody why he did it.

Since Cody was doing the work for a price agreed upon in advance, it didn't matter financially to the client just why the studs had to be sanded, but he was curious. Cody chewed on his pipe, looked at a two-by-four he had just smoothed down, and told the poet he simply felt better about doing things that way. Said it felt more finished to him. That's all he said, nothing more. Cody's Way.

The day after he heard that story, Carlisle went off to find Cody Marx. His wife said he was working on a new house northeast of town in the hills up toward Russian Gulch. Carlisle pedaled his bicycle out there, saw Cody's old pickup truck parked outside, and could hear the tapping of his hammer inside. He was working alone. That was his custom, unless he needed some dumb muscle for a day or two to help him with heavy work.

Carlisle stood off to one side, watching the old man work, shaky in the presence of a legend, trying to gather himself. The pipe was going, and Cody was humming softly as he trimmed a door. After a minute or two, he turned to use his miter box, saw the boy, and staggered backward a step.

Right off, I'm already in the hole, Carlisle said to himself. Cody was in his late sixties, and Carlisle was thinking that he could have caused the old man to have a heart attack.

Cody recovered, though, and said, "Yup, whaddya need?"

Carlisle was a nervous supplicant, but he got some words out. "I'd like to work with you and learn to be a carpenter."

"Don't need any help, can't afford it any- ways." Cody leaned over the miter box and cut a piece of molding for the door he was working on. That done, he held up the wood to test how well it joined with the horizontal piece already in place across the top of the door. The joint looked perfect to Carlisle, but Cody took a half sheet of fine-grade sandpa- per from his hip pocket and sanded down the cut. Satisfied with the fit, he nailed the molding into place, countersinking the nails in preparation for filling in the holes later on, behaving all the while as if Carlisle were merely a can of wood preservative off in the corner.

The carpenter sorted through a pile of molding and said without looking up, "You're Wynn McMillan's boy, ain'cha?"

"Yes."

"How old you be?"

"Twelve."

"Thought you mowed lawns and such."

Carlisle steadied his pubescent voice, which tended to bolt upward just short of an octave right in the middle of words, and said the lines he had rehearsed: "I want to learn to work with my hands, making things that last. I want to learn a trade and become a craftsman."

He worried that what he had said sounded a little too elevated, too formal, especially in the way he'd squeaked it out. But it was the best he could do. In mentioning "craftsman," however, he had picked the right word.

"Ya know that word *craftsman* has nearly dropped out of the English language, don't you?"

Carlisle said nothing. The old man sorted molding.

There are moments in a life when the future pivots on the slim and critical fulcrums of gut-level decisions by those possessing the power to give or withhold the things you want. That morning, as it turned out, was one of those moments for Carlisle McMillan. Cody was sorting, Cody was humming, and Cody was thinking.

"You play football or anything like that?"

"No. I don't have time, and I'm not interested anyway."

"Then you'd be available on Saturdays and after school during the school year?"

Carlisle's pulse rate escalated twenty points. "Yes, sir."

Cody returned to sifting through the pile of long, slender pieces of wood, speaking without looking at Carlisle. "I watched you mowing a lawn across the street from where I was working about six weeks ago. Thing that impressed me was how you finished up on your hands and knees, clipping the few blades of grass your mower couldn't reach."

He looked up at Carlisle for a moment. "Finishing is what it's all about, in carpentry . . . and in life, for that matter. At the other end is the phrase that injects cold fear into the bones of all home handymen: 'Prepare the surface.' Most people don't prepare the surface correctly, and that's another aspect of good craftsmanship and life in general. So whether you're doing life or carpentry, if you prepare the surface, carry out the finishing, and do everything else in between in the right way, you got things covered. Craftsmanship is a matter of attitude first, technical skill after that. Follow me?"

"Yes, sir, I follow you all right."

Cody straightened up and looked straight at the boy, squinting. "Dollar an hour. You start by doing cleanup work, since that's always part of both preparing the surface *and* finishing. Tomorrow, right here, seven a.m., ready to work. Need a ride out here?"

"No, sir. I have my bike."

The Legend carried a piece of molding over to the door, humming. Carlisle took that as a signal to leave. On his way home, pedaling fast, breathing hard, lifting off, he already felt like a craftsman. Just being around Cody Marx did that to a person. The anchor chain was parting.

Wynn McMillan had been mildly upset

with the arrangement. Not that she had anything against Cody Marx, but Carlisle was av-
eraging more than a dollar an hour doing
lawns and boats, and his earnings were important to a household where things were always lean. Yet she listened while Carlisle told
her all the reasons why he wanted to work
with Cody. And Wynn McMillan understood.

She smiled then. Carlisle never forgot
how she had smiled and what she had said.
"Be the finest carpenter Mendocino ever
produced, Carlisle, if that's what you want.
We'll manage somehow."

Some of Carlisle's best years were those
he spent working alongside Cody Marx. He
grew to love the old man. Loved him for his
skill, for his outlook, for the fine work he did.
But it ran deeper than that. Carlisle had no
father, Cody and his wife had no children, so
the bond was a natural one. Carlisle never
even considered that in the beginning, but
later on came to believe that Cody had. As
was true of men in those days, Cody felt he
knew some things worth passing on to
someone, and that someone had turned out
to be Carlisle. During the years the two of
them worked together, he tried his best to
teach Carlisle everything he knew. All of it.

With his first couple of paychecks from Cody, Carlisle bought a pair of dark blue bib overalls and a tan workshirt, exactly like those Cody wore. That year at Christmas, his mother gave him a black lunch bucket and a red metal thermos that were almost identical to Cody's. In the years after, to this day, in fact, his lunch and his coffee have ridden in that battered bucket and battered thermos, the artifacts of his learning days, a way of reaching back to the strong hands of Cody Marx and the understanding ways of his mother.

During the first two years Carlisle worked for Cody, he called him nothing but "sir" or "Mr. Marx." It was like apprenticing yourself to a Zen master, and the master was to be given the respect due him.

On Carlisle's fourteenth birthday, they were remodeling the inside of a lovely old drugstore downtown. Carlisle reported for work at six-thirty in the morning. He learned early on that when Cody said "seven," he really meant a half hour before that.

He said, "Good morning, Mr. Marx," as always, his voice mercifully beginning its decline into a steady pitch at the upper end of the baritone range.

Cody had been tamping down his first pipeful of tobacco for the day, cocked his head toward Carlisle as he lighted it and between efforts at getting it to draw properly asked, "This your birthday, is it?" He knew that, somehow.

"Yes, sir." Carlisle was grinning, proud of being fourteen and working for Cody Marx, proud of his burgeoning skill.

Cody bent over and reached into a brown paper sack on the floor. Out of it he pulled a new leather tool belt, stiff and light brown. When he held it out, Carlisle could see old but still serviceable hand tools protruding from various pockets.

"Happy birthday, Carlisle. I just want you to know it's good working with you. And, by the way, I think you're due a raise to a dollar fifty. One other matter: I'd prefer it if you'd call me 'Cody' from here on out. Now let's put these ceiling joists up correctly so we can get on to greater things."

Carlisle had tears in his eyes as he strapped on the belt. Partly because, as Cody intended, he took the present to be a symbol of progress in his long climb to skill and understanding and partly because

Cody had said Carlisle worked with him, not for him. That was important.

Over the years, through windows not yet closed and doors not yet hung, Carlisle could hear the high school marching band practicing late on autumn afternoons. If Cody and he were working in the evenings to get a job completed, he sometimes could hear the crowd and the public address announcer over at the football field. From the gabled ends of Mendocino, he watched other kids go to the beach on summer afternoons and sail their parents' boats in the mornings.

None of that bothered him. In fact, he would not have changed places with them, not for anything. He was creating things of permanence with his hands. For that's what Carlisle loved helping Cody Marx do all over Mendocino County, California. They prepared surfaces, finished, and did everything else in between. More than that, and most of all, they did it right, working to close tolerances, following Cody's Way. People smiled when Cody's truck went through town, Cody driving along in his blue bibs and tan workshirt, talking with the boy who was dressed just like him.

Carlisle worked steadily with the old carpenter until he graduated from high school,
and he still worked with him part-time during his first two years at Stanford. When
Cody had a job requiring more than two
hands, Carlisle would catch a bus up from
Palo Alto. During the ride he would study his
textbooks, thinking what a poor substitute
they were for the taction of fine woods moving through your fingers and the pleasure of
standing back and looking over good work
when it was finished.

Cody had started mumbling about retirement, but Carlisle didn't believe it. Then on a
Thursday afternoon, Carlisle's mother telephoned. In a soft, halting voice, she told him
Cody had died. "They found him out at the
old Merkle place where he was putting in
some closets."

A day in a man's twentieth year coming
down, spring day, low sun running ground-
ward. Carlisle sat in his room and cried for
two hours without stopping, quietly beating
his fist against a desk piled high with books
whose combined knowledge was no more
than fleeting twaddle compared with what
Cody Marx knew and tried to pass on to
him. At that moment, Carlisle decided he

would finish at Stanford—he would do that for his mother—but afterward he would follow Cody's Way.

Cody's tools and old truck were bequeathed to Carlisle. Anna Marx turned them over to him with tears in her eyes.

As he finally prepared to drive away, she took his hand in both of hers and said, "Carlisle, you were the main topic of conversation at our house for the last eight years. Every evening Cody would have something to tell me about you, about how much you were learning, about what a good boy you are and how much it pleased him to watch you growing into a fine man. When you showed up for work in your shirt and overalls that were just like his, he came home, sat at the kitchen table, and said, 'Anna, I think I've got a son.' And then ever after he always thought of you that way. He was so proud of you. My God, how he loved you, Carlisle. He truly loved you."

Carlisle nodded. She had told him something he already knew, but it was good to hear her say it. "I loved him, too, Mrs. Marx, every bit as much as he loved me. He gave me a place in life, a purpose, and I'll try to live up to Cody's Way."

In the old truck, which still ran like new, since Cody had done the tune-ups and repairs on it, Carlisle drove slowly around Mendocino for hours, looking at all the places where they had worked together. He remembered, it seemed, every mortise, every tenon, every dovetail, every bevel and compound angle they had ever created.

He would stop the truck and wipe his eyes when he heard Cody's voice saying, "I think we can get it a little better than that, Carlisle," which was Cody's gentle way of telling Carlisle he hadn't done something right. He leaned his head on the steering wheel, thinking of the old man who had tried his best to make a decent craftsman out of him. The smell in the truck of ash and cedar and East Indian satinwood and Honduras mahogany mixed with the smoke from Cody's pipe. The memories . . . God, all the memories.

Even these years later, particularly when he was working on something intricate, Carlisle would catch himself humming. When that happened, he would stop for a moment, finger the old tool belt he was wearing, which had been mended a dozen times and darkened by the oil from his hands and the wood he worked, and think about Cody Marx. He would think about how the old man prepared the surface on a lonely, quiet boy named Carlisle McMillan.

The decrepit house on the property near Salamander was the unchiseled stone for the monument he would build to the memory of Cody Marx. He was bent on making ol' man Williston's place into something that represented the finest of all that Cody Marx had taught him. In the best tradition of craftsmanship, he would reclaim a derelict and make it live forever.

Out of habit, the bad habit he had picked up building for developers and other people caring little about work being truly finished, Carlisle found himself cutting corners and doing things just to get them done. When he realized that, he slowed down, sometimes tearing apart a piece of work that wasn't up to Cody's standards, and started over. If he had to sleep in the cab of his truck through the roar of high plains blizzards, this job would be done right.

The roof was first. In autumn, cedar shakes could be bought at a decent price. The lumberyard in Falls City had twenty-five squares ordered for a project that was canceled, and Carlisle got his shakes for even less than he anticipated. They let him sort through them, picking out the very best. By California standards, he stole them.

Standing inside Williston's place and looking up, he saw rafters and roof sheathing, with no cavity for insulation. So raising the entire roof system to create the space he needed was essential. Carlisle knew that was going to be the worst part of the entire project. It was also the most critical.

He started by ripping off the old shingles and rotted sheathing underneath. Most of the rafters were in bad shape. These were replaced with kiln-dried two-by-twelves. He built up and repaired others, nailed down one-by-threes across the rafters, and started laying the shakes, using hot-dipped sixpenny galvanized nails. And he sanded the rafters and one-by-threes, though he was tempted not to. Nobody would know, except him and Cody. But that was quite enough.

Putting in a big skylight over what would be the main living quarters and a smaller one that would let moonlight come easily into the bedroom area slowed him down. But he did it right and fashioned them so they could be cranked open from the inside when the days warmed.

That done, Carlisle worked on the interior floors, laying down well-cured, double-tongue-and-groove car siding he found stacked on a nearby farm. The farmer charged him almost nothing for it. Later on, he would put down fine wood over the planks. For now, it was a matter of getting in a subfloor he could live with in rough weather.

The siding was in bad repair, a result of cheap material from the outset and little maintenance afterward. As Cody would have said, "Looks like someone decided to kinda let this place weather in." Carlisle tore it off, all of it, along with the inside plaster, leaving the old house standing there like somebody with a new hat and shoes but naked otherwise.

Early fall rains, cold rains, hit him twenty days into the work. Still, he continued tearing and pounding, wearing his slicker and sometimes using the truck headlights and a gas lantern as he worked into the night.

As the old man said, folks from Salamander began driving out to see what Carlisle was up to. He tried to be polite and answer their questions, but he kept working while they talked.

If the roof is an umbrella, the siding is a slicker. He wanted to make the house as lasting and maintenance-free as possible, so his choice was planking, either western red cedar or redwood. Both were expensive, and as a matter of principle, he refused to use either of those in their virgin state. He simply couldn't countenance the felling of the big trees to supply planking. Of course, the lumberyard offered the standard four-by-eight sections of pressed wood with a cedar veneer. But, as he told one visitor who suggested he ought to make his life simple and use the veneer, "I worked with enough of that in my California days to last me a life-time, not my kind of material. Besides, ever see what a woodpecker can do to cedar ve-neer?"

A local retired carpenter came by to kib-itz and offer unneeded advice, of which Carlisle was already acquiring a surplus. But he listened when the man talked about a hunting lodge up in Three Forks that was being torn down. The old fellow had helped build it fifty years back and still remembered the nice redwood they used to cover the inside. Carlisle drove up to Three Forks, shuffled his feet, haggled with the demolition crew supervisor, and got what he needed. In fact, there would be enough left over for a redwood shower and hot tub later on. Maybe enough for the atrium-greenhouse he was thinking about hooking on to the south wall, once he had sanded off the glossy clubhouse finish and returned the wood to its natural state.

By mid-October, most of the siding was in place, and rolls of batted fiberglass insulation were on their way from the lumberyard in Livermore. Just in time, too, since the first snowfall had come three days before, forcing him to sleep in the truck at night.

He had also acquired a partner. A big yellow tomcat with a chewed right ear had drifted by a week earlier, stayed for lunch and then for supper, and soon became a permanent resident. The cat slept with Carlisle in the truck cab and followed him around during the day. Carlisle studied the cat. The cat studied Carlisle.

"Well, big guy, I think the name Dumptruck suits you. So if you don't mind, we'll leave it at that." Dumptruck blinked his yellow eyes. Carlisle grinned.

Near sundown on a Saturday, he walked around the house, admiring his work and feeling better about himself than he had for a long while. Cody had been fond of quoting somebody named Sir Henry Wotton, who said, 350 years back: "Well building hath three conditions: commodity, firmness, and delight." Carlisle was succeeding in the first two and had the third pretty well mapped out in his head. In addition, he was getting back to somewhere he'd been before, somewhere with Cody, somewhere quieter, somewhere that made sense.

Carlisle was hungry but too tired to fire up the butane stove and heat another can of beans or whatever was left under the tarp where he kept his food cache. Without hurrying things, it was too late to make Danny's in Salamander, so it looked like peanut-butter sandwiches and fruit with a Milky Way at the end.

While he and Dumptruck considered their dismal set of choices, he glanced down the lane and saw Gally Deveraux walking toward him through the twilight. She was carrying a large picnic hamper in one hand and a thermos jug in the other, stumbling over the ruts. He had been eating some of his meals at

Danny's over the last few weeks and had come to know Gally better, but this surprised him.

She stopped and adjusted the Stetson that had fallen over her eyes. He walked down to meet her. "Hello, Gally. What a surprise."

Her face was red and she was panting a little from the stumbling and carrying. She was wearing jeans and a shirt she had bought at Charlene's going-out-of-business sale and her winter denim jacket. In the twilight, with strands of hair trailing out from under the hat, she looked just fine, like a slightly aging sweetheart of the rodeo.

"Hi, carpenter. I didn't know if I should drive up your lane or not. Jack took off for the weekend with some of his hook-and-bullet buddies to shoot dangerous game, deer or pheasants, I guess, maybe hummingbirds for all I know. Whatever it is, if it runs or flaps, they'll shoot it. Got to keep the range free of predators and cull the wildlife for ecological purposes, as they're fond of saying. Actually, what they do is drink and drive around, trying to scare up something they can shoot from the truck window.

"He left it to me to go out and round up

some of the yearlings. I was out there on the sorrel gelding, working my tail off, when I said to myself, 'Well, to hell with you, Jack.' That's when I got it in my head to come over for a neighborly visit. Thought with all the work you're doing, you might require something in the way of food with the punch of rocket fuel." The explanation for being there came pouring out fast and up front.

"Gally, what a kind thought. I was just mulling over the virtues of beans versus peanut butter, and here you come out of the falling darkness on an errand of mercy." He took the hamper from her.

Gally laughed and wiped her forehead with her sleeve. She was sweating lightly, even though the evening was cooling fast. "There's a steady flow of reports coming in from everyone that's been visiting you. You're surprising them. The early betting leaned toward you falling off the roof and pulling out for California when the first snow flew."

The hamper held thick slices of ham, potato salad, coleslaw, apple pie, homemade bread, the works, including a six-pack of Miller's. Gally's famously good coffee was in the thermos.

They walked around Carlisle's emerging vision while he pointed out subtleties of the carpenter's trade far beyond anything Gally cared to know. But women in general have a nice way of putting up with boyish dreams, and she asked intelligent questions, nodding and smiling as he ran his fingers over redwood and fir while he talked.

Inside, they stood on the decking, looking up through the larger skylight at red bands of sundown cut diagonally by the contrails of a jet. After a long week at Danny's and a day of rounding up yearlings to boot, Gally had to be as tired as he was, Carlisle knew, but she covered it, and at that moment he began to feel differently about her, started to care about her in the way you care about a friend who is maybe a little something more than just a casual friend.

"I want to show you something," he said.

He took her over to the fireplace and pointed at a word carved into the stone on the left-hand side: *Syawla*. "I found it when I cleaned the gunk off. Williston must have tooled it in there. I remember you telling me about the legends out here, about a priestess called Syawla."

"Carlisle, that makes the enamel peel

right off my teeth. Why do you suppose he put it there?"

"Don't know. Adds a little something to the place, though. Don't you think?"

"I don't want to think about it, period."

The nights were getting cold, but Carlisle had the fireplace working. While Dumptruck slept on the hearth, he and Gally sat on stacks of lumber, laughing and talking and eating the food she had brought in her Bronco, down the red dirt road past Wolf Butte, past a lot of things. She had traveled that road with muddled thoughts about women growing older who had more or less given up on possibilities. And she looked at the man from California wearing a navy-issue watch cap, whose hair was almost as long as hers and was tied back into a ponytail with a leather shoestring; it felt good to laugh again.

After supper, Carlisle tossed more pieces of scrap lumber into the fireplace, and for a while they sat there without talking. Both of them stared at the flames, drinking coffee out of tin cups, light snow blowing through places where he hadn't finished the siding. Gally was leaning forward, elbows on her knees, cup balanced in both hands, wondering about a lot of things.

When she left about midnight, there was the glow of a small fire on the crest of Wolf Butte three miles northwest, but Carlisle didn't see it.

The next morning, an unusual amount of traffic was moving on the red dirt road, including several county sheriff vehicles and an ambulance. Carlisle wondered about it but didn't want to take the time to investigate. A little before noon, Axel Looker drove up the lane and got out. "Hear what happened?"

"No. I figured something was going on by the number of cars and trucks going by out front."

"Jack Deveraux and some of his drinking pals were road hunting on the other side of Wolf Butte yesterday. Somehow one of the guns went off in their truck and blew half of Jack's face away. Killed him on the spot."

"My God! When was that?"

"About five-thirty in the afternoon."

"I didn't know Jack, except to see him around, but I know Gally. That's just awful."

"Well, yes and no. That'd be the going opinion around here. Jack was a serious drinker and headed further in that direction. These dumb bastards around here are always mixing alcohol and guns. I won't let 'em hunt my land anymore after they shot a steer a few years ago. We used to have bullets whizzing around the house during deer season."

Carlisle was thinking that Gally had been walking up his lane with her hamper and thermos at about the time her husband had been dying. In some indefinable way, he felt guilty about what had happened, as if he'd had a hand in it.

"Nobody could locate Gally," Axel continued. "She was off somewhere until pretty late." Axel was looking at Carlisle, remembering he'd seen what looked like Gally's Bronco parked at the foot of Carlisle's lane when he and Earlene had driven home the night before after doing their weekly grocery shopping in Livermore.

Carlisle said nothing, so Axel went on. "I guess Gally's taking it pretty well. But I'll tell you what the old-timers at Danny's are saying. They're saying it wasn't no accident, even though apparently that's just what it was. But one of the old guys who's an expert on the Wolf Butte legends said, 'There ain't no accidents out there. It just looks that way. Always.'"

CHAPTER EIGHT

The first big snow held off until late October, coming softly then in the middle of the night and settling on Carlisle McMillan's new cedar shakes while he slept. Around dawn the wind kicked up, and he awakened to the rattle of plastic sheets fastened over unfinished windows and doors. He got the fireplace going, ate some bread and jam, and waited for the coffee to brew in its pot hanging over the flames.

He had planned to install the first of the double-paned windows today, but clearly it was time for the high-efficiency woodstove that had arrived from Vermont two weeks ago. The Indian had drifted by the day after it was delivered. He came late in the morning while Carlisle was thinking about how to get 275 pounds of cast iron off the bed of the pickup and into the house without cracking it or permanently destroying his capacity to function as a male animal, or both. The stove had *Defiant* stamped on its door and looked just that way resting on the truck bed.

Carlisle had never seen the Indian before, didn't hear him coming. He stood on the other side of the pickup as if he were part of the landscape. Face like hammered copper, thin as a stipe of wild yellow clover, dressed in denim jacket and jeans and beat-up cowboy boots, white shirt with a smudge on the collar. Straight black hair about the same length as Carlisle's and a wide-brimmed hat with some kind of juju-bead hatband wrapped around the crown.

He said nothing, looking at the stove, then at Carlisle. Old dark eyes taking in the problem, taking in Carlisle, taking in the universe for all Carlisle knew.

"It's a heavy son of a whore," Carlisle said, looking at the stove.

The Indian nodded. "We could rig up a travois out of these long two-by-fours and a couple of crosspieces."

That's all he said. That's all he had to say. Carlisle knew the problem had been solved.

The Indian might have been fifty, he might have been seventy. Carlisle couldn't tell. But he was tough and strong for his size. They wrestled the stove off the truck and onto the drag, then moved it to the steps, where Carlisle walked it gingerly across the rotten porch floor he hadn't gotten around to fixing yet.

Carlisle offered the Indian a beer. They sat on the tailgate of the pickup, legs swinging back and forth, sipping and talking a little. The Indian was intensely curious about the house and what Carlisle was doing. Said he sensed some kind of positive magic in all of this.

"I have these strong feelings of ancestral worship when I look at your work. Why is that?"

Carlisle felt a little shiver and swung his head toward the Indian. He had not spoken of Cody Marx to anyone for years. But he decided the Indian would understand the story. He told him, and while he was talking, the Indian would slowly move his head up and down from time to time.

After Carlisle finished, the Indian said, "When you have closed up your house, I will come by to chant good words over this sacred place. I will bring Susanna with me. Do you know her?"

"I'm not sure."

"She is the white woman who lives in a little house by the elevator in Salamander. She may be white, but in her own way she thinks more Indian than many Indians do. She has her own vision—not an Indian vision, since that is impossible to achieve without being an Indian, but her way has much in common with the Indian way. She has strong medicine within her, and I will ask her to also say words over the tribute you build to your Cody Marx."

"I think I know who you mean, though I've never met her." Carlisle knew exactly whom he meant.

After that, the Indian started coming by every few days to check on Carlisle's progress. Always on foot, always by himself. Sometimes he brought fresh bass or catfish from the Little Sal and cooked lunch for them over an open fire. Sometimes he sat on the floor cross-legged and played a small wooden flute while Carlisle worked. Carlisle liked the sound. Somehow it fit this country, so he asked the Indian if he would teach him to play.

When the Indian came again, he brought an extra flute, saying it was Carlisle's to keep. "Begin by holding it like this, then blow across the opening here very gently. At the beginning, do not try to play any song, do not even try to put your fingers on the holes made for them. You should concentrate on getting a sound from the open position so pure that it alone makes your heart ache. It will take you months to do that, but I will help you. When you see the image of a lone coyote coming from the sounds, then you will know you have it right. So long, Builder. I will come again."

In the years Carlisle knew him, the Indian never referred to Carlisle as anything but "Builder." Carlisle, in turn, called him "Flute Player," since the Indian had never offered a name. The Indian didn't seem to mind.

Masonry was not Carlisle's strongest skill, but in the northwest corner of the main room, he'd mortared together a nice brick heat shield that ran halfway up the wall. The brick, coming from a historic street the Livermore City Council had decided to pave, would both protect the wall and absorb heat that would be released long after the stove had died out. He had enough materials left over to build a hearth two bricks high for the stove to sit on, leaving plenty of clearance all around it.

With the snow piling up outside, he set seventeen brown paper sacks in a line along one wall. In each sack were the parts for one step in the installation of the wood stove. Cody had taught him to operate this way when doing something that involved a lot of pieces.

As Cody said, "People dump all the parts out and rummage through them as the need arises. That's not only inefficient, but also small parts have a tendency to run when you're not looking. There's a whole creation separate from ours that's full of random parts that have escaped that way. Partition the job into stages, put the right parts for each stage into its own bag, and everything works out as it should."

Seventeen steps, seventeen sacks. Two days of wrestling uncooperative metal and cutting his hands, and it was done. Just in time, too, since a high-pressure front followed the storm, as things tend to occur in the high plains, with hard, bright sunlight and a sharp drop in temperature. Carlisle heated the stove to a low burn and let it cool. He did that again and again, curing the cast iron so it wouldn't crack when he built the first big fire in it. Then he put down the first real fire, and the stove cooked away, double burning the gases as it was designed to do, filling the entire house with good radiant heat, and Carlisle began installing the last of the windows.

Autumn was volatile. Four days after the snow fell, it had melted. The house was closed in except for hanging the front door, a solid-core mahogany prize that had been tossed on the junk pile up at the hunting lodge where Carlisle acquired his redwood siding. He had the job under control and rested for a moment, sitting on the doorsill and looking out across the prairie, coffee cup beside him.

A black hat was coming up the lane. Under it was the Indian carrying a small drum over his shoulder, and the woman was with him.

A black shawl over a dress of lavender-colored wool. High boots and a flaxen sash knotted on her left hip, the ends of it hanging to her knees. She was wearing a headband that matched the sash. The bounce of sunlight off her silver necklace raced ahead of them as they came on, walking easily, talking to each other.

"Ho, Builder."

"Ho, Flute Player."

"Builder, I have brought Susanna Benteen with me."

Carlisle took the hand she held toward him and looked at her. She was like nothing he'd ever seen. Beauty all right, not American beauty perfect, not the starlet or the magazine cover, but a calm, slow, haunting kind of beauty.

Her lips were full and well-defined, high cheekbones and a softly pointed chin, all of it edged and set off by the thick auburn hair. In some way he could not yet grasp, she was whole and was aware of her wholeness. You could call it quiet beauty or you could call it a hesitant nobility. You could say all of that about her and many other things and still chafe at your inexactness. There was no adequate description for a state of affairs where someone simply *was*.

Carlisle could not fit her into any category. Hanging around California for most of his life, he thought he'd seen about every possible variation of woman, but Susanna was her own tribe numbering one and no more. She looked at him straight, evenly, smiling a little.

The Indian examined the door Carlisle was working on, running a hand along the vertical edge of it, looking it up and down, speaking while he did so. "Susanna and I talked yesterday. We decided that today seemed favorable for your efforts at closing up the house, and it appears we were right. Is that not so?"

"You're right on schedule," Carlisle said. "Once I get this door hung, the place will be full tight against all weather."

"Very good, Builder. Then Susanna will prepare for her blessing, and I will carry out mine while you continue your work. I have convinced her to perform the special ceremony she did when I asked her to bless my house last year. She was reluctant, but I have told her much about you, and she now has agreed to do this as a favor to me."

"I am honored." Carlisle wanted to say more, but he felt rattled by the very presence of Susanna Benteen.

Susanna and the Indian went inside while Carlisle retrieved one of Cody's old planes and shaved the door perimeters a little more in several places. Testing, shaving, sanding, testing, until it swung perfectly into place with a soft, sure click. He wanted to look at Susanna Benteen every five seconds or so but forced himself to concentrate on the work.

"May we use the fireplace for this occasion, Carlisle?" She had a smooth, confident voice in the alto range.

"Yes, of course. Want me to get it going?"

"I prefer to do that myself, if it's all right."

"That's fine. The two of you do what you need to do."

She got the fire under way while Carlisle gathered up tools and swept the floor. The house was all wood but was beginning to feel as though it had the strength and mass of concrete. Tight, solid, with a force of its own. Anyone could feel that, just standing inside and looking around. Two and a half solid months of work, and Carlisle was pleased. Proud, in fact. This place would go on forever, or just about. Outside, he could hear the Indian sing-chanting and moving around the perimeter of the house. "Hey-ah-ah-hey! Hey-ah-ah-hey!"

His blessing complete, the Indian accepted a beer. But Susanna chose the red wine Carlisle offered her and thanked him politely as she took it.

With a low sun slanting through the front windows and catching dust motes in the air, he opened a beer for himself and sat on a nail keg. The small lumberyard in Livermore had had three of these kegs sitting in a back corner and had given them to Carlisle for the asking. In Marin County, such kegs sold for $80 in stores catering to rustic home decorating.

Darkness came, and Carlisle drank his second beer, half watching the woman take small pouches from her macramé bag and arrange them in a semicircle near the fire. The house originally had been built as a post-and-beam structure in the same fashion as an Amish barn. Carlisle had always liked this system, since all of the roof weight rested on the posts and beams, and walls bearing no load could be moved reasonable distances without the complications of headers and crossbeams. He had torn out all the inside partitions, leaving the interior completely open, with Williston's fireplace standing free about a third of the way in from the rear wall.

The only light came from the fire, a large

warm fire, and the Indian moved to where he could rest his back against the south wall, sitting cross-legged with the drum in his lap. He started to play. Soft, easy strokes, tapping the drumhead with his fingers. This continued for maybe five minutes, sound reverberating in the empty spaces.

The Indian was chanting now. The woman had gone behind the fireplace, out of view. Carlisle was enjoying it, sitting in a wash of pride within the house he was creating, listening to the Indian. A year ago he would have been impatient, wanting the ceremony to move on, but his careful work here had quieted him. He noticed that even his pulse rate had slowed over the last few months.

Carlisle wondered for a moment what Cody would think about all this hoodoo and decided he would be pleased. His concern was building to suit the purposes people had in mind.

Gradually the volume of the drum increased as the Indian played with more intensity, using his palms, his voice rising at the same time. Carlisle nearly dropped the can of beer he was holding when Susanna Benteen came from behind the fireplace.

Except for a necklace with a silver falcon hanging from it and large hoop earrings that matched the necklace, she was naked.

And she was not a bit self-conscious about her nakedness. That much was clear. She walked slowly to a position in front of the fireplace, brought her legs together, and raised her arms toward rafters that were still bare and had insulation stapled into place between them.

To Carlisle McMillan, her body looked as if it had been turned on the lathe of a master craftsman. She was all of the women who had ever appeared in his heated boyhood fantasies wrapped into one live, obviously healthy woman who began to dance in front of Williston's fireplace. She executed slow pirouettes at first, her long hair swinging in the firelight, her feet making no sound on the raw flooring.

As she moved, she bent gracefully to the small pouches on the floor and tossed powder of some kind into the fire, transforming the flames to green, then blue, then intense ocher. The Indian kept chanting, and she began to answer his words with chants of her own, until the drum and two voices merged into a wild but unified composition.

Her body was shining from the fire and her exertion, and Carlisle could feel his own sweat starting to run down his back and chest. She danced with more thrust and power now, her bare feet slapping the planks, earrings catching the firelight. Carlisle alternated between wanting to have her and being caught up in the magic she and the Indian were creating.

It went on and on, and Carlisle began to feel himself changing. Something had moved through the room and sought him out. The sounds and images were working on him: woman dancing, firelight, woman, old hands on old drum, firelight, woman. She began clapping her hands in syncopated time to the Indian's drum, almost in the way of a flamenco dancer. Her eyes locked on Carlisle's, stayed there. She became a figure of faded, limpid amber, and he could see the breath in her lungs and the wine moving in her blood. He could see all of this, could see for a moment all the way out to a transparent forever that disappeared in the moment he found it.

A crescendo was reached, the drum stopped, and Susanna walked gracefully behind the fireplace. Silence. Carlisle looked at the Indian. His head was bowed, his hands still. The only sound was from the crackle of burning wood.

After a few minutes, Susanna Benteen came around the fireplace, her clothing in place. The Indian rose: "The hearth has been blessed, and this place is now a sacred place. We did not pray only to the wood and brick, but also to you, Builder. We prayed that your hands will be guided by the six powers as you work and that your tribute to your Cody Marx will be completed as he would want. Walk here and let the house be glad."

So saying, he swung the drum over his shoulder and opened the door. Carlisle recovered enough to thank them and offer them a ride in his pickup, but they declined. He watched them walk under the yard light and down the lane, light snow beginning to fall. The Indian, the woman, her long shawl around her, one end of it cowled over her head. They disappeared into the snow, eight miles from Salamander, into some other stretch of consciousness they understood but which Carlisle McMillan knew he did not.

As he unrolled his sleeping bag and

placed it near the fire, he noticed a small sculpture of carved basswood on the mantel. It was a naked woman with flames coming from her hair. The Indian later would tell him it was a representation of Vesta, Roman goddess of the hearth. The white medicine woman had asked the Indian to carve it.

Carlisle lay in his sleeping bag, thinking of the woman's body and how it shone in the firelight while she danced to sounds from wrinkled hands playing on tightly stretched goatskin, the perspiration from her breasts falling like sweet rain onto the hearth when she turned. Regretting his lack of sensitivity about blessings and ceremonies, he found himself simply wanting her.

CHAPTER NINE

Thanksgiving. Carlisle's first in the high plains. Thelma Englestrom was back from the hospital and running Danny's again. Gally helped her serve a free Thanksgiving dinner to all the older folks having nowhere to go and to those of any age who could not afford one. She left when Thelma was closing up for the day and drove up the lane to Carlisle's place shortly after two o'clock. It was bright cold and the Chicago Bears were losing in the third quarter.

"Happy Thanksgiving, Carlisle. It's nice to be invited out." She was smiling. Gally had been spending long hours cleaning up the affairs surrounding Jack's death and working on getting the ranch sold. Except for a few words in Danny's and at the funeral, she and Carlisle had not talked since the night her husband was killed. Two days ago, he had asked her if she would like to have Thanksgiving dinner with him.

Carlisle fastened a small turkey on a spit he had rigged in the fireplace. She watched him. "Think it'll work? Looks a little wobbly."

"Some things work, some don't," he replied. "This contraption lies about in the middle of that continuum, I'd say . . . sort of like life itself. If it doesn't work, I'll crucify the bird on a cross of two-by-fours, then we'll burn him at the stake and have peanut-butter sandwiches."

"In that case I'm praying it works," Gally said, laughing. "Peanut butter's okay, but I'm not real fond of crucifixions, marriage to former bull riders included. Sorry, that's an awful thing to say. I'm supposed to be in mourning, but somehow I can't seem to get in the mood. Jack was a good man at one time but ended up being something a lot less than that."

Carlisle looked up at her from where he squatted near the hearth. "Well, I understand the new etiquette books have considerably shortened the formal mourning period, so I believe you're absolved in this case."

He plugged in the motor, and the turkey spun slowly, balanced perfectly on the spit. He looked up at Gally Deveraux and shrugged, then wiggled his eyebrows and grinned. "What do you think?"

"I think you can delay the cross building for now."

The turkey went around while he basted it with a mixture of red wine, butter, and a little garlic. Gally wrapped baking potatoes in aluminum foil for later placement in the coals, then worked on a tossed salad. Carlisle fiddled with the radio, couldn't find a station that suited him, and slipped a Vivaldi tape into the deck. He set two nail kegs by the wood stove and opened bottles of the imported beer he had bought for the occasion. They sat there while the rotisserie motor groaned under the turkey's weight.

Gally looked good, real good. Everybody had been saying how she looked better after Jack's death, sad and tragic as it was (mostly for Jack and not for Gally, some of them added quietly). Gally looked as if she had been relieved of a heavy load. She had put on a little weight, just enough, and her face seemed to be losing the drawn, sad look she had carried for a long time.

Carlisle had never seen her in anything except ranch clothes, but today she had on black wool slacks that did good things for her body and a soft yellow turtleneck sweater, her hair held up by three small combs fastened in the back. Carlisle was wearing his old construction boots, but the green plaid flannel shirt he had bought for the occasion worked pretty well with his faded tan corduroys.

"What are you going to do now?" he asked. "I heard you put the ranch up for sale."

"Well, first off, I'm going to try and get the place sold. There won't be anything left, even if I can sell it, since there are two mortgages on it. Jack inherited the ranch debt-free from his father, but we had hard times four years running. That's when the first mortgage was taken out. Then Jack got it in his head he was a brilliant gambler. He took out a second mortgage and went to Las Vegas with the idea he could win enough to get rid of all the debt. He stayed a month, went back again, and finally came home broke. High-stakes poker did it.

"I don't know for sure what I'll do once the ranch is gone. Maybe move to Casper or

Bismarck, look for work of some kind. Maybe go back to college, I've always felt bad about not finishing my degree. I was going to be a high school history teacher."

Carlisle said nothing. The moment didn't call for anything from him.

"I shouldn't be quite so negative about Jack. When I first met him he was some combination of pirate and cowboy, a real romantic figure. He did pretty well at rodeoing in his younger years till he got busted up bad and had to quit. He was never the same after that. He pretended to like ranching and tried to make a go of it, but what he really liked was riding bulls, and he was good at it. When I first met him I loved to watch him do it, and I married him because I loved him and tried to keep on loving him for a long time, but he just pulled away from me and everything else, except his drinking buddies."

And when it came to drinking buddies, she remembered that Harv Guthridge had called her two weeks after Jack's death and asked her out. She'd said no and told him not to call anymore. He'd laughed and slammed the phone down.

She looked at Carlisle, kind of a sideways look. "You ever been married, Carlisle? Or if that's a sore spot at all, forget I asked."

"No sore spot. I've never been married, to my mother's dismay. I came close to it once, six or seven years ago. She was an elementary school teacher, from southern Illinois. She married young and got divorced, moved to the Bay Area from the Midwest. We waltzed around for a couple of years, but I was in a blue funk in those days and pretty hard to get along with. She went east one summer with a group of other teachers and got swept away by a naturalist at the Smithsonian."

He paused, smiled, looked at Gally. "Janie is better off with her naturalist than with an itinerant carpenter. I've never doubted that. I still think about her, though, off and on, now and then. She was a good person."

Carlisle took a drink of St. Pauli Girl, read the label, moved on. "You from out here? I mean, is this where you grew up?"

"No, I'm an Iowa girl. A small town in the northern part of the state. My dad ran a hardware store there till he died a few years ago. My mother moved to Austin, Minnesota, and lives in one of those retirement communities. She seems happy about it, but the thought of winding up in one of those places kind of makes me want to set a deadline on my life—say about fifty. Which, come to think of it, isn't all that far off."

"Well, as a friend of mine, Buddy Reems, and I used to say when talking about death and retirement, 'Don't die dumb.'"

"Sounds good. What's it mean, not dying dumb?"

"We made a list of ways we didn't want to die. Number one was don't die in a hospital, don't let that happen. Number two was being tail-ended by a '71 Cadillac in front of Kmart because a blue-light special on men's underwear was commencing. It went on from there."

Gally began to laugh.

"The third fits right in with what you were just saying: being hit by flying debris from a rotary lawn mower operated by an overweight sixty-seven-year-old Rotarian in a planned retirement community. I'm noticing all of this doesn't sound as good as it did when we made it up one night in an Oakland bar. Beer talk tends to run that way."

"What would be some good ways to die, then?" she asked, still giggling about his list.

"Well, we had a little more trouble with that part of it. Falling off a roof after nailing down the last shingle on the best house you've ever built, a spear in the chest on the African veldt, that sort of thing. This definitely has the ring of boys and beer to it now that I'm saying it, slightly embarrassing, in fact. Besides, I figure all this arrogance about living and dying will shift a bit as I get a little older. Let's change the subject."

"Well, I don't see as there's anything wrong with a man being a boy once in a while, long as you get over it. Strikes me that a lot of the boys don't take that next step."

"Yeah, it's not much fun growing up, so we beat it back long as possible, forever if we can pull it off."

"Women understand that. We see it all the time, living with the boys." She grinned.

"I'll bet you do. And as I've always said, to understand boy-men, you've got to understand gear."

"Gear?" Gally smiled. "Tell me about gear."

Carlisle was squatted down, putting more wood on the fire, talking over his shoulder. "Men like gear, all kinds of stuff. We like bags, too, since we've got to have someplace to put the gear. Then we like to sort the gear and pack it in the bags and go off somewhere."

"Now you're really making sense. I understand that, having lived with Jack for over twenty years."

"When I was little—four or five—back in Mendocino, I wanted a doll buggy. That worried my mother, I think, but she found one for me at a rummage sale. One of the wheels wobbled, but I didn't care. It was a vehicle to cart my gear around. I carried rocks, screwdrivers, and a hammer in it. Other stuff, too.

"My mother stopped worrying when she saw that. When I got older she used to kid me about it, saying, 'Carlisle, your truck is just a grown-up version of your doll buggy, a way to haul all your stuff around.' I'd say she was right."

"Your general theory of gear explains a lot of male behavior." The fire crackled and splashed light across the smile on Gally's face. "Jack had bags and gear. Except he liked to take the gear from one bag and put it in a different bag, kind of a domino effect. After that he'd go off somewhere, hunting or fishing."

"Yeah, repacking gear is an important part of it. You get to handle it a lot more often that way." He opened his cooler and set two more beers on the floor beside them. "In that small town where you grew up, I'll bet you were homecoming queen, right?"

Gally smiled again. "I was first runner-up. My dad claimed it was a scam job, that the girl who was picked got it because she was going with the quarterback on the football team. What I never told him was that *I* was going out with the quarterback, secretly. My dad was something of a local football legend himself, enough said. Lord, that all seems like a long time ago, trivial and childish."

Though, she reflected privately, it hadn't seemed all that trivial or childish when she and the quarterback took a six-pack and, even though it was chilly, went skinny-dipping in the Shell Rock River after the homecoming game, down by where Elk Creek flowed into the river. But it seemed that way now. The quarterback was clumsy, so was she. It was inelegant, overall. But you get by those things even though they hurt a little when you call them up.

Late in the afternoon, Carlisle positioned

two sawhorses in the middle of the room and laid one-by-twelves over them. Instant table. Sunlight was coming through the south windows, and the turkey turned out pretty well. Dumptruck had his own plate in the kitchen while the radio played. The talk between Gally and Carlisle ran mostly to local things, and he happened to mention the old dance hall on the edge of Livermore.

Gally looked out at the slanting light. "Oh, Carlisle, that place is so special. Let's go over there. It won't be dark for a little while. We can be there in half an hour. I want you to see it up close. We can do dishes when we get back."

"Sounds good to me. Let's fire up the truck."

Twenty-five minutes later, they pulled up next to the Flagstone Ballroom, sitting on the shore of a small lake. The old place was in bad repair, shuttered and peeling in a raw, windy sundown. Not all that big as those things ran, maybe twenty thousand square feet including service areas.

"Kind of looks like one of Mrs. Macklin's pies on the second day, doesn't it?" Gally laughed.

Carlisle nodded, peering through a crack

in the rear door. All he could see was old sinks, big ones. Must have been the kitchen. He went around the building and found another opening. Enough light was coming through holes in the roof and other places that he could make out the floor and the dark contours of booths surrounding it.

"Jack used to bring me dancing here when we were first married."

He turned and looked at her standing in gray light, looking slim and fine in her slacks and sweater with a light mackinaw over them, a few strands of black hair with a little gray mixed in blowing across her face, trying to see her as she might have looked on a summer evening in the Flagstone Ballroom twenty or so years ago. The lake behind her was developing thin ice along the edges, and her face was turning pink from the stiff, cold wind coming in over the water.

"You probably have trouble seeing me as a young girl in a pretty dress dancing the night away in this place."

It was a declarative sentence, but she meant it as a question. "I don't have any trouble at all seeing that, Gally Deveraux. Tell me about it, anyway."

"By the time I moved out here, the Flagstone was on its last legs. But Jack and I came here a lot. Mostly on Friday nights, that's when the country bands played. Sometimes I'd talk him into bringing me on Saturdays when the big bands took over. My dad had a huge record collection of all the old bands—the Dorseys, Glenn Miller, Artie Shaw—so I was raised around that kind of music. Jack never much cared for it, said it was hard to dance to, but what he really didn't like was that a completely different kind of person from him came on the big band nights. Jack never wore ties, except those little string numbers once in a while, and most of the people who came to big band nights here dressed up. But sometimes he'd bring me. Then he'd spend the night complaining that you couldn't do the Texas two-step to what he called gringo music."

Carlisle leaned against the Flagstone and laughed, thinking about Jack and the look he must have had on his face when a band rolled into "Stardust."

Gally was under way, talking fast, talking to the wind as much as to Carlisle, and he let her run. "I remember how these big shutters would be swung up and how the lake looked with moonlight across it. There were moving lights in the ceiling that flickered on the floor and on the dancers, and on Saturday nights the bands played all the old songs: 'Sunrise Serenade,' 'A Foggy Day,' 'Stella by Starlight.' Things like that.

"The Saturday night bands had names you wouldn't believe, names like Glenn Boyer's Honey Dreamers. Icky, huh?" She was grinning and looked almost beautiful standing there, reeling in the memories, moving through old doorways she needed to walk through again.

"By the mid-sixties, things were changing fast. To keep going, the place booked rock 'n' roll bands, mostly. For some reason, though, it just kind of died out, all of it. The Flagstone closed in 1966. They had a big farewell party, and lots of the musicians who played here over the years came and played one more time. People drove all the way from Florida and California just for that one night. I was only twenty-five and wasn't from around here, but I'd spent a lot of nights in this old place by that time.

"I remember they played 'Auld Lang Syne' at the end, and we all cried, except for Jack, who was hoping they'd finish up with

'San Antonio Rose.' He was drunk and kept on hollering for that: ' "SannnAnnnntonnnn-iooooRosie," *one more time*.' The musicians playing that night probably had never played 'San Antonio Rose' in their entire lives, but Jack kept on hollering for it even after the band left the stage."

She stopped for a moment, thinking how she'd taken off her clothes in the truck that night when she and Jack left the Flagstone, sitting on his lap and steering the truck while his hands moved over her, the two of them wobbling back and forth along the roads of Yerkes County, headed toward a place called home.

She looked serious for a moment. "I loved him then, Carlisle, I truly did. He was a young girl's dream, I guess."

"I'm sure you did. From everything you've told me, I can see why."

"But I came to hate him, and that's not right."

Gally had tears in her eyes, maybe from the wind, maybe from her memories. She was leaning back into them, hearing a big band play "Early Autumn" again, seeing the lights on the floor, feeling what it was like to be a young woman when the big sky was like the curve of a cowboy's shoulder—no, some combination of cowboy and pirate—looking out through open windows when he turned you, looking out at moonlight over warm water lapping on the lake shore, thinking none of this will ever change.

Carlisle smiled at her. "I'll take you dancing sometime. Would you like that?"

She walked over and put a mittened hand on his face. "I'd like that very much." That's all she said, and they walked slowly back to the idling truck and the warmth of its heater.

They cleaned up the supper leavings, and Carlisle made a pot of coffee. Talking for a while longer, smiling at each other across Carlisle's jury-rigged table. He was thinking that Gally Deveraux was a damn fine woman. He fixed her a plate of turkey to take home with her, and they stood on his front porch for a minute or two, looking out across the great spaces where they lived. Gally had stopped thinking of Carlisle as a possibility, thought of him now as a man, a good man. Whatever his weaknesses were, he was strong in all the right ways, far as she could tell. There was a part of her that wanted to stay with him tonight, more out of companionship than anything else, but somehow that didn't seem right, yet. Besides, she wasn't ready to be turned down, and she wasn't sure how Carlisle felt about her in that way.

She stood on her tiptoes, put her hand on his face, and kissed him softly. "Good night, Carlisle. Thanks for Thanksgiving, it was real sweet. And thanks for going over to the Flagstone with me. I feel good about having done that, remembering those better days with Jack and feeling better about him and our life together because of it. I want to go home tonight and reflect on that some more. I think I'll just concentrate on remembering the old Jack and try to forget about that other person I lived with all these years."

Carlisle touched her hair, bent over, and kissed her, then leaned back and said, "Good night, Gally. Drive carefully."

She started to step off the porch but turned instead and took hold of his shirt lapel with her thumb and finger. "Carlisle McMillan, I like being around you, and I like the way you kissed me. Sometime, when I get myself sorted out a little more, I may suggest we get to know each other a bit better. I hope you won't be offended if I do."

"Gally, I don't think there's anything you could say that would offend me. Now take your turkey and run before *I* suggest what I think you're talking about."

She started the Bronco and rolled down the lane. Carlisle watched her make the turn onto the dark road, watched the Bronco's taillights move off to the north past where Syawla and the Keeper were supposed to live. When she was gone he looked northwest, then looked again. He went back inside and fetched his binoculars and focused them. There was a small fire burning on the crest of Wolf Butte.

CHAPTER TEN

The Saturday following Thanksgiving was so unusually warm for the season that it lulled people into thoughts of an easy winter, just before the storms regrouped and slammed them upside the head. Carlisle had something in mind for the house and went to the Little Sal, poking along its sandbars, looking for driftwood. He smelled the smoke from Susanna Benteen's fire before he saw her.

The river narrowed there, with twenty-foot bluffs rising on either side. She was sitting beneath a rock overhang, a small fire before her, looking at the water. He almost backed off but instead stood quietly. She seemed to be concentrating on something, and he didn't want to disturb her. And, to be perfectly honest, he wasn't sure he wanted to be alone with her. Carlisle was comfortable around women, but there was something about this woman that unsettled him, and, of course, just as unsettling were the images he still had of her dancing across the wooden floors of his house.

In convincing her to perform her special blessing, the Indian had attributed to Carlisle more cosmic awareness than he deserved. That's how Carlisle saw it. A fully mature consciousness, he supposed, would dwell on the goodness she and the Indian bestowed upon this place and upon him, Builder. But he had coveted her and was stalked by his recollections of her naked body as she danced, images that were reinforced and sharpened by echoes he still could hear in the shadowy, resonant corners of the house he was building. The Indian's drum and the slap of her bare feet on raw lumber possessed infinite half-lives of their own.

Susanna Benteen, however, was not the kind of woman you telephoned and casually invited out. She seemed neither approachable nor unapproachable. That scale didn't work in her case.

Also, he suspected she and the Indian

were locked into each other in some powerful way, operating on a level of understanding that probably was beyond him. Whether
she was the Indian's woman or not, he
wasn't sure. But he liked and respected
both of them and was not about to interfere,
even if he had known how.

While he was thinking about moving up-
river again and leaving her alone, she turned
her head. For a moment she merely looked
at him, then she smiled and called out,
"Hello, Carlisle," almost as if she had been
expecting him.

He walked toward her. "Sorry if I bothered you, didn't mean to."

"You're not bothering me. Come join me.
We don't have many nice days like this one
left."

It was the first time he had seen her wear
anything but long dresses. That day she
was in old, snug jeans and a beige sweater,
dark green mountain parka, and well-
traveled hiking boots. The auburn hair was
braided, and the braid hung straight down
her back, almost to her waist.

"How is the house coming along?" she
asked.

"Fine, real good. I'm out here looking for

a special piece of driftwood to make into a stair railing."

"The river makes a bend about a mile upstream. A lot of wood piles up there in high water, then stays when the water recedes. Have you gone by there yet?"

"No, but I'll take a look. Thanks."

"Where are you from, Carlisle? I noticed your license plates are from California."

"I grew up in Mendocino, but I lived in the Bay Area for the last fifteen years."

"I was there once, in Mendocino." She was watching the last leaves of autumn float by, curled and brown.

"When?"

Susanna Benteen pursed her lips and looked upward, thinking. "Six years ago. I had heard it was a nice place, so I stopped on my way down from Seattle."

"You from Seattle?"

She turned her head and looked at him. "No, I'm from all over, I guess."

The river gurgled where it tried to push back the bluffs. A hawk drifted far in the west, high and lonesome looking. A light breeze ruffled the water's surface.

"You've traveled a lot, then?"

"Yes, a lot," Susanna replied. "My

mother died when I was four. My father was one of those itinerant scholars, an anthropologist, who roamed the world living off grants and contracts. I went with him." She held the tip of a stick in the water and watched the small eddy it created, thinking back to her girlhood for a moment.

A rock was jabbing into Carlisle's hip, and he shifted over a little. She tossed the stick in the water and watched the current take it downstream. "It was a strange, remarkable childhood. How did you come to live in Yerkes County, Carlisle?"

"Drifted in here, on the run from all the craziness. It seemed quiet and open, so I decided to stay and build something worthwhile for a change."

"It looks like a fine house. The man you call Flute Player told me about your work even before I saw it."

"Thanks. I appreciate you and him coming by to give it your blessing."

She smiled at him. "How did you feel about the blessing? It was loosely copied from an ancient rite I once saw a shaman perform in East Africa. The statue of Vesta was my idea."

How could he answer that? Tell her the

truth about what he really felt, about the drumming and how her body looked? End run, coward's way: "Well, it was pretty different from anything I'd seen before."

Susanna Benteen smiled sideways at him. "Yes, I'm sure of that. But how did you *feel* about it?"

Moment of truth. His stomach was jumping. He let out a breath, staring across the river, avoiding her eyes. "Honestly, it was the most erotic thing I've ever seen or heard or read about. That's as straight as I can put it." He felt better having said it and turned to look at her.

The green eyes looked at him calmly. "It wasn't intended to be, but I think I understand." She blinked once. "To be honest, I had some of those same feelings midway through the ritual, though I didn't when it started. The years traveling with my father, the time spent in old cultures, made me comfortable with nakedness, mine and others'. Sometimes I forget that and take it for granted. But I admit, I saw the way you were looking at me and saw things beyond the ritual, just as you did. Men and women can't escape that, I guess. Some push of the genes, something from a long way back."

Carlisle got to his feet, a little unsteady. "Sun's going down. Be dark in a couple of hours."

"Does darkness bother you?"

"No, but my expedition isn't finished. The piece of driftwood . . ."

"I hope you find what you're looking for. I enjoyed our talk."

"Thanks, so did I." He walked back up the shore. It was full night when he stepped onto his front porch, carrying a long, pale gray piece of driftwood over his left shoulder. Susanna was still sitting by her small fire, under a bluff, near the river. She was thinking about Carlisle McMillan, about the end of autumn and the beginning of winter, about the strange old feelings that came to her almost every night and urged her toward something she was trying hard to understand.

His first winter out on the high plains was one of Carlisle's best. Short prairie days of compressed light, weather alternating between stone gray afternoons and mornings of luminous, brittle cold. With the house snugged down and the woodstove cooking away, he worked on the inside, the phase of construction he always liked best. Even though he was not short-changing any part of the building, somehow the opportunities for craftsmanship were most easily seen and done on interior spaces.

After Thanksgiving, Gally pulled out to visit her daughter in Casper, leaving the ranch in the keeping of a hired man. Her daughter was pregnant with her third child and having a hard time, so Gally stayed on to help her. She sent Carlisle a Christmas card, saying she missed his company and that she would return after the baby was born, early in February.

In November, after the crops were harvested, Axel Looker had put in an all-weather road for Carlisle. He had stopped one day while Carlisle was standing by the main road, looking at the sorry condition of his lane. The rains of autumn combined with traffic had turned it into a strip of deep, muddy ruts twelve feet wide.

Axel leaned out his truck window. "Hi, neighbor. Looks like you could use a good path up to your house."

Carlisle nodded. "I'm standing here thinking about how to get it done."

"No problem. You order out some gravel from the Guthridge Brothers pit, and I'll pilot my baby 'dozer down here. I can have it done in a day or two."

Indeed, Axel did have it finished in two days. A nice little road banked just right for moisture runoff, with gravel spread evenly over the base he'd constructed. Carlisle offered payment, but Axel Looker refused.

"With the crops in, I've been drivin' Earlene nuts just hangin' around thinkin' of things to do. That being so, she's drivin' me nuts 'cause I'm drivin' her nuts. Puttin' in your road was a family vacation of sorts. Sometime I'll have some carpentry work you can rough up for me. Till then, don't worry about it."

After a heavy snow, Carlisle would hear Axel's big Steiger tractor working in the lane, scooping snow with a front-end loader and dumping it off to the sides. When Carlisle stepped out, Axel would wave, red-faced and apparently having fun, feeling the power of his iron underneath him, taking a short and separate vacation from Earlene.

Gally returned from Casper on the fifth of February. She phoned Carlisle in late afternoon, an hour after getting home. "Hello, carpenter, how're you doing?"

"Gally! Good to hear your voice. I'm real good, hammering and sawing as usual. How's your daughter?"

"She's fine now. Got the baby here in good shape, got Sharon organized and moving forward. Lord, I'm glad I don't have three little ones to look after. She has her hands full and will for the next eighteen years or so. . . . Carlisle, I missed you. I picked up some things at a Custer deli on my way in, thought I might stop by if you're up for an evening of beer and pastrami?"

"I am indeed. Come over anytime."

"Okay. I have some reentry things to clean up here. Be about two hours or so. All right?"

"Great. See you then."

Gally Deveraux bathed in her old claw-foot tub, lying back in warm, soapy water, hair pinned up. The countryside was somber that time of year, hunkered down and trying to outlast winter's pounding that made the high plains seem like Siberia. From the tub, she could see the sky through her bathroom window, the color of gray mud, looking low and wet and ominous.

It felt good to be home, and she lay there for a long time thinking about her daughter, then about her own life and what she might do with it. Then about Carlisle McMillan. She put her toes on the faucet and wiggled them happily, then reached for her razor. She shaved her legs and stepped out, feeling uncommonly feminine and slightly wicked for some reason, the way she used to feel in the early days when Jack still called her Easy, the way she had felt that night riding home from the Flagstone, naked on Jack's lap.

Carlisle was on his stepladder when he heard the Bronco come up his lane. When she knocked, he yelled, "Come in, but watch the stepladder when you open the door."

Gally tentatively moved the door inward, felt it bump against the ladder, peered in, and squeezed through the opening. She looked up at him. "What are you doing up there in the air?"

He looked down at her and grinned. "Decided to put in a small loft. Be down in a minute, soon as I get these last few nails in the railing and countersink 'em."

Gally went into the kitchen, took the food

out of paper bags, and put it in the fridge. She looked at Carlisle's backside. He was stretched up, hammer positioned in his right hand, nail steadied with his left. He had a baseball cap on backward with GIANTS lettered on the crown, brown hair hanging straight and long. His flannel shirt was untucked in the back, sleeves rolled to the elbow. She watched his right forearm position the hammer, saw the muscles in it flex. Three easy shots of the hammer and the nail was driven home, solidly, perfectly. He reached in his tool belt, took out a punch, and countersunk the nail.

He came down the ladder and walked over to her, smiling, and put his arms around her, hammer dangling from his right hand. "Hello, Gally Deveraux. Nice to see you."

She hugged him, smelled sawdust and perspiration, felt the muscles in his back, and, without even thinking about it, tucked his shirttail in. That, she thought, is intimacy, tucking in a man's shirttail.

She pulled back and grinned up at him. "I missed you, Carlisle."

"Same here, Gally. It's been quiet since you left. Dumptruck's pretty much decided to just sleep out the winter, far as I can tell."

"Not a bad strategy, I'd say. Animals understand how to roll with nature. We keep trying to fight it. Hungry?"

"Nope. Thirsty, though."

"I can fix that. Along with pastrami and rye and coleslaw and other things, I picked up some St. Pauli Girl. Big splurge, homecoming celebration and all."

Taking a six-pack of Bud from the cooler at the deli, she had seen the St. Pauli Girl and remembered that's what Carlisle had bought for Thanksgiving. She returned the Bud to the cooler and took out the St. Pauli Girl, feeling extravagant, hoping Carlisle would be home that night.

"Carlisle, you have chairs! Three of them, folding ones."

"Yeah, church basement stuff till I figure out something else. When it comes to furniture, function dominates form for the moment. Plus the fact they remind me of going to catechism on Saturday afternoons when I was a kid. Wynn, my mother, had given up her father's Presbyterian ways and joined the Catholics."

"How'd that go for you?"

"The nuns used to whack our knuckles with a ruler if we couldn't answer their ques-

tions, simple ones, such as 'Who is God?'
Fifteen years later, I had a philosophy professor ask the same question on a final examination, and I still couldn't answer it. Still
can't." He was stretched out in one of the
chairs, legs out in front of him, right ankle
crossed over the left. He leaned forward,
unfastened his leather tool belt, and laid it
on the floor beside him.

"How did you answer the philosophy
professor's question? Or did you just leave it
blank?"

"No, I thought about it for the entire
exam period, tried several different slants,
none of which worked. Finally I simply
wrote, 'God Is.'"

"What happened?"

"I got a B plus."

Gally smiled. "Smart move, Carlisle.
Most people would have written sixteen
pages full of blather. Your answer was like
your carpentry, just enough, never too
much." She pulled off her boots and sat
cross-legged in a chair, elbows on her knees
and facing him. She wiggled her toes underneath white socks. "Where did you go to
college?"

"Stanford."

"Wow, that's the big leagues. Expensive, too."

"I had a tuition scholarship. Got some government help and did carpentry part-time. It worked out."

"Did you graduate?"

"Yes. I did it for my mother. I wanted to please her, so I stayed with it."

"What was your major?"

"Started out in engineering. I could handle it, but I didn't like it. Switched over to art with an emphasis in graphic design, took a minor in English lit. It was okay. But all I ever wanted to be was a carpenter, ever since I was a kid working with Cody Marx, the old fellow I told you about."

He grinned and took a long drink of St. Pauli Girl. "I think a shower is in order for me. I even have one of those now in the unfinished bathroom. Put some music in the tape deck if you like. There's a stack of tapes over on the kitchen counter."

For an instant Gally wanted to say, "Can I watch you shave?" She liked watching Jack shave in the early days. There was something about it, something faintly erotic. But she smiled and caught herself, saying nothing. She sorted through the tapes and put one into the deck built into Carlisle's small radio. Willie Nelson laid out a few guitar licks and sang about time slipping away, rolling into "Stardust" after that. In the background, she could hear the shower.

Beer in hand, she walked around the house. Carlisle had an eye for spareness and restraint, for elegance. And he truly was a perfectionist when it came to building. The window trim fit so perfectly that the places where boards joined were almost indistin-guishable, hairline cracks at most. The small loft was a nice idea, she thought. She mar-veled at the curved stair railing leading up to it, a piece of driftwood apparently, debarked and sanded and finished until it was as smooth as polished steel. The fireplace mantel was a four-by-six slab of oak five feet long. He had carved long, graceful, asymmetrical scallops on the outside edge.

She examined the figurine on the mantel, something she hadn't noticed before, and saw it was a naked female, flaming hair sprouting from the head. She held it in her hands, ran her fingers over it, noticed the de-tail on it, right down to tiny nipples and the absolutely correct curve of perfect buttocks. She put it back and looked at the word

Syawla chiseled into the fireplace stone, shivering a little.

Carlisle came out of the bathroom in jeans and a red sweater, gray wool socks, and moccasins. He walked over to the woodstove and opened the front doors, putting a screen across the opening after laying two large pieces of white oak on the fire.

"I have the fireplace plugged with insulation for the winter, too much heat goes up the flue. But this open-door stove arrangement works pretty well as a substitute when you're not too worried about efficiency, which I'm not at the moment."

Pastrami sandwiches and coleslaw by the fire. Easy talk. Laughter. Willie in the background, Jerry Jeff Walker after that. Beer and Mr. Bojangles. Firelight and land stretching somewhere close to forever outside. She asked him about the figurine on the mantel.

"The Indian—the fellow I call Flute Player, think I mentioned him to you—and Susanna Benteen came by to bless the house. They brought the little statue as kind of a housewarming present. Said it represents Vesta, the Roman goddess of the hearth."

Something inside Gally bristled. Susanna Benteen, the witch or whatever she was. A gurgling inside, some old and basic female thing called competitiveness. She had experienced those feelings before in her life, sometimes when she watched Jack slow-dancing with a pretty young thing from Falls City. Other times, too, when she was younger and the high school quarterback was paying attention to someone else. Jealousy turning into some kind of thin, hot venom. The old instinct from far back, competition for the best males, the prime ones, the ones who seem to carry the best traits for survival of the species. Unseemly, but there it was.

Carlisle saw something in her eyes or her face. "They didn't stay long, just came by for an hour or so and did their blessing. It was kind of them, though I'm not sure I grasped all the hoodoo that was part of it." Nothing was said about the sweet rain that fell from the rounded breasts of Susanna Benteen.

Wind came up, low *whoosh* turning into a subdued roar that faded, then came again and stayed. But inside it was warm. A little after midnight, Gally cracked the front door and peeked outside.

"Carlisle, look at the snow!"

They had been talking, neither of them bothering to check on the weather. A heavy, wet snow had begun falling quietly two hours before. Three inches of new stuff on the ground already and visibility was approximately to the edge of the porch.

"Looks like you stay the night," Carlisle suggested, peering over her shoulder. "No way anybody would want to drive through that. Besides, I don't think you can get your car down the lane, let alone up Wolf Butte Road to your place."

She closed the mahogany door and leaned against it, standing there in her jeans and white socks and yellow turtleneck sweater, smiling at Carlisle McMillan. The same sweater she had worn at Thanksgiving, the only good sweater she still owned and kept wrapped carefully in a plastic bag. Black hair with silver gray strands, hanging long, brushed, and catching wavering light from the stove.

As with a lot of women, Gally Deveraux underestimated herself. She was no raving beauty, but she had a slim, long-legged way about her. Easy, as Jack said. Kind eyes and a nice face.

Carlisle walked over to her, reached out, and put his right hand on her neck, underneath the sweater, his thumb touching her face just in front of her ear. He slowly massaged her skin and smiled back at her. Good skin, soft and warm. She could feel the calluses on his hand.

Gally ran her fingers across his cheek and nose and eyelids. He leaned into her, pinning her against the door and kissing her slow and soft. She kissed back, same easy way at first, then with an intensity she hadn't felt for a long time. Arms around the carpenter's neck, pressing her body against him, curling one of her legs behind one of his.

She lifted his sweater and ran her hands across the muscles of his back, then pulled up the sweater in front and kissed his chest. "Carlisle," she whispered, "I want you so much. I've thought, fantasized about it, dreamed of it." She was a little short of breath. His hand was wound tight in her long hair.

He picked her up, her arms still around his neck, and carried her through the living room and behind the fireplace to the bedroom area. He laid her down and began kissing her breasts, her stomach. Eventually all the undressing got done, as it always does. And not long after, they were where both of them wanted to be.

They were a little clumsy at first, but some better as time went on. He rested himself on his hands and looked down at her. He pulled her to a sitting position, put his legs around her, her legs around him. He caressed her hair, and she tilted her head, feeling his tongue move across her throat and across her ears and his teeth biting her gently on her shoulder, hand sweeping slowly down her hair and then winding it tight in his fist again.

Gally Deveraux's long and lonely times were ending. In this far place, they were ending with the warmth of Carlisle McMillan inside her.

Christ, how she loved having this man inside her. Her body came up involuntarily, bellies touching then and words from his mouth she heard but didn't hear and hearing then only her own breathing mixed with his and feeling his long hair brushing against her breasts. Gally Deveraux was becoming herself again.

Carlisle sensed that things were meant to be as they were that night, almost seamless. She felt small beneath him, fragile, and smelled and tasted of the high plains and big open country. He kept his movements slow and gentle, letting her feel him, letting him feel her. Keeping it at the level of slow delight for a long while. Dancing with her, traveling the far places with her, that kind of moment when you get as close as you ever get to whoever the person is. And from the kitchen, Elton John telling them both that Daniel was gone on a plane.

Later, lying in bed, Carlisle could see the naked backside of Gally Deveraux in the bathroom, through the open door. She was brushing her hair and quietly singing an old tune that Jerry Jeff had sung earlier, something about desperadoes waiting for a train. Dumptruck purring, walking around on the bed.

Later on, in bed together again. Not having sex, making love. Gally Deveraux riding on top of Carlisle and smiling down at him. Carlisle smiling back and sliding his hands across her breasts. Letting go, music playing out in the kitchen, letting go . . . she arched her back, his hands across her stomach . . . far country, far places, wind and buttes and land rolling like the sea . . . the carpenter and Gally Deveraux.

The next day, holding hands over breakfast. "Lord, Carlisle, it's been so long, I forgot how nice it can be. All those good loving things. Maybe a little depravity mixed in, too, and that doesn't hurt, does it?"

Carlisle waved a piece of toast smeared with orange marmalade. "Gally, the world can never have too much true depravity, 'long as it's combined with those other things you mentioned."

She smiled. "I made a decision this morning. I was lying there while you were still sleeping, and I thought about what I want out of my life. On the way in from Casper yesterday, I stopped at the college in Spearfish and asked about going back to school, about what it would take. They'll count some of my work at Bemidji State years ago, so it turns out I can become a history teacher in two and a half years. There's something called a Pell Grant that'll help with the money. Maybe I can get the ranch sold, too. So I'm going to do it, start this fall. What do you think? A near forty woman going back to school, dumb or what?"

"No, Gally, not dumb . . . smart. Real smart."

"It's only a few hours from here, so we can see each other on weekends sometimes. Think so?"

"No question about it. I'll go down there, you come up here, we'll meet halfway. It'll work."

Gally came around the table and sat on Carlisle's lap, touching his hair, looking at him. "You know, I wouldn't be thinking about going back to school if it hadn't been for you. You changed your life. I saw that and figured I could change mine. You inspired me. I feel like a new person, Carlisle, and you're responsible for it."

She cocked her head. "What's that? Sounds like a road grader or something."

"That'd be Axel Looker on his Steiger tractor. All-around good neighbor, champion driver of big iron, and ace scooper of snow from my lane." Carlisle opened the door and waved to Axel, but Axel had finished scooping and piling the miniblizzard on either side of the lane and was bouncing up Wolf Butte Road toward Earlene.

"Well, I can tell you this, Carlisle McMillan, what went on here last night won't be our secret very long. When Axel hits Danny's, there'll be some snickering at the corner table about my Bronco being parked outside your house with five inches of new snow on it. By the way, I have to get going. I told Thelma I'd be in to work at Danny's today. Four-wheel drive'll get me there. In fact, four-wheel drive probably would have gotten me home last night when we first noticed the snow." She was smiling a crooked smile.

"Maybe. On the other hand, I think it was a wise move to stay overnight."

"So do I. Got a broom, carpenter? I need to sweep off my vehicle."

"I'll do it while you pull on your boots."

Dumptruck on the porch, smelling the air, shaking snow off his paw, licking it. Bronco swept clean, Gally smiling.

"Stop into Danny's sometime, Carlisle. I'll sneak you a little something extra when Thelma isn't looking."

"Right in Danny's? On the counter, against the fridge? Where?"

"After last night, anywhere you want, carpenter."

"Okay, I'll see you soon. Take you up on it."

The sun was blinding, reflecting off the new snow. She put her arms around him, and he hugged her back.

Her Bronco hit Wolf Butte Road, fish-tailed a little despite the four-wheel drive, and turned toward Salamander. Carlisle went back inside, Dumptruck following him. He strapped on his tool belt, feeling better than he had in a long time, fifteen years or more. After a sip of coffee, he climbed the stepladder, while Dumptruck with his tail over his back and in one of his wild moods ran up the loft stairs and looked through the balusters at Carlisle, blinking, purring.

CHAPTER ELEVEN

The old man, though two decades older than me, had more stamina than I did when it came to serious drinking. Around eleven and with Sleepy standing behind the bar and giving no sign of ever closing, I said, "Well, I sure appreciate all the information, but I don't want to wear you out. Maybe we could pick up here in a day or two."

"Don't worry about me," he replied. "Don't often get a chance to drink good stuff, and besides, a codger my age could be dead by tomorrow."

I slipped a new tape into the recorder.

"When Carlisle McMillan looked up at my window his second night in town and waved to me, I kind of jumped before waving back. I shouldn't have been too surprised, however, since I'd got a close-up look at him in Danny's that morning and decided right then and there that he was probably a fella who didn't miss too much. Something about his eyes, old-looking for a guy his age, like he'd seen a lot of things and knew a lot more than he let on.

"So that winter, twenty-some hours after a medium-size Dakota howler had quieted down, I was sitting in Danny's reading the restaurant copy of the *High Plains Inquirer,* which has pretensions at being our state newspaper. Salamander's crack street department, consisting of one Merle Bagby, had gotten things plowed out, enabling the morning coffee crowd to reassemble after a day's recess due to inclement weather.

"Gally was getting things ready for the noon dinner folks while the morning coffee crowd talked about the storm. When she stepped into the kitchen for a few minutes, Axel Looker hunched over and proceeded to tell everyone at his table and the next that when he'd scooped out Carlisle's lane the previous day, Gally's Bronco had been sitting there with an accurate measurement of the total snowfall lying on it.

"It was quite a burden on their logical skills, but the boys managed to deduce that she must have been there when the snow began. *Ipso facto,* as my ol' geometry instructor from Salamander High was fond of saying, Gally had arrived at Carlisle's sometime before the snow and stayed over.

"That alone was enough to place Carlisle and Gally at about position eight on the ten-point Salamander scale of degeneracy, the standard way of judging such events in a location where the main pleasure of the flesh is eating. By the time the ladies' church groups had processed this information, another point for dalliance had been tacked on. That much accomplished, speculation then turned toward the quality and quantity of the experience.

"Beyond that, watchers at Danny's counter remembered noticing what they believed to be extra mashed potatoes on Carlisle's plate when Gally served his meat loaf and hot turkey sandwiches. That clinched it for sure, and the bell at the top of the ten-point scale resounded with a clang that bounced off Mert's station and ricocheted along Main Street for some days.

"Local students of behavior claimed to see a change in Gally's whole demeanor and said that she was even more friendly than usual. The evidence was, in short, overwhelming, and the conclusion was reached and unanimously agreed upon that Carlisle and Gally were now lovers, though Bobby Eakins would probably have said it differently. But then it's necessary to spread newspapers for Bobby Eakins when he can't be let outside. The matter of Gally and Carlisle settled, Salamander turned its attention once again to lesser issues, such as death and politics.

"I did notice, however, that quite often on Saturday nights, after she'd closed up Danny's at six, which was the Saturday closing hour, Gally would load a picnic hamper and big thermos into her Bronco. Then I'd watch her drive west out of town, doubting she was going on a solo picnic by the Little Sal and believing instead she was headed toward Carlisle's."

The old man nodded hello to a pair of cowboys who had come into Sleepy's. They were followed by Harv Guthridge, quarry owner and lover of women whose pelts were hung when he was finished with them. Harv waved to the old man, and the old man simply responded with an unenthusiastic, "Harv."

He looked at me, then over at Harv. "Never figured out exactly how, but Harv screwed me out of my workmen's comp after I got hurt digging stone for him . . . the sonuvabitch.

"Anyway, as I was saying, it took Carlisle McMillan a little over a year to get his place finished, working all day, every day, though here and there he took a small piece of outside work just to tide him over. Between getting my junk mail at the post office and listening to the conversation at Danny's, I was able to stay pretty much even with his progress. Being a geezer with a bad leg and not much going for you has its advantages. For some reason people talk right in front of you, like you're not there, saying anything, figuring you for a decrepit old bird that has no one to gossip with anyway. That's a mistake. Old men like me don't give a hoot'n-hollerin' shit what people say or think. Want truth? Look to old men and little kids.

"The number of people bothering Carlisle and asking if they could look around while he was finishing his house was such that he finally ran a small announcement in the *Salamander Sentinel* in late summer. Said that he'd hold an open house on the following Saturday and Sunday between noon and six for all those who wanted to tour the place. Gally asked if I wanted to see what Carlisle had done and offered me a ride. Since I hadn't been out of town for over two years, I took her up on it, partly to see the house, partly just to look at the countryside.

"It was well worth the trip. Gally acted as general hostess with Marcie English, who lived down the road a ways, helping her out. They served coffee and cookies, with punch for the kiddies, who ran down to the creek to watch the minnows. According to Gally's count, two hundred and fifty-seven people of various ages, stripes, and religious preferences came to tour and gawk, while a few turkey buzzards wheeled around looking at the older folks. Carlisle, being of increasing sensitivity, even installed temporary wheelchair ramps and other conveniences so we folks with certain physical limits could get up into the house.

"Kathy and Arlo Gregorian came, and everybody remarked how fast little Myrna was growing. Leroy came, so did Orly and Mrs. Hammond. Huey and Fran Sverson came, Beanie Wickers did not. The Injun and Susanna Benteen drifted by late on the second day when the visitors were about gone and helped with the cleanup.

"Bobby Eakins said, 'Shit, ya seen one house, ya seen 'em all, and I'm not going.' But he did, and he was real quiet and respectful when he walked around. Word about Carlisle's undertaking had spread to Falls City forty miles southeast, bringing some people in from that great distance. The Better Homes and Garden Realty folks over there had gotten wind of the project and sent their local representative, Cecil Macklin, to check things out and see if Carlisle might be interested in selling, now that he'd finished the place. Cecil asked Carlisle if he was building something called a 'spec home' and said he had an unidentified buyer who might be interested in the property. Carlisle grinned, said no and thanks anyway, while he walked away, shaking his head.

"Under the influence of Carlisle's hands, the decrepit Williston property had been transformed into the best damn place I ever seen. It had all the look and feel of a fine piece of cabinetry, except this was an entire house and grounds. I was 'specially interested in the hardwood flooring he'd just recently installed inside. It'd come from the gym floor at old Salamander High. And I stood there remembering the underhand shot I'd sunk that took down the Livermore Chiefs in the finals of the county tournament, January of '34.

"Next best to the flooring, I liked the little atrium thing he'd put along the south side, which you could enter either from the main house or through an outside door. Well, it wasn't so little, since it ran just about the length of the house and stuck out some ten feet. Had a brick floor in it, redwood siding like the rest of the house, and for the roof a kind of sloping latticework arrangement of eighteen-inch, wood-framed pieces of glass. Carlisle had calculated snow loads, runoff, and all the rest, so by using smaller pieces of framed glass at the proper angle, he'd avoided the problem that all the boys at Danny's had said would ruin it.

"With the help of both Susanna and Gally, who by that time had become somewhat friends, Carlisle had stocked the atrium with hanging greenery of all kinds, plus plants and flowers in pots and tubs. There also was a miniature garden that produced more vegetables than five people could eat. Said he'd found that idea in a book lent to him by Susanna that dealt with a concept called gardening by the square foot. Scattered around in amongst all these plants were little benches where you could sit and enjoy all the growing things. I was sitting behind a rubber plant when I happened to see Alma Hickman stick a big red tomato in her purse, after first glancing around to see if anybody was looking. I was, but she didn't notice me.

"Now, you got to appreciate that most of the new places around here, of which there are few, are mostly double-wides from the discount trailer place in Falls City or prefabbed jobs from the Great West company in that same location. People live with so much natural space around 'em that they apparently want their homes chopped up into little tiny rooms and hauled in one-half at a time on the back of trucks. That's one theory. More likely, it's so's they can say they've got a living room, a dining room, a kitchen, three bedrooms, and so forth. Kind of seems like that puts 'em in a higher class of citizen, far as I can tell from listening to the radio ads for those things.

"Understandable, then, the fact Carlisle

had only two rooms in his place, one of which was a bathroom-utility room with a redwood shower, the other of which was everything else, kind of unsettled them. The place was, in a single word, spare. In another single word, it was open. He'd copied the Shakers in some respects, and a fair amount of his furniture, of which there wasn't much and all of which he'd built himself, hung from the walls when it wasn't in use.

"He'd fixed up a nice loft you reached by a fancy twirling staircase, the rail of it being a long, curving piece of driftwood he'd found by the Little Sal. Even though the house was essentially one big room, it didn't feel that way, since he'd set plants and bookcases in certain ways as to sort of section off the place.

"The women oohed and said nice things about his kitchen, 'specially the ash cabinets he'd made from scratch. His silverware and dishes and other stuff more or less formed a stew, since he'd picked up things at rummage sales and at the Goodwill in Falls City. But he had a good eye for it.

"The entire place had a sort of a polished gold amber color to it, helped along by all the redwood he'd recycled. All of it shining, all of it nice and warm. Made you want to sit down and read a book or pick the five-string banjo hanging on the wall. For some folks, however, there was one negative aspect. That was the little statue of a naked female with a wild hairdo that was sitting on the mantel. The statue upset the churchwomen some, and they were buzzing about it on the way back to their cars. The younger women, however, felt different and tended to ask Carlisle more questions about the house after they'd seen the statue, smiling at him all the while they asked.

"Out the back door was a deck with a wooden hot tub large enough for several people. The binoculars boys swore they'd seen both Gally and Susanna in the tub at the same time, with Carlisle nowhere around, though they couldn't be sure, since the angle of view from the road was a little awkward. Some even claimed that Marcie English had been in there one time with Susanna and Gally.

"Leading off from the deck was a raised wood walkway, about six inches above-ground and resting on genuine forty-three-inch footings, no less. The walkway led to a ten-by-fifteen workshop matching the house in its color and details, even up to its shake roof. That little building contained fold-down workbenches, cupboards, and hooks for all Carlisle's tools. And Carlisle McMillan had a lot of tools.

"Something else interesting was Carlisle's bat houses. The image most of us have regarding bats is our mothers waving brooms around the living room on a summer evening while family members were covering up their hair and screaming about rabies and Dracula. But Carlisle knew bats eat insects, and one way to keep your yard somewhat free of them was to have bats as neighbors. With that in mind, he'd installed houses for them on the southeast side of his oaks, about fifteen feet up. Said it might take a while for the bats to move in, but they would, they would.

"Over the main doorway was a symbol, neatly carved into the wood. Most people were reluctant to ask what it meant, probably afraid they might find out, I'm guessing. Underneath the symbol on the doorway were some words: *For Cody*. Carlisle said he'd prefer not to talk about what that meant, and everybody respected his feelings, though Cecil Macklin, being the extra sharp Realtor he was, made the observation that such customizing lowered the resale value of the house considerably.

"All in all, it was quite a weekend. Some people came both days, bringing a picnic lunch with 'em the second time around. The county conservation people had helped Carlisle design a small dam, backing the creek up into a nice one-acre pond, and folks sat there by the water talking to people they hadn't seen for years, since they'd been spending all their time watching television instead of visiting, like we used to do.

"I went both days, too, naturally, riding with Thelma Englestrom the second day. Mostly I sat by the pond, feeling the grass, looking at the water. With no personal transportation I was pretty well locked into Salamander, and it felt good sitting there in sunlight and just watching some smallish hawks making their rounds near a patch of trees across the road from Carlisle's place. Couldn't identify 'em for sure, but remembered seeing those kind of birds a long time ago, but not lately.

"Carlisle seemed to enjoy it all, explaining, pointing out, answering questions. Some of us noted he'd touch Gally in little ways now and then. Bobby Eakins claimed he'd been watching once when Carlisle walked by and ran his hand over her bottom when he thought nobody was looking. Bobby said he had put a move on Gally once or twice, even though he favored what he called 'less experienced women,' but all she'd ever done in response was pour hot coffee on his hand, claiming afterwards it was an accident.

"Now, the folks from Falls City are a different crowd. That's the county seat, and along with having a community college, they've been successful at attracting some industry, not to mention doctors and other professional people. After hearing about Carlisle's work, the *Falls City Observer* sent over a reporter to observe, along with a photographer to photograph. They did a real complimentary article on the house and Carlisle, calling him one of the great craftsmen of the high plains.

"After that, Carlisle had all the work he could handle in Falls City and surrounding areas. People said you had to put up with his slow, methodical way of working, but that the result was worth it. Since he chose to work only about four weeks out of six, you had to wait till he was ready. They also re-marked that you dasn't tell him exactly what you wanted or, worse, show him a picture from *House Beautiful*. What you did was try and say what role the new spaces would play in your life. Then, in the words of a Falls City physician's wife, 'Stand back, leave him alone, and he'll give you perfection.'

"Word was also that the women liked to watch him work. Said he always wore a red or yellow bandanna tied around his head and that he had real nice fingers. They'd peer out their windows at his long, lean body and guess that he had muscles in all the right places. One woman told her bridge club that Carlisle would run his hands over fine woods just like he was caressing a woman. That got him even more work once her comment was repeated in the right circles, though Carlisle had no idea that any of this was going on.

"In general, then, this Cody, whoever he was, had a lot of influence in Yerkes County and somewhat beyond. People started re-thinking their ways of building, though Sala-mander folks stuck with their double-wides and prefabs. Some said Carlisle's tastes were 'too California' and 'too expensive' for them, although it was generally known that he'd spent less than $4,000 in building materials, furniture, and assorted houseware items in bringing his own project to completion. That figure worried some of the local lumberyards and building suppliers, but it needn't have, since there's always enough mud-brains around to pay full retail price for new green wood on the verge of warping, not to mention other similar amenities.

"So Carlisle at least had the respect of a good many folks, even though he was not one of us in Salamander and never would be. He lived apart from us, geographically and mentally. It wasn't that he was unfriendly or uppity or anything like that. You just somehow knew he had different priorities from the rest of the universe. You just knew it.

"Still, he'd bring Gally into Leroy's on Saturday nights when Gabe showed up with his accordion. Gabe'd play all the old polkas and two-steps and country tunes, just like people wanted. But about every tenth song he'd play one for himself. At first the yahoos would yell, 'What'n hell's that crap, Gabe?'

"Then Gabe, the yellee, would look at the yeller and say real quietly, 'It's a tango, you dumb bastard.' After that, they wouldn't ask anymore.

"See, Gabe'd been part of the liberation of Paris and had been left behind there to guard the place when the armies moved east. He'd spent every night in the little cafés where tangos were all the rage with aficionados. And he'd learned how to play them. Learned how to play them real well.

"If the door to Leroy's was propped open on a summer night, I'd sit next to my window and listen to Gabe play, the music drifting over the crowd, across the street, and up to me. I'd been in Paris, too. I'd heard the tangos. And I'd listen, remembering the French girl I fell in love with and . . ."

The old man's words angled down to silence, letting the thought go unfinished for a moment. He drank the last of the amber truth before him and clenched his jaw for a few seconds. Rolled his lips in toward each other, tightening them, ran his hand across thin gray hair.

He looked up at me. "Christ, how I loved her—her name was Amélie—and she loved me, too. But Ike sent us on to Germany, and it was a long time before I could get back to Paris. I looked for her, for two months I looked for her, but she was nowhere to be found.

"That was pretty much the end of my great passion. Oh, I eventually married a Livermore girl and had a daughter. But it was never the same. Never the same as lying in a Paris attic on a cold, rainy day with a woman you'd fight the whole goddamned German army for. Never the same.

"So I always liked it when Gabe'd play the tangos. I'd listen and look down the main street of Salamander, way out to the countryside, watching the heavy blue twilight coming down. And I'd be thinking of Amélie and remembering how it was to be young, with rain on the rooftops of Paris and music playing.

"Gabe also liked to play 'Autumn Leaves,' which originally was a French song. He'd treat it real gentle, stark, real sad. And I'd lie in my bed then. I'd lie there remembering Amélie and Paris, bringing back the feeling of her against me and wondering if she was still alive and what she might be doing, my eyes getting a little wet as I moved on toward sleep . . . still thinking about how it all kinda got away from me."

CHAPTER TWELVE

Early summer, and Carlisle had the house
finished except for some minor plumbing
and electrical work he wanted to complete
before his open house. That allowed him
more time for Gally and other things he had
been thinking about. In the spring, he'd
come across plans for a five-string banjo in
a copy of *Mother Earth News*. He laid up a
prototype, studied it, and figured out some
improvements. A vintage Gibson four-string
was lying in its case at a Salamander garage
sale. He cannibalized it for the tone ring and
fitted the ring to a laminated maple rim he
built up and finished on a lathe he rented for
a day. The neck was hand carved out of a
scrap of mahogany he'd picked up at a construction site in Falls City, and he laid the
frets with micrometer accuracy.

It sounded pretty good, real good, in fact, even though he didn't play all that well, learning as he did from some books and tapes he'd ordered. Good enough for Dumptruck, apparently, since the tomcat didn't complain too much. And Gally liked to hear Carlisle play and sing "Way Out There" or "Buffalo Skinners" on Saturday nights after they'd had a few beers.

As the old man said, Carlisle was taken with the music of Gabe O'Rourke. Most Saturday nights, Gabe would bring a guitar player with him, a fellow who got around real well on the ebony fretboard of a forty-year-old Martin New Yorker. Both of them were sophisticated musicians, and that surprised and pleased Carlisle, who decided he had underestimated what was possible out there on the high plains.

They played a fair amount of stuff familiar to the locals, but now and then they'd get lean and tight and play—Carlisle couldn't believe it at first—a tango. The real street stuff, direct from the cafés of Argentina and Paris all the way to Leroy's in Salamander.

In Carlisle's early years, a fellow named Luis occasionally dropped by Wynn McMillan's house in Mendocino. Luis was a tango dancer, right down to his slicked-back dark hair and insolent ways. One evening, Carlisle chewed on a stick of red licorice and listened while Luis explained to the assembled members of Wynn's salon how the tango was the one dance having universal meaning attached to it.

According to Luis, the movements of the tango represented the male's domination of the female. He argued furthermore that this dominion extended to the male's brutal attitude toward nature, as contrasted with the nurturing instincts of females. Before he had finished, Luis had constructed a semi-coherent theory of how the entire history and behavior of celestial space could be found in the movements unique to tango dancing.

Carlisle was eleven when he heard Luis's lecture, after which Luis had supported his notions by giving an exhibition in the living room. His partner was a voluptuous watercolorist, who was all too willing to be dominated, or so it seemed to Carlisle's inexperienced eyes. When Carlisle looked back on it, however, what fascinated him most was that Luis had his own theory of the macrocosm. Granted, it was different from anything Carlisle's science teachers ever mentioned, but at least Luis had a theory. Whether or not serious scholars could buy into it was a different matter, but it seemed to impress Wynn McMillan's friends.

As far as Carlisle could tell, and he was just old enough to guess about these things, Luis didn't care half as much about his ideas as he did about tangoing off into a Mendocino evening with the watercolorist. And that's exactly what he had done.

A few years later, and in a foolish moment that made him cringe when he remembered it, Carlisle had the temerity to mention Luis's notion to Cody Marx and asked if Cody thought there was anything to it. Cody had looked at him, puffed on his pipe, and said two things. First, Cody said his own ideas weren't too well formed on either the universe or tango dancing. And second, he indicated he'd be grateful if Carlisle would just tango on out to the truck and retrieve the miter box. Carlisle had let it go after that.

Gabe handled the tangos perfectly. Played right, as Carlisle liked to say, they had a certain spare, minimalist quality to them, very much like Sir Henry Wotton's criteria for good workmanship in construction: commodity, firmness, and delight. At first, the locals would hoot when Gabe started into one of the café songs. After a while, though, they came to understand he was serious about the playing of them and quieted down when he reached back and played an old tango.

Carlisle believed the accordion was a maligned instrument, possessing a distinctive voice that nothing could match. As the night moved along and Leroy's cleared out a bit, Gally and Carlisle danced together, nice and slow. Gabe knew some of the old standards, so that endeared him to Gally. She'd request "Stardust" and "I Remember You" and "September Song," the good tunes from her Flagstone Ballroom days. Gabe knew them all.

Carlisle always asked for "Autumn Leaves," one of his favorites. Gabe just tore it and him to pieces in the special way he treated it, caressing the tune in the same way Cody ran his hands over a cabinet in the moments he was finishing it. The guitar player would slide quietly in and out of minor seventh and augmented chords behind Gabe and would toss in little runs complementing what Gabe was doing on the accordion.

The run of it was that Carlisle had settled down in a place called Salamander. He and Gally danced at Leroy's and drove around the countryside, made love in Cody's monument, and cooked for each other, made huge bags of popcorn and went to the Livermore drive-in theater. When she'd ask, he would take the five-string off the wall and roll into rudimentary clawhammer picking: "My ol' man was a farmer on the Yerkes County line / Had eighty acres of bottomland and ramblin' on his mind . . ."

Once, on a whim, they cranked up his truck, stowed a couple of bags in the box under a tarp, and drove 984 miles to Las Vegas, where Gally had never been. Devil Jack had promised he'd take her sometime but never did.

They stayed in a hotel called the Barbary Coast and played blackjack. In his wilder years, he and Budddy used to haul out of San Francisco for Vegas or Reno to play blackjack on a regular basis. Late on a Saturday afternoon, with Gally's hand on his shoulder, he put down a green chip at a $25 table and ran it up to a little over $900 in ten minutes, playing head-to-head with a female dealer named Irene who could lay out a hand once every six seconds.

To Carlisle's way of thinking, a good run like that had both the purity of Bach and the juice of a modest sexual experience. When the cards turned against him, he cashed in and waltzed Gally down to a pricey store, where he bought her a new dress, shoes, the works. That night, with Gally looking slim and chic in her new outfit and Carlisle dressed in clothes left over from his Stanford days—gray tweed jacket, charcoal slacks, white shirt, and striped tie—they had dinner in a little restaurant approximating the kind of elegance Gally had only read about in magazines.

After dinner, Carlisle had taken her dancing in a real nightclub, as he'd once promised to do. The best part for him of the blackjack, the dinner, the dancing, was seeing Gally enjoy herself, listening to her quiet laughter, watching her puzzle over the menu in Michael's. They had made sweet love late at night, Gally all warm and giving and whispering in his ear about how content she was and how much she wanted him. He felt the same way and told her so. They pulled out for Salamander the following morning, singing along with the truck radio, watching the western cordillera moving toward them.

Gally packed off to Spearfish in August, started classes, and wrote to Carlisle, "It's wonderful. I feel like I'm eighteen again. I even went to a football game and sang the school fight song. Come visit me, carpenter. I miss you."

It slowly occurred to Carlisle McMillan that he had come to Salamander with a single purpose: to avoid the great economic colossus called progress. He wanted it to pass without noticing him, leaving him mostly whole and mostly sane in Yerkes County.

So Carlisle thought he'd figured it out. Lay low, do good work and not too much of it, clean up your vocabulary, find a solid woman. Simplify, keep things uncomplicated. It seemed to be working.

And he developed an interest in T-hawks. He had noticed the little hawks on the first day he walked his property. During the time Carlisle had been working on the place, they floated overhead and in the distance or perched in the high branches of the small forest across the road from him.

Birds are one thing to the casual eye, feathers and whatnot, including some degree of magic and perfectly designed for what they do, which includes rustling up the interest of cats named Dumptruck. The little hawks of Yerkes County that caught Carlisle's attention appeared to be immature birds of a much larger species. Yet they did not seem to be growing, and there were no larger hawks hanging around the small forest. Daily observations through Carlisle's binoculars confirmed all of that.

He bought a general guide to birds. Nothing. Then a more specialized one on raptors. Still nothing. On page 247 of a third book from the Falls City Library, hawks only this time, something appeared that caused him to shudder a little. There was a brief entry regarding a small predator called a Timmerman's hawk, or T-hawk. The description of the bird noted it was about half the size of a red-tailed hawk. And the entry closed with this: "Once common in the northern Great Plains, now generally believed to be extinct due to habitat loss. For reasons unknown, T-hawks established an intense fidelity to a particular forest and periodically engaged in flocking behavior instead of the more common territoriality. Destruction of local habitat was tantamount to destruction of a T-hawk colony, since they refused to breed after that and would not migrate in search of new habitat."

Carlisle read the passage again and recalled his dislike of the word *extinct* from the first hearing of it. When you said the word out loud, the sound was like that of a hammer striking cold steel.

He studied an artist's rendering in the book, then watched the birds overhead through his binoculars, repeating both steps several times. That's when he began to get excited.

His next move was to poke around the science department at the community college in Falls City. One of the biologists was willing to hear him out. Skeptical at first, he eventually became mildly excited after listening to Carlisle and drove up Carlisle's lane later that day, equipped with serious binoculars.

He looked. Studied Carlisle's hawk book and one of his own. Looked again. Carefully did all of that, back and forth, back and forth.

"Carlisle, I think you may have made an important discovery," Daryl Moore said, looking up from one of the texts and out toward the small forest. "The scientific community has believed for some time that the T-hawks disappeared decades ago. The little fellows, more properly known as *Buteo timmermanis*, were named after a nineteenth-century zoologist, H. L. Timmerman, who first identified them as a separate species. It looks to me like there's a mating pair and some young ones in the little grove over there. Hawks are extremely territorial, and there's not enough space in that patch of trees to allow more than one pair, though some flocking behavior apparently does occur at times. We must get an ornithological specialist out here right away."

Carlisle looked at Daryl Moore and said, "Tell you what, you take credit for finding them, if indeed that's what they are. I'm doing my best to sequester myself out here, and the last thing in the world I want is to attend some academic convention and relate how I was sitting on my porch drinking beer, asking my cat, Dumptruck, for his considered opinion, and simply watching the little predators for the sheer hell of it."

The biologist started to protest, but Carlisle cut him off. "Mr. Moore, you're the one who made the positive identification. I was just guessing. I'm not looking for tenure, so maybe this will do you some good, while it won't do anything for me. Just say a friend tipped you off about some little hawks living in that grove and that your scientific sense of smell got the rest done."

"Oh, I really wouldn't feel right about that." Daryl Moore appeared a little astounded.

"Okay, I'm now denying that I ever saw the birds before you came by. They're all yours, Moore. Fly with it."

"Well . . . thank you, Carlisle. If you really feel that way."

"I do. Now go call your expert and coauthor a paper with him or her. You'll all have fun with it. So will I, in my own way."

For a while, there was a lot of dust on the road in front of Cody's monument. Mostly field vehicles, old Internationals and Jeeps, with lettering on the sides indicating they were from one scientific institute or another. Carlisle started to worry about this commotion disturbing the T-hawks, and Moore agreed, henceforth doing what he could to subdue the flood of hawk experts.

Eventually, papers were written about the new find, but directions to the exact geographic location were withheld in the best interest of preserving what was probably the last refuge of the little raptors. And Carlisle no longer had to ask various scientists carrying notebooks and telephoto lenses longer than his arm to please move their vehicles so he could get in and out of his lane.

Carlisle and Moore were interested in purchasing the parcel of land where the T-hawk forest was located. As it turned out, the federal government owned the land and was not interested in selling, since most of it was leased for grazing rights. But things were quiet, and the T-hawks seemed happy, so Moore and Carlisle shut down their efforts at that point. Moore, however, began working with the Raptor Coalition to get the T-hawks on the endangered species list.

Ornithologists reasoned that if one pair of T-hawks was still in existence, there might be more. After an intensive search, two more pairs were discovered at locations within a hundred miles of Yerkes County. That was all, six adults and their young, a total of fifteen birds. The survival of the little hawks was a tenuous ride on the back of a dragonfly.

Carlisle was a happy man. He had Gally and useful work to do. He had Timmerman hawks overhead, Dumptruck on the porch railing, and songs to sing. Plus, to be honest, he still had thoughts about Susanna Benteen from time to time. It was the way of all men. And Susanna Benteen clearly was a woman worth thinking about. In working together on the layout and content of his greenhouse, she and Gally had become friends. Sometimes in a summer dusk, he would come home from working in Falls City and find them in his hot tub out on the deck, drinking wine and mildly annoying Dumptruck by their very presence.

When it came to Susanna being naked, Carlisle averted his eyes more out of self-preservation than propriety. Those feelings about her had never left him since that night a year earlier, when she and the Indian had shooed away whatever evil spirits might be lurking in his house and replaced them with good ones. Gally was one thing, Susanna something quite different. Not better, he told himself, different. Just for an instant, he'd catch Susanna watching him. When their eyes met, however, he turned away.

Later, Susanna and Gally would appear on the front porch, dressed, looking poached and cheerful. Susanna would always ask Carlisle to sing "Whippoorwill John," and he'd get out his banjo and muster up his wavery baritone: "Whippoorwill John, he runs like a moon through the canyonlands . . ." Often the Indian would appear out of the twilight, and the four of them would sit there watching the T-hawks and Dumptruck as he made his evening rounds of the property, letting the night kind of settle in on its own terms.

Carlisle was fascinated with the stories and legends surrounding Wolf Butte. On a rainy day in late summer, just before she left for Spearfish, he and Gally had parked the truck and walked across grassland toward the butte, which sat about a mile off the road. It was a day very much like the one when he'd first arrived in Yerkes County, cold rain and low clouds moving across the face of the butte.

"Where are the burial mounds?" Carlisle asked.

"I think they're around on the other side." Gally pulled the hood of her rain jacket over her head and shivered. "Carlisle, this place gives me the creeps. It's pretty close to where Jack was killed, and that plays on my nerves, too."

Carlisle looked up the wall of the butte. Thirty-two hundred feet above him was the crest. "Where did that professor fall?"

Gally was uneasy, ready to leave. "I know he was looking over the burial mounds and that he didn't fall from Wolf Butte. On the other side and about a half mile farther northwest is a smaller butte, so that must have been the one."

Carlisle wanted to walk around the butte and look at the mounds, but Gally would have none of it. "You go if you want, I'll wait in the truck."

"No, that's okay. I'll come back some-time by myself. I can understand why this place makes you jittery."

"I'm not that superstitious ordinarily, but I think it's a real strange coincidence that all those people, including Jack, have died out here and the way those old stories about this place seem to stick in people's minds. And that stuff about a priestess called Syawla and something or someone called the Keeper. It really makes my skin get crawly when I think about it."

They took a different route back to the truck and passed a sign bolted to a metal post facing the road: PROPERTY OF AURA CORPORATION, KEEP OUT.

Carlisle studied the sign. "Kind of an odd name for a company, don't you think?"

"Yes. Just like everything else in this place."

The rain turned to a light mist, and Carlisle let the wipers run one sweep across the windshield before shutting them off. He looked again at the butte. It was shrouded in a combination of mist and foggy clouds moving around and over the face and crest, but he could still see the fuzzy outlines of it.

"Gally, did you see that?"

"What?"

"I thought I saw someone or something moving on top of the butte." He got out of the truck and stood for a moment, resting his arms on the open door. "I'm sure I saw something up there. Suppose it's the Keeper?"

"Come on, Carlisle, let's go. I really want to get out of here."

They were too far away to hear the sound of a flute coming from the crest of the butte, but if the weather had been clear, they might have seen a woman dancing there.

CHAPTER THIRTEEN

After his open house, Carlisle's phone began to ring. It rang two, three times a day. A school superintendent in Livermore wanted an addition to his present house, in Falls City a surgeon's wife wanted a new kitchen, and a biochemist wanted an entire home built. Cody's Way: (1) Do good work at a reasonable price and you never will want for work. (2) Be selective when you can; if your work is good enough, they will wait for you.

With Gally away at college and his own house completed, Carlisle began to follow the carpenter's trade in the fashion Cody had trained him and wondered again how he had ever strayed from that path. But he knew: the lure of the short run, always that. He was politely selective, accepting projects he could do himself or with a bit of extra muscle he hired on a day-labor basis, driving his truck along the roads of Yerkes County with his tools neatly stowed and his dreams nearly so.

Carlisle McMillan was content, spelled lowercase and good enough left that way, a swagman come to rest. If something approaching ecstasy were not in the cards, then contentment would do. That's exactly what he was thinking on a January evening when Susanna, the Indian, Dumptruck, and he crunched through the snow around the pond and wondered how the bluegills were faring beneath the ice.

Three days later, the plans for a new interstate highway were announced.

The old man from above Lester's was sitting at his usual stool when Carlisle came into Danny's. He shoved a copy of the *Inquirer* along the counter toward Carlisle and said, "Mr. McMillan, I think you better take a look at this."

Carlisle stared at the six-column scream passing for a headline: AVENUE OF THE HIGH PLAINS PROPOSED. He flipped to the maps on the second and third pages, running his index finger along the route. The road came slanting northwest out of New Orleans and formed a quavering diagonal all the way to Calgary, Alberta. The quavers obviously were necessary to include Little Rock, Kansas City, and Omaha. The *Inquirer* had gone all out in its graphics, showing in exquisite detail just how the three-hundred-yard-wide strip of four lanes plus a grass median would traverse the state.

The route made a wide swing to include Falls City and Livermore, missed Salamander by six miles, and flowed relentlessly right up the county road in front of Carlisle's place, right through Carlisle's property, right through the little forest of T-hawks, before bending northwest and crossing the middle of Gally's land. Other customers were watching Carlisle, watching disbelief and anger fighting for control of his face.

"Carlisle, take the paper with you if you want." Thelma Englestrom was not smiling when she said it.

He spent all day studying the maps, reading the four accompanying articles, and thinking. The road featured a sharp and apparently unnecessary curve southeast of Falls City, allowing it to pass close to there and Livermore. That made him suspicious, which made him even angrier. He had seen this crap before, all over California. Somebody had diddled the route, and where there was diddling, there was money involved.

What Carlisle had not seen in his previous experience with highways was how fast they were going to move on this project. Tentative bids were already being let to contractors in six states plus Canada. The first round of public hearings was scheduled to begin in two months, where comments about the proposed route would be discussed. Given the condition of the high plains, with its industry and soil both eroding and its water about gone, something had to be done and done pronto. That was the official party line.

Pork was floating in the barrel right up to the brim, something for everybody. United States senators and representatives were swelled up over the economic benefits the road construction itself would bring to their districts. In addition, oil could be piped from the Arctic to Calgary and shipped from there to New Orleans refineries by truck, taking up slack caused by a decline in the Texas and Gulf fields. So truckers and oil companies and New Orleans would gain.

As with the sea islands connivance and

its arithmetic of woe, this project had its own self-reinforcing elements. Approval had not yet been given for drilling the Arctic, but how could that proposal be refused now, given all the money that would be spent on a highway to haul the oil? And if the Arctic was to be pillaged, the oil must somehow be delivered. Therefore the highway was essential.

That last piece of genius collared support from the drillers, makers of drilling equipment, truck manufacturers, and a range of other interests, including labor unions. But Carlisle suspected the Arctic drilling was really secondary. Highways, the idea of them, at least, had their own internal momentum, the vague idea that concrete invariably brings nirvana with it. Get a major highway through your state, and things will be just fine.

And a little sop had been thrown to the environmentalists. Part of the plan was a proposal to buy all of Axel Looker's and Gally Deveraux's properties. A new antelope and buffalo restoration project would be started there and eventually would be known as Antelope National Park. Something for everybody.

The governors of the lucky states were orgasmic, slathering their support for the highway across the newspaper pages, touting the incredible propellant to economic development it represented. As they saw it, tourism would flower, the small towns would be resurrected, the fat towns would get even fatter, population would rise, and so forth. The gleeful howls continued for page after page.

Carlisle read it all, then read it again, his gut sinking. Gally called from Spearfish that evening.

"Carlisle, I'm just sick about this highway affair. I've been pushing back the tears all day over what it'll do to you. I talked to Thelma earlier, and she said everybody in town believes it's the deliverance of Salamander."

"Gally, I hate to tell you this, but Salamander is already dead and doesn't know it. A bloody strip of concrete running six miles away isn't going to mean squat to that town. If anything, it will just make it easier for the locals to drive to the shopping centers in Falls City. Thelma and others may want to believe that garbage, but it just isn't true. I'm sorry to be so blunt, but this is just another rusty nail in the coffin of my dreams, and I'm sick of these bastards and their obvious intent to turn the entire world into a desert of concrete and baubles."

Gally was silent for a moment and then spoke quietly, defensively. "This is real complicated, Carlisle. You can pick up your tools and go where the work is. A lot of us can't do that, and we have to survive, too. I can't pick up my land and move it, and I'm about a hairbreadth from bankruptcy court. Thelma can't pick up Danny's and move it. You can build another place, can't you?"

"I can build another place. The T-hawks can't."

"But if it comes down to birds versus humans—"

He interrupted her. "I'll say it again, Gally. The highway is not going to help Danny's or Salamander. If it benefits anyone besides the contractors and cement industry and you—and Axel if he feels like selling, and he probably doesn't have any choice—it will be the towns that already are doing well, plus Stuckey's and Ramada and Texaco and all the rest of that crowd that's bent on homogenizing the planet."

"It's the town's only chance, Carlisle. What else is there?"

"If I were an expert on these things, there would be people lined up at my door from here to Yellowstone. I only know two things. First, the highway's going to hurt Salamander more than it will help. Second, this project has got a bad smell to it. Behind all the trumpets, there's some bad music playing. I can feel it in my gut, and it doesn't have anything to do with bringing more customers into Danny's."

Across the road, T-hawks were coming in from their day's work. The crickets were under way, the air was cooling, and Carlisle squinted west through a perfectly trimmed window, into pink orange afterglow.

"Gally, I admit I've got a bias about these things, but there's something real artificial about what's happening, not just in terms of this highway piece of crap, but all over the place. Highways, condos, bad construction that passes for new houses, fast-food-bad-food, shopping malls full of junk that nobody really needs, all that stuff. Capitalism has turned into trinketism, and we're ruining this country."

Carlisle was in full spate now, furious,

angry at Gally, at the world. "Somebody's convinced us that *more* is better, but nobody's talking about more of *what*. Just *more*. More is better because less is worse, and the argument seems to end there. We think we know what we're doing, but we seem to be outrunning the bounds of our ability to see what we're doing, with no reckoning of long-term consequences. We need a Department of Forever, or something like that, people taking care of the long run. I don't know, none of it makes any sense to me. All I do know is this country may have lost its capacity for outrage, but I haven't. I can down bad porridge only so long, and I'm going to fight this highway on behalf of myself and the T-hawks, mostly for the birds."

Again, Gally was silent; the line from Spearfish seemed to have been severed for a few seconds. Carlisle could hear her breathing, though, and she obviously was thinking, choosing her words.

"Carlisle, I don't know what to say to you. I'm terribly sorry, truly I am, for what may happen to Cody's monument. You've created an Eden for yourself, and I cry when I think of the highway coming through and destroying it. But I don't have your anger about the way the world is going, and I'm not strong enough to change such things even if I did. I wish I were there so I could put my arms around you, but I have an examination tomorrow."

"Well, at least the highway will solve your problem, Gally, getting your land sold. That's something good that'll come of this."

"What are you going to do?"

"I don't know. There's a professor at Stanford who is supposed to be a real warrior when it comes to these kinds of things. Saw an article about him in the alumni magazine last summer. Think I'll call him."

"I've got to go and study for my exam. Can you come down this weekend?"

"I don't know. Frankly, I'm probably not a very good person to be around right now. So maybe it's best I don't. I'll call if I change my mind."

"Okay," she said pensively. "I have plans for Saturday night, but I'll cancel them if you decide to come down. Carlisle . . ."

"Yes," he responded, voice gruff and impatient, as if he had other things to do of more importance than talking to Gally Deveraux.

"I care a lot for you."

Carlisle sighed, eased off. "I know you do, Gally, and I feel the same. Good luck on your exam."

CHAPTER FOURTEEN

In his office in Falls City, Ray Dargen was addressing a group of local businessmen. "Boys, didn't I tell you this was a chance to do some real business? I told you to trust your good buddy Ray, didn't I? The road's going through here, just like I told you it would, and—"

"Ray," one of the men intruded, "it's not a sure thing yet, is it? The plans we've seen are labeled *proposed* route."

Ray Dargen grinned confidently. "The road's going to go through here, just where the plans show. Ol' Jack Wheems, my senator friend and head of highway legislation out there in our nation's capital, guarantees it." Dargen swung back and forth in his leather swivel chair, hands folded across his curving stomach, content with the power he had and even more content thinking of what was to come.

"You're absolutely sure there's no way we can get in trouble for buying up all that land last year?" asked another man, a Falls City doctor.

Dargen snorted and waved back their fears with his right hand moving in a generous sweep through the air. "Nothing wrong with a few of us making a buck or two outta something that was gonna happen anyway. Like the Bible says, go forth and prosper."

Dargen paused and tried to remember if those words, in fact, came from the Bible and was pretty sure they had. Nobody in the group corrected him, so he went on.

"'Course, we'd all just as soon our foresight didn't appear as public record in the *Inquirer*. Now let's stop worrying and go over one more time how we divvied up these land purchases so none of us appears to have been buying property in amounts that might draw attention."

The owner of a trucking company was sitting on Jill Remington's left and had spent the evening admiring her breasts while he talked at her. His eyes toggled back and forth from her face to the downward sweep of her neckline. He droned, she was bored. But she locked a pleasant half smile on her face and pretended to be interested (God, don't these men ever talk about anything except politics and business?).

Yet Jill Remington was pleased that Senator Jack Wheems had invited her to the intimate dinner party. His wife and the conservative people he represented back home prevented him from taking her to restaurants, but he liked to show her off when he could do it in relative safety. Tonight had been deemed modestly secure by the senator's aides, who disliked Jill simply because of the senator's interest in her and the political risk that interest represented.

On her right, at the head of the table, the senator was leaning over and talking to a New Orleans road builder. "Nah, we don't expect any trouble out there. Those poor bastards in the high plains are so desperate they'll do anything to get help. We'll probably run into some problems from environmentalists in the Louisiana wetlands and maybe farther on north where we're going through the edge of a national park, but that can be managed. I'm still quietly lining up votes on the Public Works and Transportation Committee, but we should be ready to announce the final route by sometime next year, which, of course, will be the route we've already decided on."

"Listen, Senator, if you need more money for the final push, give me a call," the road builder offered.

"Thanks, we might. I'll let you know. One way or the other, we'll get it all taken care of. Cal Akers over at the Chamber is spearheading this for me, and Cal knows how to stomp ass when he needs to. Behind that born-again bullshit of his is a real gunslinger."

The senator tapped his cigar on an ashtray, shook his head, and let go a nominal laugh empty of humor. "Jesus, when those poor country folks see what the Mexican trade agreement's going to do to their little hopes and dreams of attracting industry, they'll crap bricks. The Mexicans'll work for nothing or close to it, and the agreement'll just pound those little shitburgs out west deeper into the ground with a croquet mallet, but they're dying anyway, and that's an altogether separate problem."

The others up and down the table nodded their assent.

"What is it Cal Akers says?" Senator Wheems paused, looking up at the ceiling where the smoke from his cigar drifted through the bangles of a crystal chandelier. "American technology used by Mex labor to make products we'll sell to the Japanese and Europeans. He calls it the Rio Grande Initiative. Good title."

Jill Remington, gazellelike and head canted, was on time-share, listening to the senator and nodding while the trucker talked to her, counting on her breasts to provide filler for the well-practiced, innocuous words she said back to him. Tonight she was an object and knew it, disliking the role and yet glad at the same time she didn't live out in that high plains area the senator called West Jesus and assorted other names.

"Ever been to Toledo, Jill?" The trucker leered, and the red flag in her brain, with "Question Has Been Asked!" printed on it, flipped to attention. Jack Wheems was looking over at her.

"No, I never have. Is it nice?" That, she figured, would be good for another ten minutes of mindless rambling by the trucker. She glanced at the senator; he puffed on his cigar and winked at her.

The trucker looked at her breasts, reloaded, and continued. "Little lady, we're just going to have to get you out there and show you . . ."

While he talked, Mexicana flight 32 bumped onto the runway at Dulles with Cal Akers, executive director of the United States Chamber of Commerce, on board.

The day after Jill Remington's education on the pleasures of Toledo, Ohio, and with the dregs of his travel fatigue swept away by the Christian Businessmen's Breakfast he had just attended, Cal Akers briskly entered his offices on Capitol Hill. The Mexicans were coming around on the trade agreement, and he could already visualize shoals of factories lining the border. Let the supercilious Europeans and the buzzing little Jappos suck on that prospect.

"Good morning, Jill."

"Good morning, Mr. Akers. Welcome back. How was the trip?"

"Super, Jill. Just super. What's the message board look like?"

In Cal Akers's world, everything was always super in spite of one failed marriage, a second headed in that direction, and a possible bankruptcy flowing from investments he had made in a chain of jewelry stores. Over the last six years of working for Cal, Jill had come to hate the word *super*.

"I've stacked them on your desk in the order they arrived, Mr. Akers. Mr. Flanigan at the High Plains Development Corporation has called several times. Also, Senator Wheems called and needs to talk with you right away."

"Raise him for me. Then we'll try Flanigan."

The senator was riding his big horse, lathered up and rolling. A night on Jill Remington consistently did that for him. "Cal," he roared, "get your buddy Bill Flanigan out there in West Fuckup to talk with this Ray Dargen, whoever he is, and get the son of a bitch calmed down before he wrecks this entire project. Harlan—you know, Senator Sterk from out there—tells me Dargen got a bunch of people together and they've secretly been buying land along the proposed route prior to the announcement last week. Been doing it for the last year or so, from what Harlan tells me. Christ, I knew it was a mistake for Flanigan to show him the route this early even if Dargen is a state highway commissioner."

Akers flinched at the senator's vocabulary, which echoed the way he used to talk before he stopped smoking and committed to Christ. "Who is Ray Dargen? Never heard of him except for the one time Flanigan mentioned him on a phone message he left for me on my answering machine."

"Ray Dargen's a real bad person, Cal," Jack Wheems replied. "According to Sterk, Dargen skates around on his own private grease rink, one of the old-line guys who hasn't figured out the world is changing. He's not all that bright overall, but he's shrewd-smart, and he's so mean that he bullies people into doing what he wants. Nobody likes to confront him 'cause he's got no conscience and no qualms about doing anything, no matter how nasty it is. While ago he got a Falls City woman who was running against Harlan tossed out of the primaries by printing up an anonymous flyer alleging she used dope and was screwing a Puerto Rican guitar player while letting her husband watch.

"It was all lies, but nobody could trace it to him. Dargen also contributes a lot of money to Harlan's campaign pot, and you know Harlan's a good friend of mine. I also happen to know that Dargen owns a big chunk of land out near a place called Wolf Butte. He bought it about fifteen years ago, so Harlan says. Something to do with trace elements of gold found in a stream near there. How that all fits into this I'm not sure."

"Okay, Senator. I'll call Flanigan right away and check on it." Cal Akers hung up and asked Jill to get Bill Flanigan on the line.

"High Plains Development Corporation, Mrs. Andrews speaking."

"Mr. Akers at the United States Chamber of Commerce is calling for Mr. Flanigan." Jill wondered if Mrs. Andrews, whoever she was, had ever been balled by a senator.

Mrs. Andrews had not been balled by a senator, though she'd seen several of them on television. Aside from one careless and fumbling moment after the senior prom, there had been only her husband, and he had lost interest ten years ago.

Margaret Andrews was drooping. She had spent the previous night helping her daughter deal with the baby's croup while her son-in-law watched a football game on television. She had known it was a mistake when Marilee dropped out of cosmetology school and got married to a certifiable loser. Somehow, though, with the faith of mothers everywhere, she had hoped it might work out, still did.

"Mr. Flanigan is on another line. Would you like to leave a callback?"

"When he's free, please have him call Mr. Akers."

"I'll give him the message."

"Thank you. Good-bye."

"Good-bye."

Jill buzzed Cal Akers. "Mr. Flanigan is busy right now. I left a callback."

"Thanks, Jill." Cal Akers rapped his pen on the desk blotter. Geez Louise, you could never get anybody anywhere anymore.

In ten minutes, Bill Flanigan returned the call. Akers picked up the phone, pulling up his best smiley voice as he did it. "Bill, how are you? I'm sorry to be so slow about get-

ting back to you. I've been over on the Hill
and down in Mexico City for a week, working on what we're calling the Rio Grande Initiative. It's moving along, even though the
liberals are all fussed up about cheap labor
and environmental stuff.

"Anyway, I just wanted to fill you in on
the highway project and check how it's going on your end. Things are moving fast
here, faster than I thought they would. The
good senator's swinging a meat ax on this
one, calling in his chits, beating the crap out
of anyone getting in his way. The Canadians
are on board now, and New Orleans has
helped form a national coalition of oilmen
and truckers.

"We had some problems with the federal
planners and engineers. The planners have
been whining that they don't have enough
money to maintain existing interstates, let
alone build a new one. The engineers are a
separate case. They don't like the big swing
in the road to include Falls City and Livermore. The senator himself went over and
talked to them two days ago. Told them if
they expected any more money for concrete
in the next ten years, they'd better get their
minds straight on this project. That seemed

to do it. There's still some bitching, but they're getting in harness."

"Any chance of the road coming through Salamander?"

"None. We gave it a shot, like you asked, but the engineers really screamed on that one, so I let it drop. Anyway, we both know that little pond's drying up, and a road won't help it. Right now it looks like we're staying with the proposed route, which will miss Salamander by about six miles, coming cross-country northwest from Livermore and then cutting over Forty-two and on up a dirt road to the north, same as we talked about before. Looks like a clear shot across open country after it leaves Livermore, which helps to minimize property acquisition costs. What about things out there? You see any problems?"

"Well, the Salamander thing would have helped, but we'll smoke it by them, tell them the spin-off from the highway will be good for the town, even though it's six miles west of them. The farmers and ranchers'll scream like hell about it cutting through their land, but they can be handled. One other possible problem just came up. Word has it that the Sioux consider the area around Wolf Butte sacred land, even though they don't own it. They did own it a long time ago, but that was inconvenient for the government and gold miners, so it got kind of slipped over into other hands. The Indians still feel proprietary about it, however. We've had similar problems with other development projects. Somehow we'll work it out, give 'em the modern-day equivalent of beads—a truck-load of beer or something—or just blow it past 'em, whatever it takes."

"Good. Listen, Bill, the main reason I called is a fellow named Ray Dargen who is apparently buying up land along the high-way route. That's got to stop or at least be cranked up six more notches of secrecy. Apparently Dargen has been a force in get-ting the highway through your area, but the whole thing might collapse or at minimum get held up if he doesn't quiet down."

"I just got wind of that, Cal. Whatever bad things you've heard about Ray Dargen are not only right, they're probably not bad enough. Also, he's a state highway commis-sioner. Frankly, I hate to be in the same car with him, always feel sort of like I'm cheating someone in some undefined way just by talking to him. You can see him licking his lips and rubbing his cologned hands every time the highway is mentioned. In general, he's incorrigible, plus he's a big supporter of Harlan Sterk. But I'll talk to him, try to get him shut up."

Akers continued. "Jack Wheems mentioned something about Dargen owning property near a place called Wolf Butte. Something to do with gold. Know anything about that?"

"No. I'll see what I can find out, though."

"Okay, I'm counting on you. Bill, I've got another call coming in. Just wanted to let you know how things are going here. Keep the faith and stay in contact. If everything continues the way it is now, we'll announce the final highway plans in a couple of months."

"That sounds great. We appreciate your help. I'd like to talk with you sometime about this Mexican trade agreement I've heard you mention and what impact it might have on us out here."

"Sure thing. I did ask the senator about that, however, and he doesn't foresee any real negative impact on your area. In fact, he thinks it might open the door for additional wheat exports. Gotta run, Bill."

When the light on her phone console flashed off, indicating Bill Flanigan was finished with his call, Margaret Andrews was still thinking about her granddaughter and worrying about what kind of job her son-in-law could find to support a family over the long haul. Things just seemed to be falling apart out there, jobs disappearing and people leaving. Mr. Flanigan, though, had told her that better times were on the way and had winked when he'd said it. She trusted him and hoped it was true, feeling the sunlight of a high plains autumn on her hands from the window beside her, she sat with fingers clenched, knowing winter was not far off.

She wished that her son-in-law had gone to college instead of working at Guthridge Brothers Sand & Gravel over in Salamander and hanging around Sleepy's Stagger Inn up in Livermore all night. She figured he would probably get laid off when cold weather arrived, then flop around the house drinking beer and watching game shows, yelling about what he could do on *Wheel of Fortune* if he just had the chance. When she had offered to pay his tuition so he could attend Three Buttes Community

College right there in town, he'd laughed and gone out to change the oil in his car. She had made the same offer to her daughter, but Marilee had wanted to attend cosmetology school and fiddle with hair the way she'd always done with her own. The pregnancy changed all that. And once again, Margaret Andrews thought about winter approaching, even though the sun was coming through a window and lying warm upon her hands.

CHAPTER FIFTEEN

"Your guess is right. They'll go after you using eminent domain." The professor of environmental economics at Stanford was talking by phone to a man named Carlisle McMillan somewhere out in the high plains.

"The Fifth Amendment allows for the taking of private property for public use as long as fair compensation is provided. When it comes to acquiring right-of-way for interstates, the law is quite specific. The secretary of transportation is authorized, and I'm quoting the law here, 'in the name of the United States . . . to acquire, enter upon, and take possession of such land or interests in such lands by purchase, donation, condemnation, or otherwise in accordance with the laws of the United States.' In this case, accordance means they have to compensate you, but they can take it."

"There's nothing I can do, then?"

"You'll have to use other defenses. In fact, you have to go on the offense. From what you've said, I gather there's been some doodling around with the route. I've seen that before, plenty of times. Carefully study the engineering data, make them justify the route they've chosen. At least fifty percent of the time they can't do it. I'll send you some materials that'll give you a good idea of how to go about it."

The professor watched students walking by his window in Palo Alto, red knapsacks, blue knapsacks, and glanced at his plane ticket for a conference in Melbourne. "Then there are the birds you mentioned, the T-hawks. Tell me a little more about them."

Carlisle described how he and Moore had identified the hawks and what had transpired since then.

"Are they on the endangered species list?" the professor asked.

"No, because everyone thought they were already extinct, but they've been nominated as candidates. The Raptor Coalition is working on that." Carlisle leaned against the door of a phone booth in Falls City. He was a third of the way through a garden room addition for a local attorney and trying to concentrate on his work, while anger over the road kept coming in waves, subsiding, then coming again.

"That's too bad." The professor sighed. "A species considered endangered or even threatened, which is the next lower level, is a powerful weapon in situations like these. That's the general thrust of the Endangered Species Act, and this highway clearly will destroy habitat.

"But I'll remind you, the first law of highway engineering is this: The shortest distance between any two points is always through a forest. The problem is that no legislative authority currently protects species that are candidates for the protected list but not yet on the list. And the process of getting a species listed is slow and uncertain. A recent report showed it will take the government ninety-four years merely to review all the plants and animals currently requiring attention, partly because the Office of Endangered Species is underfunded and understaffed.

"Along with that, the U.S. Fish and Wildlife

Service, which manages these things, is subject to all kinds of political pressures. Even if
you do eventually get the birds listed, that's
no guarantee they'll make it. Of those currently listed, one-third continues to decline in
numbers. Also, the FSW spends most of its
money on species with high visibility, those
that have a lot of sexy, public appeal, such as
the bald eagle, and I suspect your birds are
not in that category."

All of it sounded pretty grim to Carlisle.
"Well, what do you suggest?"

"There's a pretty good chance you can
get the highway stopped, at least for a while,
on the technicality that the original environmental impact statement was inadequate.
That's been done in the past. If you have the
resources, first get an injunction to halt construction temporarily on the basis of the
statement, and, second, file a lawsuit to
push the birds onto the endangered list. If
the birds get on the list, you're just about
home free. Notice I said 'just about.' There
are various legal and political shenanigans
that can be pulled to circumvent the list, but
as I said before, it's a powerful weapon.
Have you got, say, twenty or thirty thousand
dollars for a lawsuit?"

"No."

"Does the Raptor Coalition have that kind of money?"

"I don't know, but Daryl Moore, a biologist at Three Buttes Community College, mentioned that the coalition is talking about an injunction, so maybe they do have the money."

"Okay, that's a start," the professor said, checking his watch and fingering his plane ticket for Melbourne. "Let the coalition work on the environmental aspects of the problem, since that takes a high level of technical expertise in the natural sciences and the ability to move rapidly. Also, very few federal projects have ever been stopped purely on environmental considerations. You concentrate on the route, try to show why the proposed route is not the optimum one. That's your best strategy. Listen, Mr. McMillan, I'm catching a plane for Australia in less than two hours, so I have to run now. Good luck. I'll have my secretary send you the materials I talked about earlier, which is a detailed, rigorous approach to analyzing route selection, and call me again if you need to, anytime."

"Thanks very much, Professor Weinstein. It looks a little bleak, but you've been very helpful."

"Glad to be of some use. Hang in there. The bastards hate intelligence and commitment. They're not prepared to deal with those qualities. Let me warn you, though, this kind of thing can get rough. There's a lot of money at stake, and that's all they care about. I generally wade into these battles figuring they'll get at least an R rating. Gotta go. Good luck."

Rough. The professor had said it could get rough. It started to turn that way four days later when word got around that Daryl Moore and the Raptor Coalition were trying to block the new road because of some damn birds. And that Carlisle McMillan was spending a lot of time in the Falls City Library, studying all the documents related to the Avenue of the High Plains and intending to do what he could to prevent the highway from coming through.

Carlisle's mailbox was run over on a Wednesday night. The following day, an anonymous letter arrived: "GO BACK TO CALIFORNIA, FAG! YOU'RE NOT WANTED

HERE." A gravelly, ominous voice on the phone that same night whispered, "Better keep that cat of yours inside."

"Bill, *what on earth is going on out there*?" Cal Akers of the United States Chamber of Commerce was on the phone to Bill Flanigan, director of the High Plains Development Corporation in Falls City. "I got a call two hours ago from the senator, and he's all worked up about birds in the highway route and some carpenter who's causing trouble for us. What's happening?"

"It's hard to know where to start, Cal. A guy named Carlisle McMillan moved here from California a while back, heaven only knows why, and built a new house directly in the right-of-way. Actually, it was an old house he completely rebuilt. Of course, he didn't know the highway would be coming right up through his toilet seat. Guess he did an incredible job on the place, that's what the *Observer*, the Falls City paper, said. Called him a great craftsman in the article. Something on the order of two or three hundred people went to an open house at his place. Now half the doctors and lawyers in the state want him to do work for them. That's one thing."

"Screw the carpenter, this . . . what the hell's his name again? Miller?"

"McMillan. Carlisle McMillan."

"Okay, McMillan. We'll bury his rear end under six feet of eminent domain mixed with asphalt, and he won't know what hit him. Rest easy, Bill, that's not a problem."

"Well, the locals seem to think they can handle it in their own way. Feelings up there are running high against McMillan, and apparently there've been threats of violence against him."

"Bill, why is it we're always dealing with cretins? That kind of junk solves nothing and just brings a lot of bad publicity. See if you can convince 'em of that. Tell 'em to back off. McMillan can be dealt with. What else we got?"

"Seems while our man from California was building his house, he noticed some kind of unusual birds across the road from him in a little grove. Turns out it's a hawk that everyone thought was extinct."

"Aw, shit." Cal Akers's commitment to Christ and better living sometimes slipped in high-tension moments. "Is the hawk on the endangered species list?"

"I don't know."

"Eminent domain is one thing, an endangered species is something altogether different. The Tellico Dam project down in Tennessee got held up for four years because of the snail darter. How come we didn't know about this before? Just a minute, I've got the environmental impact statement in my files. Hang on while I dig it out." Silence, except for the soft crackle of pages turning twelve hundred miles away. "Okay, I'm scanning the document. There's a mention of Indian mounds, but they're on private land owned by this guy Ray Dargen. He's in our camp, so that's not a problem. I can't see anything about birds. When did he discover them?"

"Not long ago, from what I understand. A few months, maybe."

"The draft environmental impact statement was done quietly about a year ago, so that's why these hawks aren't mentioned. Besides, most of those statements are whitewash jobs anyway. Let me call the Fish and Wildlife Service and get back to you.

Keep the faith. I'll call you as soon as I can find out something."

"Okay, thanks, Cal. Oh, I almost forgot to mention this radical environmental outfit called EWU. . . ."

While Akers and Flanigan were talking, Carlisle was driving past the High Plains Development Corporation on his way to Salamander. He was grim, dug in, and determined to go on with this war forever, if that's what it took.

Carlisle McMillan may have been determined, but the following people were furious approaching apoplexy: Cal Akers of the United States Chamber of Commerce, Bill Flanigan of the High Plains Development Corporation, Jerry Gravatt and five other governors, twelve senators, members of the U.S. House of Representatives too numerous to mention, Canadian economic development officials, various oil and trucking company executives, cement contractors, various unions, nearly all of Yerkes County, and everyone else having a stake in the Avenue of the High Plains.

And they were all mad at Carlisle McMil-

Ian. He built a famous house in the path of their highway, didn't he? He discovered the T-hawks, didn't he? And he told that professor, Daryl Moore, at Twin Buttes Community College about the birds, didn't he do that, too? And then Moore had contacted an outfit called the Raptor Coalition, which now was asking for an injunction to stop construction of the highway until the hawks could be considered immediately for endangered species protection. If the hawks were given such status, and they surely would if the lawsuit was successful, the highway might be stopped, period, or at least require a massive redesign requiring enough time that funding might disappear. Then there was talk that McMillan had been studying the entire highway report and intended to challenge the route on grounds nobody had even thought of so far. The highway supporters' grievances were funneled into a giant vat, churning there and flowing downward and out a lower spout, where they emerged with the force of a combined virulence, all of it running directly toward Carlisle McMillan.

Ray Dargen, businessman-developer, was also mad, truculence incarnate with a diamond ring on its right pinky. Fifteen years earlier, an old man named Williston had found trace elements of gold in a creek near Wolf Butte. The county assayer owed Dargen a favor and had called him the same day Williston came to the assayer's office. Dargen then bought the claim from Williston for $3,000. Eventually, under the Mining Law of 1872, Dargen had been able to purchase Wolf Butte plus 1,500 acres surrounding it for almost nothing. That had turned out to be a little tricky, since the Indians objected to the transfer of public land containing burial mounds into private hands, but Ray Dargen used his political connections and got it done.

Rocks falling from the butte crushed the first crew of mining engineers he sent out there. Ray Dargen had not been moved. As he said to his wife, "The idiots should've known better than to camp that close to the cliff."

A second crew was more cautious, finished the work, and reported to Dargen that the gold had come from a small vein not worth the cost it would take to mine it. They had also told him there was evidence of ceremonial fires on the butte and strange symbols carved into the rock up there, not to mention what sounded like wings late at night when they were in their tents. But Ray Dargen was interested in gold, not what he had called "Indian charms and other whoopee."

So he was stuck with 1,500 acres of rolling, rocky, dry land, and he rasped his teeth whenever he thought of all that worthless ground just lying out there with nobody else around dumb enough to buy it from him. The idea of being in business was to make money, not to spend money. That's how he saw it, and he was still paying taxes on worthless property.

Two years after he bought the land, there had been quite a stir about the Indian mounds on the other side of the butte, on property he owned. The anthropologist had seemed harmless enough when he asked permission to survey and possibly excavate the site, and Ray Dargen was busy with other projects, so Dargen had given written permission for the work to proceed but said to keep him posted on what they were doing. Then it gradually occurred to him that somehow money could be made out of all this sacred Indian ground stuff. Too bad about the anthropologist falling from a butte and getting killed a while later, but that break in the action had given him time to withdraw his permission and boot the scientific types out of there.

He hadn't known what to do about those Indian mounds, but it occurred to him there was a way they could be used to make a buck, and the Avenue of the High Plains had given him an idea. He would get the ground rezoned for commercial activity and put up a theme park he would call Indian Mysteryland. Excavate some of the mounds, build a little museum to house the artifacts, and hire a curator to conduct tours and tell ghost stories. Hook the tourists off the new highway to stop and look at bones and pots and hear the ghost stories, and while they were doing that, they could eat at the restaurant he would build and put their kiddies on the rides Ray Dargen would have waiting for them.

A big outfit in the East was already designing the carnival rides and had sent him proposed names for them: Buffalo Hunt, War Party, Pow Wow, and Bad Medicine. He liked the names, along with two other suggestions the consultants made, namely Mysteryland Maze: Fun for All Ages, and the

Pioneer Chapel, where quickie marriages might be arranged if certain state laws could be tweaked a bit. The possibilities stretched before him like the high plains themselves, including stagecoach rides with mock Indian attacks and the construction of a motel on the site. Call it the Wigwam Motel. The units would be made of poured concrete and shaped like tepees. He'd construct an underground restaurant and name it the Ceremonial Chamber. Motel logo: "Stay in a Tepee, Eat Underground."

It was all coming together. A gift shop called Geronimo's Hideout—Jewelry and Moccasins for the Entire Family. One of his associates reminded him that Geronimo was an Apache, not a Sioux, and operated in the Southwest.

Dargen looked at him, chafing with impatience at such details, and said, "Well, what the hell, we'll call it something different, then. Doesn't matter. Think the tourists'll know any different or give a crap, anyway?"

There was more. Ray Dargen had discovered that a robust trade in Indian artifacts existed, illicitly gained or otherwise, and was in contact with certain museums and private collectors, all of whom were interested in discreetly purchasing artifacts from Dargen's excavations. The artifacts plus the theme park plus the land he and his associates were secretly picking up along the route would turn the Avenue of the High Plains into his personal mother lode after all. As always, he would bend things to the will of his avarice. It was that kind of bold thinking that had made this country what it was and is. That's how Ray Dargen saw it.

And then, *then,* just when it looked as if there were a different kind of gold in that property, some outside agitator named McMillan had come along and with a couple of others was fighting the highway. Dargen's first stop was to see Ralph Geigle, president of Twin Buttes Community College.

"Ralph, this biology teacher of yours, or whatever he is—Moore, I think that's his name—has got to get his mind right on this highway thing. Tell him there're lots of birds in the world for him to look at. You can also tell him I'm on the board of directors at the bank where he's trying to get a personal loan, something about getting his mother into a nursing home. Be sure and tell him that, Ralph. Hey, it's about time for your fund drive for that new building, isn't it?"

"Yes, it is, Ray. In fact, I wanted to talk with you about the fund-raising drive. And don't worry, I'll have a friendly chat with Moore. Besides, the faculty here doesn't have tenure like at the state universities."

"Good. I knew I could count on you, Ralph. If our wives keep going down to the capital and buying those expensive dresses for bridge tournaments, we've got to have a little more economic development around here. A man's got to cover his expenses, right?"

Ray Dargen stood up and shook Ralph Geigle's hand. "Let me know what you need for your fund drive, and I'll have my secretary put a check in the mail."

When Senator Harlan Sterk arrived in Falls City two days later for his monthly Listening Post Weekend with his constituents, most of it was spent with a constituent named Ray Dargen.

"Calm down, Ray. These things take time. There are such matters as law and procedure, you know."

"Senator, I'm not interested in law, and I'm not interested in procedure. What I'm interested in is business. You have any idea how much money I got tied up in properties along this highway that's supposed to be built? Enough to keep you in office for a long while. My contribution to your last campaign was somewhere over twenty thousand, and I don't give that kind of money simply because I'm interested in making democracy work better. You know that, I know that. Now our pal Bill Flanigan over there at High Plains Development tells me that Senator Jack Wheems, who's spearheading this thing, has engineers looking to see if the highway route can be changed to miss those tweety birds. Harlan, I want you to guarantee me that's not going to happen. I expect to hear from you early next week on this."

The chief engineer had studied Wheems's request carefully for a possible rerouting of the highway. "Senator Wheems, we've taken another look at the route for the Avenue of the High Plains. As it turns out, we can miss the area where the birds are causing a problem. But a big road is a system, change one part and a lot of other things have to change. It'll mean moving the highway about forty miles west of Livermore and Falls City, which, incidentally, our original calculations indicated would be a more efficient route anyhow, both in terms of construction costs and vehicle travel time, since the current route requires what amounts to a detour just to include Falls City and Livermore. Shall we go ahead and work up the alternative that misses the birds?"

"No. My good friend Senator Sterk has real problems with a route change. Let it go for now." Jack Wheems put the phone back in its cradle and turned to an aide. "Get Harlan Sterk on the phone."

"Senator Sterk is in Florida. He left a number, but he said he might be hard to reach. Want me to try?"

"No. I'll talk with Cal Akers over at the Chamber."

Akers came on the line. "Good afternoon, Senator. What's up?"

"I can't raise Harlan, so I'm talking to you. You can tell your pals out in High Plains Hickup that we've dropped the idea for a route change in the Avenue. But I also want you to tell them the funding for this highway was delicate to start with, and some members of the House Public Works and Transportation Committee are beginning to get shaky in their support of it, and if your pals aren't careful, we're not going to get any highway at all."

"Okay. I just talked to Bill Flanigan at High Plains Development. Seems there's been some violence or threats of violence involving this fellow Carlisle McMillan. Flanigan's trying to find out what's going on."

"For the love of Christ, Cal, don't those people know how to do anything right? No wonder they're falling apart."

"Tighten your seat belt, Senator. It gets even more interesting, if that's the right word. Ever hear of an outfit named EWU? It's pronounced 'E-wuu,' stands for Earth Warriors United or something like that. Well, neither did I until Flanigan called. It's a radical environmental group from somewhere out west, and they're itching to get into this. Three of them rolled into Salamander in an old van two days ago and started poking around. Rumor is they're going to blow up the Salamander water tower if the highway goes through the T-hawk habitat, and that's just for starters. I hear one of them said they might do it anyway, just to get people's attention focused on what's happening out there.

"The leader of this outfit supposedly is a guy named Riddick who's suspected of wheeling barrels of used motor oil into a Texas oil company executive's house last year while the executive was floating around in his swimming pool. When that little evening concluded, there was oil all over everything, including the executive and his wife. Riddick's not here with the EWU people in Yerkes County, however, not right now, at least. From what I hear, he's been involved in some other mischief as well. Word is he's a real bad fellow."

"Well, if that sort of thing starts happening along with the birds and Dargen's shenanigans, I can just about guarantee the works committee's going to think about sending this road money elsewhere, and there'll be nothing I can do about it. I'll get the G-men over at the Bureau on this EWU outfit. When does the public information meeting on the highway come up in Yerkes County?"

"Mid-February. It's in Livermore. Flanigan expects McMillan to cause trouble at the Livermore meeting."

"Who the hell are we dealing with, Cal? Who exactly is this McMillan, anyway?"

"Flanigan says he's really tough, Senator. He's quiet, smart, believes in what he's doing, and does his homework."

"Can't we squeeze him somehow? Financially, maybe? How's he earn his living? Who's he got his loans with?"

"We're thinking along the same lines, Senator. I asked Flanigan just that. Flanigan looked into it, says McMillan's debt-free except for a little money he owes on his property, a thousand or two. He's a builder—master carpenter, they say. It's hard to boycott him because he's too damn good at what he does, and he works for himself. The doctors and lawyers in Falls City want the work on their places done just so, and they think he's the only one around who can do it. He's out of the normal economic channels, in other words.

"Now listen to this, Senator. You know about this guy Ray Dargen. Well, Flanigan says the standard joke about him out there is that Dargen wasn't born, he rode in on an oil slick, full-grown and waving contracts.

Apparently that's easy to believe. Not only has Dargen been buying up land along the highway route for more than a year, using inside information he has access to as a member of the State Highway Commission, but apparently he also used some heavy-handed tactics on a guy who has been helping McMillan, some community college teacher.

"You know what happened? McMillan drove over to Dargen's office in Falls City a few days ago, walked in, leaned on his desk, and said real softly, so quietly that only Dargen's secretary heard it, 'Mr. Dargen, I know the fix is on, and before this is over, you'll be looking at five to ten in the slammer. You've laid out the game rules, no questions asked, no quarter given. Fair enough, padre, we'll play by your rules.'

"No kidding, Senator, that's what he said. And you know what? Ray Dargen's been pretty quiet since that happened, according to Flanigan. Apparently McMillan has suspicions about what's going on with the juggling of the highway route and Dargen using inside information to make land purchases along the route that benefit him and his partners, and he's going to push it hard, maybe right up all our asses."

"For God's sake, Cal." The senator turned quiet for a moment, thinking. "You know, in any other circumstances, I think I could grow to like this McMillan. As it stands right now, we've got to nail him good or shut him down. And the best way to do that is simply to get the highway built as fast as possible, then everybody'll forget about birds and Dargen and McMillan and go back to work."

When Jack Wheems finished talking to Cal Akers, he glanced at the calendar—six days to the end of January—and walked over to his window in the Senate Office Building, staring at the traffic below. Rush hour was almost over. He wondered what a carpenter named Carlisle McMillan was doing out in the high plains at that time of day.

What Carlisle was doing was reading a letter from Governor Jerry Gravatt.

Dear Mr. McMillan:
    Let me begin by assuring you that
I share your concern for a healthy en-

vironment where all of us can live in harmony with nature and build a prosperous high plains economy at the same time. I should very much like to discuss our mutual concerns. Therefore, at the suggestion of Mr. Ray Dargen, State Highway Commissioner, I've asked my secretary to contact you to set up an appointment where we can all sit down and reach a happy compromise on an issue that needs to be resolved. If we can just get together, I'm hopeful there is cause for optimism.

Yours truly,
Jerry
Hon. Jerry Gravatt, Governor

Dumptruck turned his head and watched with considerable interest as the crumpled letter flew toward Carlisle McMillan's kitchen wastebasket. Earlier that day, a group of men had disturbed the big tomcat when they rapped on the door. Carlisle had stepped out on the porch and looked at the four-member delegation from the Livermore Civic Boosters Club.

They shuffled their feet and got around

to introducing themselves, one of them acting as spokesman.

"Mr. McMillan, you're a businessman,
just like we are, and this highway will mean a
lot of carpentry work because of economic
growth. Don't you think you're being just a
little unreasonable?"

Carlisle stared at them, couldn't believe
their naïveté. Were they really this dumb
about what he was doing, about what was
going on with the T-hawks? Obviously, they
were, and Carlisle felt sorry for them, in a
way. He breathed twice, looked at the sky,
then back at the overcoats and said, "No."
After that, he nodded politely and closed the
door.

As Governor Gravett's letter hit the wastebasket rim and balanced there for an instant
before dropping in, Carlisle heard the sound
of breaking glass in his greenhouse. At first
he thought a squirrel had nose-dived through
it. Then he heard a rifle shot and went to the
floor, crawling rapidly and dragging a frightened and confused Dumptruck from the windowsill. He held the squirming cat and stayed
low as a third shot hit the greenhouse. After
that it was silent, but Carlisle stayed on the
floor for another few minutes before lifting

himself up to look out a corner of the window. Nothing.

The professor at Stanford had said it would get rough, maybe an R rating. He had been right. After looking at the damage and carrying in plants, Carlisle shut the greenhouse door and sat by his woodstove, wondering whether or not it was worth his effort to repair the greenhouse. Dumptruck jumped onto his lap and settled down, purring.

The following day, a Yerkes County sheriff's deputy examined Carlisle's greenhouse. "Looks like someone fired rifle shots from the road. The shell casings in the ditch are from a .30-06, fairly potent weapon. I'd say they hit what they were aiming for. The boys around here are pretty fair country marksmen, and if they'd been shooting at you, we probably wouldn't be talking right now. We'll look into it, but at the moment, you're more than a little unpopular in these parts, Mr. McMillan, and I'd watch my step if I were you."

CHAPTER SIXTEEN

One of those reaching for Susanna Benteen, and there had been many who tried and nearly as many who failed, was George Riddick. That was some years before the Avenue of the High Plains was announced.

The nomadic life has its own codes, and those who have traveled loose and free sometime in their lives, with no purpose except looking for one, come to know the signs and symbols. A certain evidence of fatigue brought on by the miles and erratic sleep, the scuffed shoes and the old knapsack beside your chair in a desert café where the afternoon sunlight angles in through dusty windows. The way you drink your coffee—slowly—and count your cigarettes and count your change—carefully—making sure there is enough, what you need for the bus that will swing open its door with a sigh and take you on to the next place, and the next after that.

In Topock, Arizona, on the California line, Susanna Benteen had waited for a bus that never came. Gracie's Cafe, where the bus stopped, would close at five, and it was already four. The place was empty except for Gracie and Susanna and the big man with a black beard, who drank coffee and twice looked in Susanna's direction, noticing the signs and symbols of the road.

A wall phone rang behind the cash register. Gracie answered, then walked over to where Susanna was sitting. "Missy, I'm sorry, but the bus broke down in Kingman and won't be coming until tomorrow. There's no place to stay in Topock, but if you can make it over to Needles, you might find a room."

The road was like that, and Susanna Benteen had learned to roll with it and was trying to think this through. She had been in similar predicaments many times in her life. The overbooked Pan Am flight out of Delhi on a Friday night, with the next available flight not until Tuesday. The train that had stopped at a country station fifty miles south of Brussels, the passengers forced off because the Brussels terminal was already filled with stranded trains during a winter storm. The time her father's truck had broken down a hundred miles from Olduvai.

The teapot before her was almost empty. Susanna poured the last of the hot water into her cup and considered her options, which were close to zero. Outside, three men sat on an old car, laughing, spitting into the dirt, looking in at her now and then. A winter sundown was only thirty minutes away, the Mojave light dropping fast. Traveling alone had its benefits, but for a woman this kind of situation was not one of them. A man could walk outside, kick a few tires, and offer to pay one of the boys for a ride over to Needles. A woman found risk in that, and with good reason. Unfair, but the way things were. Susanna didn't like it, but she understood it.

The big man at the counter walked over to her. "Look, I'm headed for Flagstaff, but I'll be glad to run you over to Needles if you're stuck."

She looked up at him. He'd been polite to Gracie when he had ordered coffee. Some risk. She measured it, looked at him again, and said, "Thank you. I'd very much appreciate that. . . . I could pay you something for your trouble."

"No need for that. It's not far. My name is George Riddick."

He picked up her knapsack and held the door for her, and they walked to his van. The boys outside kicked their tires, spat, and winked at one another, malignant and knowing. As Susanna and the man walked past, one of them said, in a voice intentionally made loud enough for Susanna to hear, "Good thing you made your move on that cute little piece when you did, beard. We were just one step away from it."

Riddick put down Susanna's knapsack, turned to the man, and slapped him hard across the face, hard enough to make him stumble and nearly fall. The other two straightened from where they'd been leaning against the car, the hormones beginning to chug upward: a fallen companion, honor in the desert, all of that. Riddick looked at them, grinned, and waited. When they didn't move, he picked up the knapsack, opened the van door for Susanna, and put the knapsack by her feet. She was shaking a little.

The man had acted with a raw, instant violence that unnerved her.

The van smelled of cigar smoke. Tools were scattered about, old coffee cups tossed on the backseat. He turned the ignition key and looked over at her. "Sorry about that garbage with the yahoos, but I've got a short fuse when it comes to smart-asses."

The tightness in her stomach eased a little, but not much. She clutched her hands in her lap and decided talk might help. "Do you live in Flagstaff?"

"No, south of there in the mountains, near a place called Sedona. Ever hear of it?"

"Yes. I was there once, just passing through. It was quite beautiful."

"Where you headed?"

"New Haven . . . Connecticut. I lived there before my father died, and I have a few estate matters yet to settle."

"I can take you as far as Flagstaff if you want. You'll be able to get a bus out of there with no problem."

Three hours later, they made the turn south outside of Flagstaff, and Susanna went on with George Riddick to his place in the mountains. In the two months she spent there, he did not touch her or even try.

George Riddick lived an ascetic's life born of an anger that never left him, and sex was no longer part of that life.

But through the years, she knew he was out there taking care of the business that mattered to him. She was always aware of a dark presence roaming around behind the occasional newspaper article reporting some horrific violence done to the people and organizations Riddick hated. Neither the rumors nor the articles ever mentioned his name, yet she knew it was him, an avenging wrath from the galaxies in an old Dodge van with balding tires and rust dripping from the fenders. Remington 12-gauge pump shotgun with a shortened barrel and a 9-millimeter Beretta pistol, both wrapped in oilskin and riding behind his driver's seat where he could reach them easily. Riddick in stained khaki pants and a worn flannel shirt, paratrooper boots, and his black ball cap with "Earth Warrior" hand stitched on the crown. Old army field jacket with a strip of electrician's tape above the right breast pocket covering the space where his name was stenciled. And the cold cigar in his mouth and the heavy, gray-flecked black beard that grazed his chest when he nodded his head ever so slightly.

Along the thread of environmental radicalism, from quiet protest to civil disobedience to hard violence, George Riddick had no comparison. He was off the scale. Susanna had come to that understanding in the time she knew him, and the savage, relentless intensity with which he pursued his ends had frightened and yet fascinated her in a way that was almost sexual.

The Sierra Club? He called them politicians, Kens and Barbies in $300 Patagonia jackets. How about PlanetFire and their summer rallies, their botched attempts to blow up transmission lines running from power plants in the Southwest? Riddick scorned them as dilettantes, monkey wrenchers who read Edward Abbey and played games in the shadows, assaulting technological manifestations rather than the destroyers themselves.

He once said to Susanna, "I am what comes along when everything else has failed. There's nothing very admirable about what I do, it just has to be done. If prevention is not possible, then retribution is next best, and if the retribution is certain enough and hard enough when it comes, then eventually it may become a kind of prevention based on fear."

Riddick had been out there before, putting his life on the line. Two purple hearts and other medals, all of which he had thrown into the garbage years ago. He had been there all right, leeches and snakes and malaria and little men in black who carried their weapons and rice down trails worn smooth beneath the Cambodian jungle canopy. In the early days, the M-16s hadn't worked right, jamming at critical moments, so Riddick arranged to have a 12-gauge Remington pump shotgun smuggled to him. He sawed the barrel short and used that, crawled through the jungle and became a killing machine, making the world safe for economic development and biotechnology.

George Riddick had no plans beyond the afternoon before him or the night or the day following. Nothing more to do than spend his life running symbolic hoses from the outlet pipes and smokestacks of the defilers of nature back to the executive offices.

He had ways of doing that, George Riddick did. Ever drink a large glass of influenza-green number two from your outlet pipe? Ever breathe plastic bags full of dog-hockey brown taken from the top of your factory's smokestack, the one you stuck a short way across the border in Matamoros to avoid the tougher U. S. environmental laws?

Ever eat a slice of yellow, maggoty dolphin your tuna-fishing fleet suffocated in its nets a week before? If you had run into George Riddick in the right circumstances, you would have, for certain you would have done that. The executive world of good hotels and neat annual reports would not have prepared you to deal with the malevolent, elemental force that was George Riddick. And you would have been well motivated to drink sincerely, breathe deeply, and chew intently. Motivated by the Beretta poked in your crotch, by the sound of your twelve-cylinder Jaguar being bludgeoned to its original molecules, and by the sight of your wife gagging as she tried to swallow pieces of her mink coat while her head was being shaved.

George Riddick had left behind him a ragged and random trail of traumatized corporate executives and government administrators, many of whom had retired after their only encounter with him. In good resorts of the Caribbean, word about Riddick passed from beach chair to beach chair. The villa at Jumby Bay cost $1,400 a night and kept the native islanders repulsed, but nothing could save you from Riddick if he decided to come. That's what they said, rum punch in hand, shuddering a little in the warm sunlight.

George Riddick understood that rich people seldom were affected by the problems they created. Others were, people and animals alike, but lawyers fought it out in abstract terms far from the everyday reality of designer executive offices. George Riddick made sure you suffered the consequences of your decisions, physically and emotionally. They said he was an unanticipated echo of the things you had done and that you would think hard before doing them again after his violation of your spirit and your manhood.

As Riddick said to Susanna Benteen, "I simply provide an additional outcome to the bad choices certain people make."

Yes, George Riddick had been out there, and he was still out there with a sticker pasted across his dashboard that read PUN-

ISH THE BASTARDS! If you breached the standards he had raised single-handedly, he would be coming. Not for a while, but he would be coming your way . . . eventually. And as he passed through the Mojave from time to time, he remembered Susanna Benteen and wished his mind had been in a place where he could have had such a woman for his own.

CHAPTER SEVENTEEN

THE OLD MAN:

"As I came to find out, Carlisle McMillan and I shared at least one other conviction in addition to liking Gally Deveraux, which was neither of us cared much for flocks of men in matching blazers, calling themselves community representatives or something like that. You know 'em, easy to spot. They're the guys with shit-eatin' grins in grainy black-and-white newspaper photographs, always standing behind a mayor or governor or some other suit at ribbon cuttings in honor of recently constructed shrines to human ingenuity, Mammon, and the Army Corps of Engineers.

"I dislike 'em mostly because they're always so goddamned cheerful. Don't get me wrong, there's a severe shortage of happiness in the world, and I'm all for good cheer. But if you look real close at those pictures, you can see l-u-c-r-e printed right across their carefully flossed teeth. It comes through even in bad photographs. Their abundant cheer flows not from seeing a good sunrise over the Little Sal or simply by being given another day of life, but from the sweet dreams of money with which they'll do something to make even more money. Just what they're going to do with all this money is not clear to me and maybe even not to them.

"The other thing I notice is that these ribbon cuttings almost always have something to do with the destruction of nature. The little matching-blazer army is 'specially fond of projects such as highways, dams, nuclear waste dumps, and gigantic bridges, real big schemes of any kind that are being paid for by taxpayers other than themselves and seem to do great amounts of damage to nature. They use the word *progress* a lot in talking about these matters, though that's recently been replaced somewhat by *economic development.*

"They only wear their precious blazer outfits when the bag's outta the cat. That is, when the project has been completed or is too far along to stop. In the early stages, they're involved in espionage and plotting, so they keep a low profile. That way they're able to surprise the general population with the wonder of these ventures when the projects emerge full-blown and ready for construction. Moreover, surprise has the value of cannonballing the projects right through the guts and out the other side of anyone having the impertinence to raise questions about the merits of a particular majestic enterprise relative to its cost."

I smiled at the old man's words and checked the small tape recorder I had laid next to his breakfast plate. I had seen the blazers. Everyone had.

The old man chewed his over-easy eggs, took a sip of coffee, and continued. "Their main forum for handling opposition of any kind is an exercise in phony democracy called the public hearing. I went to one of these meetings once when they was thinking about putting a big dam across the Little Sal. See, plans are made by bureaucrats, engineers, and selected movers and shakers. After everything's already been decided, a public hearing is called for the purpose of what's gracefully labeled 'soliciting citizen input.'

"But the big thinkers don't really want input from citizens. If common folks had too much input and asked hard questions about who really stands to benefit from dams and highways, the things might never get built. The hearing is just a slick way of getting people to *think* they've had some say, which they have, except their *input* has nothing to do with the final *output* and therefore is of no value, not to mention being useless.

"The planners know this, so it's kind of a delicate balancing act to con people into thinking they've had a voice in the matter without letting 'em screw up the big dreams. That's why the local leaders sit in the audience at these hearings and pretend they're just regular citizens. They're also watching for any real troublemakers so they can identify them and report to the main propeller heads, who are from out of town.

And I can tell you, Carlisle McMillan got their attention right away, because Carlisle, unlike most of the sheep, is not cowed by anybody, seems to me. More than that, he absolutely hates experts. And understand, experts are the key to the entire scam of the type we're talking about here. At the hearings, ordinary people ask sort of simple questions, like 'Couldn't Denver find another source of water rather than damming up the Little Sal and pumping all the way from the high plains to the eastern slope? It's a pretty good fishing river, and some of us would hate to see it spoiled.'

"At that point, the suits go into high gear. It's all been intricately choreographed, 'cause there's too much profit riding on this to leave anything to chance. The moderator of the hearing says something like 'I'll turn that question over to our expert, Larry Software, a PhD in engineering from the Massachusetts Institute of Technocracy with two thousand years of experience in such matters, a staff of four hundred and sixty graduates of Ivy League schools, and a computer bigger'n this town.'

"Dr. Larry, who's at the front of the room, has about twenty volumes bound with plastic spirals within arm's reach. These are collectively called *The Report.* Expert Larry rises, puts his hand on the stack, and says, 'I hope all of you have had time to read and consider *The Report.* On pages one sixteen through two ninety of volume twelve is the benefit-cost analysis for the project. Of course, in volumes fifteen and sixteen, along with some useful notes in the two-volume appendix to *The Report,* is our multiple-criteria decision model, in which we have included our set of alternatives, our prioritized criteria, and the utility weights we have assigned to these criteria, along with estimated outcomes of each alternative in light of the criteria. Oh yes, you may also have noticed our discount rate justification in volume eleven. Using all of this, we ran one hundred and eighty-two million simulations on our giant Crawdad 290FXZ computer, constantly adjusting and testing our probability estimates and examining the model's sensitivity to parameter changes. Clearly, the only feasible alternative is to dam the bejesus out of the Little Sal so the people of Denver can have all the water they need for car washing and theme parks.' "

The old man shook his head. "I ask you now: Is the citizen who likes to fish the Little Sal smarter than Larry Software, his Crawdad 290FXZ, and his cast of hundreds? Hell, no. In the course of Larry's mental enema, our fisherman is more than sorry he ever got to his feet. He hasn't read *The Report*

'cause he didn't know it existed, and anyway, he'd rather be bass fishing than plow-
ing through that stuff, so he wouldn't have
read it even if he had known it existed. But
he stands there, nodding from time to time
so he won't look too stupid, all the while being secretly aware that what Dr. Larry's really
saying is, 'I'm sticking this project right up
your sweet ass, you little toad, so sit down
and shut up.'

"Besides that, the governor is all for it,
which the moderator mentions about every
three minutes, so whatever project we're
talking about must be all right. The governor
wouldn't be governor if he didn't know what
he was doing, right? Also, some folks feel
generally uncomfortable in opposing things
a smart man like the governor supports, as if
it were sort of unpatriotic to behave that
way, and they'll buy the whole shitaree, regardless of what it is, on that basis alone.

"Trouble was, as I said before, Carlisle
McMillan was not awed by experts. Quite
the opposite. He'd seen these counterfeit
proceedings before in California. So when
the newspaper our state counts on lifted off
in ecstasy about the new highway, Carlisle
took one look at the maps on the second

page and knew he had trouble. In addition to a general map showing the proposed route from New Orleans to Calgary, our reporter included a series of smaller maps that broke the state down into sections. And there it was: a nice, fat line right through Carlisle's thirty acres northwest of Salamander and the grove across the road from him.

"Accompanying the maps was some of the most breathless prose you'd care to read, courtesy of the state's Department of Economic Development, describing in some detail the almost overwhelming benefits the new road would bring us. One main idea underlying the project was to provide a highway link between the terminus of an oil pipeline that would be built from as yet unexplored Arctic oil fields all the way to Calgary. Then tanker trucks would haul the cheap crude from Calgary to refineries in Texas and New Orleans, the economies of which had fallen on hard times. Boy, that was brilliant. Use lots of oil to haul oil, creating your own demand in providing the supply.

"Of course, there were other much advertised benefits, such as getting farmers' grain and livestock to markets and providing

more incentives for giant Tokyo-based elec-
tronics corporations to locate plants out
here, which, as we all know, they was just
itching to do, except for the lack of a modern road system and rattlesnakes crawling
around on the sunburnt greens of our nine-
hole golf course. Tourism, it was suggested,
would explode, as people desiring to visit
Salamander and its many attractions, such
as Leroy's and the post office, could now
get here more easily.

"Some even mentioned the possibility
of putting a collection of boutiques in
Lester's TV and Appliance building, if the old
codger—that being me—living on the second floor could be evicted. And these bud-
ding entrepreneurs were assured by lawyer
Birney that, indeed, residents of Codger-
dom have no rights of any kind regarding
anything, and eviction was no problem.

"I had that part all figured out, however,
and wasn't worried in case it came to eviction by force. I had a plan. Among the sou-
venirs collected during my waltz across Europe in the winter of '44 was a live hand
grenade. Did it still work? I was guessing it
did. Even if it didn't, I figured the eyeball

shock factor would be almost as good as an actual explosion.

"I could visualize it all, dwelt on it. The plan was as follows. I'd be sitting on the steps to my apartment, grenade concealed in my lap, pin pulled out. I'd be holding down the lever on the grenade, and I'd have a string leading from the grenade to a broomstick hidden behind me. I estimated Fearless Fred Mumblypeg, town cop and eviction master, would be in the lead, coming up the stairs with lawyer Birney right behind him, followed in turn by all the right-thinking commercial wizards about to lose their financial asses on a dumb idea.

"I imagined hearing Fred's voice, 'We have a warrant . . .' Everybody would be packed in the stairwell behind him, looking up at me. Just as he'd get the words going, I'd swing out my little present on the broom handle so it was dangling right in front of them and yell *'Shit on a stick!'* I also thought about following that with *'Kill 'em all, let God sort it out!'* My old platoon sergeant used to say that second part, though I admitted to myself it was a little overused, and I was hoping I'd think of something better at the moment of truth when the storm troopers came up my stairs. I figured I would, since I'd be watching Fred go to his knees while lawyer Birney was trampling the fat red blazers behind him, and all of that would have been inspirational, I'll tell you that.

"But there I go digressing again. The point is that the list of good things expected to flow from this great highway was virtually endless and was repeated almost every day by our state newspaper, supplemented on Wednesdays by a semiliterate piece in the weekly *Salamander Sentinel,* making even more extravagant promises, though it printed the maps upside down two weeks running.

"Now, the local excitement over what they named the Avenue of the High Plains was understandable, since Salamander was dying. I'd been conducting a death watch for fifteen years, though the decline had set in long before I began my observations. The real issue was whether anything could be done to save the patient. My personal opinion, and understand I ain't no expert at all on these matters, was that nothing could be done. We were too far gone for resuscitation, kind of like a cinder: not quite ashes, but incapable of further combustion.

"And I felt bad about that. Salamander was a pretty good place at one time. Still is, in some ways. But it'd become increasingly clear to me that we'd borrowed our days out here ever since Eble Olson drove a stake into the ground in 1896 and named the town after the Little Sal, which in turn had been named by the horse soldiers. Those latter fellas swept through here waving the flag of Manifest Destiny and pretty much decimating the original inhabitants, clearing things out for the white settlers.

"In terms of historical context, I should point out the Indians were gutsy, but they weren't no match for the thirty-seven-millimeter revolving cannon invented by one Benjamin Berkeley Hotchkiss of Watertown, Connecticut, or the rapid-fire gun designed by Dr. Richard Jordan Gatling. On top of the firepower, there were broken treaties and land grabs that'd make Genghis Khan blush, not to mention the missionaries working to convince the heathen that Christianity was their true path to salvation, whatever that was.

"What really got the Indians, finally, was that we just took away their main resource by killing all the buffalo, completely wiping out the last herd of northern bison up on the Cannonball River in 1863 using the combined forces of the military, mercenaries, and the Sioux's old enemies from the woodlands, the Cree. Heck, the government even gave medals to the buffalo hunters for their role in helping to put down the Indian threat.

"Still, I remember what things used to be like when I was a boy out here in what at one time was called the West River Country. 'Specially I remember Saturday nights. The farmers and ranchers would come to town, make a stop at the local produce house to sell eggs or a few chickens for pocket money, then proceed along the street for groceries and haircuts and hardware and what-have-you. We used to call it daughter-and-egg night, since that's mostly what the farmers brought to Salamander.

"The town band would be playing in the little gazebo down at the park, and people would buy popcorn from the red, white, and blue wagon there, munching away while they listened to 'Stars and Stripes Forever' and other favorites. Kids'd be running around, old folks'd be talking, and in between was the complicated dance eventually leading to new family formation.

"All the while, however, the clock was ticking and the interest on our note was piling up, though none of us was aware of that. We just took it for granted that things would go on forever in a more or less happy fashion, only getting a little better over time through the miracles of agricultural chemistry and improved farm implements.

"With the band playing its version of 'Gary Owen,' which was Custer's old marching song, and the melodious hum of Main Street on Saturday nights, things seemed pretty good. We didn't have any idea the tallyman was coming toward us. He was lean and tough and gaunt in the face, but he was a long ways off, and we couldn't make him out yet.

"Understand, mister, this is triple-hard country. That's for sure. Thin soil, short grass, and scarce water. The early mapmakers didn't call this area the Great American Desert for no reason at all. Without the dreams of empire, it probably wouldn't have ever been settled. But the federal government picked up the flag of Manifest Destiny where the horse soldiers dropped it and handed it off to various fast guys who flipped it around, showing everybody the Jolly Roger on its backside.

"The feds stayed in the game, however, giving us land under various congressional acts, along with subsidies for high-priced irrigation systems and for crops that already were in a condition of surplus. Naturally, being bribed to do something, people tend to do it. And being encouraged to drain aquifers that take maybe a hundred years or more to get filled up again has a tendency to leave the aquifers empty after a time. Similar thing happens with soil when you let it blow away in the wind or wash into the rivers through bad farming practices and overgrazing. Problem is, there's some fundamental law at work when it comes to water and soil. It goes like this: When it's gone, there ain't no more, at least for a long while.

"A professor from an eastern college came out for a visit and said, 'It's all over, folks.' Told us, given what had been done to the land and water, we had maybe thirty years left, no more.

"He proposed turning this part of the Union into something called a 'buffalo commons,' the idea being that the feds ought to resettle people out of here, let the towns other than those along main highways just go back to nature, and populate the place with buffalo and other critters that could do a better job of managing the place than humans.

"Personally, I thought it was a pretty good idea. Of course, not everyone felt that way, and some of the boys threatened to *resettle the professor* if he didn't get his smart ass back to wherever his league of ivy was located. Bobby Eakins called the professor a head-egg and said all them thinkers were crazier'n shit. Bobby said he himself had been driving around the countryside in his Blazer and plenty of water was gushing from the irrigation systems.

"But the plain truth was that we'd used up the water, pretty well mangled the soil, and generally had caused a shower of destruction on the place. Still, the money from U.S. taxpayers kept on coming to us, for which we were sort of grateful and sort of embarrassed, all at the same time. Everybody knew these subsidies were nothing more than money doled out to people to keep 'em doing what they were doing when our beloved market system said they ought to stop doing what they're doing. Naturally, we objected to that way of thinking about it, since it sort of smelled like welfare, and we got short fuses out here about welfare chiselers and government interference in general. So we kind of disguise all of this through the use of terms like *agricultural programs* and *farm policy*."

I halted the old man's historical lecture while I turned over the recording tape. He went to the bathroom and returned with two fresh cups of coffee.

"I always have myself a good chuckle," he said, "at the debates in Congress over agricultural programs and the arguments involving what they like to call 'saving the family farm.' That creates kinda warm, fuzzy pictures in the minds of urbanites. You know, Gramps by the woodstove, chickens pecking around the barnyard, square dancing in the Town Hall on Friday nights, lemonade on the porch swing, the last refuge of old-time values, including something referred to as the *real* America.

"Actually, to my way of thinking, we're in the manufacturing business out here and have been for a long time. Pittsburgh makes steel, Seattle builds airplanes, we manufacture grain and meat. No difference between what we do and, say, oil refining or Detroit's assembly lines. Just visit any big cattle operation or the packing plant over in Falls City and watch 'em shred animals to pieces if you got any doubts about that. Axel Looker, for example, owned two thousand acres and rented another thousand. Axel didn't have no chickens pecking around his barnyard. Matter of fact, Axel didn't have no barnyard.

"What he did have was a new prefabbed ranch-style house, some prefabbed metal sheds for his big equipment, and a small forest of prefabbed silver MFS grain bins so he could store his grain and sell it at just the right time. And Axel wasn't worried, because if grain prices didn't get to where he wanted 'em, he just backed down and let the government take it off his hands. If prices did go up, however, he wasn't obliged to share any excess profits with other taxpayers.

"By the way, Axel's wife bought their eggs and frying chickens over in Livermore at the Piggly Wiggly, instead of locally at Webster's Jack and Jill. While she was shopping, Axel would be downtown, checking in at the brokerage office to see how the futures markets were doing. The Farm Bureau in particular doesn't like to talk about those things, preferring the Hollywood version of the lonely struggling farmer against the greedy banker, all the while the bureau's supporting programs driving the last few real family farmers and small towns to the wall.

"Along with farming and ranching, we're also in the resource extraction business in a funny kind of way. It seems to me that extraction is when you take something out and don't put anything back. So we've been using both soil and water at a clip far exceeding their natural replacement rates. That is, we're sort of in the mining business as a byproduct of our main activities. In this case, we're mining soil and water. Not too much worry about that, however, 'cause if the soil and water problems got too bad, we were all pretty certain the U.S. taxpayers would want to bail us out to save the family farm, even though we caused the problems in the first place.

"Fortunately, we've been pretty good at hiding all of that up until the last few years when some outsiders began asking rather pointed questions about our viability out here. Our congresspersons, however, have been real effective at selling the rest of America on the idea of preserving a bucolic life that don't exist anymore, maybe never did. It's a highly useful myth that's turned into an outright lie.

"Along with that bad news are all the other things that've been working against the Salamanders of the world. With agriculture getting bigger and bigger, due partly to the generosity of Congress and their flows of money out here, there are less country folks to produce kids and buy things. People of childbearing age leave, except for a few, and if you ain't got enough kids, you ain't got schools. And if you lose your schools, you've ripped out the heart of the community. The few remaining kids ride yellow buses long distances to endure what passes for education in these United States. So contrary to popular belief, the money just oozing its way out here don't help the small towns at all, just the big landowners and the big agribusiness firms. It just seems to go on and on, and it don't ever get better, only worse.

"Every so often one or two of the retail people in Salamander would make a try at stirring us up. The young woman who took over the variety store in '76 was that way. She formed a development group, pushing ideas that seemed pretty alien to the locals. Even got some advisers from down at the university to come up here, study things, and make recommendations.

"And, boy, the townspeople thought those professors were really queer geese. One argued in favor of what he called 'boot-strapping our way up,' which was like talking a foreign language to most of us. It went completely against the advice we'd been receiving from the governor and his economic geniuses, all of 'em hoping Salamander might attract a big meat-packing plant or, better yet, a laser research facility.

"Problem is, industry ain't too excited about coming to a place where there's no labor force, a decrepit sewer system, and a declining water supply. Executives take one look at Salamander's golf course with its sunburnt greens and rattlesnakes, which I mentioned before, and they choose something a little spiffier.

"Anyway, Charlene Lorenzen struggled with her variety store, while the locals were shopping at the Falls City Wal-Mart, and tried to get us all foamed up about making

Salamander into what she called 'a place where people will want to come and live.' I admit she had some interesting ideas.

"For example, since you can buy a house in Salamander for almost nothing, she suggested we provide a haven for struggling artists and writers. They'd pay their rent by giving lessons to all the locals and generally creating a more intellectual and artistic feel in the community. The boys at the elevator and over at Leroy's had fun with that, saying the only thing worth painting around here was Alma Hickman's cheeks and yellow stripes on the highway.

"Charlene talked about some other ways of getting things going, such as building a new sewer system and redoing our municipal water supply. But when it came to raising taxes a little to pay for them, nobody was interested. One problem with having a town full of older folks, though I'm generalizing a bit here, is that they're not inclined to make investments in a future they're going to miss.

"One of the economics professors who came calling at Charlene's invitation made a lot of sense to me. He said Salamander was not going to attract major industry and pursuing that particular course of action was a waste of time. Instead, he argued we should get into what he called 'vest-pocket manufacturing.' Said all we had to do was visit some of the industries in Falls City or other such centers of economic excellence and see what two or three of us might produce in the way of subcomponents for the larger products being manufactured there. Said that producing a high-quality product at a reasonable price was a no-fail strategy every time. He pointed out that every new job in Salamander was a major addition and that we didn't need all that many new jobs to keep Salamander going.

"He also said we needed to decide what kind of place we wanted to be and then work toward that. To those accustomed to government largesse and laissez-faire, all at the same time, that seemed awfully managerial. One possibility he offered, which went along with what Charlene was thinking, was simply to define Salamander as a bedroom community, kind of a suburb, for Livermore and Falls City and then work on making it the best possible place to live and raise a family.

"Among other things, he suggested the

local implement dealer ought to move all his rusty combines off vacant lots on Main Street, since that detracted from the appearance of the place. That was an unfortunate suggestion and got him on the shit list of not only the implement dealer, but also the many folks here apparently seeing rusty farm machinery as objects of beauty. That's the only reason I can figure out why they dump 'em in ravines on their farms, so they can have a pleasant evening's stroll down to look at the 1942 hay rake lying there on its side.

"The professor's list of things to try seemed endless to those who saw none. He kept saying, 'You don't have to be fancy, you just have to see the possibilities.' Most of us had trouble with that second part, but we were polite to him during the free noon meal at Clyde Archer Legion Post 641 and wished him a safe trip back to the university.

"After a while, Charlene got kind of tired of people telling her that every new idea she or somebody else suggested wouldn't work in Salamander. You could see it in her face. Finally, she sold off her remaining stock at bargain prices and closed her variety store. Last I heard, she was operating a home-decorating shop in Falls City and doing real well.

"In any case, talk on the street and at all the local gathering places was about the new highway. U.S. Representative Larkin held a press conference in the Legion Hall where he extolled the virtues of concrete and traffic and economic development along with its sidekick known as progress. He even mumbled about how maybe the highway could bring about a reopening of the mines over in Leadville.

"Looking out at a fairly grim horizon, then, the only hope the residents of Eble Olson's town could see was the proposed interstate highway. It wasn't ever made quite clear just how the road would benefit Salamander, but all the experts said it would, leaving the exact nature of those benefits to our own fertile imaginations.

"For a while, Carlisle and one Mr. Moore, a professor over at the community college, plus a group of outsiders interested in hawks and their well-being, stopped the highway dead by filing a lawsuit to halt construction while the U.S. Fish and Wildlife Service was trying to figure out whether or not to list the T-hawks as endangered, since they was almost extinct. In spite of our collective intent to destroy virtually everything in the name of improved shopping malls and other features of the good life, it seems some do-gooders, long of hair and bereft of love for their country, got some laws passed years ago saying you couldn't destroy the habitat of animals if their species was near to passing into oblivion.

"There were several months there when the little T-hawks appeared to be a severe roadblock, in a manner of speaking, and caused considerable hand-wringing in all the papers. Various creative solutions were hatched over beer at Leroy's. Several of the boys said there weren't many of the birds anyway and about ten minutes of shotgunning could turn an endangered species into an extinct species, in which case it wouldn't be endangered anymore. There was a certain logic to that, I had to admit. But there was also the risk of about twenty years in jail and a fifty-thousand-dollar fine, which sort of cooled things off.

"Instead, they got some bumper stickers printed up that read, MY FAVORITE BREAKFAST? FRIED T-HAWK. That sort of mindless poop appeals to people without minds, so pretty soon almost everybody in Salamander had one of the stickers on their cars and store windows. Fellow named Ray Dargen pasted one on the door of Danny's, but Thelma scraped it off that night with a razor blade.

"Unfortunately, Mr. Moore got quieted down pronto when the president of his little college said the highway was clearly in the best interest of the school and that Mr. Moore's support of the highway clearly was in Mr. Moore's own best interest. Moore, however, was a gritty fella and hung in there behind the scenes for the duration with Carlisle.

"Things got pretty dicey. Word was that funding for the highway was getting shaky, and that only increased the level of frustration with those opposing the road. Eventually, our congressfolks said they'd support oil drilling on the continental shelf near Santa Barbara, California, in exchange for voting on a bill that somehow or another exempted the T-hawks from protection, which was made easier by the fact that two other pairs of hawks had recently been found in locations southwest of here. Bird lovers testified in Washington, D.C., that the additional T-hawk habitats were also being destroyed and that it was vital to preserve the Yerkes County site. You could hear 'em scream from here to the White House, but it didn't do 'em any good, and truth went marching on.

"At first, some of the local ranchers and farmers who objected to the road cutting through their land were on Carlisle's side, though they admitted to being a little uncomfortable aligned with radical environmental causes. More than that, they were afraid the locals would start calling them *'T-bird,'* which is what Carlisle was being called behind his back.

"Axel Looker led this group opposed to the highway going near or through their land. But when Axel saw the money being offered for his property, he sat down and did some figuring, 'penciled it out,' as the boys around here like to say. The generous offer would allow him and Earlene to retire in Florida, which they'd been wanting to do for some time. When Axel withdrew his opposition, the coalition folded. Axel also let it be known that he would no longer scoop out Carlisle's lane in the winter.

"It'd be unfair to imply that Carlisle was

completely by himself in this, though it was pretty near to that. One ranch couple in particular, Marcie and Claude English, hung in there with him. But they were kind of outcasts anyhow, since they were deep into something called 'holistic resource management,' which they claimed would restore and preserve the grass out here for decades more of grazing. For those raised on Genesis and its reassurance that we humans are to have dominance over everything God created, that all sounded like something a little to the left of Satan. Besides, the idea was thought up by a fellow from Africa, and everybody knew Africa wasn't doing well. But Claude and Marcie were kind enough to have Carlisle over for dinner a number of times during all of this and refused to budge, forcing the government eventually to use assorted legal atrocities on 'em.

"Carlisle and his buddies held up progress on the road for several months, but their options were steadily declining. And I knew the final public hearing over at the Livermore High School gym would be worth attending to see if Carlisle had anything else left in his arsenal. So I'd been fishing around with Claude English—groveling, as a matter of fact—and he offered to take me the following Tuesday evening.

"I'd guessed it was going to be a real shootout and thought about wearing my old army helmet, just for fun. But I was afraid the great business minds trying to turn Lester's into a trap for all the tourists supposed to blow into Salamander, following the concrete trail we'd lay for them, would use mental incompetence as grounds for my eviction.

"In that case, my worst fear was they'd send me out to the Yerkes County Care Facility, which Bobby Eakins called 'the Boweling Alley.' So I decided to remain as inconspicuous as possible.

"Claude and Marcie picked me up the evening of the highway hearing. Susanna Benteen went with us. That was kind of fun, since I'd never been close up to her, let alone talked at all with her. She was real nice, asked me a lot of questions about my life and times, laughed real genuine when I tried to get off a little joke or two.

"She wasn't at all distant like I thought she'd be, and it gave even an old guy like me goose bumps just to be riding along in the same car with her. Something kind of haunting about her, like she'd seen about everything there was to see. And, of course, she was just plain fun to look at, like a good painting or something, and I got to wishing I were a little younger. Did that just for a moment, then settled back and enjoyed the ride on a crisp February evening."

I could see the old man was a little tired from all the talking and suggested we take a recess until the following day, giving me time to transcribe my notes. Around eight o'clock the next evening, I met him again and bought a beer for myself and whiskey for him.

"Where was I?" he asked when we had settled in a booth.

"You, Susanna Benteen, and Marcie and Claude English were on your way to Livermore for the public meeting."

He nodded, took a sip of whiskey, and got his thoughts organized.

"Well, picking up where I left off, the Livermore gym was hot and didn't smell too good. Radiators hissing, people fanning themselves. Bowing to public demand, the school janitor opened the side doors, letting a breath of fresh air into the place. But those sitting near the doors started complaining about the draft, so he closed them again, leaving all three hundred and fifty of us to breathe a recirculating swirl of greed, hostility toward Carlisle McMillan, and old jockstraps.

"The ground rules for the meeting were as stifling as the air in the Livermore gym. Each person was given an allotted speaking time of ninety seconds and could rise only once, thus curtailing honest discussion of any kind.

"Things got started with a statement read by one R. M. 'Highway Bob' Hawkins, who took a sip of water and then introduced himself as executive vice president of the state's Associated General Contractors. He pointed out that for each dollar spent on construction, a spin-off of two seventy would be generated by something he called the multiplier effect. He also said that for every one million spent on road construction, sixty-seven workers would be put on various payrolls, meaning that something in the neighborhood of about forty-five hundred jobs would be created in the state by just the construction activity itself. He finished up by saying, 'There's no question that the great driving machine of our economy is construction. It's the real pump primer that gets those waves of economic benefits rolling.'

"At that point, Claude English rose and said that if construction generated so many good things, why didn't the state just build a bunch of pyramids and solve everybody's problems? A good part of the audience laughed, even though they all knew Claude didn't have his thoughts together on the highway project. Still, he was one of them, had been for a long time, and a little joke was all right. The moderator rapped his gavel and called for order.

"Following Highway Bob's chest thumping and Claude's comment, the audience was treated to statements supporting the highway by the Falls City Chamber of Commerce, the Yerkes County Development Authority, the Livermore Boosters Club, the Farm Bureau, and the High Plains Development Corporation. Bill Flanigan of HPDC looked serious when he said that his group had carefully weighed all things pro and con about the project before coming down in favor of the road passing through Yerkes County, also noting there just weren't many cons to be found, if any.

"Marcie English then got to her feet and

tossed up a nice soft one for the experts to shoot down. Her voice was a little shaky, not being used to speaking in public and all, and her main argument had to do with preserving the family farm and not taking land for road construction. The moderator smiled and thanked her for her input, as he called it, reminding her the Farm Bureau was in favor of the road, and looked around the room for the next pigeon.

"There was silence for a few seconds. Then Carlisle McMillan, looking awfully tired from trying to fight the highway and earn a living all at the same time, stood up, stated his name as required, and got his endgame under way. He simply asked the experts to prove the selected route was the best one based on the criteria they had listed in volume twelve of the report. He'd acquired a copy of the report, all fifteen volumes of it, and had spent a lot of time reading and calculating, using instructions supplied by a Stanford professor, he later said.

"The moderator, a public relations specialist from the State Highway Department, gave Carlisle a condescending smile and said the selection involved sophisticated mathematics, implying Carlisle should sit

down and be a good boy because the figuring was way over his head.

"Carlisle, showing no signs of discom-
fort, replied, 'I think I'm capable of understanding the calculations, and I'd like to see
them demonstrated.'

"That set everybody off jibbering and
booing Carlisle. See, most folks don't even
like the word *mathematics*. The very mention of it usually is enough to cause a run for
the exits by the general public. So when
Carlisle stood his ground and asked for
proof, there was a lot of mumbling about his
gall and how they all wished he'd go back to
California, where smart-asses who understood mathematics belonged in the first
place.

"Things got more interesting at that
point. The moderator conferred privately
with Dr. Wendell Hammer, chief brownshirt
for the propeller heads. After that, the moderator, red in the face and stuttering a little,
said that the person who'd done the calculations wasn't in attendance that evening.
Carlisle said that wasn't his cart to haul and
suggested that certainly others present
were capable of showing why the proposed
route was best, given they were so strongly in

favor of it. More huddling up front. Over in the amen corner, the local leaders were highly agitated.

"Dr. Hammer got pushed to the forefront of things and tried to smoke it by Carlisle with a bunch of technical gibberish involving stuff with names such as 'social utility functions' and 'discount rates.' Carlisle took it all in and said his personal calculations conclusively proved that another route forty miles to the west was the best one, based on the criteria presented in the report itself, and that he'd be happy to demonstrate that fact. He also said, and I wrote this down pretty much word for word: 'The discount rate used in this study is far below the true cost of capital for the project. I'd appreciate knowing how you chose the rate you used. It's not realistic, and anything approaching a realistic figure will produce a benefit-cost ratio favoring the western route even more. Furthermore, I can prove the western route is better even using the crummy numbers you experts have put in for the discount rate.' "

The old man chuckled. "To those in attendance, this conversation between the good Dr. Hammer and Carlisle was like a battle between androids employing light

swords and ray guns. Nobody had any idea
what the two of them were talking about, including me, 'specially when Carlisle used
the word *sophistry* as part of his criticisms.
Besides, everyone already knew the proposed route was best since it included Livermore and Falls City, and why all the fuss
over an extra fifty million dollars in construction costs anyway? Somebody else, the nation's taxpayers, was footing the bill for that.

"The moderator tried to invoke the meeting rules on Carlisle, saying, 'I think maybe
we've heard more than enough from you,
Mr. McMillan,' at which point the crowd ap-
plauded.

"Carlisle was not moved by meeting
rules. He said, 'My questions have not been
answered, and I have a right as a taxpaying
citizen of Yerkes County to have them answered.'

"Now it's important to understand that
the majority of the crowd were Yerkes
County taxpayers, and then there was an
outsider, Carlisle, who just happened to be a
taxpayer, and somehow there was a difference. People began to shout at Carlisle to
sit down and shut up, and things were at the
point of getting out of control. Some folks

were putting on their coats and walking toward the door, shaking their heads at all the stupidity.

"Carlisle obviously had Dr. Wendell Hammer bolted to the wall defending something he wasn't sure of in the first place. The good Dr. Hammer tried to recover by giving us all an earful of mouth and ran around Carlisle's questions twenty-seven times before melting into a pool of butter. After more clustering up front, the moderator declared the meeting suspended and said it'd be continued the following week when additional mathematical specialists and their capitalist running dogs would be flown in from Vienna to testify in favor of the proposed route.

"It was a long week for everyone, especially Carlisle. The newspapers pounded away at the need for economic development and how the highway was a crucial link in those plans. Bill Flanigan put out a statement saying that the highway would ensure sustained economic development in the state for the next twenty-five years.

"On the Wednesday following the meeting, a young T-hawk with a twenty-two-caliber bullet hole in its chest and wire wrapped around its neck was found hang-

ing from a streetlight in front of the Salamander Post Office. Stapled to its right wing
was a note scribbled in crayon on a piece of
butcher paper: *'IT'S THESE TWEETIES OR
US!'* The *Inquirer* printed a photo of the
dead hawk swinging in the winter breeze
and ran an editorial condemning the action
and pleading for calm and good sense, neither of which was to be found anywhere in
Yerkes County.

"Merle Bagby, Salamander street commissioner, cut the hawk down only three
hours before Carlisle stopped for groceries
at Webster's Jack and Jill. Carlisle was carrying two sacks out the front door when Bobby
Eakins and a few others came out of Leroy's
and started calling him names. They said he
should take his ass out of here and go back
to where all the other stinking hippies lived.
Carlisle ignored him until Bobby pushed him
up against the plate-glass windows of Webster's. Carlisle dropped his sacks of groceries and told Bobby to knock it off, at
which point Bobby took a swing at him. He
missed, and Carlisle cold-cocked him right
onto the hood of Mrs. Macklin's Dodge.

"Whether that was a mistake or not is
still a matter for debate. But the result was

that Hack Kenbule proceeded to beat the crap out of Carlisle right there on Main Street. Carlisle was strong in his own way but not all that big in the frame. Even though Hack was running to fat, he was bigger and stronger and a lot meaner than Carlisle. He'd also had several Grain Belts before the ruckus started, and with the crowd egging him on, he might have killed Carlisle if Thelma Englestrom hadn't run screaming out of Danny's and got the fight stopped with the assistance of Jim Webster.

"Jim helped Carlisle pick up the groceries and provided new grocery sacks for him and got him into his pickup. All the while, the crowd that had poured out from Leroy's and Danny's was jeering Carlisle, except for Huey Sverson, who just looked real sad. Some also noticed Arlo Gregorian was standing off to one side, not saying anything. While this was going on, Bobby Eakins was still lying across the Macklins' car hood and, for once, was quiet.

"Carlisle, pretty battered in the face and looking like he hadn't slept for months, came to the public hearing when it was continued the following week. This time the experts had computer printouts that were longer than the proposed highway and held them up for everybody to see. Then the engineers took over and explained all the technical details one more time.

"Carlisle stood his ground and, as some privately said afterward, seemed like he beat the bunch of them on the basis of logic and numbers. He kept hammering away at how the route selected was not the best one according to their own standards and how their discount rates and benefit-cost ratios were dead wrong. The engineers fiddled with all the pens in their plastic shirt-pocket protectors, shuffled their feet under the table, and looked at one another with tight lips, as if they knew Carlisle was right. But the main suits just absorbed the blows as they'd been taught by all their years in politics. The problem was, you see, Carlisle was arguing with those in control of the microphone, and that's always a losing battle.

"Besides, when people want something, intellectual fine points, including proof, don't count for much in the end. Two days later, the State Highway Commission and the secretary of transportation voted in favor of the original route involving the great curve of concrete coming by Falls City and Livermore. At the same time, they announced construction had already begun in the southern states and would begin in Yerkes County as soon as weather permitted, news that was greeted with overwhelming cheers throughout the county.

"The locals all agreed the choice was well considered and that democracy had been served. After all, democracy is based on majority rule, isn't it? And the majority favored the proposed route, didn't they? Some of a zoological bent kindly observed that it was too bad about the T-hawks, but they also pointed out that extinction was just nature's way of saying good night. I heard that in Danny's.

"On the same day the highway decision was announced, the *Inquirer* ran a back-page article saying that sinkholes were forming in various parts of the local countryside due to fast-emptying aquifers underneath the ground, according to a study by state geologists. Meanwhile, the cheerleaders got out their blazers and sent them to the cleaners for a little sheep dip, preparing themselves for the numerous ceremonies in which our forthcoming prosperity would be celebrated and praised."

CHAPTER EIGHTEEN

A week after the highway decision, Carlisle was sitting by his woodstove, thinking about his next move, not that he had any moves left. Maybe just pack up and leave.

Gally Deveraux had called a few days earlier from Casper, where she had spent Christmas with her daughter. She had heard about the highway decision and said how bad she felt for Carlisle. Her voice was soft and caring, but things had subtly altered between them. He had been completely wrapped up in work and the highway fight, and she had been immersed in her classes. And though she hadn't said as much, Carlisle sensed she might have found someone else.

They had met a few weeks before at a motel halfway between Spearfish and Salamander, but something was different. Gally was different; changing fast. Carlisle was different; his anger over the highway had made him grim and uninterested in all the great ideas Gally was picking up from her studies, ideas she wanted to talk about with the intensity of a woman finding herself. And because of the planned Antelope National Park, which would include her land, it seemed as if Gally's financial worries might disappear.

She especially wanted to talk about the professor she had for a course in colonial history, how brilliant he was, how much time he was willing to spend talking with her outside of class. It was ending, what she and Carlisle had together. Both of them knew that. Nobody's fault, just the way things work out sometimes. When they parted at the motel, they held each other for longer than necessary, but neither of them mentioned getting together again.

There was not much keeping Carlisle in Yerkes County. The highway would take his house and the birds. He closed the wood-stove doors after putting a couple of splits of oak on the fire and sat there with Dumptruck on his lap, feeling a little sorry for himself, trying to figure out his next move. Become a gypsy again, maybe do that. Find another place. Flight as a possibility.

He was thinking about finishing the dining room table. The table was supposed to swing down from its vertical position against the wall to horizontal on heavy brass hinges from an old church door. But he had never figured out an aesthetic and yet functional way of locking it up on the wall when it wasn't in use. What was the point? It would be gone when the highway came through. No, he thought, do it anyway, finish things, do it right. After that, fix the atrium glass. Get the body in good shape for its burial.

He was standing there looking at the table, confronting the old classic trade-off between form and function. The simple hook he had been using was inelegant. Something just as simple was needed but with a little more style. Dumptruck kept jumping on the table and going to sleep and had to be moved each time Carlisle wanted to swing the table up and eyeball the problem.

Somewhere around four in the afternoon, sun going down, Dumptruck shifted from sleep to a state of alertness, ears pricked. A moment later, Carlisle heard the crunch of snowy footsteps. He walked quickly and quietly to a window and looked out: Susanna Benteen, alone. As she stepped onto the porch, Carlisle opened the door. Light snow was falling.

She was smiling, her face reddened from wind and cold. "Hello, Carlisle. I guess a belated Happy New Year is the greeting for today. Is it all right if I come in?"

"Of course, and late Happy New Year to you, Susanna. Can I take your cloak?"

"I think I'll leave it on for a while. The walk was fun, but I'm a little chilled at the moment. A hot cup of tea would be nice, though." She looked around the house. "What are you doing to the dining table?"

"Trying to figure out a way of latching it to the wall properly."

Carlisle was talking from the kitchen area, getting the tea ready, thinking. Susanna didn't seem as formidable to him as she once had. In the process of building his monument to Cody Marx and suffering through the highway wars, he had become completely his own man. That made Susanna's strong sense of herself less threatening to him.

And their talk by the river over a year ago had somehow cleared the air between them, for Carlisle, at least. He had said his words plain and true, she had understood. Plus she had been coming by regularly with Gally or the Indian over the past year, and the tension Carlisle had felt in her presence was mostly gone. Mostly. There was still the matter of a desirable woman, and that tension never goes away. He recollected this was the first time she had ever come to his place alone.

"What's the problem with the table? Oh, I see. You're trying to figure out a different way to hang it on the wall." She was bent over, examining the hinges.

Carlisle carried two cups of steaming tea from the stove and handed one to Susanna. "I'll figure it out, just a matter of time."

"I saw something like this in Iraq once. I'm trying to remember how they did it. Can we sit by the stove until I warm up?"

Susanna sipped her tea, green eyes looking over the rim of her cup at Carlisle McMillan, auburn hair spilling out from under the hood of her cloak.

He looked back, but it was still difficult for him to sustain any sort of prolonged eye contact with Susanna Benteen. "What are you doing way out here on a cold January day?"

"I stayed all night with Marcie and Claude English. They're real nice people and have me over once in a while. You know them, don't you?"

"Yes. I met Claude originally when I bought my subflooring lumber from him. They had me over for dinner a few times during the highway mess. Good folks, smart folks."

"Marcie and I are interested in intensive gardening. We met at the Salamander Library one day while we were both looking at the same section of books. They wanted me to stay on through tonight, but they have small children, and I always feel like I'm putting them out a bit when I stay for long, even though Marcie says that's not so. Besides, I felt like walking. I started off for Salamander, then got the idea of coming by to see if you were home, see how you're doing after the highway battles."

"I'm glad you came. I'd invite you to stay for dinner, but I'm afraid I don't have much in the way of anything to eat. Been sitting around here feeling sorry for myself and didn't get into Webster's Jack and Jill this week."

"Carlisle McMillan, carpentry may be your game, but cooking when there's nothing to cook is one of mine. I learned those skills during the years I spent on the road with my father."

"You once said he was an anthropologist, correct?"

"Yes. Sometimes we were three hundred miles from the nearest main food supplies, in the Australian outback or in some mountain pass in Bolivia. I remember my father's long face that Christmas morning in Bolivia, looking at our food stocks. I was only fourteen, but I put on my coat and went hiking around until I found a farmer who sold me a pretty rough-looking chicken. I made it work, though, with some canned vegetables and potatoes. Mind if I look through your larder? You can always make soup, no matter how thin the pantry seems."

"I'd be grateful if you did. I can promise a decent bottle of red wine if you can cobble up anything at all from what's in there. Worst case, we can have the wine and skip the food if it comes to that."

Susanna smiled and removed her cloak. "It won't. That's something I can almost promise you."

She was right. A half hour later, good smells were coming from the kitchen area while Carlisle stared at the dining table, still thinking about how to fasten it to the wall. Concentration was difficult with Susanna twenty feet away in front of his stove. The images of her dancing across the floor upon which he was standing kept rolling through his head.

She hummed, her hair hanging long with a slight curl to it, silver hoop earrings dangling, and looked over her shoulder at him. "How's it coming, the table? Any great ideas yet?"

"A few ideas, none of them great. Something smells good over there."

"It came down to soup. Were you aware you had all the makings for homemade bread mixed in among jars of jam and cans of old roofing nails?"

"No . . . I did?"

"You did, and I'll have it under way in a while. There is something basic about the smell of baking bread. Something from a long way back." Dumptruck was rubbing against her legs, purring.

"You've got that right. And I just figured out how to hang the table. A one-by-four piece of carved redwood hinged on the wall that locks into a cradle built for it on the underside of the table when the table swings up. I think it was the prospect of baking bread that did it."

He walked over to a window and looked out. Then cracked the door and looked again. Women and big storms seemed to arrive at his place at the same time. He pondered that coincidence for a moment, then let it go. "Susanna, the snow's really building up out there," he called. "Want me to run you into Salamander before it gets worse?"

"No, I'm making soup and baking bread. The storm will take care of itself. It doesn't bother me if it doesn't bother you."

By eight o'clock supper was ready, and Carlisle had roughed out the assembly for hanging the table on the wall. It hung there now, precariously, and he swung it down. He set the table with plates, silverware, and two stubby candles hot waxed onto small scraps of pine. A tape went into the radio's deck, and he turned off the lights. "Not bad, huh? The place looks pretty good."

"It looks very elegant. Just right. And somehow it's sort of comforting having a table saw within reach."

Astor Piazzolla went to work in the tape deck of the radio: tangos. Carlisle had ordered the tape after listening to Gabe O'Rourke play the tangos in Leroy's. Susanna held up her wineglass: "Here's to Bolivia."

"Bolivia it is, may she thrive and prosper and supply tourists with colorful blankets."

Susanna laughed. "I learned to tango once, got pretty good at it, too, if I do say so."

"Where was that?"

"Argentina. I was on the road by myself, and stopped there for a while. After my father died, I took off to see what I'd missed in my earlier days of traveling with him. That's all I thought about back then, the next railroad station, the next bus to a place I had never heard of. The road gets in your blood."

She looked away for a moment, toward the radio, and remembered the Argentine who had taught her the tango.

Carlisle watched her when she turned, the auburn hair shifting and then coming to rest softly in a slightly different way on her neck and shoulders. She touched her mouth with a napkin and looked at him again. He sat there in a blue workshirt and old black sweater, sawdust on his jeans, looking back at her.

On the third finger of her right hand was an opal-set ring. Another, plain and thin and gold, circled her index finger, and a jangly silver bracelet hung from her wrist. A silver falcon dangled from the chain around her neck; he had seen it before and remembered it. Her dress was wool, cream colored, and the patterned yellow-and-brown scarf lay with studied informality on one shoulder.

She reached across the table and put her hand on his. The opal ring was cool on his skin. "I've been thinking about your predicament with the highway, Carlisle. May I suggest that in your anger and sadness you're missing something."

"What am I missing?"

"Your tribute to Cody Marx is not wood and nails, windows and doors, the material objects surrounding us here. The real tribute is that you built it for him in the way he would have wanted it built. And in the process you rebuilt yourself. He would understand that instantly, but I think you've somehow missed it. Based on what I have heard you say about Cody Marx, he would appreciate a tribute but not a monument. There is a difference."

Carlisle grinned. "Good point. You're right, Cody doesn't need a monument. I've been concentrating on the output, what the house represents and what the highway will do to it. Cody always focused on journeys rather than destinations, on craftsmanship rather than objects, knowing that good process eventually leads to good product, if you're not in a hurry. I understood that once, got it back when I was building the house, and then forgot it again. And Gally Deveraux once said something to the effect that, if I want to, I can strike camp and be gone with the morning. Build another tribute if I have to. But I somehow don't feel like I have to do it again."

Susanna Benteen smiled then. "I like that . . . be gone with the morning. Stay light, portable. I try never to accumulate more of lasting value than what I can carry onto a bus or train in one suitcase and a bag over my shoulder. I still remember the Bushmen of the Kalahari. They could do that, strike camp and be gone in less than an hour with everything they owned."

"Were you there in the Kalahari with your father?" Carlisle's face was almost incredulous. Distant places, places he had only heard about.

"Yes." She began laughing. "They admired his portable radio. On the day we were leaving, he offered it as a gift. The Bushmen shuffled their feet and politely declined. It was too heavy to pack and not necessary for getting through the day and the night following, which was the time frame on which they based their lives. They took only what they could carry easily, stayed light. The radio was only portable to us because we had a Land Rover, not to the Bushmen, though."

Susanna tore a small piece of bread from the hot loaf. Piazzolla moved into "Nuevo Tango," weaving the song around a January wind, which probed for cracks in Cody's tribute and found none.

"How about coffee by the stove?" she

asked. "I'll fix it if you'll clear the table. Seems a fair trade."

"Deal."

Carlisle tossed pillows on the floor next to the woodstove. Susanna concocted something from regular coffee, bitter chocolate, cinnamon, and a small splash of whiskey. After the coffee, they poured more of Carlisle's red wine. Susanna was quiet, staring into her glass. Carlisle had difficulty keeping quiet around her, as if he needed words as a nervous reaction to her presence. There was some old force made of equal parts darkness and light within him, and he could feel it moving. A woman, her presence, what to do next. He wondered if women ever had the same feelings.

"Susanna, do you know anything about Wolf Butte? All sorts of legends float around about that place. Since I've been on this land I've noticed what looks like a fire up on the crest, usually very late in the night, just before dawn."

She slowly brought her eyes up to his, looking at him with the directness of an arrow. "Yes, I know about the legends of Wolf Butte. 'Stories' is a better word, I think. 'Legend' carries the sense of being not true or overly romanticized. In the case of Wolf Butte, however, what you have heard is mostly true. It is a place of great power, the Early Ones knew that. If you're asking about the people who have died out there, they died because they came to alter what the Keeper believed should not be tampered with."

She took a deep breath, reached into her bag, and brought out a curved, dark green comb. She held it between her teeth and pushed her thick hair up high on top of her head and fastened it there with the comb. Carlisle watched her, she smiled at him.

"Have you heard about the professor who died near Wolf Butte while preparing for an archaeological dig?" she asked, settling herself against a cushion.

Carlisle nodded. "Yes."

"That was my father." She said it evenly.

"Jesus," Carlisle whispered.

"That's how I came to Yerkes County in the first place, to do a little private investigating of his death. The explanations all seemed a little too pat, too tidy, to explain a careful man walking where he had walked many times before and falling. My father was used to rough country, knew how to take care of himself, and I was suspicious. He had told me that academic reputations were threatened, that the dig at Salamander Crossing, as the place was called, might disprove widely accepted hypotheses of the overland migrations by early peoples. Quite a bit was at stake. And the dig was shut down immediately after his death."

"How did your investigation turn out? Find anything?"

"No, nothing. Then I met the man you call Flute Player. Since then I have been to Wolf Butte many times with him. He knows every rock and tree and crevice there. And he has convinced me that my father died because they were going to excavate the burial mounds. He says many people have died out there over the years, that the Keeper of the butte has a way of watching over things. And you know what is strange? My father would understand that kind of power and would believe in it. In that light, his death makes sense to me because it would make sense to him."

"Why did you stay on in Salamander?"

"Inexpensive living, a big peaceful countryside. I settled in, focused on living my life rather than worrying about my father's death all the time. To be honest, I didn't have much money. Because my father bounced around so much, he didn't leave a lot in the way of a death benefit from his retirement program. What little there was I spent on my travels. I get by."

"Where were you before you came to Yerkes County?"

Susanna Benteen gave him the direct gaze she seemed to have invented. "Traveling, on the road for most of seven years, stopping here and there for a while. Before that I lived for three years with a man named Andrew Tanner on the Spanish seacoast . . . San Sebastian. He was a freelance journalist, a war correspondent."

"Hell of a life, Susanna." Carlisle was shaking his head slowly and feeling a brief surge of unexamined envy toward a man named Tanner. "Let me ask you something else, if you don't mind. It's a little impertinent, I suppose, so don't feel compelled to talk about it if you don't want to."

Susanna Benteen smiled. "I don't feel compelled about much of anything. What is the question?"

"Do you know who the Keeper is?"

"No. And that's the truth. But I believe something is out there."

"Do you think it's the Flute Player? Is he the Keeper?"

"I truly don't know. But there is a powerful force in and around Wolf Butte, I know that much."

"And you're aware that the highway route goes within three hundred yards of the butte and through part of the burial mounds on the other side of it."

"Yes, I know that. The Flute Player is worried. He says the Keeper has big medicine but that it may not be powerful enough to stop what is coming this time."

"What about the Indians in general? You seem to think like an Indian. Can't they do something?"

"Carlisle, I must gently disabuse you of some notions you—and others—may have about Indians and about me. It's not really your fault. Neither our media nor our educational institutions know or teach much of anything accurate about Indians. The Indians have a lot of problems, including unemployment, extreme poverty, crime, broken families, alcoholism. And diabetes is rampant, apparently something to do with genetics and diet combined. I don't know if they care one way or the other about the highway. From what I understand, the laws are complicated when it comes to artifacts, and in this state the owner of the land can do pretty much what he or she wants to do with it, including the disposition of archaeological finds.

"Also, my father taught me to beware the 'noble savage' view of traditional peoples. Whites tend to have a mythic view of Indians. We like them just fine in our romanticized and somewhat imagined past, that idyllic time before the white man came, living a life supposedly full of freedom and harmony with nature. If I told you that some Indians kill bald eagles, which are an endangered species, for their tail feathers, you might begin to shift your views, even though the tail feathers are used in religious rituals. And if I told you that many of the eagles are killed to get feathers for the manufacture of curios that are sold to tourists, and that occurs all the time, you probably would vehemently disapprove. It's all a good deal more complicated than most people understand.

"Beyond that, there are many aspects of Indian culture and belief that are close to my own view of things. That's why the Flute Player accepts me in the way he does. But I am not some New Age mystic driving to sweat lodge ceremonies in a BMW and trying to be a weekend Indian. I am not an Indian, and I can never be an Indian. The Indian way is a separate view of life and nature that is difficult for whites to understand. And, in the same fashion, Indians cannot become like me. I have my own beliefs and my own ways of behaving that have come down to me from an unusual childhood. I lived for years in tribal cultures over much of Africa, Asia, South America, and, to a lesser extent, the American Southwest. My ways are not the ways of the Indian. They are *my* ways, but there are some similarities."

Carlisle was slightly chagrined. "Well, the lecture was deserved."

"I didn't mean to lecture. I just wanted to get a few things straightened out." She smiled warmly, sipped her wine.

"In any case, all of this is hard for me to get my hands around, Susanna. Your father, the Keeper, people dying over there at Wolf Butte, the highway, the birds, an outfit called the AuRA Corporation."

She looked at the ceiling. "What does the word *aura* mean, in the dictionary sense? It's something surrounding a person or a thing, something that has a quality all its own."

"Yes, I'd say that's pretty close."

She canted her head slightly, thinking. "It reminds me of Aurora, Roman goddess of the dawn and the rising of the sun."

Carlisle fetched his old college dictionary, thumbed it, mumbling, "A . . . a-r, a-t, a-u . . . here it is, 'aura.'"

Susanna reached over and tapped the page. "Look at the beginning of the 'Au's.' What's there?"

He ran his finger along the columns, then smacked the book with his hand. "Au is the chemical symbol for gold!"

She smiled. "I thought so. My high school chemistry is a little dusty, but I remember reading somewhere that the symbol for gold was taken from the Roman goddess's name. Now, doesn't the corporation that owns the land spell its name with a capital A followed by a lowercase u?"

"You're right again. That's how it's spelled."

She smiled, looked at him. "So what do

we have now? Is AuRA just a clever spelling of the word *aura*, with a play on the symbol for gold? Or does it have some other meaning?"

"I don't know. But I think you might be on to something."

"I don't know, either," replied Susanna.

Carlisle was silent for a moment. "Maybe we ought to talk with Flute Player."

"And maybe we ought to talk with some of the more militant Indians at the reservation or with the American Indian Movement people down at the capital. I met Lamont Crow Wing once. He's a fist beater with AIM. There might be more that can be done yet. At the moment, though, I'm too tired to think about it. Do you have something I can sleep in?"

"Clothing or a bed?"

"Both, please."

Susanna was about six inches over five feet, seven less than Carlisle. His worn gray sweatsuit might do it, he decided. He handed it to her, and she went into the bathroom, coming out a few minutes later looking just fine, sleeves rolled up, pants ballooning and draping to the floor. Susanna knew how to wear clothing, gave it her own twist, and appeared ready for a lunar fashion show when she had put it together.

"You can have the bed, Susanna, I'll toss my sleeping bag up in the loft."

"No, I prefer the sleeping bag. I practically grew up in sleeping bags."

She carried the bag up the curving stairs, stopped halfway along, and looked down at Carlisle, her free hand on the rail. "Good night, Carlisle. I admire the things you construct, but I admire you and your craftsmanship a great deal more."

Carlisle lay in bed a long time before sleep came, thinking of Susanna, of what she had said, listening to the storm and to Dumptruck talking softly as he moved from under the stove and padded up the loft stairs. The stove needed serious help by four in the morning. He pulled on a sweater and jeans and padded toward it, trying not to disturb Susanna. Approaching seven on the Beaufort scale, the wind pounded like a great flat hand smacking his redwood siding as he opened the stove door and laid pieces of cured white oak onto the coals. The heat began to rise again, and he squatted there, letting the warmth come into him.

"Good morning, Carlisle." Susanna was leaning over the loft railing, whispering.

"Good morning, Susanna. Sorry if I woke you."

"You didn't. I awakened some time ago. I've been lying here listening to the wind. Would you like coffee?"

"Yes, but I'll fix it. You can sit by the stove while I do it. Or maybe you prefer tea?"

"Thank you, I do prefer tea," she said, wrapping the sleeping bag around her and stepping barefoot down the loft stairs.

Carlisle flipped the radio on at low volume, interested in the weather report. It came in the form of bulletins every few minutes, a droning recitation of school closings and Big Medicine. Twelve inches of snow had fallen already, with another twelve to eighteen inches on the way. Winds would reach forty miles per hour by evening. Back over to music, Merle Haggard singing about the road. Too early for Merle, bad day for the road, so he punched in an old tape that had Paul Winter playing his soprano saxophone in the Grand Canyon.

Susanna sat on a pillow with the sleeping bag wrapped around her, sipping tea, looking at Carlisle McMillan resting on one elbow, drinking coffee. "What are you thinking about, Carlisle? You're thinking about something."

He was thinking about firelight and goatskin drums and a woman dancing. On a blizzardy February morning, he was thinking about sweet rain.

He didn't answer.

"Carlisle, would you like to make love?" She said it straight and unadorned, but she spoke quietly and smiled.

He smiled. "Yes. I've wanted to make love with you since I saw you moving through my headlights on my first night in Salamander."

"I sensed as much. And I have felt the same about you. First, I must bathe. Then I'll use the remainder of the wine to fix us something nice to drink."

Carlisle tried to cover a slight shaking of his hands when he handed towels to her, while she carefully and precisely took various items from her shoulder bag. The witch of Salamander, green eyes and old ways. She walked toward the bathroom, smiling at him, stopped, and took his hand, looking up at him for a moment.

The shower came on, and Carlisle leaned against the kitchen wall, listening to it, imagining her standing under the water. Ten minutes later, Susanna came out of the bathroom wearing her cloak for a robe, the hood down, hair loose and falling to the small of her back, the silver rings dangling from her ears.

"A shower is in order for me, too." She had left a small bar of sandalwood-scented soap in the bathroom. Her hairbrush and green comb lay near the sink. A small bottle of perfume with no label was next to the comb. Her toothbrush and a container of baking soda next to that. Womanly artifacts and the high scent of female from a long ways back somewhere. He took the stopper from the perfume bottle and smelled flowers and sand and wind along the Tigris.

He let the water beat on him. The water hot, the fierce wind outside . . . Susanna Benteen. When he was finished, he pulled on his jeans and sweater and went into the living room.

"I'm up here, Carlisle." Her voice came down from the loft.

She had arranged pillows, blankets, and the sleeping bag into a warm cradle occupying most of the small loft. She was naked, sitting on and among the pillows, legs curled underneath her. A single candle was set in the empty wine bottle, incense was burning somewhere. Cradled lightly in her hands was a yellow feather. If Syawla came to earth, she would look like this, Carlisle thought.

She delicately pointed the feather to a thin, almost invisible scar starting between her breasts and curving down for six inches over her right rib cage. "A mama baboon did that when I was twelve. I was playing with her baby, and she became nervous, wanted the baby back."

The wine, warmed and spiced. Breasts full and lifting when she reached up and inserted the feather in her hair, smiled, and then removed it and laid it to one side. "I found it along the road during my walk out here."

The evolution of night into day was smooth and nearly indiscernible, the storm disallowing anything other than a deep gray to form outside. Susanna was taking him along corridors of the senses he had never walked or even contemplated walking. There was a ritualistic quality to her lovemaking, a sense of progression trellising him upward toward something he could not see or even imagine.

Her face in his neck, lips in his ear, she whispered words of her own over and over until it became a mantra of sorts, and he stopped thinking about the body against which he moved. Making love with Susanna Benteen was to have her become a presence in your mind as well as a physical entity touching you.

She raised her body to meet his, both of them glistening with sweat, her face losing its composure and going slack from the rise of her sexuality, her hands sliding along the moisture on his back. He bent her like the wind bends sienna wheat in a high plains summer and eventually came to know that loving Susanna Benteen took you as near to Truth as you can get without dying.

And the woman lay there as the callused hands of a craftsman moved over her, hands upon her in all the places she wanted them to be. She touched the neck of Carlisle McMillan as he moved over her, ran her hands along the veins and arteries there, the beat of his blood in her fingertips, her words coming in small bits of Swahili and Arabic, in Navaho and Sioux, as she looked up at him.

The hours of the day compressed and expanded. Sometimes the two of them lay silent for a long while, side by side, her hands moving across his face and chest and shoulders while he did the same to her. And they whispered to each other in an old sweet language that seems profound in those moments but is difficult to recall later on.

The storm continued for another thirty-six hours. Susanna and Carlisle talked and cooked and made love, and sometimes they slept. Susanna mentioned she used to paint in watercolors but had to leave her easel behind in one of her moves.

"That can be remedied," Carlisle said. He put on his parka and boots, tied a rope to the back door so he could find his way home through the blizzard, and waded to his workshop, staggering and thrashing about in deep snow. He stomped in through the back door while Susanna held it open, snow on his eyebrows, carrying pieces of ash and an array of Cody's hand tools.

CHAPTER NINETEEN

The only sound, aside from first wind rising, was the occasional brush of Carlisle McMillan's leather jacket against the boards of his workshop when he shifted his weight. Two weeks after he and Susanna Benteen had first made love, he was hunkered down there, his back against the exterior north wall, covered by the quiet darkness of a high plains winter. He looked out across his pond. Every day, sometimes several times a day, he broke a hole in the pond ice so the animals could find water in hard weather. The hole would freeze over, and he would do it again. Somewhere under the snow was a new summer cactus blooming and the sweet smell of western rains. Somewhere under the ice were bluegills suspended in the cold and waiting for a warmer sun.

A young doe came out of the T-hawk forest across the road. She moved quietly through starlight and over open ground north of Carlisle's house, circling in toward the pond. He could hear the faint crunch of her hooves across white silence. The doe paused, knowing he was there watching her, in his boots and old jacket and navy watch cap, long hair blowing only slightly. He breathed slowly, quietly.

An owl rode in on night wings and landed in one of the bare oaks near the house, head swiveling. The owl knew the field mice had tunnels under the snow. The owl also knew they left the tunnels sometimes.

Just short of the pond the doe stopped, her breath turning to foggy, transient puffs in the cold. She stamped a foot quietly, in the way whitetails demonstrate uncertainty, then came to the small piece of open water after a minute or two. She drank a little, lifted her head to look in Carlisle's direction, drank some more. He did not move. She needed water, not alarm. She would have enough of that when the bulldozers and chain saws came in two months.

Forty thousand feet above the doe,

above Carlisle McMillan, were the blinking lights of an overnight jet heading west through the northern sky. Seattle? San Francisco? Over the curve of his thoughts came the sound of a morning train, distant, almost not there. A week ago, the final decision to push the highway through had been made. In the years to come, only temporary silence would be here, silence until the next pair of headlights flashed in the darkness and the next set of truck tires rolled along the Avenue of the High Plains. The owl would be gone, the mice would be gone. All of it, the doe, the house, the pond, all of it would be gone.

Seventy feet away, in the house, Susanna slept. She would stay with him for a while, leave, then return a few days later. There was more than a trace of impermanence about her, as if she might come into high plumage and take flight at any time.

Carlisle understood. You didn't hold Susanna Benteen, you simply moved parallel with her for a while. When it came to relationships, Carlisle guessed that forever was not part of her vocabulary and tried to accept that. Still, when she left him he was empty, and he never truly had felt that way before. He had cared for Gally, a rich feeling of warmth and friendship. But he and Susanna made something beyond what he had ever known. To touch Susanna Benteen was to move your hand across space and hear your voice ask the old questions. There were no answers, but the asking of them was enough.

Love was not a word Susanna used. She was capable of love and, in fact, could love profoundly. Carlisle sensed that and could find it sometimes in how she touched him or looked at him.

The doe finished drinking, looked again toward Carlisle, and began walking back toward the T-hawk forest. First sign of red in the east.

A few nights before, snuggled against the curve of Susanna's back, he had dreamed: It was midafternoon in Africa, in Sudan. A child was dying there, belly swollen in the last stages of hunger, flies clustered on its open mouth. A mother, holding the child, would brush away the flies, hoping only that death would come soon to the child, and to her. But the child first. God, in Your mercy, please let it first be the child, then me; the child suffers more.

In the dream, Carlisle was engaged in strange travels. He imagined a cosmic filmmaker, six thousand trillion miles out, the distance light could travel in a thousand years Earth time. Androgynous, skilled beyond human comprehension, and with a penetrating intelligence lodged in a brain three feet in diameter, the creature of Carlisle's fancy was sitting on a massive throne suspended on whatever passed for atmosphere in its lonely place. The terrain was flat, so perfectly flat that from its throne the creature could see for a hundred miles in all directions, and nothing moved out there.

Attached to the creature's throne was a machine humans would call a camera and lens, but of such power and proportion that to call it that would do the instrument injustice. Two hundred meters high and forty meters in diameter was the camera, with the lens affixed at the top and reaching out sixty meters at a right angle to the camera mechanism. The creature manipulated its machine by thought alone, wherever or whatever the creature thought about, so to that place or thing the throne, the creature, and its digital image machine turned, swinging easily, silently.

Years before, the creature had filmed Cleopatra moving slowly across an Egyptian courtyard, gold bracelets flashing in sunlight, her lips parted as Antony came toward her. The photograph was cropped, Antony taken out, the likeness of Cleopatra retained and enlarged and hung on the infrastructure of the machine next to a long-range portrait of Eve that the creature had been studying for years beyond the counting.

A thousand years out, a millennium following the death of Carlisle McMillan, the powerful lens might probe a turning Earth lit in longitudinal sequence as the day raked westward over it. Over the Ganges Fan and the Java Trench, over men and women hauling in empty nets on a beach of Ocean India, over a child and its mother in Sudan. A man leaning against a shed at first light, half a world away, would come later. The camera would find the doe and the owl and the man, focus and magnification controlled by the creature's thought, zooming in on the man as the creature willed it, down to the level of the man's eyes and face in exquisite detail. The filmmaker would study the images later, editing, keeping some, eliminating others, its judgment hard-pure and implacable.

The man would be discarded. Self-pity unmistakable in the eyes of the man, and the creature would match that against those pulling empty nets onto a tropical coast, match it against a woman and child dying in the Sudan. Struggle would be paramount in the creature's value scheme; self-pity would be of no interest and, more than that, a matter for condemnation. The creature would have been watching for a long time and might recall that one hundred million years ago there were no flowers in the place where this man crouched by a small building. Now the man had geese beating their way north when Earth tilted in the spring and flowers after that, and the creature would have seen them on earlier film and wished flowers would grow around its camera throne. It longed for the sight of geese moving through end-of-winter skies. But the creature's place was cold and dark and arid, colored only in black shadow where the thin yellow from its own distant sun fell upon it and the equipment. Self-pity had no place when the stomach was full and there would be flowers again, and geese again. The creature rumbled those words in its mind, as it sorted, tossing images of the man aside.

Carlisle jerked to wakefulness, breathless and overwhelmed.

Not a pretty picture of me. That's what Carlisle thought, and remembered then the diamondback rattlesnake in what the old travelers called *mauvaises terres,* "evil lands," the Badlands today. He had come through there once. It had been cool, and the diamondback had crawled onto the road, stretching out on the pavement's warmth in the late afternoon. At first, Carlisle had thought it was a crack in the pavement. Then he saw the patterned back and swerved, letting his truck pass safely over the snake. There was traffic, tourists spending an hour in a place that never counted hours, counted in years by the millions if it counted at all.

Carlisle had stopped his truck, pulled a long-handled broom from his truck box, and walked back to herd the snake across the road to safety. Cars, vans, motor homes running past him, Carlisle frantically waving and pointing at the snake. Drivers adjusted, missing the snake, waving back at Carlisle. The snake would have none of it, wrapped itself into a coil in the midmost of the road, and began striking at vehicles as they passed over or around it, driven by the preservation instinct, self-defense, not anger. Humans would have called it courage if the snake had been one of them.

Blind stabbing instinct or not, Carlisle had admired the snake, six pounds of flesh rearing up and fighting back against tons of indifferent metal and rubber. He had approached to within ten feet of the diamondback when a Winnebago motor home ground the animal into a stew of red and yellow, disembodied tail flicking. A man's arm had come out of the driver's side as the vehicle moved on down the road, fist closed, middle finger extended, hand pumping up and down. Darwin is Darwin, screw you and your snake, Jack, whoever you are. Lunch at Wall Drug, Doris, just up ahead?

Carlisle watched the doe leaving him, thinking: Nothing's going to be left when we get finished, not diamondbacks or old lions or men ill designed for the times of which they are a part. I, at least, can move camp, dodging the machines for a while.

At first he had thought his strategy didn't work. Then he decided it was working pretty well until the highway project came along. As

Susanna said, maybe just call that part bad luck, the highway.

Try again, she had said. "Like the Stoics, you must try to assume a posture of noble indifference toward chance. Try to slough off the road as just plain bad luck."

He knew what he needed to become was cryptozoic. *Crypto* as in "secret" or "hidden," *zoic* as in the way certain kinds of animals live, such as raccoons and coyotes and deer. These animals have learned to exist alongside civilization, while remaining apart from it.

Carlisle wondered if it was still possible for him to live alongside civilization and yet be somewhat apart from it. Find a slice of quiet in the layers of noise, conduct a raid into the noise now and then for some work, take the gold, and run like hell back to the quiet place. The Indians had a name for it. They called it "shapeshifting." Carlisle had tried it once on the high plains, and it seemed to be working. He would make another run at a cryptoreality. Stay in the tunnels of a separate world as much as possible, watch for the owls when going out in the open, hope for some better luck next time. Flight was no good. You couldn't escape it, whatever "it" was. He remembered words by the anthropologist Loren Eiseley: "In the days of the frost seek a minor sun."

Carlisle had done it once, found his own small sun; he could do it again. It was not a perfect strategy, but it was next best to simple and didn't involve self-pity.

The doe reached the end of the lane and crossed the road, moving into the T-hawk forest. Sunrise, smoke from the woodstove lying almost flat in the wind and streaming toward Salamander eight miles away.

Carlisle, still resting against his toolshed, looked down at his hands. With their prehensile virtues, they swung one of the best hammers anywhere. Man, the tool user. He reached down to feel the old tool belt Cody had given him, a talisman of sorts, and remembered he was not wearing it.

The smart-money boys thought they had neutralized him once and for all, counting coup while galloping across their legal documents like a little cavalry in business suits, armed with deceit and visions of a New Jerusalem out there on the prairie. Susanna had convinced him there was more to do. He wasn't finished yet. He didn't have much hope that anything could save his house or the birds now, but whatever it took, he wasn't finished. He was getting ready to ratchet upward again, turning like a river.

It had taken a little digging, but thanks to Susanna figuring out that AuRA was related to gold, Carlisle's further research had turned up the interesting fact that Williston had filed a mining claim decades ago for Wolf Butte and the land surrounding it. Mr. Ray Dargen had subsequently purchased that claim. Two years later, the land itself had been bought from the federal government by the AuRA Corporation. Susanna added the clincher: "Au" plus the first two letters of Ray Dargen's Christian name, and the result was "AuRA."

Carlisle had already uncovered some of that information earlier but had trouble sorting through the records. AuRA was the key. It was easy when there was a name to hook things together. The Three Buttes Land Corporation owned AuRA, and Three Buttes was a subsidiary of the RAYDAR Corporation, Dargen's holding company that served as an umbrella for his operations. Moving on from there, Carlisle found what he earlier suspected: Some of the locals and their friends had not only machinated for a route passing near Livermore and Falls City, which it didn't need to do if the shortest route was a concern, but they also had advance word of the project and bought land in key locations along the right-of-way. Land they bought for a hundred bucks an acre would be worth twenty or more times that when the interstate came by. The Three Buttes Land Corporation had made a sizable chunk of these purchases.

Today, Carlisle decided, he'd try to find the Indian, see what he had to say, see if the Sioux could be roused to do something. He looked at the sky, grinning upward, remembering the millennial filmmaker of his dream, and leaving it with one final enigmatic image, which might give the creature pause as it edited and discarded a thousand years from now. And he was quiet inside, the heart of Carlisle McMillan was quiet once again, and he hummed to himself as he walked toward the house, watching the T-hawks lifting off at sunrise from their little forest across the road, feeling distant signals from a place deeper than his bones. He looked toward Wolf Butte and could see what looked like the faint waver of a fire on the crest.

Susanna was still sleeping. He took off his clothes and slid in beside her. She turned and snuggled her face in his neck, running her hand along his back. "You're cold," she whispered drowsily and rubbed against him, putting one of her thighs between his. He ran his hand slowly over her legs, her breasts, her hair.

CHAPTER TWENTY

Morning tea near the woodstove, and Susanna's green eyes were looking at Carlisle McMillan.

Carlisle said, "I think you're right. It's not over yet. Let's find the Indian and talk with him. Do you know where he might be?" His energy was back, and Susanna could feel it in him, the intensity.

But there were things you would tell your lover and things you would not. Some things belonged to you, not to him. Susanna knew exactly where to find the Indian, but she was reluctant to say anything. The Indian had treated her in a special way, let her see and feel things she was sure he did not generally share with others.

Finally, Susanna replied, "Carlisle, this is going to sound a little like one of those bad western movies, but let's go outside and build a fire. If the Indian sees it, wherever he is, I think he'll come."

She knew the Indian would indeed see the fire. From the crest of Wolf Butte, you could see whatever you wanted to see.

Twenty minutes later, Carlisle grinned at her as he heaped scrap lumber on a fire he had built near the pond. "Do we dance around it or just let it burn?"

"Sometimes, Carlisle, you sound just like the locals." Susanna shook her head slowly, but she was smiling. "Just let it burn for a while." Two hours later, there was a knock on the door.

"Ho, Builder."

"Ho, Flute Player."

Carlisle asked the Indian about the burial mounds and what laws might be available to protect them. The Indian knew nothing about law and said so.

"I do not live on the reservation, and I am somewhat apart from the tribe. But I will ask, though the People are discouraged about being able to do anything about anything anymore." The Indian stood on the porch and talked with Susanna a few minutes, then left.

Three days earlier, an official-looking car had come up Carlisle's lane. Important legal notices usually arrived by registered mail, but the formal notice that his property was being taken for the highway was delivered in person via the county attorney, who was flanked by two state troopers. Those on the side of economic nirvana were taking no chances, Carlisle thought, smiling to himself.

Dumptruck, sitting on a windowsill, had caught on right away and hissed when they got out of the car. But Carlisle had nothing against these guys. They were simply doing an unpleasant job, acting as the big dog's tail. They seemed a little surprised he was polite and offered them a cup of coffee.

They hesitated, then accepted and came inside. Susanna had been painting near the woodstove, standing in front of her easel and wearing an old shirt of Carlisle's as a smock. He introduced her, and she provided the visitors with a nice smile. That was the only way Susanna Benteen knew how to smile.

Carlisle had watched them take it all in. The wood on which he had expended more than a year of his life, sun coming in through the skylights, Susanna, Dumptruck, the five-string banjo hanging on the wall. Now and then, he caught them glancing in Susanna's direction while they talked. She was, after all, a kind of quiet legend in Yerkes County, and none of them had ever spoken to her before. Later, Carlisle and the men had stood on the front porch for a few minutes, looking west to the T-hawks' forest.

"It's a damn shame, them taking your place," one of the troopers had said with true sincerity in his voice. Then he added, "Don't quote me, though."

Carlisle smiled. "Thanks. I won't quote you, don't worry."

The county attorney asked, "Do you think this road's really going to do anything for Salamander?"

"No." Carlisle said only that, and the county attorney let it go.

The same trooper who had spoken earlier looked at Carlisle as they stepped off the porch. "Like I said, I'm sorry. It's a shame." He held out his hand.

Carlisle nodded and shook the trooper's hand, then did the same when the other two men offered theirs.

After they'd gone, he looked over the official notice stating he had until April 30 to clear out of the house he'd built for Cody. That gave him a little over two months to pack and move. He could do it in one day. As he laid the notice on the mantel next to the statue of Vesta and stood there thinking, Susanna put her arms around his waist from behind and rested her cheek against his back. A week ago, she had sent a letter to a man named Riddick living in the Wilson Mountains of Arizona. She said nothing to Carlisle about the letter.

A few days before Carlisle's eviction date, the Indian stopped by. He argued that one final symbolic gesture concerning the highway was in order. At first Carlisle objected, not being inclined toward what he saw as token behavior.

But, listening, he decided the Indian was not talking about tokenism. Symbolism, yes, but not tokenism. The Indian spoke of Crazy Horse, the great Sioux warrior; and Sweet Medicine, the Cheyenne medicine man; and Chief Joseph of the Nez Perce. He talked about long, forced marches through the snow and the smell of burning villages. To the Indian's way of thinking, the highway was not an isolated occurrence, but rather a plain and obvious continuation of what had gone before. Now, however, as he pointed out, the whites had turned on their own, distrusting anyone making a try for freedom or asking for consideration of ideas beyond the white man's customary way of doing things.

"Builder, we must proclaim again that some of us stand for another way. If we want to be certain our deathbed memories cause us to smile, we must stand for that other way, just as Crazy Horse and Sweet Medicine and Joseph did. As in your culture's tale of the man Odysseus, someone has chosen to open the bag and release all the contrary winds against people such as you and me, or so it seems. But if we cannot have the winds with us, then we must let it be known that we will at least not bend, no matter how hard they have chosen to blow, no matter if they are winds from the graveyard. We must, in our own way, shout into those winds, even if our words are blown back into our faces and are heard only by ourselves. If you find that idea uncomfortable, then I have misjudged you."

Carlisle had talked to the Flute Player several times about the Lakota Sioux somehow blocking the highway to protect the sacred ground. Maybe they could save that much, if nothing else. But the Indian would say only that the People were considering it. Carlisle and Susanna drove down to the capital and met with Lamont Crow Wing of AIM, a tough veteran of the Indian struggles. He had been at Wounded Knee with Frank Black Horse, Loreli Decora, and the rest when the federal government laid siege to it in 1973. He'd been part of the protest in 1972 after Raymond Yellow Thunder was beaten, stripped from the waist down, and paraded around an American Legion dance in Gordon, Nebraska, where the celebrants were invited to kick Raymond Yellow Thunder, after which he was stuffed in a car trunk and died there.

Lamont Crow Wing was no soft reservation Indian. That was obvious. In an old workshirt, jeans, and surplus army boots, he sat behind a gray metal desk and looked at Carlisle, then at Susanna.

"Of course, I have heard about what's going on up in Yerkes County. I respect you for your struggles, Mr. McMillan. But let's talk straight. I do not care about your house. It is unfortunate the highway will destroy your home, but from our point of view, that's all it is, unfortunate.

"The highway is a complex matter for us. Even within a given Indian tribe there is much controversy over the best path to the future for us. Some traditionalists hold out for the old life ways, others see an acceptance of white attitudes toward economics and development as our only hope for survival. In other words, if you go down to the reservation, you might be surprised to find support for the highway in some quarters. Unemployment is a serious problem for us, and some believe the highway will bring new jobs. Also, some of the tribal leaders can be bought off easily. That's already happened in the past, and it will happen again.

"The T-hawks—that's sad, and pardon me if I'm overly blunt, but you people worry about the extinction of a few birds while we worry about the extinction of entire cultures. We are being obliterated, just as surely as if the horse soldiers were still slaughtering us with their guns. It's a little slower now, but no less painful."

He listened when Carlisle argued that

saving the T-hawks would save the burial mounds and vice versa, then Crow Wing repeated much of what Susanna had already said about the Indians' problems. He finished by saying, "A lot of the People have just given up and don't think it will do any good to try to stop the highway by legal means, in spite of the burial grounds near Wolf Butte. We have no faith in white man's law, and there's no reason why we should, given our past experience with it. However, just to make you aware of it, AIM has filed a request for an injunction to halt the road while the disposition of artifacts is discussed. Because of the speed with which the highway project has proceeded, we were late in the filing and have little hope our request will be granted. Concern for the past is no match for the promises of economic development."

Lamont Crow Wing grinned sardonically, looking straight and firm at the man and woman across the desk from him. "You know what we used to sing as part of our ghost-dance ritual? 'The whites are crazy / The whites are crazy.'"

He promised, however, to talk with some other members of AIM and certain of the reservation Indians about the highway, the birds, and the burial grounds. He was mostly concerned about the burial grounds and said so. Carlisle had not heard from him after that.

On a cool April morning, under heavy clouds and threat of rain, Carlisle and the Flute Player formed a two-man picket line just north of where Route 42 intersected the red dirt of Wolf Butte Road leading to Carlisle's house. Construction workers and machines had reached the intersection and were preparing to move up the road, doing initial site work for the heavy construction to follow and taking dead aim at Carlisle's place and the T-hawks. Word had flashed via the Yerkes County telegraph that he and the Indian were out there obstructing progress, and inside of forty minutes around two hundred people had gathered, creating a traffic jam nearly blocking 42.

Huge yellow machines were moving back and forth in what seemed to be almost random patterns to a casual watcher. If the earth could have talked, it would have been screaming as tons of it were dug and pushed and loaded and hauled. The scene resembled a military battle: red dust rising into the air, the roar of trucks and earthmovers and bulldozers, people shouting, men operating jackhammers tearing up Route 42 where it would be rebuilt to accommodate an exit from the new interstate highway, allowing tourists to visit Antelope National Park and Ray Dargen's Indian Mysteryland.

As Carlisle would later say, "In spite of how you feel about road construction, you have to admit there's something awful virile about it, all those big machines, all that power. In terms of dominating nature, it doesn't match nuclear weapons, but it's next best."

Carlisle was dressed in faded jeans, his old leather jacket, and work boots, his hair reaching to his shoulders, yellow bandanna tied around his head. The Indian wore his standard uniform of jeans and denim jacket, black hat and cowboy boots, western shirt. Each of them carried a small wooden flute, and they stood side by side, directly in front of a bulldozer that had crossed Route 42 and was beginning to move up the dirt road.

Carloads of people were still arriving. Most left their autos on the highway, turning it into a parking lot, and walked up to within fifty yards or so of where Carlisle and the Indian had positioned themselves. People were talking to one another, nodding, pointing at the two, shaking their heads. A few were smiling and laughing, most were not. Somehow, what was occurring moved Carlisle's earlier arguments from the level of easily dismissed abstractions to a hard, obvious reality.

More red dust rose into the air, drifting over the spectators, and far back, locked in the traffic jam, were the sirens and revolving blue lights of state patrol cars. Ralph Pluimer, on-site manager for F. J. Remkin & Sons, contractors for the portion of the road within the state, moved forward and spoke to Carlisle and the Indian, thinking he could frighten them into giving up their foolish stand. "I'm asking the two of you to please get out of the way. But I'm only asking once. After that, it's your asses, not mine." Carlisle said nothing, the Indian said nothing.

Pluimer turned and walked away, motioning for the lead bulldozer to move forward. The driver, wearing a blue baseball cap and mirrored sunglasses, shifted gears and the machine jerked toward Carlisle and the Indian.

A woman from the crowd, Marcie English, ran to Carlisle and the Indian, crying, pulling on Carlisle's jacket. "Carlisle, this is insane, you're going to get hurt. Please stop. It's over, can't you see that?" Though she was screaming, the noise of the approaching machinery almost overpowered her words.

"Go back, Marcie. Dammit, go back! I don't know what's going to happen here."

Carlisle tore her hand from his jacket and she retreated, wiping her eyes on the cuff of her rain slicker. He could see Susanna Benteen off to one side, about thirty yards away, a look of concern on her face. Susanna had serious reservations about the wisdom of this demonstration and had said so. But Carlisle and the Indian had already decided they were going to do it.

The Indian began to play his flute, its timbre cutting through the roar of machinery, his melody counterpointed by the wail of state patrol sirens back along the highway. The lead bulldozer was thirty yards in front of them and moving forward. Carlisle brought up his own flute and began to play, the two of them harmonizing on a short, repetitive melody.

Rain began, turning the raw earth to a slimy red gumbo. WFC Television had arrived from Falls City, a cameraman and a reporter positioning themselves behind Carlisle and the Indian. A photographer and a reporter sent by the *High Plains Inquirer* to cover the destruction of the T-hawk forest joined the television crew.

Rain coming harder . . .
    Clank of machinery . . .
    Sheriff's department strobe lights off to one side, coming across open ground from the east . . .
Bulldozer treads turning bright red, earth color . . .
    Sirens . . .
    Men yelling . . .
Ralph Pluimer shouting at the bulldozer operator: "We've put up with these sonsabitches for too long . . ."
    Bulldozer coming on . . .
Carlisle and the Indian playing their flutes . . .
    Cameras filming the Indian and Carlisle and a person known as the duck-man

standing beside them who
was wearing a large overcoat
with a bulge that seemed to
move around beneath the
gathered lapels . . .

Reporter excited, gabbling
into her microphone . . .

State trooper forcing his way
through the crowd and attempting to drive a patrol car across
the increasingly muddy terrain.
Other troopers running, slipping, sliding, toward Carlisle
and the Indian . . .

Ten feet from the Indian, Carlisle, and the
duck-man, the bulldozer stopped, distorted
images of the three men reflected in the
rain-washed blade, elongating their faces
and bodies into otherworldly shapes—a
little tin-pot army from another time. Still the
Indian and Carlisle played their simple
melody, and the duck-man clutched his
coat lapels, pulling down his knit cap with
his other hand. The bulldozer beginning to
inch forward again. The operator dropped
the blade and began to push a growing
mound of earth toward the three men.

Simultaneously, four state troopers reached the Indian, Carlisle, and the duckman, and a fifth began shouting angrily to the bulldozer operator, who stopped his machine and shut off the engine. The rain began to fall with more intensity. Suddenly, the entire construction site was quiet. All machines were shut down, everyone simply was watching. It was absolutely silent, except for the rain and the voices of state troopers talking to the three protesters. One of those watching from back in the crowd was a big man with a black beard, who wore an old green army jacket and a cap with EARTH WARRIOR on the crown. People stood apart from the stranger but glanced at him and whispered to one another when he walked over to the witch and talked to her.

A patrol car worked its way across the mud and halted twenty feet from where the conversation between the troopers and protesters was taking place. Carlisle was shaking his head in response to the words directed at him. The Indian continued playing and was ordered to stop by one of the troopers.

He continued anyway, and the trooper yanked the flute from his hands, shouting at him, "What the hell do you think you're do-ing?"

The Indian replied, "I am watching the buffalo."

The duck-man was silent, still clutching the lapels of his overcoat with both hands and his eyes flicking rapidly in all directions. There was agitated movement beneath the coat.

Carlisle, the Indian, and the duck-man were handcuffed, taken to the patrol car, and put in the backseat, while a trooper held the mallard duck and wondered what to do with it. Susanna Benteen offered to take the duck, and Marcie English, in turn, took it from her, saying they would keep it safe on their ranch.

The doors on the patrol car were slammed shut, and with red lights flashing and siren howling, the car fishtailed across red mud, back wheels spinning. Through the mud-splattered rear window, three blurred heads could be seen as the patrol car maneuvered through the crowd and onto Route 42, heading toward Livermore. The same thought was on everyone's mind: This surely must be the end of the Yerkes County highway war, and it had come down finally to the mud-and-rain-blurred images of two handcuffed, long-haired men and another one regarded as the town crazy riding east in a state patrol car on a wet April morning.

When the reporters asked for comment from the bystanders, most refused. Some were clearly pleased that Carlisle and the Indian had been arrested, others just shook their heads and turned away when attempts were made to interview them. Marcie and Claude English refused to talk. Susanna Benteen had disappeared.

One Mr. Gabe O'Rourke, however, did respond tersely to a reporter's question. When asked what he thought of the drama that had just occurred, the accordion player offered only the following enigmatic statement: "It was a first-class tango. One of the best I've ever seen."

So the Builder and the Flute Player and the duck-man made their stand, a symbolic stand, but not a futile one. Carlisle understood that when he saw their reflections in the bulldozer's blade. They had lost but not succumbed. They had shouted into the wind.

Public records show a man named Carlisle McMillan and another identified as Arthur Sweet Grass, who gave his age as "old" when asked by the booking sergeant. Told that was unacceptable, Mr. Sweet Grass changed it to 105. They were charged with a misdemeanor and jailed for a few hours, then released when Carlisle paid their nominal fines for creating a public disturbance. It should be noted, however, that Mr. Sweet Grass indicated he was perfectly willing to work off his fine in jail time. After attempting to interview the duck-man, the magistrate recommended he be released with no charges filed against him.

Afterward, sitting in Carlisle's living room area, Susanna said, "Arthur was right, it *was* worth doing. At least you stood for something besides concrete. He once said that if you cannot fasten your message on the horns of a buffalo, then send it on the wings of a butterfly. At least you sent a message, even if it rode only on a butterfly's wings."

And the people of Yerkes County would remember the stand and talk about it for years to come. How a white man and an Indian and a man dismissed as loony had challenged the bulldozers, flutes playing, refusing to be moved by the arguments of progress, even when it was clear to almost everyone else that the white man and the Indian and, of course, the duck-man were wrong. On top of that, the *Inquirer*'s photographer eventually won a Pulitzer for his shot of Arthur Sweet Grass, Carlisle McMillan, and a man in a long overcoat reflected in a bulldozer blade.

Heavy rain halted construction on the highway for six days after the Indian and Carlisle were arrested. When work resumed, Susanna and Carlisle drove west of Salamander, parked the truck, and walked across the fields of early May to a hill overlooking the T-hawk forest and the place Carlisle had built for Cody.

They found a spot where the warming sun hit the earth nice and soft, sitting there and watching the first of the Caterpillars crawling north along the gravel road. The driver wore a blue ball cap and mirrored sunglasses. Behind him was a truck carrying men with chain saws.

When the Cat turned into Carlisle's lane, Susanna wrapped both her arms around one of his, tears running down her cheeks. He gritted his teeth, listening to the Cat-skinner shift his machine into successively lower gears. The driver never paused, just kept shifting down and moving up the lane, a grinding, surreal, unremitting symbol of something called progress. Susanna was digging her fingernails into Carlisle's arm without even realizing it.

The bulldozer crushed into the atrium first and hit the south wall of Cody's tribute thirty seconds later. Carlisle could hear the splintering redwood shriek as nails he had hammered one by one wrenched free, the house first leaning, then twisting into a grotesque shape. And he thought about Cody and about all the long days in the sun and nights he'd slept in the truck with a yellow tomcat while snow blew around them, working by the light of a gasoline lantern, sanding and smoothing, preparing the surfaces and finishing, and doing everything else in between in the right way. He could see the piles of lumber he had scrounged and Gally coming up a twilight lane and Susanna naked in the loft with a yellow feather in her hair. He could see it all, and all of it was disintegrating as he stared down at what had been his thirty acres.

In less than ten minutes, the place was leveled. After that, the workshop went down in one push, and the bulldozer moved toward the pond. The dam was earthen, so it was no problem, and pond water flooded into the creek channel. Down the lenses of his binoculars, Carlisle could see bluegills washing through the cut. While the bull-dozer took care of the pond, a workman started a chain saw and began cutting the two oaks standing near where the house had been. They came down easily, crushing the bat houses as they hit the ground.

Across the road, T-hawks were rising into morning air as men moved into the for-est with chain saws. At the entrance to Carlisle's lane, two men in yellow hard hats were leaning over a car hood, looking at a large map they'd unrolled.

"Carlisle, I can't watch this anymore. Let's go." Susanna got to her feet as she said it.

He nodded, kicked a clod of dirt, and walked off with her. Looking back once, he could see the bulldozer scraping soil into the pond. It would be filled and leveled in a few hours. Workmen were randomly tossing the remains of Cody's house and the workshop onto trucks, and T-hawks were circling high above the whine of yellow chain saws held steady by men in orange hard hats. Carlisle wondered if the T-hawks wondered. Maybe, maybe not.

By day's end, there would be no remaining signs of Williston or Carlisle or the T-hawks, and Carlisle decided without even thinking about it that one small token gesture was in order. He picked up a rock and threw it as far as he could toward the bulldozer. The rock fell an eighth of a mile short, bounced twice, and was still. At the same moment the rock came to rest, the water tower in Salamander exploded in a roar of orange flame and crashed onto the county maintenance shed next to it.

The mature hawks were in a frenzy, trying to coax the young ones, not yet ready to fly, into the air away from the toppling trees and whine of the saws. Susanna Benteen tugged at Carlisle's jacket. "Carlisle, *please* let's go."

Carlisle refused to move, frozen there, breathing hard with emotion and nailed to where he stood. At that moment, the blast from a shotgun brought quiet with it, and everyone looked down the road. None of them had seen the old rusted-down Buick turn off Route 42 and begin moving up Wolf Butte Road. It came slowly up the red dirt, toward the T-hawk forest. On it came, straight toward where the engineers studied site plans. The chain saws had shut down, workmen wondering what role the Buick and a shotgun protruding from its driver's-side window played in their morning's work. They stared at George Riddick as he dismounted from the car. The gun was pointed upward, the butt of it resting on his hip.

Riddick wiggled a cold cigar in his mouth and looked at the men. "Good morning, gentlemen. Now we're going to have a discussion about options. And your set of choices is pretty thin. In fact, there is only one: Get the hell out of here."

He brought the shotgun down from his hip and chambered a shell, the hard *shick-shick* of the forestock's slide underlining his words. George Riddick pointed the Remington toward Route 42 and spoke with quiet firmness. "All of you get moving. Now." With those words, a ragged band of hard hats began running down the road toward Route 42.

There is a thin and tenuous line between outrage and radicalism. Carlisle had tee- tered on that border, stepping tentatively across it when he and the Indian and the duck-man had made their stand. But George Riddick had walked across that line a long time ago and kept on walking into territory where few had ever walked and kept on go- ing to a place where his mind no longer functioned in normal ways. And what hap- pened to him personally was of no concern to George Riddick.

Over the years, two things had protected Riddick. The first was the sheer boldness of his ways. People simply didn't expect other people to behave as he did, such as the time he walked into the headquarters of Continental Cyanide, tore up the telephone switchboard at the main reception desk, and instructed the receptionist to open the locked glass doors to the executive offices, which she did with Riddick's hand on her throat.

The CEO had screamed at him, "This is terrorism!"

Riddick gave him a cold grin. "You're

goddamned right it is. Get ready to be terrified."

Beyond his audacity, George Riddick was a random variable. No pattern, no predictability, hard to trace, impossible to anticipate. He would lie up for months in his mountain cabin near Sedona, walking the rocky trails, rage building. Then some primeval swell would mount within him, and he would move again. Yet for all his anger and brutal methods, he had never killed anyone since his long-ago jungle days.

The previous afternoon, the local boys had sicced Hack Kenbule on Riddick, just as they had done earlier with Carlisle. Riddick was walking down the main street of Salamander when Hack came after him. Didn't work out the same as with Carlisle. Hack lasted exactly fourteen seconds, staggering around and gasping for air after half a dozen karate chops to the neck and other critical regions, after which Riddick put him through the dusty window of what had once been Charlene's variety store, with a kick in the face. Marv Umthon tried to intervene on Hack's behalf, and Riddick simply broke big Marv's ankle with one stomp of his boot, looked at Marv hopping around on one foot screaming, and decided to break the other one while he was at it. Fred Mumford, being the sole member of Salamander's police force and having self-preservation foremost in his mind, declined to arrest Riddick on the grounds that Hack Kenbule had started it all.

Two hours before Riddick appeared at the T-hawk forest, three members of EWU wheeled a barrel of chicken blood into Ray Dargen's office. Damages to the office and to Dargen's Lincoln Continental parked in back were subsequently estimated at $70,000. Dargen heard the ruckus before it got to his inner office and locked the door. George Riddick kicked in the door with his paratrooper boot, pasted Ray Dargen against the wall and poured six ounces of chicken blood down his throat, then left him vomiting on the $200-a-yard beige office carpet.

Thirty minutes after the damage to Dargen's operation, another barrel of blood was trundled into the offices of the High Plains Development Corporation. Margaret Andrews ran out the back door and used the pay phone down the block to call Mr. Flanigan, who was in Washington, D.C., expressing his concerns to a Senate committee about the Rio Grande Initiative and its potential impact on the economic future of his area.

After that, Riddick removed the license plates from the old Buick, filed off all identification numbers on the vehicle, and put the other members of EWU on the road to the mountains, telling them, "This one might end badly. I'm going to do the rest myself."

Riddick maneuvered the Buick until it was angled across the road just short of the T-hawk forest. He filled his jacket pockets with ammunition. Right pocket: double-aught shotgun shells. Left pocket: clips for the Beretta. He laid a Winchester Model 94 .30-30 on the hood of the car and put a box of cartridges beside it. Drinking water from his canteen, he waited. He had no plans. Whatever was going to happen would happen. He wasn't even sure why he was doing this, something about the end of things, something about the state of *"no more"* he carried in his mind.

State troopers arrived, looked over the situation, and called for help. Three hours later, George Riddick faced the standard array of bullhorns and SWAT teams. Fifty or sixty armed men confronted him, the bull-horns talking to him, trying to talk him down. He seemed unaware of it all.

News teams arrived by midafternoon. Five miles to the northwest, a fire burned on Wolf Butte, sending a barely discernible column of smoke rising. Riddick saw it.

Flanking movements were tried. Riddick expertly used the Winchester to hold them off, firing over their heads. He had nothing against the cops but knew they would come for him after dark. Didn't matter, nothing mattered anymore except struggle and retribution.

An hour before sundown, a line of old cars and pickups turned onto the red dirt road and moved up it toward the T-hawk forest. When the phalanx of police halted the caravan, seventy-five Lakota Sioux and representatives from other tribes, mostly members of the American Indian Movement led by Lamont Crow Wing, got out and walked across the fields to the T-hawk forest, disregarding the bullhorned orders to stop. They chained themselves to the larger trees while two EWU members with chicken blood on their clothing, ignoring Riddick's orders to leave, began hammering spikes into tree trunks as a deterrent to chain saws. After word reached the AIM office about the stand Riddick was making, Lamont Crow Wing had said, "Piss on it. Let's go do something and stop hanging out here like a bunch of res Indians waiting around for the handouts."

Darkness came. Negotiations continued with Lamont Crow Wing while spikes went into trees. A SWAT team moved forward toward Riddick's position. Men running, crouching, falling to their bellies, and talking to one another over small radios. They were within thirty yards of the junked car and with their night-vision glasses could see the Winchester lying across the hood. More quiet chatter on the radios, sweating hard and getting ready. Final assault. They checked their weapons and begin zigzagging runs toward George Riddick's barricade. When they arrived, there was nothing except the Winchester lying on the hood of the sedan.

A little way to the north of where the final assault had been made, two men sat on the crest of Wolf Butte by the remains of an extinguished fire. They talked quietly. One of them was old and wore a wide-brimmed hat with juju beads on the crown. The other wore a cap with the logo EARTH WARRIOR. They greeted the woman who had climbed the butte and sat beside them.

While they talked, a somewhat ambivalent federal judge in Falls City, worried about political ramifications, had been prodded into action by an attorney for AIM, who had continued flashing news to the judge from the front lines near the T-Hawk forest while insisting he would be held responsible for any carnage that occurred. The petition by the Sioux was granted, and the judge issued a temporary restraining order preventing highway construction through the burial mounds northwest of the T-hawk forest until questions surrounding the content and true ownership of the mounds could be settled. The judge wrote the following in issuing the order:

> Traditionally, Fifth Amendment rights regarding private property have held sway in such matters. Recent claims, however, by Native Americans and other original inhabitants of lands throughout the world, particularly the Australian Aborigines, have given the courts some pause in

allowing destruction of a people's heritage, even though the relics that are part of this heritage may be located on land held in private ownership. Therefore, the purpose of this restraining order is to allow time for litigation concerning the limits of constitutional rights concerning the disposition of such artifacts.

CHAPTER TWENTY-ONE

Ray Dargen was screaming into his car phone, his words machine-gunning all the way to Washington, D.C. The Lincoln was out of commission while the dealership struggled with removing dried chicken blood, but he still had the Cadillac, which he also treated as a depreciable asset for the RAYMAX Corporation, even though it was his wife's vehicle and never used for business.

Senator Harlan Sterk was talking quietly on the other end. "Ray, shut up and listen to me. The FBI and the State Bureau of Criminal Investigation are looking into the violence out there. We'll take care of that. But I'm telling you, Senator Wheems has had it. You overplayed it, my friend. You've done it before and gotten away with it. This time it's not going to work. I know you've been a good supporter of mine, but there are limits as to what I can do, and frankly, I'm pretty steamed up myself about those land purchases of yours along the right-of-way. To quote Jack Wheems, 'I don't give a good goddamn about what some clown named Ray Dargen thinks. This highway is a lot bigger than him *or* Yerkes County.' Wheems said that two hours ago."

Sterk continued. "What happened out there has been all over the national news. The networks keep rerunning that tape of McMillan and his friends standing in front of the bulldozer, and somehow that crazy man, we think it was this George Riddick, and his Indian cohort have captured the fancy of people everywhere, the last stand against the white man's stupidity, all that stuff. Christ, people are calling in from all over the world on behalf of those birds. The transportation committee is saying bad things about this project, and if we don't watch out, we're going to end up with a strip of concrete that ends somewhere near Falls City in a wheat field."

Ray Dargen began to whine, but Senator Sterk interrupted him. "Ray, I said shut up and listen. It looks like the Indians can hold up the project for at least six months with the restraining order. You own the land, and, whether it's morally right or not, the law is pretty clear according to a lawyer I spoke with. The land is yours, and the artifacts in the burial mounds are yours, and that's how things probably will eventually work out through the courts. But that's not the problem. The problem is this: The transportation committee is buckling under the bad public relations that have been generated out there and may recommend that the highway end at Wichita, especially with Florida crying about their population boom and the need for more road money down there. Even if that doesn't happen, Wheems says a delay of six months is unacceptable to him, since that will put us into winter and effectively amounts to a construction delay of nearly a year. At the moment he has the engineers working around the clock, looking for a way to change the route and still include the Falls City–Livermore strip. It'll be a pretty strange-looking road, but I think he's going to get it done.

"If I were you, I'd stop worrying about the highway and start worrying about my own ass. George Riddick, or whoever, is still roaming around somewhere, and your old pal Carlisle McMillan is talking to the state attorney general about those little land acquisitions along the right-of-way carried out by you and your buddies. To be honest with you, Ray, I think you're in some trouble, possibly bad trouble, and I can't help you. More than that, I can't even appear to have had anything to do with your mischief. We warned you about this. I went too far in getting Wheems to change the route to include Falls City and Livermore, given what you were trying to pull off. Now listen to this and listen carefully: I appreciate your past support, but this is where we part company. Don't call me anymore, Ray, I don't want to hear from you. My advice is to get yourself a first-class criminal lawyer and hang on. And by the way, if you run into Axel Looker out there, tell him to stop calling me, too. It's not our job to help him retire to Florida or Arizona or wherever. Good-bye."

The last three sentences of an editorial in the *Inquirer* one week later read as follows:

Businessman-developer Ray Dargen's decision to deed Wolf Butte and surrounding property to the Lakota Sioux is commendable; however, just what this means for the planned route of the Avenue of the High Plains is uncertain. In fact, the entire Avenue is uncertain at this time, which is a sad state of affairs for those of us concerned about the economic future of this state. It's unfortunate that a few radicals with misplaced concerns about the environment can thwart the progress so necessary to our collective well-being.

CHAPTER TWENTY-TWO

In the weeks before his eviction date, when the settlement over the house came to a head, Carlisle retained a lawyer from Falls City, a counselor who had fought all the land wars ever fought in the high plains. He was old and mean, the only true son of a gully rattler. And he didn't much like anybody, jamming the law and logic right up the nozzle of the state and anyone else daring to offer an opinion, making them pay Carlisle $180,000 flat for the Williston place.

Their protestations reached the level of shrieks, but the lawyer quoted Plato—"Render to each his due"—then rolled into biblical metaphor, loosely, citing Jacob's dream, saying Carlisle had lain upon the rocks of Mr. Williston's place and turned them into the gate of heaven for himself. The lawyer paraded a copy of the *Observer* article that had called Carlisle one of the great crafts-men of the high plains, pointing out that 257 people had come to Carlisle's open house, and generally made the opposition feel as if they were destroying St. Peter's Basilica.

The state countered by offering to pay that sum if Carlisle would agree to let them convert the place into a tourist information center, saying what a nice impression it would make on visitors. That gave Carlisle visions of "Rick + Tammy" hacked into the wood he had sanded and smoothed and of people going tinkle in the pond or throwing stones at the bluegills. His lawyer took care of that, too, calling for what he labeled "the complete purification of a man's monument to his teacher," by which he meant absolute and total destruction.

The bulldozers were already working in Louisiana and Arkansas, and the schedule was tight. After all, New Orleans and Yerkes County both needed saving. The money was paid with no tourist information center attached to it, after which the lawyer swept up his documents, shook Carlisle's hand, and said, "Screw 'em." His wife wanted a wall moved in their house, and he would take that as his fee, if Carlisle was agreeable.

Two days before he was required to vacate Cody's place, Susanna helped Carlisle box and haul his things to her house. Carlisle went into negotiations with the owner of the Flagstone Ballroom over in Livermore and managed to buy the old dump and a little bungalow beside it for $20,000. That was his next project. He had figured out that with the right design, a fair amount of scrounging, and some careful work, he could turn it into a real palace for Susanna and him. Living quarters, plenty of room for workshops and art studios and Susanna's mail-order business, while leaving the dance floor intact. After he had the plumbing working and some wiring done, he patched the roof and framed up temporary quarters that could be heated in winter. When Susanna's lease expired six months later, they moved themselves over to the ballroom.

After two years, and some perspective to look back on it all, Carlisle still believed he was right, right in his general opinions about the demise of Salamander and right to try to stomp the corrupt bastards who cooked up the highway in the first place. He would do it again under similar circumstances. But maybe he had made it all a little too pat, too one-sided and sanctimonious. That's what he concluded in his more honest moments.

As Susanna said to him, "Carlisle, it's hard to find true evil, but there are fools everywhere. Salamander has only its share and no more."

Carlisle knew he had positioned himself as some kind of pious champion fighting a dark empire, when all he was really fighting mostly was a bunch of people who had forgotten how to survive and had been suckered by what pyemic marketeers defined as the good life. Salamander, and Yerkes County in general, had counted on a future that never happened, panicked when it didn't.

Besides, he reflected there were good things out there. When he was considering whether to leave or stay after the highway route had been decided, he thought about that, the good things. Where else could you hear first-class tangos those days? And the county still respected him for his skills, if not his opinions. Salamander, what was left of it, remained cool toward him, but the people in Falls City and elsewhere continued to pay well for his services. You could buy gas without first paying an attendant in a bullet-proof kiosk, and in Susanna, the Indian, Marcie and Claude English, and Gally, not to mention a gutsy little guy called the duck-man, he had met some of the best people he'd ever known, people possessing wisdom and courage far beyond the flashy cleverness of Buddy Reems or the ephemeral culture of the San Francisco streets. That's why he purchased the Flagstone Ballroom and decided to make another run at his particular brand of camouflage.

When the Avenue of the High Plains was jogged west to avoid the T-hawk forest and Indian burial mounds around Wolf Butte, the idea for Antelope National Park was scrapped. So, of course, was the federal government's intent to purchase the properties owned by Axel Looker and Gally Deveraux, where the park would have been located. Facing bankruptcy and foreclosure on her ranch, Gally had dropped out of school.

Susanna, while awarding Carlisle the Recusant of the Decade Award, encouraged him to go see Gally, believing he should renew the friendship that had been important to both him and Gally. Danny's had closed six months after the highway was completed, and Gally was managing the restaurant portion of a new Best Western motel near Falls City.

Carlisle hadn't seen her for more than two years. It seemed longer than that. Lots of things seemed far back to him, farther than they really were. The Yerkes County highway war and Susanna had driven a wedge into time, splitting it and fouling up his internal abacus, making events that occurred before the wars and before Susanna seem more distant than the calendar's measure, and he hardly recognized Gally when he sat down at the Best Western restaurant counter.

They tried getting together a couple of times during the early stages of the highway battle, but, as he pointed out, there was something between them, concrete. Regardless of where their conversations and glances at each other had seemed to lead, the concrete divided them. The highway had covered their relationship with a layer of hard feelings that suffocated it for him.

Gally was facing slightly away from him, talking to a waitress, crisp, and well dressed, her hair pulled back fancylike. Just as she finished her conversation and was about to walk into the kitchen, Carlisle said, "I'll have a hot turkey sandwich with extra mashed potatoes."

She turned, surprised at first, then smiling. "Hello, Carlisle."

He was a little uneasy, asking if she had a few minutes free. They sat in his truck, and he told her that he missed her as a friend. He was sorry for both of them that things had ended a little too quickly, too hard. Gally had a nice way of touching his cheek with her hand. He remembered that when she reached over and did it, saying she understood, tears in her eyes. He was glad he'd come.

Still touching his cheek, she said, "Carlisle, we had a fine year together, and if it can't be me, then I'm glad it's Susanna."

She said her life was going well, and he believed her. The motel manager had come up from Dallas, escaping the memories of a messy divorce back down the road, and he and Gally were thinking of getting engaged. She promised to send Susanna and Carlisle a wedding invitation if things got that far. He said they would be pleased to attend.

She looked at him, serious face. "Carlisle, the highway hasn't helped Salamander at all. In fact, it's done quite a lot of harm. Just made it easier for people to drive over to Falls City for shopping and eating out, like you predicted. Can you imagine? People actually drive forty miles to Falls City to buy bananas because they're ten cents a bunch cheaper there. Don't they think about wear and tear on their cars or the value of their own time or the gas it takes to get there?"

Carlisle was silent, while Gally continued, starting to giggle. "Did you hear about Leroy's parrot?"

Carlisle shook his head.

"Well, let me back up a minute. Leroy, as you know, watched his business going to pot for years and was always trying to think of something to perk it up. That's why he hired Gabe for a while on Saturday nights.

"After he decided Gabe cost too much, he got the idea of using a bullhorn to entertain the crowd. Said he'd seen some comedian on television using one. Every so often he'd pick up this stupid bullhorn and announce to one and all that so-and-so's pizza was ready. He even tried to tell jokes through it. The problem is, of course, Leroy's no comedian, as we all know.

"After a while, the boys starting grabbing the bullhorn when Leroy wasn't looking. It got pretty bizarre, not to mention tasteless. By nine on Saturday nights, they'd start trying to sing along with the jukebox through it. By eleven, things would degenerate, the drunks wrestling for control of the bullhorn so they could make announcements such as 'Hey, Alma, how about comin' over here and sittin' on you-know-what for a while?' For heaven's sake, you could hear them clear out on the street, so Leroy doused that idea. Next thing he tried was dwarf tossing. Ever hear of that?"

Carlisle had an incredulous grin on his face. "What tossing?"

"Dwarf tossing. Leroy didn't invent it. Seems it was all the rage for a while in some spots around the country, though it's unlikely it'll be an Olympic event anytime soon. At one end of his place, Leroy piled up three or four old mattresses. The idea, from what I gather, was to see how far you could throw this dwarf from Falls City who hired himself out for the occasion. Hack Kenbule, of course, eventually held the all-time record for the event, at least at Leroy's. Marv Umthon was rankled by that, but he was still hobbling a bit from what that wild man Riddick did to his ankles, so he couldn't match Hack's great achievement. Anyway, that silly stuff lasted until people started complaining about the insensitivity of the pastime, even though the dwarf didn't seem to mind too much.

"Then while Leroy was downstate at the hospital he got to talking with some psychiatrist who owned this parrot named Benny. Seems these birds have a life span of just about forever, decades, at least, and taking one on is a major commitment. Not only that, they're really tough *hombres*. Leroy claimed they can break a broomstick with their feet. Apparently, the parrot had attacked the psychiatrist's wife in a fit of jealousy, chewed her up real bad, and the psychiatrist had brought her down to the hospital so the doctors there could take a look at her wounds.

"Leroy bought the parrot for two hundred dollars, a steal, he maintained, figuring it would be a real draw at the tavern. It was for a while. The first day he had Benny, he took him into the bar and set him on a chair. Benny the parrot promptly hopped down on the floor and started walking around, mumbling to himself, so Leroy said."

In the telling of this, Gally began laughing so hard that tears ran down her cheeks. It was contagious, and Carlisle was laughing, too, even before she had the whole story out. Just imagining a parrot named Benny walking around the tavern floor and grumbling like Leroy was funny enough in itself.

"Now, Carlisle, remember that big, mean, ugly tomcat Leroy had? The one that used to sit on the jukebox and hiss at customers? Remember him? Leroy called him Bar Rag."

Carlisle nodded.

"Well, Bar Rag comes strolling into the room that first day Benny was walking around on the floor inspecting the place. The cat sees the bird, goes into one of those belly-to-the-ground-little-short-steps routines that cats are famous for, and begins sneaking up on Benny. About the time Bar Rag is only a few feet from Benny and is picking up speed as he moves in for the kill, the parrot turns, sees the cat, and yells, '*Hi!*' "

Gally was shaking with laughter. So was Carlisle, lying across the steering wheel of his truck and choking on the mental pictures he was forming while Gally talked.

"Leroy said Bar Rag was in the middle of his charge but stopped on a dime and actually flipped over backwards when the bird yelled *'Hi!'* at him. According to Leroy, Bar Rag started running for the back door, accelerating all the while like a space rocket, and busted right through the screen. That was three months ago, and Leroy hasn't seen him since."

By this time, Carlisle was slumped against the truck door, hands over his face, roaring with laughter. "What—"

"Wait!" Gally gurgled through her laughter, dabbing at her eyes with a handkerchief. "I'm not finished. Leroy's traffic improved, just as he'd hoped. Everyone wanted to see the bird that had run off Bar Rag. Pretty soon there were all kinds of people standing around with Grain Belts in their hands, just watching Benny to see what he'd do or say next. If nobody was paying any attention to him, Benny would swoop through the tavern screeching, 'Watch the bird! Watch the bird!'

"Also, it turned out that Benny had picked up quite a bit living with the psychiatrist. People'd be at the bar talking, and

Benny'd be sitting up on the Budweiser sign hanging from the ceiling, listening. After a while he'd start talking right into the conversation nearest him, saying things such as 'It's because of your mother, you'll just have to work through it,' and all that therapeutic stuff.

"Everybody thought this was pretty funny, except Bobby Eakins, who for some reason never liked Benny. He said, and I'm quoting him: 'I come in here to drink, not to get analyzed by a bird. I get enough of that shit from Leroy.'

"Leroy claimed parrots are sensitive and that Benny knew Bobby didn't like him. One evening, Bobby was into his third Grain Belt when Benny came walking down the bar, stopped about three feet from Bobby, and stared at him, head kind of twisted funny, eyes blinking, and says, 'Aarrk, *hi!*' "

Gally was imitating the way Benny must have looked, and Carlisle started roaring again, seeing in his mind the face-off between Benny the parrot and Bobby Eakins in his fertilizer cap.

"Bobby says, 'Get the fuck outta here, ya asshole bird,' dips his fingers in his beer, and starts spritzing Benny. Those in attendance said it was something to watch. Before Bobby could even flinch, Benny had Bobby by the ear with his beak and was tearing it right in half. Leroy grabbed Benny, Benny chomped down on Bobby, Bobby's screaming and crying and bleeding. It was a real mess. He got his ear sewn back on okay, but there's a big ugly red scar there, and his earlobe hangs kind of funny. Leroy finally got rid of Benny, sent him somewhere to a pet store, and Bobby refused to drink at Leroy's anymore, mostly because of the grief he received from the other local heroes, who took to calling the parrot 'Bobby's Bird' and saying things like 'You and the parrot can work it out, Bobby. Aarrk, good thing it wasn't an eagle.'"

Carlisle was still shaking his head and wiping his eyes. "How's Leroy doing now?"

"I guess you haven't heard. After Gabe, bullhorns, dwarf tossing, and parrots, Leroy decided it was time to forget the whole thing. He retired about a month ago and closed the place. Threw one final party, however, on the last Saturday night he was open. I went to it, and it was fun, though I have to admit, I kept thinking of all the good times you and I had there. I'm not trying to bring up what we talked about before, just telling the truth.

"By the way, at Leroy's closing, a lot of people asked about you. They never cared much for your position on the highway, but they do respect you for standing up for what you believed in. A number of them said that. Even big ol' Hack Kenbule said he had second thoughts about the pounding he did on you when you were just trying to save the house you built. He didn't mention the T-hawks, of course, since that's not something that Hack can get hold of. In any case, it was a good time, Leroy's farewell party. Even Beanie Wickers came slinking in. I hadn't seen him since the night you saved him from losing his manhood to Huey's knife. Before it was over, he and Huey shook hands and had a beer together, but Huey said that's as far as it went and that Beanie was not allowed to dance with Fran, who in the meantime, I noticed, was dancing real close with the co-op manager and blinking her eyes at him."

As she prepared to go back to the restaurant, Gally turned serious. "Carlisle, do you remember the old man with the bad leg who used to live above Lester's? The one who came into Danny's for lunch every day and read the paper?"

Carlisle knew whom she meant. The old guy watching the decline and fall of a high plains village from his second-floor window.

"About six months ago, he fell down those steep stairs to his apartment and broke his good leg. They hauled him out to the Yerkes County Care Facility since he had nowhere else to go. That craphead Birney got him evicted from the apartment and convinced the social services people they ought to keep him out at the home. After that, they tried to turn the building into a boutique, but you were right, Salamander is not Lourdes, and nobody's driving six miles off the interstate to buy machine-made quilts and cornhusk dolls. It lasted about six months. Word is that Cecil Macklin lost his financial tail on the enterprise.

"Anyway, I go visit the old man every couple of weeks or so. I feel just awful bad for him. He's very smart in his own way, and they're using drugs and television to make him into a vegetable. He's never talked much about himself all the years I've known him, but he's real depressed now and spends his time looking through some old shoeboxes where he keeps his memories. He showed me the silver star he got for fighting at the Arnhem Bridge in Holland during World War Two. Said he killed three Germans that day and took a small piece of shrapnel in the leg. Now this great land thanks him by shoveling him off to the county farm and treating him like shoddy from the packing plant. I guess the Veterans Home has a waiting list a mile long, so he can't get in there, and it's not much better. Maybe if you get a chance, you might stop in and say hello. He's desperate, I can see in his eyes."

As Carlisle drove back to Livermore, his old anger ginned up again. What the hell kind of place was this country becoming? he asked himself for the thousandth time. Money all over the place for $150 basketball sneakers demanded by whining worshippers of people with decent jump shots and not much else. But apparently nothing for old people, dying babies, T-hawks, and everything else that needed tending.

He talked with Susanna about it. A few days later, he drove over to the depressing mess generously labeled a care facility. Out of sight, out of mind, old folks drizzling and babbling. Some of them because they were genuinely ill, some of them because of the way they were being treated.

Carlisle found the old man. He was standing, supporting himself with a cane, and looking out the window of the room he shared with two other men, both of them bedridden. The room smelled of bodily functions, and the window had heavy institutional wire fronting the screen.

"I'm Carlisle McMillan. I'm not sure if you remember me, but I used to see you in Danny's now and then."

The old man nodded and brightened a little. "Oh, yessir, I know who you are, Mr. McMillan."

He looked tired, run-down, sinking. Bedroom slippers, dirty trousers, soiled long-sleeved shirt cut off at the elbows and never hemmed.

"How's your broken leg?"

"It's comin' along real good. Don't make much difference, though, since I don't have anywhere to go anyhow. Birney and his redcoats took my apartment away. That's about all I could afford. Got myself in a pickle, a small one by modern standards, big to me."

They walked outdoors and sat in the

sunlight. Carlisle noticed as they talked about the weather and things in general how the old man's mind seemed to crank slowly upward, his diction becoming better, and he made reference to world events, talking about them in kind of a rough, humorous, semiphilosophical way. He was raw-smart, as Gally had said. Carlisle mentioned the reconstruction job he and Susanna were doing on the old Flagstone. The old man's face lightened, and he said he'd spent a lot of his evenings at the Flagstone, met his wife at one of the Saturday night dances.

Carlisle asked him, "Know anything about billiards? The real stuff, table with no pockets, three balls, run the cue ball off three cushions to make a carom and go to heaven?" Gally had once told Carlisle the old man was the best three-cushion billiards player in the state years ago and regularly cleaned out the hustlers who occasionally stopped in Salamander, looking for a little traveling money.

Crooked grin on the old face. "I banked a few cue balls around the green felt in days past. Got my first car that way, took it off a drummer selling ladies' undergarments back in '38 who didn't know when to lay down his cue and give up. Hard to find a true billiards table now, since the game's too difficult for the Pepsi generation. They want to play pool and call it billiards, which it ain't."

"Tell you what," Carlisle said, smiling. "During one of my salvage expeditions, I found this great old billiards table at a tavern over in Leadville. The slate's perfect, the cushions seem fine, new felt required, beautiful hand-carved mahogany for the structure. It'd been covered with canvas for years. Thing must weigh a thousand pounds, but I took it apart and hauled it back to the Flagstone. Thought I'd set it up at one end of the dance floor, which should allow for plenty of cue space.

"Right beside the Flagstone," he continued, "is a small house, a bungalow, really, where the ballroom manager lived. I bought it as part of the property. I hear Gabe the tango player is getting pretty wobbly and needs a place to live, you need a place to live. How about the two of you sharing the old place? Gabe can work off his rent by playing a little music, you take care of yours by teaching me to play billiards. If you want, you can help me refurbish the Flagstone. I'll have lots of sanding and finishing work, but that'd be up to you. I checked with the social services people, and it's okay with them. They need the space out here, and besides, you have a reputation for not taking your quiet-medicine and being uncooperative in general. What do you think?"

The old man looked at Carlisle, real hard. Got tears in his eyes. Carlisle got some in his, too. "First thing you've got to learn is how to hold the cue properly. Most people never do learn that. It's a game of physics and geometry, skill and treachery. That'd be right up your alley, wouldn't it, Mr. McMillan?"

Carlisle nodded, chuckling. "It'll take me a few days to get the old house in livable condition. How about I pick you up a week from today, first thing in the morning? That'll give you a chance to pack and say goodbye."

The old man whacked his cane against the bench they were sitting on. "Both of those things'll take exactly twenty-three seconds combined. I'll be ready."

Then he started to sob. "Mr. McMillan, I don't know what to say. I'm dyin' out here, and I'm not ready to die yet, and now you're comin' along with this good deal and ploppin' it right in my lap when I'd given up seein' anything but bad custard and white-coated bullies."

He really cut loose, crying hard, his despair flowing down and away from him. Carlisle reached over and took hold of the old man's arm while the man pulled out a wrinkled blue handkerchief from his right hip pocket and held it over his eyes.

He tried to talk again, still choking. "Been thinking, in fact, about how I could squirrel up enough of this dope they hand out here to get it over with once and for all, if I didn't reach a state of complete senility before then." Pointing with his cane, he said, "I'll be ready, Mr. McMillan, on the front porch over there, belongings in hand. Can't stop thinking now about the Flagstone and how I can help you rebuild her. Probably find my footprints at various places on the dance floor. I can help you put the billiards table together, too. Done it before."

Carlisle smiled, started to say more, then left it where it lay. "See you in a few days."

When Carlisle went for him the following week, the old man looked entirely different. He was standing on the porch when Carlisle pulled up at the care facility, shaved, clean shirt and trousers. At his feet was a small, tan cardboard suitcase with brown stripes and a bad crunch on one side. Four battered Sears shoeboxes were tied together with twine and stacked beside the suitcase. On top of the boxes was an army helmet. Carlisle helped him into the truck and put his belongings on the seat between them.

"This is Dumptruck." Carlisle grinned, gesturing with his head to the tomcat lying along the top of the seat back.

"I met Dumptruck once before, during the open house at your place several years back. He sat on the grass with me by your pond. We talked a bit and watched the little hawks flyin' around. Liked him then, like him now."

He held out his hand. Dumptruck sniffed it and slid off the seat to sit on the old man's suitcase, purring.

Carlisle shifted gears and drove away from the Yerkes County Care Facility. The old man was talking about billiards tables while he petted Dumptruck. "Hardest thing is to get the slate level. Gotta get it real level. Without that, you can't play a precision game of billiards, can't truly engage in geometry, physics, skill, and treachery. And that's what it's all about, Mr. McMillan, leveling the slate and playing with precision. Yessir, I guess that's what it's all about in everything."

CHAPTER TWENTY-THREE

There is an evening highway coming out of New Orleans and bending northwest all the way to Calgary. Long stretches of it run through the high plains, over short grass and thin soil, past the buttes and a scattering of little towns lying along or a few miles either side of the road. Travelers often comment on the oxbow shape of the highway in Yerkes County, how it swings east and runs north past Falls City and Livermore, then abruptly heads forty miles west before resuming its northerly direction, as if desultory minds had drawn the route.

Fifteen miles or so up the highway from Livermore and west of a town called Salamander, a town that's nearly gone now, is an exit onto Route 42. If you take that exit, turn off 42, and drive north along a red dirt road, you'll pass a small forest where little hawks are lifting off for their twilight voyages. They made it through the Yerkes County War, barely. Now there is talk they'll be netted and put into a captive breeding program in the San Diego Zoo, far from their evening forest, since only four other adults of their species can be found in the continental United States. Across the road and back in a field from the hawks' forest are the ruins of what might have been a house at one time.

Farther up that same dirt road, which turns to a sticky red gumbo in the rain, is a monolith called Wolf Butte sitting a mile back from the road, its rumpled white face partially obscured when low clouds are draped across it. Stop and get out of your car, miles from the nearest little town. Stand there for a moment. Silence. Easy wind comes, goes, comes again.

Notice the hawk sitting thirty fence posts south of you. This is sacred ground, so claimed Sweet Medicine. You believe it. Anyone who comes alone to this place believes it. There is nothing out here that cares about you, about whether you live or die or pay your bills or dance on warm Mexican beaches and make love afterward. There is nothing except silence and wind. And they do not care, for they will be here long after your passing. That much they know.

Just as the cloud moves off Wolf Butte, and before another one comes, you might think you glimpse a figure moving along the crest of the butte. If you carry good binoculars, first-rate equipment with multicoated glass and all the rest, you'll be able to see the figure is a woman. She is indistinct—the distance, the mist. But you can see her dancing, turning slowly, arms raised. Long auburn hair hangs down and touches the bare skin of her shoulders, touches the slow arch of her naked back, swinging with her as she moves. But your glasses won't be good enough to see the detail of the opal ring on her left hand or the silver bracelet around her wrist or the silver falcon hanging from the chain around her neck. Another cloud will come onto the butte, and she will disappear. A pair of dark eyes twenty feet behind her and out of your vision can still see her, though.

Better you move on now, keep going. You probably shouldn't say anything about what you've just seen. It could have been a trick of the mind, anyway. Even if it wasn't, one does not meddle in such matters. That was known long before the horse soldiers rode through here on their way to the Little Big Horn. That was known a long time ago.

If you drive along the road another quarter mile, you'll see a sign set back twenty yards in the grass: PROPERTY OF THE LAKOTA SIOUX, NO TRESPASSING.

You turn to the person traveling with you. "It's getting dark, maybe we should go back to that Best Western we passed near . . . what's that town called? . . . Livermore? The guidebook says there's a restaurant attached to the motel. The book also mentions there are all kinds of strange legends about this place. Supposedly late at night you can see a fire burning up on that butte over there."

The person next to you replies, "Yes, let's do go back. There's something kind of creepy out here."

You nod, saying nothing about what you saw or thought you saw through the binoculars.

Near where the interstate highway passes Livermore, an old dance hall sits on the edge of a lake. If summer has come and the wooden shutters are swung open, it's possible to stand on the dance floor, look out across the lake, and see lights from traffic moving north and south on the highway.

The shutters are open tonight, and music is playing. An old man sits in the second tier of booths up from the dance floor, back in the darkness, a glass of Wild Turkey on the table in front of him and a fine baby boy named Cody Robert McMillan on his lap. A tomcat known as Dumptruck sits by the old man's glass, licks his right front paw, and purrs as the old man pets him. The cat stays just beyond the grasping fist of the little boy, who reaches out and burbles, "Kiddy."

The old man is smiling, thinking about the hand grenade he had hidden in a shoebox and was preparing to use on a lawyer named Birney and Birney's associates. When Carlisle McMillan bailed him out of the care facility, he left it with a fellow inmate there, just in case things got too bad. That other resident of the place was also a veteran and grinned when the old man gave him the grenade, saying he would know what to do with it if the time came.

Carlisle McMillan is three years into his rebuilding job on the old Flagstone Ballroom. He estimates it will take another two years, maybe more, before he's finished, with all the other outside work he has to do. Tonight, however, he is resting, at the request of Susanna Benteen. She has organized a celebration, something to do with nothing at all except moonlight across the water outside.

At the east end of the dance floor is one of the best billiards tables anywhere, rebuilt and recovered, with a playing surface five feet wide and twelve feet long. The old man is convinced it must be the same table on which he won his first automobile in 1938. Carlisle is coming along on the game pretty well. It's not a game you learn quickly; still, he's coming along. He understands the skill and physics and geometry parts all right, but, as the old man says, Carlisle is a little light on the treachery end of things.

Understand, however, Carlisle has been busy with other projects, not leaving him as much practice time as he needs. Along with his regular carpentry work and refurbishing the Flagstone, he has a little furniture manufacturing operation under way. Fixed it up with the county so the able-bodied folks at the care facility could help with the finishing work. Nothing heavy, just the details requiring a lot of care.

Some of the old people can even do the work sitting up in bed. They love the challenge of accomplishing something. Carlisle's a stickler for quality, says it has to be done right, and they're learning. Pays them a fair wage, too, part of which goes into a fund that has dramatically improved the quality of food served out there. He puts the small profits from the enterprise in a special account and says he's going to build a better place for Yerkes County old folks someday, just in case he needs it himself.

Then there's the book he's writing. He is titling it *Scrounging—Old Things for New Lives* and has signed a contract with a regional publisher. Carlisle needs photographs for the book, so he bought a used camera, a 35-millimeter Nikon, to take the pictures himself. He seems to have a natural eye for it, even Susanna says that, and she knows about such things. Now he's started roaming the countryside, taking photos of just about everything that is old but can be made to live again, and is building a darkroom over in one corner of the Flagstone where the coat-check area used to be.

The other matter that required some of Carlisle's time was cleaning up the last bit of wickedness surrounding the highway construction. He didn't give up on that, kept pushing hard until the state attorney general's office investigated questionable land purchases along the right-of-way. Three convictions for fraud and conspiracy came out of it. All parties received probation, but the fines and bad public relations bankrupted two of them. Ray Dargen suffered a stroke shortly after his conviction and moved to Arizona. Carlisle let it go after that.

When Carlisle's mother, Wynn, comes to visit, and she visits regularly now that she has a grandchild, the two of them carry their glasses of wine out by the lake and make a quiet toast.

"To ancient evenings and distant music," Wynn always says, raising her glass and reciting words she had heard a long time ago from the father of Carlisle McMillan.

Things are working out for Gally and the motel manager. She wears a diamond on her left hand, and the wedding is coming up in a month or two. Sometimes Carlisle drives over to the restaurant, oscillating slowly back and forth on a stool, half listening to the traffic on the new interstate outside.

And Gally Deveraux smiles at Carlisle McMillan. If it's a quiet time in the restaurant, they sit together over coffee and talk in the way they used to talk when they sat on stacks of lumber in a house Carlisle was building. Those were other times, when they stared into Mr. Williston's fireplace while snow blew in and around them, talking about their lives, trying to halt the flow of liquid into the crust . . . and doing that, eventually.

Tonight, however, there is music in the Flagstone Ballroom. Lying around the ballroom are lumber and light fixtures and a better furnace than the old one that came with the Flagstone. Carlisle and the young fellow from Livermore he's taken on as an apprentice are going to install the furnace before next winter. But it's summer now, and a nice breeze is blowing in from the lake.

Hanging high on the wall at the lake end of the dance floor is a piece of wood with the symbol of Vesta on it and the words *For Cody* right below the symbol. Carlisle had sawed it out from over the door to his place before they brought in the bulldozer.

Gabe O'Rourke is pretty elderly now, but he and the other old man have a lot of fun talking about their Paris days and arguing over what color the walls ought to be in their bungalow beside the Flagstone. While the others are working on refurbishing the ballroom, Gabe practices his accordion off to one side, providing background music for the hammering and occasional soft cussing. Some days Carlisle carries a lawn chair down to the lake for Gabe so he can fish for crappies near a partially submerged brush pile. Gabe likes to watch the little bobber dance along just below the surface when a fish takes the bait. When the other old man limps down to fetch him in late afternoon, they clean his catch and have the fish for supper along with their fried potatoes.

And, Lord, Gabe still loves to play the tangos. Sometimes the other old man will ask him to get out his accordion late at night, when the two of them are sitting around in the bungalow. He plays the Paris songs. Plays them real sweet and watches his friend walk to the window and look out across the lake, wiping at his eyes when he thinks Gabe isn't looking.

Neither of them say anything to Carlisle

when Susanna goes off by herself for a time without mentioning just where it is she's headed. They think it's a little odd, but both have chalked it up to modern times and male-female relationships being different from what they remember. But when she's here, which is most of the time, they like to watch her face when Carlisle comes home in the evening after a long day and climbs out of an old green truck with KINCAID PHOTOGRAPHY, BELLINGHAM, WASHINGTON printed in faded red letters on the doors. She goes out to the truck to meet him, puts her arms around him, and leans her head on his chest. He's sweaty and slumping a little from the hard work, an old and well-mended tool belt lying over his shoulder.

Tonight, Susanna helped Gabe onto the old bandstand on the north side of the dance floor and provided him with a chair and a small table for his beer and ashtray. The old accordion has never sounded better than it does right now, with twilight moving over the high plains. She and Carlisle are dancing twenty feet off to one side of Gabe, near the windows overlooking the lake. While a new sun moves westward over the longitudes, across Ocean India and Sudan, a huge and distant camera following the light, Carlisle turns to Gabe and says, "A slow tango, my good man, if you please."

Gabe nods, takes a shot of beer, puts down his Lucky Strike, and starts into the song—real haunting, real spare, firm, having a certain amount of both commodity and delight. Susanna taught Carlisle the basic tango steps a while ago, and everybody had a good time watching him stumble around while he was learning. He's not much of a dancer, but he gets by. Now Susanna, she's altogether different. As Gabe likes to say, "I don't know where she learned it, but Susanna dances a real sweet tango."

Susanna is wearing a full-length gown she made, spaghetti straps and pale lavender in color, fitting her real snug. She's five months pregnant with her and Carlisle's second baby, and the roundness of her belly shows clearly from beneath the dress. She has her auburn hair piled way up on top of her head, with lots of silver draped all over her, including large hoop earrings. The place is lit softly by sixty-year-old overhead lights, creating changing patterns on the dance floor and reflecting from her earrings when she moves her head just right.

Susanna is all silver and softness, Carlisle is wearing clean-washed clothes for the occasion, tan military-style shirt and khakis. Still has on his work shoes, though.

Gabe's playing real good, leaning back some in his chair, eyes closed. Carlisle takes Susanna in his arms, and they move across the floor, looking just fine. Susanna smiles up at him when he bends her back a little in the way of the tango.

Up in the second tier of booths, a big yellow tomcat brushes against an old man who is listening to the music and looking out open windows toward an interstate high-way. The old man runs his hand slowly along the cat's fur, but he's not really thinking about cats or highways. He's vaguely watching Carlisle and Susanna, looking through them and beyond them, out across the lake, past the truck lights heading toward Calgary, out across time.

Eight hundred miles southwest of old men and old dance pavilions and tangos in honor of moonlight or whatever, a van lies on one side underneath a stand of oaks. The man who owned it died a year ago in a stream of bullets fired by federal agents. It is said he kicked open the door of a cabin, waved a shotgun, and was gunned down when he threatened the agents.

As it all comes about then, a van slowly turns to rust in the Arizona mountains, a high plains twilight gives way to darkness while Carlisle McMillan bends Susanna Benteen gently backwards, and an old man is half listening to another old man play a tango. The music floats out of the ballroom window and merges with the distant sound of traffic moving up and down what is called the Avenue of the High Plains. The old man is thinking about a woman called Amélie, and a city called Paris, and about where it all went . . . and how fast it all went . . . when you weren't looking real close.

AUTHOR'S NOTE

Though this story stands by itself, it is a continuation of two of my other books: *The Bridges of Madison County* and, especially, *A Thousand Country Roads*. Those of you who have read the previous books will be somewhat familiar with certain events and characters. For anyone who might be interested, *A Thousand Country Roads* details Carlisle McMillan's search for his father, Robert Kincaid, who played a central role in *The Bridges of Madison County*.

ACKNOWLEDGMENTS

Thanks to all the friends who read versions of this book and offered helpful comments. And to my editor and publisher, Shaye Areheart, for her good humor and incisive suggestions. And to Ken Watt, who owned a parrot named Benny and probably does not remember me, but I remember Ken and his Benny stories from a California evening nearly thirty years ago. Much gratitude is directed toward my agent, David Vigliano, who not only marketed the book, but also made several good suggestions about improving it.

ABOUT THE AUTHOR

Robert James Waller lives quietly with his wife, Linda, and their dogs and cats on a small farm in the Texas Hill Country, where he pursues his long-standing interests in writing, photography, music, economics, and mathematics. In the Texas evenings, he wades remote Hill Country streams, fly-fishing for bass and trout.